"That

"Do n
rolled his

"Fool
led softly as his blade popped one free. "Hah! One of these and a man's set for life," he said softly.

The breath caught in Eddis's throat. The skeletons along the south wall were stirring, and a wordless gasp of warning behind her assured her the others were as well.

Against the Giants
Ru Emerson

White Plume Mountain
Paul Kidd

Descent into the Depths of the Earth
Paul Kidd

The Temple of Elemental Evil
Thomas M. Reid

Queen of the Demonweb Pits
Paul Kidd

Keep on the Borderlands
Ru Emerson

The Tomb of Horrors
Keith Francis Strohm
(2002)

Keep on the Borderlands

Ru Emerson

KEEP ON THE BORDERLANDS
©2001 Wizards of the Coast, Inc.

All characters in this book are fictitious. Any resemblance to actual persons, living or dead, is purely coincidental.

This book is protected under the copyright laws of the United States of America. Any reproduction or unauthorized use of the material or artwork contained herein is prohibited without the express written permission of Wizards of the Coast, Inc.

Distributed in the United States by Holtzbrinck Publishing. Distributed in Canada by Fenn Ltd.

Distributed to the hobby, toy, and comic trade in the United States and Canada by regional distributors.

Distributed worldwide by Wizards of the Coast, Inc. and regional distributors.

GREYHAWK and the Wizards of the Coast logo are registered trademarks owned by Wizards of the Coast, Inc., a subsidiary of Hasbro, Inc.

All Wizards of the Coast characters, character names, and the distinctive likenesses thereof are trademarks owned by Wizards of the Coast, Inc.

Made in the U.S.A.

The sale of this book without its cover has not been authorized by the publisher. If you purchased this book without a cover, you should be aware that neither the author nor the publisher has received payment for this "stripped book."

Cover art by Alan Pollack
Cartography by Dennis Kauth
First Printing: November 2001
Library of Congress Catalog Card Number: 00-191032

9 8 7 6 5 4 3 2 1

ISBN: 0-7869-1881-0
UK ISBN: 0-7869-2674-0
620-T21881

U.S., CANADA,	EUROPEAN HEADQUARTERS
ASIA, PACIFIC, & LATIN AMERICA	Wizards of the Coast, Belgium
Wizards of the Coast, Inc.	P.B. 2031
P.O. Box 707	2600 Berchem
Renton, WA 98057-0707	Belgium
+1-800-324-6496	+32-70-23-32-77

Visit our web site at **www.wizards.com**

THE KEEP

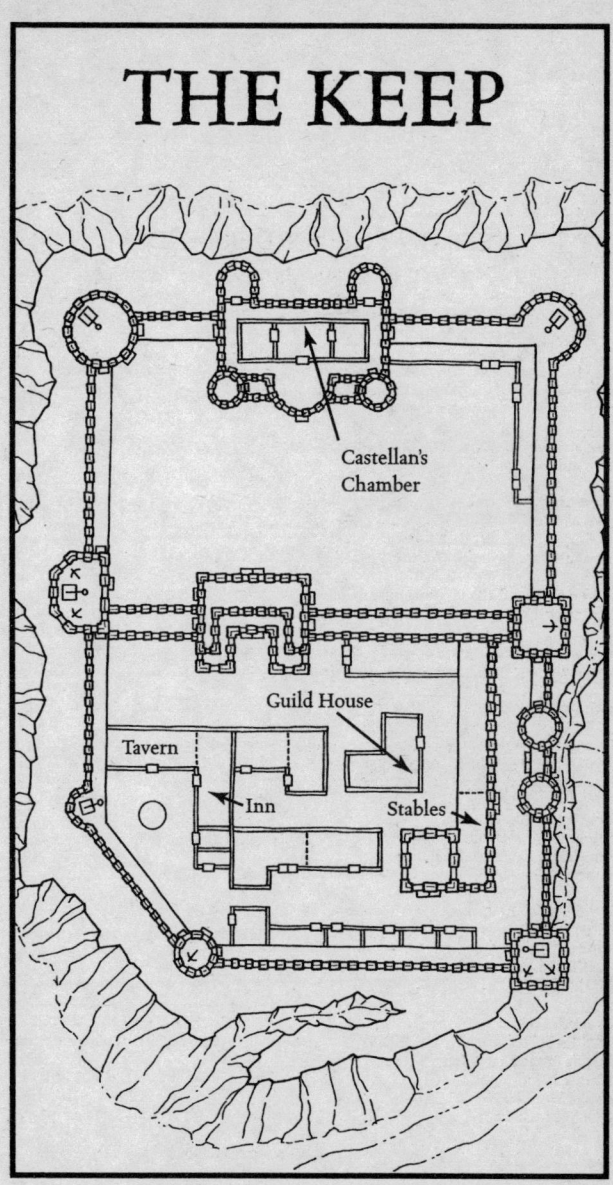

I

Autumn came late to the southern borderlands of the realm. Dry, rank patches of grass on either side of the road bore signs of frost, and meadows that a month earlier were hock-deep in fragrant clover and wildflowers had been turned into a grayish waste. North of the road, scrubby brush edged a burned-out forest. South, a distant copse of trees marked a source of water—most likely a stream. A few bright red or yellow leaves fluttered in the light breeze, but most were gone, leaving pale branches to stand out sharply against the clear morning sky or the thick fir-woods beyond them.

The sun, barely risen, cast long shadows and shone straight in the eyes of the small company of armed men who rode guard on three covered carts. The six horsemen wore mail and swords, and strung bows lay across several saddle-bows. Early light glinted red on a sheaf of iron-tipped boar spears clutched by a gray-bearded man seated next to the driver of the lead cart. He, like the riders, gazed all around, his eyes never still, keeping tense watch. Keen-eyed guards rode behind the last wagon and the four saddled and bridled horses tied to it.

Aside from the clop of hooves on the dusty road, the occasional creak of leather or wheels, it was very quiet.

The lead horseman swore under his breath as sun struck him full in the eyes. He adjusted the brim of his leather cap and edged his mount nearer his companion—a man much younger but like enough to be his brother.

"Hand me that bow, Blorys, and fix your hat," he ordered tersely. "Rotten watch you'll keep, with your eyes full of sun-fire."

Blorys nodded and complied with the order, shoving loose bits of red-gold hair off his brow and under the chain-mail coif. He reached for the bow, then froze.

The leader held his breath, listened intently, but heard nothing except horses and wagons.

"Gone quiet out there, Jerdren," the youth murmured. "Too quiet. And there was a hawk took flight from that dead tree yonder, near the bend. I don't think we're what startled it."

Jerdren nodded and glanced around. Nothing and no one visible.

"Ambush, you think?" He kept his voice low.

The horses slowed to a walk and the wagon drivers eased back to stay in place behind them. The four mercenaries Jerdren had hired days earlier were right where they belonged—two flanking the wagons, two at the rear.

"Not much of any place to hide along the road this near the Keep," Blorys replied.

He glanced at the blackened trunks and fallen trees to his left. The Keep's men kept trees and brush cleared back from the road. South, there was no cover this side of the distant stream.

"There—" he indicated ahead with his chin— "I'm thinking, just around the bend ahead."

"True. Big rocks up there, as I remember. I smell a trap, Blor. You back down and pass the word. Casual and quiet like. No sense tipping our hand, is there?"

His brother gave him a sardonic grin. "I know how it's done, Jers. But I'm staying right with you unless you swear not to charge out on your own."

"Hah." Jerdren grinned. "You think I'm damned fool enough to ride into a horde of thieves by myself?" The younger man rolled his eyes. "Anyway, this near the Keep, it's more like your hawk's found something to—"

A resonant hum interrupted him. He threw himself sideways, flat against the horse's neck, as a long, black-fletched arrow whined through the air and buried itself in the first wagon. The driver shouted in surprise and dragged back hard on the reins, pulling the horses and the cart off balance briefly. His companion readied one of his thick-hafted spears for throwing and came partway upright.

"Stay down!" Blorys ordered sharply. He fitted an arrow to his string and shook the quiver resting by his knee, making certain the other shafts would slip out easily. "Nice of 'em to warn us!" he said.

"Nice? Stupid, I'd say!" Jerdren said tersely and slid his sword under his leg, leaving both hands free for his bow. "Let's hope our hide merchants remember what I told 'em to do if we're jumped."

He urged his bay gelding forward at a trot, and Blorys on the dapple mare came with him.

It was quiet once more. One lone maverick up there, or an over-excited fool in a company waiting to take the caravan as it passed? Jerdren wondered. He wagered the latter. A quick glance showed him the wagons were close together, their hired men taking up positions along the left flank and behind the last cart.

He and his brother came around the bend, holding the right side of the road—as far from the rubble of boulders and hillock as they could get. The silence held, and even with the early sun hard on the boulders, he couldn't see anything but stone, dirt, and a few scrubby bushes. Jerdren slowed to a walk.

"No one there," he murmured and sent his eyes ahead to the next possible danger—a low, bald ridge marking the path of a dry creek. He caught his breath sharply. Something metal flashed in the sun, then dropped out of sight on the far side of the ridge, maybe four strides back from the road.

"Saw it," Blorys said quietly.

"Nice and easy," Jerdren replied. His face was grim.

A clatter of hooves broke the silence. Six men on dark hill ponies broke cover some distance ahead, fanned out across the road, and at a sharp command spurred forward, howling and bellowing. Each carried a heavy-bladed short sword high, ready to hack. Behind them, another six rough men on foot piled out of the brush, bows and javelins in hand, and behind the ridge, others were shouting threats and curses.

Jerdren had to shout at his brother to be heard. "Think they're trying to distract us?"

Blorys shook his head grimly, tucked the reins in his belt and drew back on his bowstring. "Trying to scare us into surrendering, more like!"

Jerdren laughed at that. "Picked the wrong caravan then, didn't they?"

His first arrow barely missed one of the horsemen, falling just short of the men on foot, who, for the moment, were staying put. One of the riders—a bull of a man with a wild black beard and long hair spilling from under a metal cap— shouted another order. The horsemen split, three to each side of the road as their footmen launched a volley of arrows, then closed ranks again. One knocked Blorys back as it slammed into his shoulder, but it fell to the road, foiled by his hardened leather vest.

The riders stopped at a sign from black-beard—close enough to be clearly heard but out of reach except for a very good, or very lucky, arrow shot.

The mercenary leader stood in his stirrups and shouted, "Give up your wagons, you men, and we'll spare your lives!"

Jerdren bared his teeth in a humorless grin as the footmen came up behind the riders, stopping several horse-lengths back. "Come and take 'em, why don't you?"

"Don't be fools. There ain't enough of you to even slow us!"

"Twelve men? Twenty, even?" Jerdren laughed. "Bad odds for you, I'd say!"

He turned partway in the saddle and drew down on the nearest rider. The arrow went low and right, hitting the man's upper arm with a metallic clank. The fellow snatched at the wobbling shaft and threw it aside.

"Armor!" Jerdren hissed at Blorys as the riders started forward again.

The younger man nodded once, then loosed his own arrow. It hit metal and flew wide, but he had another already to the string. Jerdren drew a steadying breath and took quick aim. He might have time for a second shot before shifting to his sword. The first arrow creased the leader's horse, sending it rearing and plunging as the man swore and tried to get it under control. The second shot slammed deep into a bandit's unprotected throat. Blood splurted, and the sturdy hill pony panicked, half-turned, and threw his dying rider. The man next to him veered around the fallen man and aimed a kick at the riderless animal. A mistake on his part; the frightened beast spun into him, and the dangling reins tangled around his boot. He went flying, lay momentarily dazed, then pawed his sword from the dirt and clambered to his feet.

Jerdren was ready for him. Teeth bared in a savage grin, he ripped the short sword from its sheath and brought it down in a slashing blow. The raider staggered back, folded in half over his torn belly, and fell across his already dead companion, gasping and wheezing.

Other men came from the north now, on foot, swords and javelins ready. Jerdren gritted his teeth. Time those armsmen he'd hired back up north earned their pay. He could only hope he'd chosen well, as the remaining riders swept up and joined battle with the two brothers.

Two men converged on him, grinning as they brought their swords down. Jerdren drew his horse to one side and kneed it forward, bringing his blade down hard against the nearest fellow's unprotected neck. With a grunt of pain, the man fell forward and slid limply to the ground. Jerdren came back around sharply and slashed backhand at the second man—a sinewy fellow with a beard nearly as red as his own. Blades clashed before red-beard drew back, trying to find a way under his opponent's guard.

Jerdren's eyes flicked briefly left and right. The hired guards were keeping the bandits away from the wagons still, and up along the road, the footmen were moving nearer. They wouldn't risk getting trampled, he thought, and he kneed his mount forward as he thrust. His enemy parried the blow, but the effort left him off-balance, and before he could recover, Jerdren slashed across the man's face, opening a long, nasty cut just below the eye. Blood ran down his cheek. The fellow cursed raggedly, drew his horse aside, and came around, his sword ready to thrust. Jerdren slashed downward across it with the flat of his own, slamming it into the man's unfortunate mount. The horse neighed frantically and staggered back, a thin line of blood darkening its pale gray coat.

Jerdren kneed his horse again, bringing the blade around hard as he rode past red-beard then checked and turned back. The hill pony reared. A bright-red arc of blood shimmered in the early sun as his rider slid down the beast's withers and fell to the road, where he lay still, sword still clutched in his fingers. The pony bolted back past the carts.

A quick glance assured Jerdren that the footmen hadn't come any nearer. There were men down beyond the carts and north of the road. He didn't dare take count just yet. One man lay limp across the neck of his pony and just beyond them, Blorys was fighting the last of the riders. Someone back along the wagons was howling in pain.

One of his hired men shouted, "All but two of 'em down, back here!"

"Stay alert!" Jerdren bellowed back.

A wail of agony was cut short as Blorys brought his hand down hard, two-handed, and cut deep into the man's neck. The pony spun halfway around and bolted back toward the rough line of bandits still waiting up-road, dragging his rider. The foot fighters drew back, and several of them turned to run.

Jerdren's exultant laugh stopped them. "Going somewhere? Cowards!"

Two of the men turned back, their faces dark with anger, but the third—a thin, beardless creature clad in greasy leathers—caught his breath on a sob, threw down his spear and fled down the middle of the road. The mercenary laughed again and urged his mount into a gallop, left hand wrapped around the reins, sword in his right. Blorys's angry shout came after him, but he ignored that and clove a path through the scattering footmen, riding down the unfortunate fellow and dispatching him with one hard, slashing backhand. He fought his excited horse to a halt, brought him back around, and grinned at the remaining spearmen and archers, most of whom simply stared back. A warning shout from a hatchet-faced older man brought two of them around to face the charging Blorys. The younger man was cursing steadily, and he cast his brother a furious look before engaging the two ragged but determined spearmen. Hatchet-face drew back a pace, apparently watching for an opening.

I can't get at him without going through Blor, Jerdren thought. He ducked as an arrow soared just over his head, slapped aside a spear with the flat of his blade, and turned toward the other two hulking brutes who clutched their spears and watched him grimly.

"Man on a horse has all the odds against footmen, hasn't he?" he asked cheerfully. With a flash of teeth, he dropped from the saddle and sketched them a bow. "Like your chances better this way?"

Behind him, Blorys cursed, and one of the footmen cried out in pain.

The two men facing Jerdren glanced at each other, then shouted, and both charged him. Jerdren slapped one spear aside with a backhanded, flat-bladed sweep, sending its holder staggering, briefly off balance. Before the man could regain his feet properly, Jerdren ducked, coming up under the shaft of the second spear and grabbing it, hard. He yanked, thrusting with his blade at the same time. The man wore no armor, not even hardened leather. The sword went through his belly, stuck briefly in bone, then ripped free as Jerdren let go the spear and dropped back, yanking hard on the hilt. The mortally wounded man fell, clutching his belly. Jerdren was already pivoting on one heel, bringing the dripping blade around in a hard, flat, two-handed swing.

Droplets of blood flew from the blade, glittering like rubies, before the weapon slashed through an upraised spear haft and through the robber's neck. Jerdren didn't even bother to see if he still lived; he was already across the road, ready to aid his brother.

But Blorys was off his horse, reins in one hand and bloody sword in the other, as he nudged each of the three men with a booted foot. The hatchet-faced man groaned faintly. The others were silent and rolled limply away from the pressure.

A sudden stillness reigned once more, except for the wheezing of the wounded man at Blorys's feet, the faint sobbing of someone back among the carts, and a woman's frightened weeping coming from the lead wagon. Jerdren bit back exasperation. *I warned that hide merchant not to bring his lady, didn't I?*

He walked back to the lead wagon, his bay gelding now quiet and trailing after him.

A keen look around assured him that the road, at least, was clear. There had been fairly heavy fighting along the north side of the caravan, and he could see two fallen men beyond the third wagon. Two of the hired men were injured, but neither of them too badly. One sat pale and quiet as one of his fellows bandaged an oozing cut on his brow. The second tended to his own forearm, a bloody bandit's arrow at his side. A third man lay still and pale beside the middle cart.

"Fell from his horse," one of his comrades told Jerdren. "That one there—" he pointed to a dead bandit some paces away— "busted his head with a stone. Last thing he ever did." Brief silence, which the man broke. "We took two of 'em prisoner, but one's not likely to live. Bad cut in the leg."

"I'll deal with them shortly. You did well, you men," Jerdren said. He raised his voice a little as he turned toward the lead wagon. "Lhodis! Hide merchant! How're your people there?"

Blorys came up, leading his mare, a dripping sword in his free hand. A trickle of blood ran down his cheek. His eyes were dark with anger. Jerdren held up a hand as a tremulous voice came from the lead wagon.

"We're . . . fine, swordsman! All right, I th-think."

"Good! Everything's taken care of! We'll move on as soon as we can. You and your folk just stay inside there! Nothing out here you need to worry about." *Nothing you need to see, either, hide merchant,* he added to himself. *You* or *your lady.*

Blorys dabbed at the cut on his cheek and cleared his throat ominously. Jerdren held up a hand for silence. "Later, brother," he said. "We need to clear the road, and get moving."

"Clear the—damn it all, Jers," the younger man said flatly. "And if there's more of 'em?"

"After what we did to the ones who showed themselves?"

Blorys sighed faintly. "It's a point," he conceded.

"We'll post three men for watch," Jerdren said mildly and glanced at the nearest of his hired men. "Pick two fellows with good eyes and make sure no one's sneaking up on us. Can't leave all these dead men on the road for the next party to find. Rest of you, help me and Blor get 'em a ways off the road."

"Search them?" the armsman asked.

"Search? Look at them," Jerdren replied sourly. "Poor ragged brutes—well, get 'em moved and search 'em if you please. We'll split anything that's found. Make a pile of their weapons, though. We'll take what we can of those. Keep men can always use the metal to melt into new blades, if not the weapons themselves, and they'll pay well for that kind of thing." He raised his voice slightly as the men began to move off. "Remember, main thing here is we clear away the bodies and get moving again! I want to make the Keep well before midday!"

Men scattered. Blorys went with three of their hired men to get rid of the footmen, while three of the others dealt with the dead and dying riders, and fastened the two remaining hill ponies to the back of the last wagon. Jerdren squatted down next to the two prisoners. Behind him, mercifully, the woman's weeping died away, and it was quiet in the carts.

Two rough-looking men stared back at him. One whimpered, clutching his upper leg. Someone had wrapped a length of cloth around it, but blood still seeped around his fingers, and both the fabric and his breeches were soaked. The other sat cross-legged in the road, his face blank, fingers clinging to a broken bow.

"Well," Jerdren said finally. "I wonder what we do with you two. Suppose we could gut you, same as we did for your friends, here. Or maybe you'd prefer to run for it? Of course, you'd have to go now, before I change my mind."

The second man laughed harshly and indicated his wounded fellow with a jerk of his head. "How far do you think *he'd* get? How far'd I get, for all that, until you ran me down?"

Jerdren shook his head. "He's no threat to me or those who hired me. Take him if you like, leave him if you'd rather. But go, and take a message with you for any of your kind still alive out there and thinking caravans like this one are easy pickings. Tell them how many dead men you left behind."

"Hah." But the bandit got stiffly to his knees and leaned over to speak quietly against his fellow's ear. The second man simply clutched his leg and watched blood seep between his fingers. His eyes were half-closed, and his face deadly pale. After a moment, the first man got himself upright, with the help of his shattered bow, and glanced at Jerdren.

"I'll tell 'em. They won't listen, but I'll tell 'em."

"Do that," Jerdren said evenly and stood to watch as the bandit limped up the road and into the dry creek bed. He vanished into the shadows of the burned forest some distance north.

Jerdren walked to the head of the wagons, turned to look back along them, then bent his gaze to the blood-smirched road to find any arrows that were still whole and true. He pocketed three arrowheads that could be remounted on new shafts and shoved a nasty-looking, well-balanced, broad-bladed dagger into his belt. Something like that would do a lot of damage, no matter where you stuck it in a man.

Most of the dead and dying robbers were well away from the road. One wounded hill pony lay thrashing feebly in the ditch south of the road. "Save poor Blor the pain of this," Jerdren muttered as he found the big neck vein and drove his dagger in deep. The animal fell back and lay still. His brother hated seeing a horse suffer but hated having to dispatch one even more.

"And how we're to get *you* moved," the older man told the dead beast, "I don't know." A dead horse wasn't as nasty a mess as ten or more dead men, but he'd rather not leave any bodies behind.

He climbed back onto the road. The hired men were making a pile of swords, daggers, spears, and the like behind the last wagons, and one of the hide merchant's apprentices was helping stow the cache. Jerdren wiped his short sword and sheathed it, then checked his bay gelding over carefully before mounting. Blorys rode up to join him.

"Ready, Blor?" he asked.

Blorys shrugged. "Almost. Lhodis and his woman will probably have bad dreams for a while, but they didn't actually see anything, and they weren't hurt."

"They'll be fine," Jerdren said shortly and gave the sign for the wagons to start. "I *warned* that man about bringing his woman."

"He's no worse than most of the merchants, Jers," Blorys reminded him. His gaze stayed on the north side of the road, searching as they rode. "One reason they hire men like us for journeys into the wilderness. Like this one, remember?"

"Yeah. I know." Brief silence. "There's blood on the road, but there's not a thing we can do about that."

Blorys grinned briefly. "Pray for rain."

"Hah. By tomorrow, it'll be buried under dust anyway."

"That pony—"

"Be realistic, Blor. The dead men and horses will all be gone before we reach the branch in the road at the foot of the Keep. Captain of a band that ill-manned won't last long as captain if he doesn't bury his dead, and they'll want the horses for the meat."

His brother merely nodded.

Perhaps another hour of steady riding, with no sign of pursuit or another ambush, and the lead men relaxed a little, slowing the pace to give the horses some rest.

"You owe me a pair of silver pence, Brother," Jerdren finally said. "Remember? You bet me we'd never see a fight the whole way to the Keep, with all the men we hired."

"Hah," the younger man replied sourly. "You owe *me* a silver. For throwing yourself into the thick of things back there and trying to get yourself killed."

Jerdren eyed him sidelong.

"I keep telling you, Jers, I *like* being a younger brother. I've gotten used to it, nearly thirty years' worth, and I don't mind if you leave me behind when we're tottering, white-bearded old men, but—"

"What? You think I was in any danger from those footsore . . . those hacks?"

"They had the advantage of numbers and a sneak attack, Jers. Some of them were pretty good—how do you think I got cut?" The cut on his face still seeped a little blood, but it wasn't deep or very long.

Jerdren grinned. "All right, a few of 'em. For the most part, they were underfed, scrawny brutes, probably not much good at hitting a standing target and lousy at moving ones."

"So what? Men like that hunt in packs, Jers! To make up for the lack of skill! If there had been another twenty waiting out there—"

"Well, there weren't," Jerdren broke in. He glanced sidelong at his brother and grinned. "Besides, you were close enough, guarding my back, right?"

It was an old joke, but Blorys wasn't smiling.

"You know not to count on that, Jers. I had my hands full—we all did." He touched the drying cut, winced.

"I'll clean that when we get in," Jerdren said.

"I can manage." A tight little silence.

Jerdren turned away from him to look out across the southlands, beyond the frost-killed meadow to the thick forest, the steep hills and the purplish hint of mountains beyond. Same unchanging thing day in, day out. Year in and year out. He sighed faintly.

"I'll be glad to see the last of this one," he murmured to himself.

Blorys heard him of course. The man's hearing was extremely keen. "Glad? Why, brother? It's a long ride, but we have decent horses, and this time at least the clients are friendly folk—unlike some we've guarded. It's good pay, and Lhodis didn't even argue the additional coin for the extra wagon and for the hired men. And *he* suggested the hazard fee, which we just earned, I think. . . ." His voice trailed away. "You're bored again, aren't you, Jers? Like back home in Sedge when we were growing up, and later in the army." He waited. His brother shifted his gaze from the south hills to the road and said nothing. "Jers, I thought we'd worked it out. There's enough variety in hiring out, we take different routes—I thought this time you'd last at something."

Jerdren opened his mouth and closed it again. Finally he shrugged. "Maybe I'm not done with it yet, Blor. After all, you still enjoy this."

"Yes, but we also promised each other that one wouldn't tie the other down. Doesn't matter if I enjoy hiring out if you're bored with it."

Jerdren sighed faintly and shook his head. "We'll talk about it once we reach the Keep."

"We'll do that," Blor replied mildly. He glanced around. "We should take a proper break here. Eat a little, finish off the water bottles. The land's a lot more open than at the branch-off to the Keep."

Jerdren chuckled.

"What?" Blorys asked.

"You don't really think someone would be fool enough to attack *us* at the base of that road? After the damage we just did back there? Besides, the castellan may not send armed parties out into the wilds any more, but his men can see most of that branch road from the walls. Not likely he'd let anyone get away with jumping their trade right at the front door!"

"Maybe," Blorys said evenly, "but it's gone from bad to worse out here, just in the three years we've guided caravans, and he keeps pulling back closer and closer to the walls every year. He hasn't much choice." He grinned crookedly, patted his brother awkwardly on the shoulder. "Sorry. You know all that, same as I do."

"Never mind," Jerdren replied easily.

They took a proper meal break in the open, then halted again briefly where the Keep road branched. Here the woods pressed closer and jumbled piles of boulders and slabbed rock were everywhere. The hired men kept watch up and down the road so Lhodis, his cutter, and two of his apprentices could mount the horses that had been tied to the rear wagon. The remaining merchant folk redistributed themselves in the three wagons, to make the hard climb as easy as possible for the teams. Blorys dismounted to help adjust stirrups and girths. Jerdren sat his bay gelding and kept a careful eye on the east woods and the road threading its narrow, rutted way through the trees. Eventually it vanished into tree shadow where the woods came down to meet it.

Jerdren glanced up as the sun went behind a cloud, and a light, chill wind blew between his coif and the back of his neck. The air felt damp, all at once. Rain or perhaps even snow by nightfall, he thought. Snow was something he'd only appreciate from inside the Keep's tavern, with a good mug of ale in his hands and a belly full of the taverner's best stew warming him.

Blorys had finished with the horses and stopped to talk briefly with the gray-beard who was running the a careful check on the last of the wagon-brakes. He called the hired men in and went over to join his brother, who was still gazing down the east track.

"Wonder what's out there, these days." Jerdren said.

"Nothing a clever man would want," Blorys replied.

The older brother roused himself. "What?" he challenged. "You don't believe in the fabled riches of the east? All the tales we heard back in barracks?"

Blorys grinned. "Parnisun's Castle made of gold and gems? No. And you don't either. Any road as rutted and narrow as that doesn't lead to a palace, unless it's one like the Ogre King's house of bones."

"Be something to see, anyway," Jerdren said thoughtfully.

"No ogres," Blorys said firmly. "No east road. Let's go. It feels like it's about to snow out here."

2

Late afternoon sun glimmered pale through thin, high clouds, and a chill breeze gusted fitfully. At the base of the Keep road, four horses stood close together with their heads down and tails to the wind. One rider sat his mount in the middle of the east road, keeping watch all around them. Two men—a graying man clad in a priest's robes and a black-haired youth in novice yellow—stayed in comparative shelter with the horses, a little apart from the others. The novice spoke now and again. The priest occasionally nodded his head or signed for silence. The elder man was composed, his face serene. The youth tugged at his garments or shoved hair from his face, his fingers never still. He started as a strong gust moaned through the rocks.

A short distance away, the remaining two members of the small company drank from their water bottles and shared a wafer of crisp travel bread. One was a medium-sized, dark-skinned man who wore foreign-seeming armor of woven, hardened leather, reinforced in places with metal, the whole painted in dark red and black. His companion, a slender woman, topped him by half a head. She wore dark, service-able leathers and a plain cuirass under a thick, black cloak. Both were extremely watchful, in their own ways. The man used little but his eyes, now and again easing partway around on one heel, his movements sparing and graceful. The woman paced, her head moving sharply as she gazed around, a long, pale braid whipping across her shoulders. She brushed crumbs from her cloak with impatient fingers.

"We will go soon, I think," the man said. His common speech was soft, slightly accented, his voice low and resonant. His cheekbones were high, his eyes golden-brown and tipped up at the corners. He looked young and vigorous from a distance, and only at close range could one make out fine lines around his eyes and a few gray hairs in the neat beard. "The horses do not require much more rest, since we did not push them hard today. Not even the packhorse of the priests, laden as it is. Even *your* horse—" He ducked his head politely as the woman rounded on him. "Your pardon, Eddis."

The woman's mouth quirked. Her eyes were deep blue, and as she looked at him, some of the fire went from them. She was still visibly nervy.

"All right, M'Baddah. Apology accepted, my friend. I know. You're doing your best to get me over that stupid horse of mine. Feather! What fool would name a foul brute like that?"

"His previous owner, who wished to find a buyer for the brute, as you call him? A buyer like his current owner, who chose for pretty and for price, rather than testing him thoroughly first, as I suggested at the time. The horse *is* an attractive fellow, and when he wishes, he does indeed move smoothly as a feather."

"Hah."

That was just like M'Baddah, Eddis thought. Trying to talk her out of a foul mood. It upset the clients, he reminded her. It took her attention and her energy from things that mattered—such as keeping the clients safe. Hah, she told herself.

Not one client so much as scratched in my care! And as for my moods—well, my clients know what they're getting. By now, they should know. I've got a reputation, after all. *A corner of her mind was uncomfortably aware he was probably right, but she was too cold and stiff and—yes—nervy, to be soothed just now.*

"Sure. Until it decides to balk at something like a leaf or a rabbit, and I'm flat on my back in the middle of the road!"

"My Eddis, please. This just now was not a leaf, was it?"

"I—all right, it wasn't."

It had raised the hair on *her* neck: A pale slash of road suddenly darkened and sticky with blood, and a dead pony in the ditch, just around a bend in the road, where it would startle anyone, never mind an idiot horse.

"I, myself, was caught by surprise," M'Baddah admitted. "So much blood, still fresh—an ugly riddle."

"Hardly that, M'Baddah. I've always thought that stretch of road looked like a good spot for an ambush."

"I agree. Likely the caravan that has stayed half a day ahead of us since the pass. I would say from the signs that those who laid the trap lost the battle."

"No broken, burned-out wagons, anyway. Whoever they are, they might have shoveled some loose dirt over the mess they left." She shivered as a gust of wind billowed her cloak. "I thought our novice there was going to faint." She sighed angrily. "Wretched horse. I could've broken my neck!"

"It takes time to bury such a mess, my Eddis. You know that. Perhaps those folk had no choice but to flee the area at once. I think we will learn what happened at the Keep."

"No doubt," the woman said dryly. "In other words, we should get moving, right?"

M'Baddah shrugged, a wide and graceful gesture of his

hands. She glanced over at the priests. The novice stood with his head bent as the elder held out a cloth-wrapped bundle and murmured a prayer over it or to it—she couldn't tell which. Each day at this hour, he'd broken the thing out for prayers, and it took time. Just now, she was cold and cross and ready to reach the gates up there and be done with riding for the time being.

"*I'm* ready. How much longer is *he* gonna take?" she growled.

"He is paying us extra to make stops for his rites," M'Baddah reminded her quietly.

The priest lowered the bundle, checked its wrappings, and handed it to the novice to restore to the box on the packhorse's back. The youth brought all three mounts back with him.

"There. An hour or less, and we deliver the clients safely, and all is well. I sell Feather for you, or we trade him—"

"Blessed right we do," she replied shortly. "In case you forget, M'Baddah, the brute *has* thrown me the last two mornings in a row."

The foreigner smiled. His eyes glinted. "Then, I shall kill and cook him for you, as payment for his crimes. And, how does my Eddis like her roast horse—hot through only, or dark and dry?"

Eddis turned to stare at him, her jaw slack. He raised an eyebrow and waited.

Her lips twisted. She finally laughed, and the tension went from her body and her eyes. "All right, M'Baddah, you win! They're ready. Let's get these two safely inside the Keep."

He patted her shoulder and moved onto the road to signal the guard in.

"Anything, M'Whan?" he asked as the rider drew close.

"No, Father."

He also wore red and black painted armor and carried a shortbow at the ready. M'Baddah's son, M'Whan, was a paler, younger copy of his father, at least physically. He had only joined them two journeys before, and to Eddis he still seemed shy or unsure whether he belonged with them. For a while, she hadn't been sure of that either, but it was a small enough favor to grant M'Baddah. The older man had traveled with her from the first and had proven himself invaluable. M'Whan was still quiet, but he was an accurate archer, a skilled swordsman, a good hunter, and nearly as keen-eyed a tracker as his father.

The priest and his novice were waiting quietly where the Keep road branched. Eddis and M'Baddah mounted and got the company on the move once again. At her gesture, M'Whan took the lead, and she and the older guard dropped back behind the clients. The swordswoman chuckled quietly.

"Thank you, M'Baddah."

He smiled and sketched a bow.

"You know," she added thoughtfully, "when I first hired you, I knew I was getting a good tracker and fighter—and, I hoped, an all-right cook. I didn't realize how useful you'd be at breaking bad moods. Mine especially."

He raised one eyebrow—a trick Eddis found mildly annoying since she couldn't do it. "Bad—? Oh, I see. This temper, you mean. But, you could easily learn to do a shift-mood yourself, if you chose, my Eddis. You breathe deeply, from the gut, and with each breath, the four words—"

"No," she said firmly. "Thank you, but I am *not* ready for your religion, M'Baddah—or whatever it is. Not yours, not theirs, not anyone's."

They were quiet for some moments. Eddis laid a hand on his forearm. "Sorry, my friend. Everything I've said to you today has been rude or angry or both. I'm grateful you've stayed with me."

"It pleases me to stay with you." M'Baddah loosened his grip on the reins as the road began to climb.

M'Whan slowed the pace to a walk, partly for the comfort of the clients, but mostly so he could keep a sharp eye out as the rock walls closed in and the road began to twist its way up the steep cliff. A few turns on, there wasn't much chance of an ambush because the Keep guards could see just about everything, though Eddis made sure *her* guards stayed alert all the way to the gates. Including herself. *I haven't gained my reputation as a good caravan guard by taking fool's chances,* she reminded herself.

The way was narrow here, just wide enough for a cart and a rider, and there were massive boulders and rock piles everywhere. She shoved her boots deeper into the stirrups and drew back on the reins as the wretched Feather began easing to the right—and the drop-off. The road was at its steepest here, and she didn't like it much at the best of times.

"We are nearly out of this," M'Baddah reminded her. "This switchback and the next, and then it is nothing. And I will switch sides with you now, if you like."

She nodded and drew a relieved breath when he and his placid mare settled in next to her again. Heights weren't the problem, but the horse . . .

She ducked and threw up an arm to shield her head as a hail of small stones clattered down the slope, bouncing off the road, her head, and her forearm. Startled, Feather plunged sideways and tried to rear, but M'Baddah hauled him down before turning his own mount and urging it a few paces downhill where he could look for the source of the slide. M'Whan's startled, wordless cry brought him back around and stopped him cold.

Two large men had come from between piles of stone and

stood mid-road a few paces ahead of him, effectively cutting off their progress. One held a crossbow, the other a heavy, two-handed battle-axe. The young guard froze as the crossbow veered his way. The priest and novice eased left, against the cliff face, dragging the packhorse with them.

From somewhere above Eddis, a third man called down, "That's right, all of ye! Stay nice and still—and quiet!—and no one'll die! No tricks, any of you, or y'all die!"

M'Baddah held out a warning hand as Eddis glanced his way and felt for her sword.

"You! Skinny lad in the rear, I see that! Hand away from the blade, *now!*"

Eddis scowled, hand still hovering, but M'Baddah said, "He *is* almost straight above you, my Eddis, and he has a stone in his hands—a large one."

She spread one hand across her leg, signaling "Stay ready." The brute high above her rumbled a threat, and Eddis spread her hands as wide as she dared without letting go the reins. The horse was acting up, tight as she held him.

"You settle that horse down there, boy!" the man overhead snapped. "No tricks, I said!"

"Come steady him yourself!" Eddis snarled and looked up. Three man-lengths above her, a bear of a man in rusty armor straddled a slab of rock, easily hefting a boulder that would crush her, if he dropped it. His eyes went wide.

"You're no lad!"

"Bright man," Eddis replied steadily. "Except you've picked the wrong place to rob people."

"Would be," the man with the crossbow said, "if we planned on taking our time." He stepped forward, eyes shifting to the priest. "We won't. You—priest. Just hand over that box *and* your pouch, and we'll be gone."

The priest eyed him coldly.

"Or we'll kill you all and take it anyway."

The bandit gasped in pain, one of M'Whan's hidden daggers deep in his forearm. The crossbow twanged loudly. Eddis tightened her grip on the reins and threw herself flat on Feather's neck as the quarrel sang through the air unnervingly close.

M'Baddah caught his breath sharply, came up behind Eddis, and slapped her horse on the rump, sending it jerking forward. The crossbowman's weapon fell from suddenly limp hands, as he staggered back, M'Whan's second dagger buried to the hilt in his throat.

Eddis spurred up the road, drawing her sword. She and M'Baddah veered around the huddle of priests. Feather leaped again, nearly unseating Eddis as the boulder shattered on the road just behind them. M'Whan had already turned partway around in the saddle, a word steadying his well-trained horse as he drew his bow down on the man high on the ledge. M'Baddah and Eddis rode straight for the axeman, who stared blankly at his fallen companion.

She sliced at his head as she rode past, and he winced back from her—into M'Baddah's wickedly sharp, curved sword.

It took her a moment to get Feather under control and turned. The crossbow wielder lay still, and M'Baddah was dismounting rather stiffly to retrieve his sword from the dying axeman. Up on the rocks, the brute clutched his shoulder, where one of M'Whan's yellow-fletched arrows wobbled between his fingers, a dagger's worth of the shaft in his arm. He turned and staggered out of sight.

Eddis rode down to where the clients still huddled against the cliff. "It's all right, you're safe and so is your bundle. Let's go, now."

The novice clutched his saddlebow and closed his eyes. He looked sick. The priest merely nodded and tugged at the youth's reins to get all three animals moving. She let them pass, caught up to M'Baddah and his son. M'Whan was off his horse staring at his father.

"Father, you're wounded!" When he reached out, M'Baddah pushed his hands aside.

"It is nothing much, my son. Leave it. You can tend it for me once we reach the Keep walls and the inn."

It was Eddis's turn to stare. A trickle of blood ran down M'Baddah's leg. He held a short, pale quarrel in one hand, but the tip and a finger's worth of shaft were dark with his blood. "You broke the man's aim. What might have been painful is merely a scrape." Before M'Whan could protest further, the older man mounted. "Let us get these priests safely inside the gates."

"These men—" M'Whan began. He sounded dazed, and his face was white.

Eddis shook her head. "Leave the bodies. Your father is right. The priests are our concern now." *And your father,* she thought.

The younger man pulled himself together, nodded, remounted, and dropped back to take rearguard behind the priest, his novice, and the packhorse.

Fortunately, the last of the steep part was nearly behind them. The next loop of road seemed to jut over open air before turning back along the cliff face, and from that point on, the way was fairly easy. M'Baddah, despite his wound, set a quick pace, and now Eddis could see the thick, featureless south wall and the first glimpse of turrets. After another turn, more of the walls, and finally she could make out movement up there: guards and others, perhaps.

After that final climb, the road snaked east along the black stone ledge, hugging the walls before making the final plunge to the main gate. Now she could see men in polished helms gazing over the walls, and the glinting points of their tall pikes. The drawbridge spanning the dry gully was down and the portcullis up, but the heavy gates were closed. She was aware of men watching from the high, square towers, ready to launch an attack if need be. From here, she couldn't see the ballistae and catapults.

It was always daunting, riding up to this gate. M'Baddah, aware how she felt, laid a hand on her shoulder. He looked pale, and his lips were set in a tight line, but as she worriedly touched his shoulder, he managed a smile.

"We are safe. They know us, my Eddis."

"I know. It's just that . . ."

She let that go and took the lead, pulling the cap from her very recognizable hair as she dismounted at the gate. It was quiet, suddenly, leaving her all too aware of the narrow slits and round openings in the walls.

One gate opened as she stepped forward, enough to let out two men armed with pikes. One came a pace closer, smiling as he recognized her. She managed a smile in reply.

"Eddis of Caffer, and my men," she said. "You know M'Baddah and his son, M'Whan. We've brought the priest Xyneg and his novice to meet with your curate. But first—we were attacked just now, on the Keep road."

At a gesture from the near guard, the one just behind him turned and strode back into shadow. He returned a moment later with a tall officer, who listened as she quickly explained.

"Get four bowmen out here at once, mounted," he told the guard. "I'll go with them. Eddis," he added, "we'll talk of this later. Go freely inside, settle your clients and your horses and goods, get yourselves lodging and a meal. You're known here."

"Thank you," she replied. "Known" meant they were trusted—not kept in the barracks and watched until they were deemed safe, which was almost as good as known. "We three will be at the inn. The clients are to be guests of the curate and are expected."

The officer nodded as he and his fellows mounted and rode out.

Eddis felt suddenly very tired indeed. The pikeman smiled at her. "As the captain says, ma'am—"

"That's Eddis. Ma'am is my mother."

"Eddis." The smile became a grin. "You're known here, Eddis. Captain'll find you when he needs you. I'll get someone to escort the priests to the chapel."

Eddis shook her head. "Thank you, but it's a contract. We'll manage." She made certain to shove her cloak behind her shoulders as the gate opened. *Let the guard see I'm armed but that the weapons are properly stowed,* she thought.

* * * * *

An hour later, washed and clad in fresh cloth breeches and tunic from her saddlebags, pale, damp hair trailing down her back, Eddis sat cross-legged on a narrow cot in one of the inn's few private rooms, counting out stacks of coins on three squares of soft brown suede. Six extra silver to share out this time. Nice of that priest to add it. Still, we did deliver them safe, even after the surprise practically at the gates. Two extra silver went to M'Baddah as her lieutenant; one for his son, as apprentice. Still better coin than a two-season youth could expect in most companies. All in all, very good money, this trip. She folded the sides of the leather around the coins and set the packets on the low chest that held her personal things. Aside from the chest and the bed, there was no other furniture—wasn't room for anything else, except the small wooden tub they'd brought in for her bath and taken away once she was done.

M'Baddah and M'Whan stayed close by, in the large common room. Eddis stretched hard and leaned forward to squeeze water from her hair onto the stone floor. Now and again she stayed in the common room herself, but the chance of a bath and clean hair had been too much to resist.

"Getting soft in your old age, Eddis," she mumbled. "A room all to yourself with a bar for the door, and a real window." True, the window wasn't much more than a narrow slit—deliberately made too narrow for anyone to climb through, though only a madman would try something that lawless inside the Keep—unlike some places she'd stayed.

She dismissed that, gazed around the tiny room with real pleasure. Everything about it was plain, strictly functional, but neat and very clean It was much nicer than what she'd had as a girl—a corner of the main room, near the hearth, and a damp straw mattress to share with three sisters.

All the rest of her siblings—the ones who'd survived childhood—still lived in that village. Most of them, especially her older sisters, had thought her an odd child for actually enjoying the bow lessons all the village children had to take. Even the villages near the heart of the realm weren't always safe from human predators or other, worse things, but many boys and most of the girls found ways to avoid the demanding work. Not Eddis. She had shown a talent for the bow, and later for the spear, and eventually had been allowed to join the village hunters—mostly older men like her uncles.

It had taken a lot of convincing to get yet another uncle who'd been a soldier to teach her basic sword moves. She'd managed, and she'd mastered them, which was all that counted.

At the time, she hadn't been certain what she would do with such skills. A grown village woman wasn't expected to use weapons. By the time Eddis had reached her seventeenth summer, she knew that whatever else she wanted out of life, being a villager wasn't any part of it.

Her family hadn't understood. "They probably still don't," she sighed faintly. At times, she missed them very much. "But not that way of life."

Her oldest sister had wed at sixteen, was a mother at seventeen, and had never been beyond the most distant of Caffer's hay fields. It hadn't been easy for Eddis, breaking with the only way she'd ever seen or known, moving from Caffer to the nearest market town, finding enough work here and there to keep herself fed, currying horses in exchange for a corner of the stable where she could sleep, hoarding her money a copper at a time so she could haggle for that first used sword.

"Forget all that," she told herself. "It's done, and it wasn't easy, and sometimes it was frightening, and some bad things happened, but it's over. You won, and you got what you wanted, Eddis—your own company of guards, the chance to travel and be paid for it, to see new lands and meet new people. Sometimes, you get to fight. And you still enjoy all of it."

She got to her feet, shoved the men's pay packets in her belt, stuffed all but three coins of hers in her purse, and snugged the ties down. The loose money went into the pocket sewn inside her tunic. That should cover food and drink.

She shook still-damp hair back over her shoulders where it lay cool between her shoulder blades. M'Baddah and his son must be at the tavern by now. No matter. Her stomach was reminding her it had been too long since that bit of travel bread at the base of the cliff.

The tavern door was at an angle across the courtyard from the inn, just a few long strides away. Now she could smell fresh-baked bread and hear laughter. The small courtyard was cool, the air definitely damp, and the sun nowhere in sight, though it was barely two hours from midday. She crossed the area quickly, slipped through the open doorway, and paused there, letting her eyes adjust to the interior gloom.

The deep walls and strong shutters kept the place warm this time of year. The interior was one large room with plenty of long trestles and benches. There were smaller tables here and there that could accommodate six, if people sat close.

M'Baddah had taken one of the tables against the far wall, and as she started across the room, he got to his feet and pulled out a four-legged stool for her. He and M'Whan had shed their lightweight armor and now wore loose, sleeveless red tunics over black shirts and loose black pants. Both had thick pottery mugs before them. M'Badda's small knife was stuck in a dark loaf of bread. Eddis drew her stool in close to the table and handed over the folds of leather.

"A small bonus, thanks to that little disagreement on the road," she said, her voice low, and her movements unobtrusive. The Keep had the most law-abiding citizenry she'd seen anywhere, and the taverner was known to keep a close eye on his customers, as did the guards who came here. Still . . . no point in tempting anyone. The men slid the packets out of sight. M'Baddah came partway to his feet again, but M'Whan pressed him back down.

"You said you would rest, Father. A cup of pressed fruit and a small ale for you, isn't it, Eddis?"

She nodded, and he went off to the counter. M'Baddah cut a thick slice of bread and handed it to her, his face expressionless.

"Your leg is all right?" she asked.

He nodded. He didn't like being fussed over, she knew, and she kept her voice neutral.

"It is fine, and I am fine. M'Whan thinks it his fault."

Eddis shook her head. "We were in a bad spot, and he disabled and killed the one man with a distance weapon, and it's *his* fault? M'Baddah—!"

"You know his problem, my Eddis. He thinks however much he trains, and however skilled he becomes, he will let me down. I cannot persuade him this is not so."

He went abruptly quiet as M'Whan returned with two wooden cups. She tore off a bit of the dark brown, pungent bread, then washed it down with a swallow of fruit juice before topping off the cup with some ale.

"Apricots—oh, that's nice."

There was silence around the small table for some time, as they finished the bread. Eddis poured the last of the ale into the apricot juice and drained the cup.

"I think I'll last until nightfall, now."

"I asked the taverner for you," M'Baddah said. "The same stew as last time: venison in a thick broth, and plenty of tubers and carrots. And the taverner's wife still makes one pot with and one without the onions."

"Good." Onions made her ill, which had been another good reason to leave her home village. She leaned forward on her elbows. "Now. Have you heard anything yet about customers leaving here?"

M'Whan shook his head. "I asked in the stables, Eddis. They said some hide merchants came in earlier, but they won't leave until everything they brought sells—two carts of goods and another of weapons and metals."

"Weapons? Interesting. Most tanners stick to their hides. Still, they'll be fighting snow over the passes if they delay too long," Eddis said. "Not our concern. What escort?"

"I did not learn that yet," M'Baddah put in. "But I hear there is an ore-monger who wants a guard for himself and his purse in the next day or so."

"Too soon for me," Eddis replied.

Too soon for M'Baddah, she thought. Whatever special potions he carried, he'd still taken a quarrel in the thigh, and she wasn't about to head out with her lieutenant wounded. If all else failed, she'd claim exhaustion herself to keep them here until he was all right. She glanced around the room. There weren't many people around at this hour; a few men sharing a jug of wine at a nearby trestle might be either off-duty guards or armsmen. No one she recognized.

"My Eddis," M'Baddah said, "I agree there is no hurry for us. You look tired, and this season has been good to us. We can afford to wait for a client or even return north without one. Also," he added with a sly smile, "I will need time to sell that horse of yours."

She smiled back. "I know. Still, if we can find a client, a few days from now, I'd rather not—"

"I understand," he said. "You have been poor and hungry, and you choose not to be these things again." He shrugged. "It will not be a problem, my Eddis. You have a good reputation."

"We have," she corrected him.

"We, then. What?" he asked as M'Whan's gaze went beyond them, toward the door. Eddis turned to look.

Two tall, ruddy men stood just inside the open doorway, and one of them was laughing cheerfully and loudly, drawing everyone's attention.

Eddis groaned. "Oh, gods, it's Jerdren. I should have known."

"But I thought you liked Jerdren?" M'Whan asked rather anxiously.

"I do. Sort of. Sometimes. But he's . . . impetuous. Trouble. Remember the fight he started last time we met up with him?"

"I remember." The youth cast up his eyes. "Because we slept in the stable that night after getting kicked out of the inn."

"Well, that's Jerdren for you," Eddis said resignedly. "You just never know what he'll do, but you *do* know it'll be loud and probably involve fists. That's fine for some village where the worst that happens is the people around him get shoved into the stable for the night. The Keep—they'll shove you into the dungeon and leave you there."

M'Whan shook his head. "He knows that too, doesn't he?"

"I think so. Gods, I hope so. Still, why would that stop—"

A cheerful, carrying voice filled the room, silencing her and briefly quieting most of the chatter around them.

"By my father's white beard, it's never Eddis, is it?" Jerdren strode over to clap her on the shoulder. "I haven't seen you since . . ." He considered this and shrugged it aside.

"Since the ale house in Lower Vale," Eddis said, mildly enough. "The one where you and those two village louts got in a fight over the barmaid and got all of us tossed out."

"Why—so it was." He seemed surprised by this, then grinned again. "But I didn't get *you* tossed out, Eddis! Hey, no, *you* punched that red-faced brother of hers in the—"

"*I* didn't punch him until he grabbed my—never mind." Eddis scowled up at him. "Damn all, Jers, why is it that every other time we run into each other, you've either been in a fight or are about to pick one? Not just Lower Vale, but Hillside, Rivers-Edge *and* Bally?"

She slapped the table, lowered her voice as M'Baddah touched the back of her near hand. "Sorry, M'Baddah. All the same, you're a curse, Jerdren, that's what you are. And frankly, if you plan on starting a fight here, or even if you don't plan one . . ." She drew a deep breath and let it out in a hard gust. "Well, you'd better find someplace else to sit, or I swear I'll—"

"Ouch," Blorys put in wryly and offered her a shy grin.

Eddis glanced at him and fought a sudden smile. Poor man, shackled to a crazy brother like Jers.

"Fights?" Jerdren's sandy red eyebrows went up. "Why would I start a fight in the Keep? There are rules, right? Only a fool would do that, right?"

Blorys cast his eyes up. Jerdren shrugged and smiled cheerfully.

"So, that's settled. Eddis, you look gorgeous as always, and I'm tame today, I promise you, so is there room enough here for Blor and me to join you? We haven't talked in a while, you know."

Eddis edged over toward M'Baddah. Jerdren grabbed two empty stools, while his brother went for a jug of wine and cups. "How long've you been here?"

"An hour or so," she said. "You?"

"Got in around midday."

Eddis sighed heavily. "I should've known that was you. Had a little trouble on the way, did you?" she said sourly. "And left a nasty mess behind?"

"Huh?" He stared blankly. "Oh. Were the bodies still there?"

"One dead horse count? Also, lots of blood?"

"Not my fault," Jerdren said dryly. "You cut 'em to keep from getting cut by 'em, and they bleed. Fact of life."

He took a cup of wine from Blorys, drank deeply, wiped his mouth on the back of his hand, and gave her a cheerful grin. "Just trying to leave a clear road for you, Eddis."

"Yah," she scoffed. "Hello, Blorys. How's the road?"

Blorys smiled. "Same as always. This last caravan was pleasant enough. One before that, seems we fought someone or something off every single day. One before that, up on the Holderin foothills, river flooded and took half our camp downstream."

"Old business," Jerdren said, impatiently. "Same as always, same as last year, and same as the next, probably." He seemed to come to some decision, drank quickly, and set the cup aside. "Listen, Eddis," he said crisply. "You're just the person I wanted to talk to."

"Me? Why?"

"Why not?"

She held up a hand for silence and began turning down digits. "Back up north, just before that fight over the barmaid, there was something about hidden gold. About half a year before that, something about cleaning bandits out of a village. Then there was Inner Dell and the—oh, never mind!" Eyes narrowed, she leaned on her elbows and glared at him. "I know that look, Jerdren. It means you've come up with something complicated, possibly dangerous, and probably unlawful. Well, not me, not anywhere, but definitely not here in the Keep!"

"But—!"

"Jerdren, they'll lock you up here and toss the key over the walls if you steal from a shop. One of *your* schemes would probably get us *all* tossed over the walls!"

Blorys gave Eddis a tired look. "Sorry. I knew he was up to something, but he wouldn't tell me."

"Told you I would, soon as we found someone—well, like Eddis. Didn't I? Just wanted to tell it once, that's all." He turned back to Eddis and smiled.

She edged back on her stool and eyed him sidelong. "Save the charm, Jerdren. You aren't luring me into one of your schemes."

"Scheme? But Eddis, this is *official* business!"

"Sure. Look, just tell me, I'll say no, and we can go our separate ways."

"She's got a good point, Brother," Blorys said pointedly. "Tell us, all right?"

The older man grinned widely. "Okay. We got in a while back, and I settled with the clients, then went to unsaddle while Blor got us cots. So, I'm coming out and ran right into Mebros. Remember, Blor? Used to be on the gates, short man, pale beard. Watch captain these days—so, anyway, I told him about our little fight out there on the road."

"I thought," Blorys broke in, "that we were leaving that until after we'd had a chance to clean up."

"Well, he was there, and I know him. Anyway, Lhodis and his people weren't going to keep quiet about the fight, were they? And Mebros wasn't surprised. Seems there's a band of robbers holed up somewhere close by. Of course," Jerdren shrugged, "there's always been a few men here and there, but since midsummer, they've attacked when and wherever they feel like it. Ten days ago, they took a gem merchant's wife hostage, took all his money, then forced him to come here to collect the stones as her ransom."

M'Baddah stirred. "What did they do?"

"The Keep men? What could they do, not knowing where the woman was? The merchant lost his money and his gems both, but at least he got his woman back." Jerdren shook his head. "They know the guard here can't chase 'em down, whatever dirty tricks they pull. These days, there are barely enough soldiers here to man the walls. The castellan runs what patrols he can, but—"

Eddis leaned forward. "You're telling me they're just going to get away with it?" she demanded. "Because if they do, then what's next?"

Jerdren's eyes were very bright. "Well, you know, that was my thought exactly, Eddis. It seems the castellan is going to put out the word for volunteers—heroes, Mebros says—to find that bandit camp and destroy it!"

3

Blorys sighed wearily, breaking the startled silence that followed his brother's words. "Jers, you're mad."

"Mad? Why?"

The younger man merely shook his head.

"All right, Blor, it may be only another Keep rumor, but if someone's going to hunt down these bandits, why *not* us? We did all right this morning, didn't we?"

"Against a band of poorly trained, ragged men like that, we did."

"We were still outnumbered," Jerdren reminded him, "*and* set on by surprise." He drank wine, set the cup down, and began turning it between square, freckled hands, his eyes absently fixed on the contents. "Could be you're right, Blor. I *am* getting bored with the same routine, year in and year out. Sure, it takes a good man to plan a journey across the realm, especially out to the borderlands, to bring a caravan through safely."

"Or woman," Eddis remarked dryly. Jerdren gazed at her blankly and finally shrugged.

"Oh—right," he said.

"Look," Blorys said, "Mebros's always been one for spinning a good yarn. How do you know this isn't another of them?"

"Could be," Jerdren allowed, "but I don't think so. He got it direct from one of the men who watches the inner gates, and that fellow is good friends with one of the castellan's personal guard. That's not the same as market rumor, is it?"

"Save the argument for later," Eddis said. "Just tell us."

"All right," Jerdren said. "What he said is that up until this summer, there've been the usual raids on travelers and caravans. You know. A few men preying on lone wagons, harrying riders. Mostly, they've been unorganized and easily driven off. But recently, the attacks have increased, and the raiders seem better armed, better organized. Mebros says all evidence points to a large band, a camp of fifty or more men—soldier-trained."

"The men who attacked us this morning were organized, but I wouldn't call them well trained," Blorys pointed out.

Jerdren shook his head. "From what Mebros said, I don't think they were part of this local band. He says they wear a patch or badge of some kind—a bit of dark green on one sleeve. Our bunch might have been a raiding party moving through the area, or maybe men looking to join up with the local band." He waved that aside. "Mebros says it's near certain there's at least one camp close by, but it's also fairly sure they move often. Still, a large band of men, I'm thinking they'd have two or three regular sites up in the hills they go to, near the river or across rock, so they'd leave no obvious trail. Far enough away that the castellan can't afford to send men looking for them but near enough to keep watch on the road."

"That still covers a lot of rough ground," Eddis said.

"Exactly." Jerdren grinned at her. "And most of the castellan's men are guards. They're best at manning the walls here."

"So what, Jers?" his brother asked dryly. "You're suggesting that the five of us go looking for a well-armed group of fifty or more? Track them down ourselves and bring them down? That's high odds even for *you*, isn't it?"

"Well—"

"Forget it, Jerdren," Eddis cut him off flatly. "Those aren't my kind of odds. Personally, I'm still happy guarding merchant carts. The money's good, and I don't have to answer to some captain or . . . or castellan, either."

"I didn't say just us," the man protested. "The men I hired up north might want to join us, and there should be a few more like us here. Besides, Mebros says there's to be a decent reward and a call for volunteers from the guard—"

"Who are men fit only to guard the walls, according to you," Eddis broke in sharply. "I don't like it, Jerdren. Too much 'if and maybe' to your story, and besides, every time we run into each other, there's trouble. Usually started by you."

"Eddis?" M'Baddah spoke up for the first time. "Perhaps M'Whan and I should go learn what we can before you and Jerdren argue the matter further."

Why bother? she thought sourly. All the same, she at least needed to discuss things with M'Baddah—privately.

Jerdren nodded. "Sure, M'Baddah, that's the spirit! Blor and I can talk to men we know in the barracks, and we'll meet back here later. Fair enough, Eddis?"

Silence.

"Look, this isn't like running into each other some place like Lower Vale. This would be a job. We'd plan it, like a regular campaign. What could go wrong?" The gleam was back in his eyes. "You know, when Mebros told me, all I could think was, 'Why not us?' *Then*, when I heard you had just ridden in, Eddis, it all—came together. It's a chance for . . ."

"Fame, wealth and glory?" Blorys asked sourly as the older man hesitated.

"What's wrong with fame and glory, Blor?"

"What's wrong with living to a ripe old age?" Eddis asked as she pushed to her feet. "Look, M'Baddah's right. Why sit here arguing over what might be wild rumor? I want to know what's involved. What we'd have to accomplish, how much help we'd get from the Keep, what size of a reward. . . ."

Blorys laid a hand on his brother's arm. "Wait, Jers. You've had your say. I agree with M'Baddah and Eddis. Let's go learn what we can. We could meet back here later, if there's more than rumor to go on."

"One more thing, Jerdren," Eddis said. "*If* your rumor proves true, and we decide to go in with you, and *if* the castellan decides we're what he wants—or what he's willing to settle for, you and I are *equals* in this. Got me?"

"Equals—well, sure! But—?"

"That means I get equal say with you on who's chosen to go with us, how things are planned, and who sits in on the planning sessions—all of it, all the way. I am not *joining* you, Jerdren. We two are working together, or you can start looking elsewhere for your fighting force, got it?"

The man nodded. She glanced at his younger brother, who gave her an apologetic smile. "Blorys, you'll be back here maybe an hour after sundown?"

He smiled faintly and nodded. "We'll be here."

* * * * *

The wind had died away, and afternoon sun cast long shadows, warming the stone walls and paving. Eddis strode across the square and over to the fountain, M'Baddah at her elbow and M'Whan close behind. Water burbled from a central pillar, falling back into the shallow stone bowl. It was much cooler here, and quiet. Private, for the moment. Most of the local people she could see were dismantling the morning market stalls across the courtyard, while a few customers haggled over the last fruits and baskets of tubers. Eddis settled her elbows and the small of her back against the stone lip and looked at her companions.

"You hadn't heard about this mad venture?" she asked.

M'Baddah shrugged.

M'Whan shook his head.

"This Mebros could be pulling a joke on Jerdren. He'd have friends like that. Still, say it's true. Say the castellan would pick people like us to clean up these bandits, give us what aid we needed, and reward us if we succeeded. Say even that between you two, Blorys, and me, we can keep Jerdren in check. Are we interested?"

Silence, which she broke. "For myself—I don't know. I've worked hard to build this business *and* a good reputation. It's good coin, steady work. Why trade that for an unknown?"

Her lieutenant raised an eyebrow. "Because a good warrior always seeks challenge, but we could return to the road, once the task is done. For the challenge alone, I say we should go."

M'Whan merely nodded.

"All right." Eddis sighed faintly. "I just wish Jerdren wasn't involved. I hardly feel comfortable sharing a table with him in the tavern, but if he went off on some wild scheme of his own out there, it could get us killed."

"No," M'Baddah said. "We know he is . . . excitable. We plan for that. As his brother no doubt must, all the time."

Eddis looked back toward the inn and laughed. "Poor Blorys, he probably does." She turned to her two confidants. "So then, we're in. Let's split up and go learn what we can."

* * * * *

She returned to the tavern just as the sun was setting. Ruddy light moved quickly off the highest towers, and a chill wind swept across the courtyard, blowing dust and fine spray from the fountain. Eddis shivered and lengthened her stride.

It was warm inside the tavern and much busier than it had been earlier. People crowded the near trestles. She waited just inside the doorway for her eyes to adjust, her mind full of useless bits of information gathered over the past hour. The innkeeper claimed to be too busy to know about anything outside his own walls, but the man's son had heard there was to be a scouting party to look for the bandit camp. Following his suggestion, she'd talked to Khalidd the trader, but Khalidd was no help. He'd merely had the tale from Mebros. Ghor the smith was busy shoeing horses, so Eddis had had no opportunity to ask him anything.

She'd picked up a dozen or more odd rumors here and there. Someone had said there were lizardmen out in the wetlands east of the Keep, and another supposedly had proof of magic armor in a cave—which was of course distant enough that its exact location was hidden. Others spoke of an enchanted mountain cat living deep in the woods and of a frail-looking hermit who turned men into logs. Two different girls told her about a maiden held by men who'd killed her family, leaving no one to ransom her, but Eddis had heard a similar tale back in her own village. There seemed to be endless speculation about the bandits, outrage over the merchant's wife, and plenty of new tales about the attack on Jerdren's party this morning. She'd heard that three of the bandits had since been seen here in the Keep, disguised as peddlers, and that a small invading party had tried to scale the western wall of the inner bailey and would have succeeded except for the racket they'd made falling into the terraced garden beds.

There'd been a long hour then, while the guard captain listened to her story about the battle on the road and got her to identify the two dead men. The third had vanished, only a thin trail of blood to show which way he'd gone. Fortunately, they'd already talked to her clients and seemed willing to accept what she said as truth.

The aroma of fresh loaves brought her back to the moment, and now she could see M'Whan threading his way between tables, coming her direction. Off to her right, the taverner's wife was stoking a fire in the massive fireplace and two servants were moving around lighting candles and lanterns. Three half-grown boys came from the direction of the outside kitchens bearing steaming pots of stew. Serving girls followed with covered baskets of bread, and behind his long counter, the taverner turned up his lanterns and began setting out fresh cups and pitchers. Eddis drew a deep breath, sighed happily, and followed M'Whan across the room.

They'd shoved two small tables together in front of a corner bench built into the southeast wall. Blorys watched as Jerdren spread out a map, securing corners with filled wine cups and two fat candles. Light from these fluttered and cast odd shadows as Eddis took a stool. M'Baddah settled down next to her and passed her a cup.

If Jerdren had been excited earlier in the day, he was almost vibrating with energy now. But he merely glanced up and smiled a welcome before returning to his map. It was upside down from her viewpoint, but Eddis recognized the Keep and lands to the east, north, and south of it. The map properly flattened out, Jerdren jumped to his feet and began pouring a dark red wine into cups and handing them around.

"To our new company," he announced, "to Fortune's Five—and to fame, wealth, and glory!"

Eddis eyed Blorys sidelong. He cast up his eyes. "It's all he's told *me* since he got here."

"Said I'd wait until everyone was here, didn't I?" Jerdren demanded. He was grinning broadly. "Ask the lady—we're equals in this. Anyway, I went off to the barracks to find Mebros, but he's normally on the inner gatehouse, they told me. None of us would normally be let inside *those* gates, of course, but I thought, why not see if he'll come out? One of the guards sent word in for me, and while I waited, he and I talked—he'd heard about our ambush this morning, and he told me a tally sheet went up in the mess hall late today. Said it asked for volunteers—trackers and hunters, men who know the woods east of the Keep.

"Mebros wasn't to be found, but another guardsman came out with word that some parchment pusher wanted to talk to me if I was the Jerdren who came in this morning with hide merchant Lhodis."

Jerdren's eyebrows went up. "You wouldn't believe the size of that end of the Keep. Stone training grounds for two full companies to drill at the same time—not that there's so many men, these days. Terraced crop beds on all sides, up against the walls so's a company can still drill there, *and* they can eat once they're through drilling. Seems to me there's a clever man in charge here. Practical.

"Left alone, I'd've got lost at once inside the north towers, but my guide led me up a flight of stairs and inside a plain stone chamber, talking to a tall, pale fellow named Hollis. 'Undersecretary to Castellan Ferec,' he said. He knew about our set-to out on the road and said Ferec wanted to thank us himself. There's a banquet tomorrow night, Blor, and we're invited—us and our men."

"Hmmm. That might mean the castellan wants to look us over, Brother. Talk to us, see if we might be useful to him. They say it's how he does things."

"Could be. Thing is," Jerdren leaned forward to plant his elbows on the map, "I ran across Odis—that's one of the men I hired for this journey, Eddis—on my way to the barracks, early on. He and his mates already have a return job, and they're heading out tomorrow. Wanted to know if I'd give 'em good recommendation to this ore merchant who's eager to get back north with his pouch of gold. Well, I did that, and I also told Odis about this raid. He just laughed! Said the main reason they signed on with us was hopes of a chance like the ore merchant. 'Why give over an easy job with a filled purse at the end,' he said, 'in exchange for real danger and crawling through the woods?'

"Anyway, when this Hollis said we were all invited, I thought, say those bandits had set their ambush late, rather than early, then Eddis would've taken 'em out just like we did, right Eddis? And we're equals in this, right?"

Eddis stared at him. "Jerdren, tell me you didn't try to wangle us an invitation to a formal banquet!"

He smiled cheerfully. "I didn't just *try*—I got it! All five of us, tomorrow at second bell after sunset."

Eddis broke the silence. "Jerdren, I can't eat at a lord's table. I'm village!"

"So?" he asked. "*We're* village, and we left that for the army. But this castellan's no lord! He was a soldier left in charge here when the old lord went north with most of his army. When none of 'em came back, he stayed on to keep things together, that's all. Man like that won't care how you eat your soup. Besides, you wanted to know how much truth there is to Meb's rumor, and who'd answer that better for you than the man in charge?"

Eddis shook her head in disbelief. Behind her, the room was filling up, and the babble of voices was growing louder by the moment. M'Baddah said something quietly to

M'Whan, who went off through the crowd and came back some moments later followed by one of the taverner's daughters—a dark-haired, slender lass in bright blue, who smiled at everyone and joshed with most, expertly balancing a tray piled high with bowls of stew and chunks of bread.

Eddis sniffed the fragrant steam cautiously. Stew with no onion—they remembered. She tore her bread into thick strips and dipped it into the rich broth.

"Eddis? You can do this, right?" Jerdren looked rather anxious.

She chewed bread, swallowed. Finally shrugged.

"The banquet, you mean? I can—" She fell forward as someone slammed into her left shoulder.

A long-fingered hand dragged her back upright, and a reedy voice mumbled apologetically. Eddis was turning toward the voice when her belt shifted. *My purse!* She spun around the other way and snatched at the dark-haired, skinny fellow backing away from her. He evaded the grasp but went sprawling as M'Baddah stuck out a leg. Eddis was off her stool and had him by two handfuls of roughspun shirt before he could scramble up. He twisted in her grip but subsided when she transferred one hand to his hair.

"All right," she snapped, "where is it?"

"Where's what?" The face was a boy's, despite a thin smear of moustache on his upper lip and a skinny tail of beard. His eyes were very wide.

"The purse you just cut from my belt," Eddis hissed.

"Purse? Cut? I lost my balance, woman, and fell into you. I said I was sorry, didn't I?"

"Fine," she said. "Apology accepted, once you hand over that purse!" He twisted suddenly, freed himself from her grasp, and dove under the nearest trestle. Merchants and their women scattered. Eddis swore under her breath and went after him.

She flailed out and caught hold of a boot. The boy yelled as she edged forward, ready to wrap her arms around his leg, but he kicked hard, hitting her shoulder, and the boot came off in her hand. It was thin and old and smelled awful. Eddis tossed it aside and dragged herself grimly into the open and partway up.

The boy was two trestles away now, dodging through startled patrons, forcing his way past serving girls toward the door. A tray of bread went flying. Eddis scrambled onto the nearest trestle, jumped from it to the next one, scattering people and cups in all directions. Another jump. The thief was about to dive under one last trestle and gain the way out when she threw herself at him, slamming him to the floor.

He was yelling now, crying out for help as she wrapped one hand in his hair and yanked.

"Where is it?" She had to yell just to be heard. "I won't ask again, boy!"

The room went quiet around them, all at once, and the boy's eyes moved rapidly, taking in his surroundings. Suddenly he yelled, "You're hurting me, owwww! Let go!" Startled, Eddis nearly loosed her grip, but M'Baddah had come up and caught his arm. "What're you doing, woman, are you mad? I was just—I was just trying to get past your table, minding my own business and you—owwww! My hair, you'll pulling it out!"

"Not like I will if you don't give me back my purse," Eddis snarled. She was aware of staring patrons all around them.

M'Whan pushed his way through the crowd. "Eddis, I can see two guardsmen coming this way!"

"Good," she said.

"Yeah, good!" the youth said virtuously. "And when they search me and don't find anything, you'll be sorry you hurt me!"

"I found it," Blorys said as he and Jerdren came up. "I saw him toss something under our table when M'Baddah tripped him." He held up a small, thin-bladed knife and a plain leather pouch.

"That's a lie," the youth said. "You can't prove those things are mine."

"You're right. That purse isn't yours," Eddis glanced at the two solid men in guard's colors who stood quietly next to her and the youth.

At a gesture from one, M'Baddah released his hold and stepped back.

"Sir," she told the guard, her eyes still on the boy, "the purse is mine. I can tell you exactly what's in it, to the last coin. Also, there's a red fletch I saved from an arrow—the one I used to kill my first deer." She waited while one of the guards took the bag, fingered its cut strings and poured the contents into one hand. His companion took the knife, peered at it closely. Eddis kept her two-handed grip on the thief. His muscles were taut, ready to spring if she relaxed her attention.

A low buzz of conversation broke out around them once more. People were standing and staring. The guard slowly pushed the coins around on his hand, then fished out a small strip of red feathers—frayed and faded from so many years in the pouch. He snugged down what was left of the cut strings then handed it to Eddis, who freed a hand to stuff the little bundle down the front of her shirt. She stepped aside as the soldiers took charge.

"What's this about, boy?" the guard asked, mildly enough.

The youth shook his head. "How should I know? I was just going to get a fresh mug of ale, and she jumped me for no reason. Maybe you should search her, see if she's got anything of mine." He patted a cloth bag hanging from his belt and suddenly looked worried. "Maybe you should just hold onto her while I make sure *my* coins aren't missing. I had four silver pence when I came in, and I'm not feeling anything there!"

"Oh, is that so, Kadymus?" The taverner came out of the crowd. "Seems to me a lot of us have wondered how a mere 'prentice always has coin for beer and ale—and how it seems folk find themselves short at times *you've* been about." He looked at the larger of the two guards. "Sergeant Evoe," he said formally, "this lady here's named Eddis. She guards caravans, comes to the Keep often, and always visits my tavern. I've never had a spot of trouble from her. And that little knife belongs to Kadymus, I've seen him use it."

Kadymus glared at the taverner, but before he could say anything, Evoe grabbed his near arm, the second guard grabbed the other, and they hustled the skinny cutpurse away. The taverner watched them go, and as the crowd began to break up, he took Eddis's hand in both his.

"My thanks for catching him. I've had my suspicions for a time, but I'm a busy man, and he's that quick."

"I noticed," Eddis said dryly. "More fool I for wearing my purse openly on my belt like that."

"This is a lawful place," the taverner replied sternly. "None of my customers should have to worry for where a purse hangs in here. Your meal and your drink's on me tonight, Eddis," he added, and strode off to his counter.

"Nice going," Jerdren said admiringly. "I didn't realize you were that fast!"

Eddis shook her head. "I was angry. Still, if I'd been wrong about him . . ."

"Well, you weren't," he replied, "so why worry about it?" He led the way back to their table.

It took time, and Eddis was red faced by the time she resumed her stool. It seemed everyone in the tavern wanted to grip her hand and thank her. Jerdren grinned as he settled over the map once more.

"Funny, though," said Jerdren, "*you* starting the brawl, and here in the Keep of all places!"

Eddis cast up her eyes.

"Well, I laughed, didn't I, Blor? But you didn't answer me. You can deal with this dinner tomorrow night—right?"

She groaned as she resumed her seat. "If they don't have me in the cell next to that nasty little thief for starting a brawl. Yeah, Jerdren. I can do this."

4

Sundown the next evening found the party being escorted by half a dozen polite guards in dress tunics past the inner gates and across the inner bailey. Eddis eyed the stone bastion with trepidation. The place was intimidating with its narrow windows and high walls, and armed guards seemed to be everywhere. Two flanked the doors. *What if they believed that gangly young cutpurse after all—and I'm about to be arrested for brawling in public?* She tried to assure herself that she'd have been led away from the tavern at once. M'Baddah touched her arm and gave her a reassuring smile. She drew a deep breath, smiled back, and tried to relax.

She'd never before taken a meal with people of rank. *So we all don our breeches a leg at a time,* she thought. *Still, some of us pull on roughspun, and others are helped into silk.*

They waited outside the great doors while the leader of their escort spoke quietly to one of the guards. The man nodded gravely and turned to pull the door open. It was thick as Eddis's fist and appeared to be solid iron, but it was so well balanced that it took only one man to move it, and it swung silently and easily. They entered a vast, cool chamber, and the door closed after them.

"Wager those two men'll know each of us again," Jerdren muttered.

The sound echoed. Blorys tapped his brother's arm and minutely shook his head.

Eddis looked around curiously. The room was large and empty, and shadow hid the far walls. A few candles in tall sconces lit the way between the outer doors and another heavy door straight ahead. Their boot heels clicked on polished slate, and the sound echoed. It was cavernlike, she thought. Impersonal.

But the next door opened into a brightly lit hallway, its floor a warm, polished oak, the walls hung here and there with blue and yellow banners. Their guide passed two closed doors along the passage and stopped to indicate an open room dominated by a table covered in books and scrolls. Other than a grate in one wall and a door on the far side of the chamber, there seemed to be no other furnishings. A short, elderly man in green robes came from behind the table and smiled at them, dismissing the guards with a gesture.

"I am Ogric, Castellan Ferec's master of table, at your service," he said. "In a moment, I will bring you to the banquet hall. We maintain little protocol here. When the castellan enters, he asks that no one stand or bow, and you may eat and drink as soon as he gives you greeting." He beckoned them to follow and led them across the chamber into the room beyond.

This room was enormous, clearly meant for feasting. A wide trestle ran the length of the room, with three shorter, narrower tables butted against it. Whitewashed walls were hung with pale blue or yellow banners, and a length of cloth in the same colors dipped from the ceiling. Several men already sat at the main table, though the central three chairs at the head were still unoccupied. At the other tables, Eddis saw everything from graybeards in soldier's tunics to men and women she recognized from the market and the shops. Ogric led them to places at the middle table, closest to the long trestle and opposite the empty chairs. Eddis let M'Baddah hand her into the first of those before settling next to her, his son at his left elbow. Jerdren was across from her, Blor next to him. The rest of this table was mostly taken up by military-looking men, most of whom were curiously eyeing the newcomers. She glanced at Jerdren, who grinned back.

Servants came in to distribute bowls of bread. Men in dark tunics followed, ladling wine into cups. Other servants followed, pouring soup and setting out small pots of dried herbs for seasoning the steaming broth. It smelled wonderful, Eddis thought.

A sharp, echoing rap brought attention to the long trestle. Ogric tapped his staff on the floor a second time. "Castellan Ferec," he announced, and inclined his head as a tall, black-haired and black-bearded man in plain blue tunic and breeches strode into the room followed by two older men who also wore unfigured blue.

Eddis glanced across the table as Jerdren gasped.

"By my grandsire's beard," he whispered. "That's the man who called himself Hollis!"

Blorys tugged at his brother's sleeve. "The castellan? He's the man you talked to yesterday, the clerk?"

"I thought he was a clerk," Jerdren replied. "I'm just trying to recall what I said to him." He fell silent as the three men stood at the center of the trestle.

Ferec waited for the low murmur of conversation to die away. "Guests, friends, protectors, and companions," he said warmly, "eat and drink with me." He smiled at the outsiders as he and his men took their seats. "We dine first here in the Keep and turn to business later."

Once the meal began, a low murmur of conversation filled the chamber. The castellan's attention had been claimed by the man on his right. Eddis was talking to M'Baddah. Blorys got Jerdren's attention again.

"You remember what you said to him?" he asked in a non-carrying voice.

The older man shrugged. "Nothing rude," he replied in kind. "I was hoping to learn about the sortie against the bandits and put in a good word for us, remember? Odd, though. I've heard of men in power doing that kind of thing—checking men and stories for themselves, rather than waiting for a clerk's report. Never expected to be taken in that way myself."

"He's said to be a good judge of character, Jers."

Jerdren picked up his soup and drank. "Good stuff. I hope so, Blor. I guess we'll find out, won't we?"

Across from him, Eddis was nibbling bread she'd dipped in her broth.

"Gods," he murmured. "Doesn't that woman ever eat? All I've seen her do is pick at food!"

Blorys nudged him in the ribs with a hard elbow. "Be quiet, Brother, she'll hear you!"

I heard that, Eddis thought, but decided to ignore him.

Soup cups were taken away, and platters of sliced meat and bowls of dripping juices followed. Feric spoke quietly with the men on either side of him and let his guests alone to eat and drink.

Halfway through the final course—baked, sweetened apples filled with cream—the man nearest M'Whan began talking to him, too quietly for Jerdren to make out what was going on. Then the fellow beyond Blor engaged his brother in conversation. Some moments later, both Keep men rose and went around to the head table, where they spoke at length with Ferec, who set aside his cup to listen gravely. Jerdren forced himself to continue eating and drinking.

More wine was served, and as the servants came forward to remove plates and cups, most of the other guests rose quietly and left the room, leaving only the military men, the older guardsmen who'd shared their table, themselves—and the castellan and his advisors. As the outer doors closed, Ferec rapped sharply on the table. All conversation ceased at once.

"Jerdren, I heard from you personally and from the hide merchant Lodis about the service you and your men did us. And I learned this morning about your feats, Eddis—bringing those priests and their burden safely here, and personally stopping a thief so skilled none of my men had been able to catch him in the act. My thanks to you all, and the thanks of the Keep's guards and citizens.

"As token of our gratitude, my late master would have given you coin and gems. Unfortunately, he is ten years dead, and though we still hold these walls, we no longer prosper. But you deserve recompense."

"Sir," Eddis put in quietly, "there is no need. We did what we had to, nothing more."

Jerdren's boot pushed against her leg, hard, and he scowled at her.

Feric smiled. "I expected you would say that. But valor deserves recognition, and my close advisors and I believe we have found a way to reward you." He got to his feet. "If you will come to my study, we can talk further."

They followed him and his men out a different door and down a long hall, up a flight of stairs. "Men before us and behind us," Jerdren muttered to his brother. "Think perhaps they still don't quite trust us?"

Eddis nudged him and cast him a sidelong, warning look.

Feric led the way into a room at the head of the steps.

Like the old man's chamber next to the banquet hall, this was a plain room, dominated by a table piled high with rolled parchments, quills, and maps. A smaller table against one wall held two fat candles and a tray with pitcher and cups. Several cushioned stools stood about the room. The castellan took his seat behind the table and shoved everything aside but the maps. Eddis and Jerdren were shown to the stools nearest the table, and the rest chose for themselves.

There was a brief silence, which Feric broke, his eyes fixed thoughtfully on Jerdren. "Yesterday, you and I spoke for some time in this room. I am sorry if you feel deceived, but I find it often useful to use the guise of a simple clerk to learn what men think of me, of the Keep, and the way we care for what we have. Often, people will speak more freely to a mere lackey than to the leader—or so I've found."

Jerdren shrugged. "You've the right, sir, to do as you choose. Perhaps I'd have felt ill at ease, thinking I was coming here to talk to a guardsman and finding myself with the master."

"Not 'sir,' Jerdren. Castellan or Ferec. You told me something of your battle on the road. Give us the details now, if you will."

"Well . . ." He made as terse and short a story of it as he could and answered a few questions from one of the graybeards.

"Myself, I doubt the men we fought are part of the armed camp you want. These men set up a lousy ambush that fell apart almost at once. They had more men, but we came away with only a few minor wounds and killed maybe half of them."

"Perhaps," the castellan allowed and turned his attention to Eddis. Between them, she and M'Baddah described the brief one-sided fight on the steep road.

"We never got close to the big man on the rocks," Eddis finished. "The other two—there seemed no reason to stay behind and study them. There might have been more men hidden, and we had two men to deliver safely here. As for that fellow in the tavern, Castellan—that was luck only."

"We've talked to witnesses," Ferec replied. "But, as you choose." He got to his feet and paced the small space behind the desk. "Bandits have always been a problem here. In the years since Macsen left us, we've had fewer men and resources to keep the outside lands cleared of them. These days, we must be content with maintaining the gates and walls, sending out a sortie only when such men come too near the Keep. Unfortunately, these most recent raiders are brash and deadly. They seem to roam the wilderness freely, attacking whomever they choose, but whenever I have sent men to seek them out, they haven't returned. We believe they have some kind of spyhold in the ridges south of us, where they can keep watch on the road and perhaps even on our gates. So they know when we send out men after them." He sighed quietly.

He leaned across his desk, hands flattening the topmost map. "I believe we need a different kind of company, or at least, a different kind of leader—someone who can track those bandits to their hiding place and destroy it. Bring in whoever is in charge of those mercenaries, if possible. Retrieve whatever can be found of the goods and money they've stolen." He eyed them in turn. "People like you.

"This may seem a curious reward, but we will make certain you are well armed and provisioned. You will be free to choose your own company, and we will lend you men who know the nearby woods and riverlands. If you win through, half of whatever trove you recover is yours, to divide as you see fit." He paused. "If you choose, you may talk this over among yourselves and send me word."

Jerdren looked at Eddis and raised an eyebrow. She glanced at M'Baddah and his son, then nodded. "No need for that, si—Castellan," she said. "We heard rumors of this hunt when we arrived, and we've talked it over already. For my men and myself, I accept, and I know Jerdren and his brother are willing. But M'Baddah has an idea—about these spies you think may be out there."

The dark outlander inclined his head. "If I were a master of bandits, I would have such spies. Any high place that can be seen from your walls is suspect. Such men would know when any company leaves the gates, including ours."

"We thought perhaps," one of the advisors said, "you could disguise yourselves as a caravan and its escort."

"But if no such company had come into the Keep previously? It would rouse suspicion." M'Baddah spread his hands. "They say that from your east walls, a man can see all the way down the cliffs to level ground and across open meadow to the forest."

"That is why Lord Macsen chose this crag and built as he did," Ferec replied.

"I suggest, then, that our company wait for nightfall and descend first those east walls and then the cliffs, avoiding the road and the gates entirely. Your men can lower us by ropes, and we could gain the shelter of the woods before moonrise, with the bandits no wiser."

"I like that," Jerdren broke in.

Eddis nodded. "With a man on watch where we went down with a rope ready to lower, we could send back for supplies if necessary, and no one out there would know."

"I can see we've chosen well," Feric smiled. "I'll give you my letter of credit for whatever weapons and provisions you need before you leave tonight. My captains will get word out to the barracks and around the Keep that we want skilled volunteers, and you, Jerdren and Eddis, will be given passes for the inner bailey and the fortress gates, in case you need to speak with me."

He gestured, and one of his advisors distributed cups, pouring a little wine for everyone. Feric raised his in toast. "To your success, and your safe and speedy return. When you do return, we will do what we can to find a more fitting reward."

* * * * *

It was neatly done, Eddis thought. He had worked out a bargain, sealed them to it, and politely dismissed them in almost no time at all. A very short while later, they were escorted by a single guardsman across the now mostly deserted inner bailey.

Jerdren clapped his hands together as the gates closed behind them. "That went well! So, now what?"

A newly risen half moon glanced on closed doors and shuttered windows. Nearby, light came from the windows in the backside of the tavern. Torches flanked the wide entry to the chapel and a single flame flickered somewhere inside. The fountain square was quiet, the inn shuttered for the night with only a single lantern burning low before the main door. From somewhere inside, a loud snore broke the stillness, and someone else snarled a curse. It was very quiet, except for a sudden, muted burst of laughter from the tavern.

"This place goes to bed earlier than our old village," Jerdren remarked sourly as he headed for the tavern.

"At this hour?" Blorys asked.

His brother shrugged. "It's not so late, and there'll be people wanting to talk to us. After all, Ferec said he'd get word out. But there's been plenty of rumor, and with us as his guests tonight—"

"There'll be even more rumor," Eddis said dryly. "But I'm not ready for sleep, either—not after such a meal."

The great room was full, the trestles filled with people. Brief silence from those nearest the door greeted their entry, but after a moment, people turned back to their own business. Blorys went off to the taverner's counter for cups.

The tables they'd had the evening before were still pushed together, and two pale-haired fellows sat at one end.

"Willow! Mead!" Eddis opened her arms in greeting. "When did you get here?"

The two scrambled to their feet and came forward to hug the slender swordswoman, who hugged back fiercely. They were shorter than Eddis and slender, clad alike in loose deep green shirts, greenish-brown trousers, and tall, smooth boots. Golden hair fell loose behind their pointed ears to their shoulders.

"Elves," Jerdren murmured in surprise.

He fell quiet as Eddis beckoned him over, introducing everyone around as her companions drew up stools. Blorys distributed cups, and the taverner himself came over with a pitcher of wine and Eddis's usual ale and pressed fruit. He waved aside her coins and was gone before she could protest or thank him.

"We arrived late this afternoon," Willow—or Mead—replied to the swordswoman's earlier question. They were alike enough that it was difficult to tell them apart, though a closer look revealed subtle differences between their clothing and their faces. "What are you doing so far south this late in the year, though, Eddis? I thought you and your men didn't like facing the passes if there might be snow."

"We still don't, Willow. The pay was worth it, though. I wouldn't have expected you two here, myself. Last I heard, you were heading north."

"We went north. It proved to be another false lead."

"We had better luck east," Mead added.

"Same matter or another?" Eddis asked as she mixed fruit into her ale.

The elves exchanged glances. "The same matter. We finally caught up with the company that attacked Mother's clan, two years ago." There was grim finality in his voice. All dead, Eddis guessed. "One of the dying told Mead that two of their leaders had split off some time before, That they'd planned on coming this way, to harry the East Road."

"Just you two—fighting against how many?" Jerdren asked.

Willow smiled, but his eyes remained dark. "We had surprise on our side. And both of us have some skill with weapons."

"Believe it," Eddis told Jerdren. "They're good."

"Say we've learned the trade," Willow said quietly. "My half-brother is as skilled with his blades as his arrows and as clever a mage as any you'd want to meet. Fortunately, because his spells persuaded that man to talk and let Mead know he spoke the truth. We would never have journeyed so far for rumor or hearsay. As it is . . ."

"We barely reached the stables when we heard about this sortie against bandits," Mead said. "We hear you are to captain it, Eddis."

Jerdren stirred. Blorys gripped his wrist, and his brother subsided.

Eddis flashed the younger man a wry grin. "Not exactly. It was Jerdren's idea to begin with. Since that's so, he can tell you about it, if he'd rather." But Jerdren, his color suddenly high, shook his head. Eddis explained. "It's possible you're looking for the same men we're after." She let the unspoken question hang.

"We'll join you—if you'll have us," Willow said, his eyes moving from Eddis to Jerdren.

Mead merely nodded, but his dark eyes fixed on Jerdren's.

"Don't worry, Jerdren," Willow added with a faint smile. "You look like a man who hasn't dealt much with magicians of any sort, let alone one like Mead. But you have Eddis's word for our use to your party. She can tell you I'm skilled enough with swords, knives, and longbow. Mead's fast and deadly with a bow or his knives. We don't know the lands hereabouts, but we're both good in country like this—woods, hilly ground, and river-bottom. We're both good at tracking and quieter at it than most men. We can see farther and better in the dark, and we've good cause to help you, because we want certain of those men dead as revenge for the pain they caused our family. I'm willing to go for nothing but the chance of vengeance—"

"Nonsense," Eddis broke in firmly. "Share and share alike, Willow. In whatever plunder we recover, in the dangers, *and* in the castellan's offer of funds for provisioning and weapons. Tell them, Jers."

He grinned, as if pleased she'd used his nickname. "Elves as fighting companions—I admit Blor and I haven't had that chance before, but we've heard plenty of tales. It's equal shares for all who come with us," he said.

The two elves looked at each other for a long, utterly still moment.

Mead broke it. "We'll go, then."

* * * * *

Eddis opened her eyes groggily. First light was pale in her window—not enough to have wakened her. A scratching on the door panel brought her fully alert.

"M'Baddah, what?" she asked as she scrambled to her feet and hauled the dark shirt over her head.

"It is no great rush, my Eddis," his low voice came through the window slit. "I merely came to keep Jerdren from pounding at your door to waken you. He is greatly excited and babbled something about a full company or more awaiting you both, outside the tavern."

She scrubbed sleep from her eyes and felt for her trousers. "Outside—you mean, even the *tavern* isn't open yet?"

"Not *quite* yet, my Eddis."

"Tell Jerdren he's a dead man for even *thinking* about beating on my door this early, and I'll be there when I'm dressed and cleaned up. Not before!"

By the time she had replaited her hair and pulled on her boots, sunlight slanted through the little window and across the fountain square. A few merchants were beginning to set up for business. The tavern door was open, and the odor of freshly baked loaves and hot, fried meat carried her through the door, where it was almost as gloomy as it had been the night before.

Jerdren's shout of welcome hit her from across the room. M'Baddah reached her at the same moment.

"I'll kill him yet," she mumbled and let her lieutenant escort her over to the now familiar corner. Jerdren, his brother, and Willow had the table to themselves at the moment. Half a dozen hard-looking armsmen sat together nearby.

Willow laughed quietly as Eddis settled on a stool. "Are early hours as good for you as ever, Eddis?"

"Rrrrr," Eddis replied and gave Jerdren a gimlet-eyed glare. "Early," she informed him flatly, "is essential on the road. Not here."

"I agree," Blorys said. He handed her a cup and a thick

slice of pale, heavily seeded bread, shoved a pot of thick fruit spread her way, then sat back to quietly wait until she'd had a little to eat and drink. When Jerdren leaned forward to say something, Blorys tapped the man's shoulder and shook his head firmly.

Thank you, Blorys, Eddis thought grimly. Keep the man quiet, and he won't wind up wearing the pot of fruit. She finally set her cup down and eyed Jerdren questioningly.

"What's been done?"

"Without you?" he demanded sourly. "Nothing. You and I agreed—equals, remember? Those," he gestured toward the table of men, "are Ferec's contribution. I know a few of 'em, but none well."

"Fine. Let's start," Eddis said and turned to catch the attention of the nearest man.

* * * * *

By midday, they had a solid core group of thirteen and another ten men in reserve. Those going would be themselves, the two elves, and six of Ferec's men who knew the area well, who had tracked and ambushed stray men and creatures, including a burly older fellow who served as cook for hunting parties. A good part of the afternoon was spent questioning the Keep men and going over Jerdren's maps with them. There were small stray bands of men to be found almost anywhere, Eddis learned, but most of them fled if confronted with a few swords. Now and again the guards encountered a regular clutch of armed men, but they also tended to evade a fight as well.

"Possibly under orders," one of the men said.

There were plenty of rumors of other creatures, but while several of the men here had *almost* seen something neither human nor beast, close questioning by Eddis revealed few *actual* sightings.

"That's good," she said finally.

"What do you have against fighting creatures?" Jerdren wanted to know. "Take out a horde of goblins or even kobolds—they're cowards unless they outnumber you, mind—and I wager these people'd be grateful indeed."

She bit back a sigh. "Let's deal with what we know first and with the actual threat to the Keep—armed men, a company of bandits attacking caravans, if you remember? Besides, it just might take more than a few hours together out there before we're a proper band of fighters and not a collection of volunteers who don't know a thing about each other's fighting styles, skills, and drawbacks. I'd rather not take on a horde of kobolds or anything else when I don't know who or what's protecting my back."

Jerdren gave her a sidelong look but said nothing more on the subject.

"You sure thirteen's enough?" she asked finally.

"Remember what you just said about fighting styles, Eddis? The more of us there are, the more of a problem that becomes. Besides, a larger party would just be more visible, and that could make it a lot harder to sneak up on those bandits."

"Remember, we have a backup list of men here. We can always send for reinforcements if we think we'll need them," Blorys reminded them both.

"Good point," Eddis said and went over the list one more time. "Since you want a session or two of weapon practice before we go, I'm thinking we'd better have those men join the rest of us, before we go."

The castellan, true to his word, sent out one of his aides that afternoon, and the man accompanied Eddis and Jerdren to the trader's and then the provisioner's, making arrangements for the party to have funds for the journey. Eddis bought new daggers, a clutch of arrows and several new bowstrings, a spare pack for food and enough plain provisions, travel bread, dried fruit and plain dried meat to fill it. She finished the day utterly exhausted and slept the entire night without dreaming.

Two more busy days followed. Jerdren watched as each of the Keep men demonstrated his sword, bow, or spear skills, and he ran them through some basic maneuvers often enough that Eddis felt comfortable she'd be part of an organized company if someone or something attacked them.

By midmorning the next day, she, Jerdren and M'Baddah had completed a tour of the walls of the inner bailey, looking for the best place to get their people down to level ground. M'Baddah had been right, though. The only practical places for a company to descend by rope were along the east wall, where the ledge was narrow and the rocky heights steep but not undercut. Still, Jerdren insisted on a full tour of the walls, so he could check all possible spots. Maybe he simply liked being on the walls, and she had to admit the view in all directions was spectacular.

That evening, the party met in the stables, where their goods had been temporarily piled up in two stalls.

"All right," Jerdren said. "We've maps, and we've been over what plans we can make up here, but a lot may change once we're down, as most of you know. My suggestion is that you make certain of your goods now, see that everything's done up the way you want it, and that you know where things are stowed. Then each of you get an early night, if you can. We'll want one more check of the local stores tomorrow. No sense in losing your life out there because you lacked a single dagger."

"Good point," Eddis said as he glanced her way. "Tomorrow, we'll meet for a midday meal, and after that I suggest we all rest until sunset. We won't be moving all night tomorrow night, but we'll need all the reserves we've got to get down the ropes and into the trees before moonrise. Questions?"

There were none. After an extensive opening and retying of parcels, checking of weapons and belts, leather bags of goods, and quivers of arrows, the party dispersed by twos and threes. Finally, only Jerdren and Eddis were left.

"All right?" Eddis asked finally.

Jerdren shrugged. "So far," he allowed. "Ask me again, once we're out there."

5

The next night, at full dark, a party of twenty-four stood on the high east wall of the inner bailey. Thirteen of these wore dark, thick, hooded cloaks and carried packs of various sizes, as well as filled water skins, swords, and other weaponry. All but one wore armor of some kind, and Mead carried a sturdy leather shoulder bag that held his book of spells. Ten men in the dark blue of the Keep, Captain Mebros directing them, worked to secure five lengths of thick rope. The knots were checked twice, then five of the men descended to hold the lengths taut. Mardiak, the castellan's sorcerer, stood back from the edge, watching the men's efforts as he cast a spell to detect danger around the base of the cliff. A charm dangling from his right fist had already been used on the ropes and the knots.

Lets us save Mead's spells for later, Jerdren thought. Chances were, they'd need all the spells the elf had, once they were out there.

The party had been blessed just before sundown by the Keep's curate—a man as influential and important in his own sphere as the castellan in his. Jerdren, squatting on his heels atop the walls, didn't feel any different for Xyneg's blessing but had long since decided it couldn't hurt anything. Most of the Keep armsmen going with them seemed more relaxed for having been blessed, anyway. His right hand jittered against his leg—not so much nerves, he thought, as eagerness to be on their way. The first of their men were already down, the second group—including Eddis and the elves—was on its way. The last of the Keep guards next, with more rope for the rest of the way down, and then he and the last of their party would finally be on the move.

He reached the narrow ledge without incident a short time later. To either side, he could just make out the shapes of men working to secure rope while others dropped carefully down the ledge. The meadow below was kept clear all the way to the forest, and it had been watched from the walls until well after sundown. According to Mebros, that didn't leave time for anyone but a horseman at a flat-out run to cover open ground between woods and cliff. *If anyone were to be down there,* Jerdren told himself, *we'd all welcome the fight. That would settle my stomach properly.*

He could make out the nearest people in the gloom. Blor had already gone down, but there was Eddis and behind her one of the elves. Willow, he reminded himself. He and Eddis had worked out order of descent and order of travel back in the tavern. Blor and three of the Keep men were their most keen-eyed or sharp-eared men, and Mead went with them, a charm swinging from his neck. Eddis and her two men were among those who'd follow, while he, Willow, and the rest would bring up the rear.

He and Eddis had decided that earlier as well, comparing skills and reflexes as impassively as if neither were actively involved in this, and he grinned, recalling the bemused look on his brother's face at the time. In blunt fact, Eddis's eyes were somewhat better than his in the dark, her reactions perhaps a hair faster, and she was younger than he by nearly ten years, which would count both on the ropes and down there in the dark.

Truth is, he told himself gloomily as the first five moved quietly out of sight, you don't like heights, Jers. Too bad M'Baddah's idea for leaving the Keep in secret had been such a good one. At least it was too dark for him to see the drop beneath his feet. Yah. You got enough of an eyeful of the drop from up on the walls. He was still willing to wager that Eddis thought he'd been admiring the supposedly extraordinary view from the walls, rather than trying first to work past the fear—and then looking for the quickest and least distressing way down.

Willow tugged at his sleeve, indicated the ledge with a jerk of his head. Jerdren drew on his new, thick gloves, took hold of the rope held out for him, wrapped a heavy length around his forearm in case his gloved hands couldn't hold his body up, and edged his way over the edge of the cliff, where he could clamp the rough hank between his legs.

Somehow, his hands and legs remembered how to get him down a rope—and it didn't take nearly as long as he'd thought it might. Everything moved smoothly, even when his feet lost contact with the stone, and he swung loose over a drop for a heart-stopping moment. All at once, he could see dark shapes below him and felt Blor's familiar grip on his leg. Thumb and forefinger first, to let him know it *was* his kinsman, before the entire hand grabbed hold to guide him to safety. His boots touched ground a moment later, last of the five in his final group. He freed the rope from numbed calves, stepped back, tugged twice, and felt a responding tug before the knotted length began to slide smoothly upward.

It was very quiet where they stood. They were sheltered from the wind here, or it had died away. Jerdren could hear the slither of rope against stone, and someone high above quietly urged his men to haul the hanks in. Somewhere to the north an owl wailed, the sound rapidly fading as the predator flew away from them. The air brushing the left side of his face felt chill and damp: water that way, and something began a monotonous, soft creaking. Frog or insects, Jerdren thought. Likely where the water was.

The sky directly overhead was a blaze of stars, cut off to the west by the bulk of the Keep and to north and east by tall trees and rising ground. No sign of the moon down here. It wouldn't rise for at least an hour, and it was still short of half-full. They'd have plenty of darkness to get themselves out of the open and well into the woods for what was left of the night.

It wasn't actually completely dark where they stood, Jerdren realized. His eyes were finally adjusting. He could make out the difference between pale expanses of grass, darker bushes, and stubby trees. Then he noticed individual faces, with the company so close around him. He stripped off the heavy leather gloves and stowed them as Eddis edged over.

"Mead's checked already," she said, "there's no one and nothing close by."

"Good. We'll move out, then, in order," Jerdren said, as quietly, and stepped aside to let the others go ahead. He'd take up the rear with two of the older Keep soldiers who'd hunted these lands with Lord Macsen himself. Both had excellent ears. Willow took the lead, M'Baddah on his right hand. The rest moved out behind those two.

The company reached the nearest trees without incident. It wasn't any darker in the woods than it had been on the meadow, and Jerdren's eyes had adjusted well enough to the gloom that he easily made out Eddis holding up a hand to signal a brief halt while Willow and M'Baddah went ahead a few paces. Mead bent over his charm, caught his breath sharply as the thing glowed a dull red against his hand. That can't be a good sign, Jerdren thought, and reached for his sword as the mage hissed a warning. With a yell, half a dozen men leaped from the trees into their midst, and more came running from their right flank.

Jerdren drew his sword and parried an overhead blow. Somewhere ahead of him, someone cried out in pain, and he could hear Eddis cursing in a flat voice. A moment later, he went down hard, breath driven from him as a man landed squarely on his shoulders, but the fellow was thrown as he fell. He drew one of his daggers and dragged himself partway up, feeling the ground before him. A boot there—a ragged pant leg that didn't belong to any of his people. The cloth tore from his grip, but he had the man now: the pale face just there, which meant the body was . . . He swung the dagger in a slashing arc and buried it in flabby flesh. The man shocked, shuddered, and went limp. Jerdren retrieved the blade, wiped it on the dead man's shirt, and got warily to his feet.

Just to his right, one of the Keep men was driving back another of the invaders with a spear, and he could hear Blorys's voice not far away. Someone else yelled, and all at once the ambush dissolved, men running wildly toward the meadow, some going north over open ground and the rest south.

"I'm making a light," M'Baddah said, and a moment later a partly shuttered lantern cast a ruddy, dim glow over them.

"What damage?" Eddis asked as she came back toward the edge of the woods. Her sword was bloody, and there was a cut on the back of her hand.

"Winded," Jerdren replied shortly. "Blor?"

"Fine, Brother. We have one man down here, badly wounded—no," he said quietly. "One dead."

"Three of them dead and another stunned," Willow reported. He bent over the half-conscious man. M'Baddah was helping one of the Keep men bandage a nasty cut on another's forearm.

"Make it four of them dead," Jerdren replied grimly and retrieved his sword. He gazed down at the man he'd killed. Skinny, ragged . . . the fellow looked as badly off as any of those men they'd fought on the road, days before, but Jerdren didn't recognize him as one of them. He walked from man to man, checking that all his company was still here. One down already, he thought. But they were fortunate no more of them had been killed. A sudden attack like that, in the dark, men could easily have killed their fellows and not the enemy.

He was pleased to see that three of the men were keeping watch, that M'Whan stood at the edge of the woods to make sure the fleeing men kept running. He followed Mead over to where Willow had the stunned man sitting up.

Jerdren smiled down at him—it wasn't a nice smile. "So," he mused aloud. "Were you waiting for us? Just happened to be here, saw us coming, and decided we looked like a good source of supplies and weapons? Or expecting us?"

The man bit his lip, but when Willow drew a long, slender blade, he shuddered, and the words tumbled from him.

"We been here a while, out of sight of those walls. There's rabbits and such here, but it's getting colder at night. Hard to find game. We heard there were men, hereabouts, they'd take good fighters. But—" he forced his eyes from the blade and the set face behind it—"but we couldn't find 'em. Just now, we were arguing which way to go, some of us wanted to just . . . get out. And our watchman saw you coming. Seemed worth a try, maybe get a warm cloak, bread. . . ."

"He's telling the truth," Mead said evenly.

"What do we do with him, then?" one of the Keep men asked.

"I have an idea," another snarled, and the man huddled in on himself.

Jerdren shook his head. "You—if you're smart, you'll try to catch up with your friends before something gets you. Go fast enough, and go now, and I won't make you pay for our wounded and dead."

Willow hauled him to his feet. The man gazed fearfully from elf to elf, met Jerdren's eyes briefly, then turned and bolted.

"All right, people, we'd better get moving. M'Baddah, I guess there's no sense in dowsing your light. Move out ahead with it, and someone get another one going back here at the rear."

They pulled the dead enemy out to the edge of the woods, while two of the Keep men heaped leaves and pine needles over their fallen comrade. Moments later, they set out once again, with just enough light to let them walk through open forest at a decent pace. A short ways in, one of the Keep men located a deer path he knew, and they turned roughly southeast, walking at a stead pace until moonrise.

Jerdren called a halt for the night just as the moon cast pale light through the highest branches of tall oaks. They'd reached the first of the marked clearings on his map. He'd have preferred to reach the second, but two of the men had lost blood and needed the rest. There was a narrow stream here, nearly dry this late in the season, but it had enough running water to allow them to refill their bottles.

Watches had already been chosen before they left the Keep, and this deep in the trees, the air was warm and still, so they built no fire. Jerdren lay back in his cloak as the first watch settled into place. At the elves' suggestion, they had been left from the regular watches for the present, but one or the other was to be roused at once if anyone thought they saw or sensed anything suspicious, since both could see much farther in the dark than the humans.

Not that it's so dark now, Jerdren thought sleepily. It was the last thing he remembered until Blorys woke him. It was cooler than it had been, especially near the stream, and moonlight now came from the west. Jerdren checked that his sword wasn't shoved too tightly in its sheath, that his two daggers were ready to throw, and hung his strung bow from the hook on the quiver before moving several long steps out into the woods. He slowly paced around the dark camp and the sleepers, occasionally coming upon the two Keep men who shared his watch.

The moon was nearly down and the woods shadowy once more when he woke M'Whan, unstrung his bow, and lay back down. He was asleep in moments and didn't wake until sun warmed the small clearing.

He woke sluggishly and a little stiff, the way he always did, first day on the road. Didn't used to, did you? he asked himself sourly. Getting old, Jers, aren't you? It didn't help that they were traveling afoot; he'd merely traded a sore backside for aching legs. He cleared his throat and spat, staggering to his feet.

To his relief, Eddis was already up and about, and showed no signs of the bleary-eyed, irritable woman who'd broken fast at the inn two days before. At the moment, she was sitting cross-legged on her blankets, plaiting her hair. Beyond her, Willow was bent over, nearly folded in half as his long-fingered hands massaged his calves.

Guess I'm not the only stiff one this first morning, Jerden thought. If a young elf had sore legs—and Willow was a year or so short of thirty, according to Eddis—then he, Jerdren, was doing all right.

Mead leaned against a tree a short ways off, his heavy leather-bound spell book open, his lips moving silently now and again. Memorizing the spells he thinks he might need for the day, Jerdren told himself. Let's hope that if we do have need, he's made the right choices.

Blor and one of the Keep men were keeping watch, the others eating or checking their weapons. M'Baddah was rubbing salve into the arm of their most seriously wounded man, and Jerdren was glad to see the man's color was good this morning. We can't afford to start losing men before we ever find that camp, he thought. First day out, and one already gone.

Their cook came over and handed him a cold meat pie—the taverner's wife's gift to the company, but they wouldn't stay fresh for long. Jerdren took his with a smile of thanks and ate it quickly.

Eddis pulled one from her own pack and bit into it. No onions, Jerdren knew. Though how anyone could live without onions, let alone those crispy, toasted brown bits . . .

None of his business, he reminded himself as he sucked gravy from his fingers, washed that down with flat ale and a swallow of water, then pulled a tart, crisp apple from his own bag of provisions. He finished that as Eddis, M'Baddah and Blorys came over to join him for a look at the map, and a quick conference.

Jerdren unfolded the heavily detailed parchment. "Now, we're about—here, right?" He indicated a point well into thick woods. The East Road had taken a bend south and was at the farthest point from them.

Eddis shook her head. "There are four streams shown between the Keep and that point. We crossed one dry bed and stopped the night at this one. Makes two, Jers."

"Dry being the proper word," Jerdren replied evenly. He

wasn't used to having his skill with maps questioned. "We could've crossed dry, flat beds without knowing it, in the dark."

"M'Baddah would have known," Eddis countered. "I would have." She indicated a point halfway between the Keep and his finger. "I'd say we're nearer here."

"It is easy to settle," M'Baddah put in smoothly as the two co-captains eyed each other narrowly. "Ask one of your hunters. If he isn't certain, we can always send someone up a tall tree. If you are correct, Eddis, the road will be visible. If not . . ."

"I don't believe it matters," Jerdren said as the outlander hesitated. "But by all means, if we've someone good at trees."

"No point in risking a broken leg this early on," Eddis replied mildly. The tension between the two was gone. "We came straight east last night. We're going north today, aren't we?"

"Toward that hilltop," Jerdren agreed, his finger moving to tap at the indicated height.

"At worst, we'll need to angle a little east or west to make it. Though I'm still not sure why we want that hill. Map shows it covered in old forest, Jers. What d'you think we'll see from there?"

"Well, we probably won't see much," Jerdren said as he shoved stones aside and re-rolled his map, folded it twice, and stuffed it into his pack. "Thing is, we should be able to *hear* things. I grew up in hilly, wooded country, and sound carries in hilly, forested land. If there *is* a camp over a day's worth from the Keep, I doubt the men who've set it up will bother to be quiet, especially if they don't know we're out here. If they're within an hour or so of that hilltop, we should hear them. If the lines on this map are correct, or close to it, for how the land rises and falls—well, we can very likely tell where the sound is coming from."

Eddis gave him a cold look and got to her feet. "I didn't ask for a lecture, Jerdren, and I'm not a dim-witted child. Next time just tell me." She strode off and knelt to stuff her loose belongings into her pack.

"She's right, Brother," Blorys said finally. "She's not a child or a fool. Don't treat her like one."

M'Baddah had already quietly moved away.

Jerdren watched his brother go and cast up his eyes. Here I thought fighting a camp of robbers was going to be the hard part. He made sure the map was tucked firmly into his pack, got up and stretched hard, fingers digging at the small of his back.

They moved on soon after, angling north and a little east through ancient trees. There was little undergrowth here, and only an occasional ray of sun came all the way down to touch the needle-cushioned ground. More light reached them at midday, when they took a break, sharing around a skin of wine and one of water while their provisioner and cook handed out flat bread, cheese, spicy, jerked venison, and dried apple slices. The rest of the day was as quiet as the first half, and they made the top of the hill just before sundown.

The trees were an odd mix, here. Massive oaks with thick branches set far apart, as if the hill had once been a nobleman's park. In and around these, scrub oaks, fir and other trees twice as tall as the tallest of them, and thin. Spine-brush and other weedy undergrowth was everywhere.

There had been no water all afternoon. No pools, not even a dry stream bed, and as the ground rose, the dirt grew harder underfoot. Mead, who was still in the middle of the company, glanced at Jerdren once or twice and finally dropped back to join him.

"There is something wrong here," the elf said quietly.

"Wrong?" Jerdren stopped, sent his gaze around the woods, tested the air with his nose, then simply closed his eyes and *felt*. No unusual sound, but no lack of sound, either. He could hear birds high in the branches, small creatures rustling through the lower brush. Nothing that would have warned the boy Jers to back away and run for it. He finally opened his eyes and shook his head.

"Excuse me please, but I've never before worked with a magi—a mage. Or an elf. Perhaps we're not using *wrong* in the same way. I'm at home in a hilly wood, and there's nothing here to make me wary. You?"

Mead was standing very still, head cocked. He shook his head. "I am not certain what it is. My spell revealed nothing. Just—if we stay in this area for the night . . ."

Jers considered this, then shrugged and started walking again. The rest of the company was a ways ahead, and Eddis glanced back. He waved her on.

"We should have about one more hour of walking, mostly uphill. Once we're there, we'll talk again, Mead. If there's danger about, we'd be fools to camp in the midst of it."

The mage merely nodded.

They reached the brow of the hill well before sunset. There was little brush here, but the trees were closer together and smaller. Most of the Keep men were already sitting as Jerdren came up, rummaging through their packs for water and dry wafers, while others gathered firewood. M'Baddah and his son were keeping watch. Blorys knelt to cut a hole in the springy grass for the fire. Eddis just dropped her pack and was waiting as her co-captain joined them.

"Nothing much to see here, Jers, and all I've heard so far is the noise we're making. Which isn't much."

"It's enough," he said and bit back irritation that was at least half caused by tired legs and feet. "We'll listen once everyone's settled in. But you and I had better listen to Mead, first." He repeated the earlier conversation.

Eddis frowned at her fingers, then looked around for the mage.

The elf had moved away from the rest of the party and now stood with his hands against the bole of a massive oak, eyes closed, fingers exploring the rough bark. Willow eyed his half-brother anxiously, then came over to join Eddis and Jerdren.

"He said he told you, Jerdren. He still can't be specific about the threat, just that there's something. He's concerned enough that he won't be sleeping tonight."

"If . . . we were to keep going, farther north maybe, or back the way we came?" Eddis asked. "There's at least an hour of daylight left, but we could keep going after dark with lanterns again."

The elf shrugged. "He's had the sense for most of the afternoon. Whatever is bothering him, I doubt we could get far enough away from it before dark, but he still says there isn't anything close by that's any threat." Willow tipped his head back to gaze high into the trees. "The last time he had a feeling like this, we were attacked by an owlbear. Nasty creatures, and hard to kill. But there's plenty of deer and small game tracks here. You wouldn't see any, if it was an owlbear."

"We've got trackers," Jerdren said. "Men or—or whatever's around—has to leave prints."

Eddis waved an arm, taking in the land sloping down and away from them on all sides. "On this? There hasn't been rain in a long time. The ground's hard." She drew a deep breath, let it out slowly. "All the same, you're right. I'll get a couple of these men to keep watch and let M'Baddah and M'Whan take a look while we're getting settled in. And I say we keep the fire going tonight," she added. "All night."

"I was going to say as much," Jerdren replied.

Eddis merely nodded and went off to talk to her lieutenant.

Thin, high clouds began to move in as their cook got a fire going and began kneading dough for bread. Wind sighed through the high branches, though little reached the camp. Willow found a small, bubbling pool down the north side of the hill, so there was water for soup and washing. The meal was eaten in shifts, with four on guard around the hilltop at all times. Mead ate on his feet, wandering in and out of the trees, often stopping to listen.

Willow, Blorys, and Eddis took turns at listening also. The only nearby sounds were wind, and the crackle of fire, and now and again small birds high overhead.

Later, when Jerdren went down to the spring, a squirrel ran off chattering through the branches, and moments later the unmistakable bounding thumps of a deer crashing through the undergrowth brought him up short. He closed his eyes briefly as the deer moved out of hearing. Odd, he thought. There still wasn't anything that would have warned Lim to run for it or at least keep a wary eye out. Still, he'd have expected more squirrels, possibly birds lower in the branches and not just high in the firs. He climbed back to the camp, dipped his cup in the pot of tea, and got comfortable.

"If there's a camp anywhere hereabouts, we'd've heard something. I didn't, and more to the point, neither did Blor or Willow. So I'm thinking," he added with a glance at Eddis, "that we turn back south tomorrow and angle off toward the east."

She shrugged, sipped steaming liquid, then turned to look for Mead. The mage was leaning back against the great oak, staring up into its branches.

Willow stirred. "I'd like that. If there's no one out here, then we're wasting time and supplies looking." He shook out his folding leather cup, dipped up a fresh cup of tea, and carried it over to his half-brother.

Jerdren looked at Eddis again, then around the campfire at each of the men there.

"All right. We'll move out at first light. Some of you gather more wood, enough to keep that thing going all night. Make sure one of you's watching while the other gathers branches." His eyes strayed toward the now pacing mage. "He'll be on watch the entire night, but we'll keep four men on at all times. Blor, you take someone and bring back water for the morning."

"Better do it now," Eddis added. "Once it's dark, a spring like that could draw all kinds of predators."

He knows that, Eddis, Jerdren thought tiredly. His brother merely smiled, caught up the empty pot, and took one of the spearmen with him.

* * * * *

The sun was gone from sight, muffled in cloud. There would be no moon until nearly dawn, and the night was very dark. Four at a time kept watch, with one making sure the fire stayed going. Mead walked quietly around the circle of sleepers, or leaned against the oak, his fingers exploring the bark and his eyes troubled.

* * * * *

Eddis came awake at M'Baddah's light touch and sat up, shoving wisps of hair out of her face. The air was cool and still. Disorienting, she thought. I thought it was autumn, and me back home again. She'd half expected to see the familiar old bed she'd shared with her sisters, and beyond the narrow window opening, the family vegetable garden. Here instead was a campfire and ruddy light on tree trunks, flickering shadows cast by trees and branches, and armed men who moved quietly around the hilltop.

It wasn't her favorite sight. She'd grown fairly used to woods and the way a campfire made them look, but firelight hid more than it showed, and just now she could imagine all manner of things just out of sight. Don't imagine, she ordered herself flatly and rubbed her eyes.

"Quiet so far," M'Baddah whispered.

Eddis nodded and sat cross-legged to string her bow, then looked around. M'Whan squatted by the fire, cup in hand, and two of the Keep men were moving out into the night as two others came in and rolled in their blankets for a few more hours of sleep. Most of the men around the fire were merely dark, blanketed lumps, but Blorys was directly across from her, a shock of red hair spilling over his face. Eddis gathered up her bow and three arrows, making sure the rest weren't bound together in the quiver the way they sometimes got, and walked away from the light.

Mead was there, pacing around the great oak. If he saw her, he made no sign. Eddis hesitated, then went on. Better not to distract the mage, though his behavior worried her. She hesitated again just off the brow of the hill. Thin fingers of firelight flickered on a pale-barked tree, but it was otherwise dark out here. Once her eyes adjusted, she'd be able to see as well as anyone but an elf. Just don't trip on something and break your neck, Eddis, she thought. One thing for certain: Any bandits sneaking up on them might see the fire, but they'd see no better than she did, and she'd hear them coming. Every few steps she stopped, but there wasn't anything to hear. *Hope that means the other three are being as cautious as I am and not that they aren't moving. Or that something got—*

She broke that thought immediately. This wasn't the place to think about "things" getting anyone.

Back the other direction, then. She could make out more of her surroundings this time—like the line of heavy, dry brush on her left that anyone or anything would have to crash through to reach the camp from the west.

She reached the end of the brush and was ready to turn back when Mead's yell of alarm reached her, and, from the sounds of things, immediately roused the camp. Someone was bellowing orders up there—Jerdren? But another voice topped his—a rough one that didn't belong to any of their men. She tightened her grip on the bow, shifted the arrows to the same hand and, with her free hand outstretched to keep her from running headfirst into trees, clambered back up the hill as fast as she dared.

The camp looked like utter chaos, with half-wakened men scrambling from their blankets to snatch up the weapons they'd left at hand, and others charging across the open ground to protect them from the half-dozen massive brutes who came striding up from the south. They carried ugly spears and two-handed swords, and she realized with a shock that none of them were human. Jerdren and M'Baddah stood shoulder to shoulder, swords ready, just behind three of the Keep men who braced their spears against the ground. Blorys and Willow were firing arrows as quickly as they could, and as Eddis hesitated at the edge of the clearing, one of the hulking creatures howled and staggered away, two arrows protruding from its thick neck.

Mead stood with his back to the fire, halfway between it and the vast oak, staring up into darkness. Eddis looked in horror as a bloody Keep man fell from the lowest branches and lay unmoving at the mage's feet. As she set an arrow to her string and started toward Mead, the elf mage waved her back.

"No closer," he shouted. "It's a lion!"

Eddis swallowed sudden dread and backed away, eyes fixed on the tree. She was dimly aware of the fighting behind her— men crying out in pain, a clash of swords, and the bellowing of wounded enemy. There. Gods! Twice her height above the ground, she could make out see the green glow of narrowed eyes reflecting firelight. Then M'Baddah had her by the arm, dragging her away toward the fire that their cook was working hard to build up.

"Three of the monsters are dead," her lieutenant told her. He almost had to shout to be heard above the melee. "The others won't last much longer. Stay back from that tree, my Eddis. The beast came without warning and snatched *him* up before any of us could react!"

He knelt to wrap moss around one of the long branches, tied it in place, and poured a dollop of lamp oil over it. He turned away to look over the fighting as Eddis swallowed dread. The cat's eyes seemed to hold hers. Willow moved past her, bloody sword in one hand, and took up a position not far behind his half-brother.

Jerdren's excited voice rose above the clamor of fighting. "That's got 'em, men! One more of 'em bleeding and— sure enough, there they go! No, stay put!" he ordered sharply. "No point in giving 'em cause to turn in the dark out there and come against us. We'll clean up, wait for daybreak, and move out. Willow, where'd that brute of a cat come from?"

Light flared from Mead's outstretched hands, illuminating the oak and its occupant: A tawny, cream and black cat at least as long as Eddis was tall spat and snarled in fury from its perch.

"It should run from light," she whispered. Why isn't it running? Why, for that matter, had it attacked a lighted camp?

The beast vaulted onto a higher branch and edged out over the mage, ears slowly going flat. Mead fell back a pace and began another muttered spell. M'Baddah thrust one of his fresh-made torches into the fire and handed the spluttering branch to Eddis. When he started across open ground toward the oak with another, Willow held up a hand.

"Stay where you are! It has already killed one man, and you cannot reach it with that anyway."

"It's not showing proper fear of fire *or* light," Blorys said. "It just pounced, caught that man by the throat, shook him, and started dragging him into the tree. That's not natural!"

"Arrow!" one of the Keep men called out. Eddis ducked down as an arrow sang over her head and buried itself deep in the branch just in front of the massive cat. The beast snarled and snapped it with a slap of one massive paw, but stayed where it was.

"Don't flush it down here!" Jerdren ordered sharply. "It's already killed once! If we can scare it off—!"

"And how do you plan on that?" Eddis demanded.

M'Baddah handed his torch to one of the spearmen, strung his bow, and fished out one of his arrows with a thickness just behind the point. He held that in the fire until it caught, took careful aim, and fired, just as sparks exploded upward from Mead's outstretched hands. The arrow just missed the cat, but Mead's spell didn't. Eddis smelled burned hair. The cat screamed, half-spun on its branch, and leaped for the ground. It was a long blur of gold and black, flying across the clearing, then it was gone. They heard it squalling, well to the north, then nothing.

6

Eddis's legs folded under her. Her skin went chill and damp. M'Baddah dropped down next to her and wrapped an arm around her shoulders.

"Everything is fine now, my Eddis," he murmured. "The beast is gone and so are the orcs—the two who were able to flee."

Behind them, someone was building up the fire, and she could hear Jerdren calling out sharp orders.

"We'll search those brutes before we drag the bodies out of camp. Any gold or gems they might have on 'em—well, I'd say we've earned those, all of us. Eddis?"

"I'm here!" she called back, and for a wonder her voice was steady.

"Just checking! M'Baddah, we need some of that salve of yours over here. Got a couple nasty cuts."

"I will tend the wounded," Mead said as he came back into the light. "Orc blades are sometimes poisoned." He murmured something to Willow, who set an arrow to his string and stayed by the oak, gazing out northward. The mage hesitated as M'Baddah helped Eddis to her feet.

"Are you all right, Eddis?" he asked. "You look pale."

"I *feel* pale," she said and licked her lips. "I hate lions. I really hate them. They eat people! I came out here to fight bandits, not to get eaten!"

Mead smiled briefly and squeezed Eddis's fingers.

"I had forgotten that about you." The smile was gone as he glanced back toward the tree. "But there are worse ways to die. That man—he never knew what struck him."

She merely nodded, and the mage went on to deal with the wounded. Four men down, Eddis thought, and their provisioner was limping.

Get control of yourself, she thought. Jerdren would find it amusing, and she wouldn't enjoy being the butt of his heavy-handed humor.

Sure enough, there he was when she turned around, grinning across the fire at her.

"Buck up, Eddis," he said cheerfully. "We held our own against orcs, and the big cat ran off, didn't it?"

She glared at him.

"It may not have run as far as we would like," Mead said as he knelt to pour water over bloody fingers.

"It *can't* run as far as I would like," Eddis muttered. Jerdren didn't seem to hear her.

"Ah look, Mead. The animal wasn't sick, was it? Stubborn, maybe, or just simply hungry, but it did finally run!"

Mead shook his head. "It is not sick. It was startled, but only when fire actually touched it. The one who controls it may send it back against us. If I am right about why I was not aware of it until it killed, why it came into the firelight, and why it did not flee the noise or my light spell . . ."

He shrugged and fell silent.

Jerdren laughed. "Control? Someone out here in the midst of this gods-forsaken wilderness controls a mountain lion?" He held up a hand, forestalling comment. "Look, we have plenty to do between now and daybreak. If there's no immediate threat, tell us about this control later, when we're on the move."

"I cannot tell, any more than I could sense the cat earlier," Mead said. "What I felt earlier was the sense of cold, human purpose in the beast. That is gone now, but I am no longer sure that I will even be able to detect that much, if it should return. The spell is human, I think, but turned. Evil."

"A black sorcerer?" M'Whan asked.

"Perhaps," the mage replied. "But I think the man is not so much evil as mad."

Jerdren stared at the elf in visible disbelief.

"Uh, mage?" One of the Keep men came forward. "It's said there's a madman out here in the wilds. Some have it that he was one of the old Lord's priests, and others that it's only a tale. No one's ever seen him, or if they did, they didn't survive it. But I know men who've come hunting out here, and they've heard wild laughter."

"You didn't tell us that!" Jerdren said. He sounded exasperated. "I asked for any information that any of you might have, and here you hold out on me . . . ?"

"It's fable," one of the spearmen said defensively. "Just another of those tales that everyone hears but only children believe."

Mead shook his head. "The cat was real, and so is the spell."

"Well, never mind," Jerdren said finally. Another of their guards brought over two heavy leather purses that clinked when he handed them over. Jerdren poured the contents into his hand and grinned.

"There's something like—seventeen gold pieces and two red stones in all." He slid the whole into one bag, tossed the other aside, and snugged down the ties. "I'll hold this, but we'll share equally."

Eddis stowed her arrows and knelt to roll up her blankets as two of the Keep men went to deal with the body of the man the cat had killed. In the end, there wasn't much they could do but cover him with fallen oak leaves and take his spear and daggers.

"Look, Jerdren," Eddis started, "I see no point in staying here until daylight. Especially after what Mead's told us. I say we break camp now and move south again."

"What if there's more orcs out there?" he asked.

"We fight them, what else?"

"I agree with Eddis," Blorys said, one hand coming down hard on his brother's shoulder. "With a mountain lion prowling around here, you can wager there's no robbers' camp. Especially if the cat's under someone's control. Don't look at me like that, Jers. We've done what you wanted, which was to eliminate this part of the forest first. No one's going to get any more sleep, and it's nearly dawn anyway."

Jerdren's lips tightened and his color was high.

"Look, Brother," Blorys continued. "Eddis is right, and so's Mead. You're just being stubborn, and this isn't the time or place for it. You didn't know what was going to happen tonight, and no one's blaming you for picking this hill for our camp. Take a deep breath, relax, and let's pack up."

Jerdren turned to Mead. "What chance you'd be aware of that animal if it came sneaking up on us?"

The mage shrugged. "I cannot be certain, but the creatures are territorial. It fled north, so the farther south we go, the less likely it is to follow us."

"But if it's under some madman's control . . ."

"It is still a territorial animal, and the farther the lion moves from its master, the weaker the spell becomes, until it loses its power entirely."

"Oh." Jerdren scratched his head. "Didn't think of that."

"So, we should go now, and with lights," Mead went on. "Because Willow and I can see well enough to avoid trees and pitfalls, but you cannot. I have a spell that should turn aside any small band of orcs or robbers, if we stay close together."

Jerdren looked at Eddis inquiringly, his lips still tight. For a moment, she thought he was going to argue again, but he finally shrugged and turned to stuff the orc's purse in his pack.

"We'll do it then."

"Thanks," she replied. "M'Baddah, you and M'Whan keep watch, and the rest of you pack up. Leave those orcs where they are and break out a couple of lanterns. You men, we'll need the light. Move it!" She cast a sour glance at Jerdren's back. Stubborn, difficult man. She should have known he'd be like this. Just now she was sorely tempted to thump him one. She turned away and caught Blorys's rueful smile. Poor Blor, how did he manage?

M'Baddah had finished sorting his arrows and slung the red-and-black-painted case over his shoulder. Eddis left her bow strung as well, hooking it onto her quiver and freeing up her short sword. Their cook poured sand around the edges of the burning wood, leaving only one thick branch aflame for light. All around, men worked quickly, gathering up their belongings and settling their packs.

It was still very dark out, and the trees seemed to loom over them. Eddis's hands were trembling once more, making it hard to get her lantern lit.

I'd forgotten how much I dislike woods at night, she thought. *Sensible people don't belong out here. I'll fight just about anything that comes at me, but it helps if I can see it coming!*

Lantern in one hand, sword in the other, she drew a deep breath and tried to relax. Too much had happened in too short a span. Still, she'd made a fool of herself just now, snapping at Jerdren. Good leaders weren't supposed to act that way, and these Keep men didn't know either her *or* Jers well. No doubt they'd both lost face.

They moved out moments later. It was slow going at first, even with the lanterns and the elves' keen eyes to lead them around trees and snags. Near the base of the hill, they came across a game trail heading roughly southeast. Jerdren wanted to follow it, but Eddis was firmly against using it, and both Blorys and M'Baddah backed her up.

"If deer use it," Eddis said flatly, "so do the things that hunt them."

They went on through the woods, but she could hear her co-captain grumbling to himself for some time after.

The moon rose just as they came back into the area of reasonably flat ground and wide-spaced trees. Willow set a better pace here, and before long, the moon rose. Eddis could tell by the shadows that they were heading east and a little south.

Mead once asked a for brief halt so he and Willow could check their back-trail.

"There is no hint of anything or anyone following us," the mage said as he came back. "And there is no one anywhere near us just now."

"Good," Jerdren said. "Then, if no one objects, we'll find a clearing and set up camp for what's left of the night."

No one objected.

Eddis bit back a sharp retort. "I agree. Let's go." Fortunately for her temper, they found a decent clearing a very short distance on. She took first watch, and by the time she'd made a full circuit of the camp, Jerdren was rolled in his blanket and presumably asleep.

* * * * *

Morning came cool and cloudy, with a stiff breeze that blew smoke and ash everywhere. Eddis woke to the smell of burned porridge and the sounds of men moving quietly about. Nearby, M'Baddah and his son were talking quietly. She yawned, stretched and sat up, shoving loose hair out of her eyes and behind her ears.

"There's Eddis!" Jerdren's cheerful voice smote her ears. "Pleasant dreams last night? No lions?"

She gave him a cold look from under her lashes, finally shook her head. "What about your watch?"

"Dead quiet the whole time," he replied. "Mead didn't sleep at all, and he said the brute wasn't anywhere about."

"That's good enough for me," Eddis said. She took porridge and a mug of hot tea from the cook as her co-captain moved on. Thanks to the wind, the honey-sweetened porridge was covered with fine ash. She shrugged, stirred it in, and began to eat.

"We need to talk, you and I," Jerdren was back, map in hand. "Not while you're eating. I know."

"Thank you."

"I think we need to move out as soon as we can, Eddis. Maybe even cross the road and keep going south, since it doesn't seem that—"

"We need to talk," Eddis said levelly, "but not while I'm eating. Not unless there's an emergency. Finding that camp of robbers is important but not an emergency."

"But, I—"

"You're still talking. Go away, Jerdren," she said and bent over her bowl.

Silence. The man sighed and went away. M'Baddah came over to sit next to her. She gave him a smile and went back to her breakfast. M'Whan and one of the guards came in with an armful of dry branches and went out for more. Eddis finished her food while it was still warm and sat, eyes closed. She could hear branches snapping off to her left and M'Whan's low voice, then the Keep man's response. They were too far away for her to hear what they said. Somewhere closer, she could hear Blorys talking to Jerdren. He sounded rather exasperated.

"Jers, relax, can't you? The last watch needs to eat still, and we need the fire because that mush won't be edible if it isn't kept hot, you know that. We can't break camp yet, anyway. Mead needs a little quiet time to devote to his spellbook, remember? So there's no use you prodding Eddis this early"

Jerdren sighed heavily. "I know that, but if we don't—"

"It'll all get done, trust me. Meantime, there's a couple men here who can probably help you figure out where we are better than Eddis can. Remember what someone said a while ago about lizard men and boggy ground? We don't want to stumble headlong into fens and monsters. And you don't *really* want to fight lizard men again, do you?"

"I remember someone talking about lizard men, Brother, but I don't remember anything about bogs."

"Maybe that was something I heard back in the Keep, then," Blorys broke in. "I don't remember. Doesn't matter. *Not* finding lizard men is important to me. You and I are the only ones here who've fought them before. We were part of a full company, with experienced officers, and it was *still* a nasty battle! That's not why we're out here, anyway. We're supposed to find bandits, and deal with them. Remember?"

Silence. Eddis sipped her tea, eyes closed, aware of M'Baddah at her elbow. She wondered briefly if Blorys meant her to overhear their conversation, then decided it wasn't worth worrying about.

M'Whan's warning shout brought her to her feet, the empty bowl sliding from her lap, her empty cup going the other way.

"*Yrik!*" he bellowed in his own tongue.

The Keep man's voice topped the outland youth's. "Orcs, coming right at us. Between us and the camp. Twenty or more!"

"Up the tree! Do it now, man!" M'Whan yelled at him. "Father! They're coming at you from north and south!"

Eddis dove for her bow, slipped the string in place, and grabbed the three arrows she'd left next to her blanket the night before.

"Got it!" Jerdren shouted. "All right, people! Half of us over here, and Eddis, you take the north! Three lines deep, just like we practiced!"

"Got it!" she yelled back and grabbed two of the spearmen as she strode around the fire. Thank the gods they *had* practiced this maneuver, she thought as she knelt and dropped the sword belt between her knees, so she could fit an arrow to the string. Archers in front, spearmen behind, sword at the rear. It was all they had time for as several massive, ill-clad creatures burst into the clearing. Some carried short stabbing swords and round shields, one a mace, and two of them heavy clubs. She heard Jerdren yelling a challenge as her first arrow soared across open ground to bounce harmlessly off a hardened leather jerkin. You didn't factor for the wind, she told herself and sighted down her second arrow. At her right, M'Baddah was steadily firing arrows, and to her left, Willow had already brought down two of the monsters.

"Aim for the eyes and the throat!" the elf shouted.

Eddis shot again, aiming just at the massive chin of the nearest orc. The wind sent it a little offside and down, but she'd corrected properly this time. With a howl of agony, the brute went down, nothing of her arrow visible in its throat but the fletching. With her third arrow gone—it wounded the orc who was trying to avoid tripping over his dying companion—

she let one of the spearmen draw her back through their line and caught her breath. Keep men jabbed at the oncoming brutes, and two of the men fell.

Remember what you learned the one time you fought orcs, Eddis told herself grimly.

The man right in front of her brought down his enemy with a mighty thrust to the eye and lost his grip on the weapon. Eddis eased aside for him to retreat from the next orc that was charging straight at them, club swinging.

"Break—now!" she shouted. The same cry echoed from behind her half a breath later—so Jerdren was still on his feet and fighting. Orcs charged into them, but the humans and elf were no longer a compact fighting group, splitting off by ones and twos. Eddis leaped aside as one orc stumbled over the stones edging the fire pit and fell. One of the Keep men caught up the brute's club and with a wild yell, brought it down on the back of its head. The orc shuddered, then lay still, its hair and jerkin smoldering.

"Look out, Blor!" Jerdren yelled.

M'Baddah pulled Eddis aside as another orc charged across the open at a dead run, a mace clutched in its hand. The outlander spun away from an overhand blow at the last moment. Eddis pivoted the other direction, letting the orc's charge send it hurtling past her. Her sword sliced through the air and down, biting deep into the backs of its unarmored knees, severing tendons. The brute shrieked and collapsed on its back, one arm and the mace under it. Eddis reversed her grip quickly and brought the sword down two-handed, burying the blade in its throat, leaping back as blood pulsed high. It slowed almost at once.

Across the fire pit, Jerdren was fighting back one monster with slashing two-handed swings of a club. Blor was still on his feet, but she couldn't make out anything else. A wordless shout of warning from M'Baddah brought her back around as he brought his curved sword down in a hard, overhand arc across the nape of a fallen orc. Two of the creatures still stood, but neither was moving well, and both were bleeding copiously. Two others came from the trees, but they weren't running. Getting wary, she thought. They should. There were six of the brutes down and dead that she could see, and one of her people in trouble, so far as she could tell.

One of the two newcomers went after M'Baddah, who had fallen back with two of the spearmen. The other orc brought up its short sword and charged her.

She stood her ground until the last possible moment—nearly too late. Its shield clipped her left shoulder hard, and her arm went numb. She pivoted, but already off balance, she went to one knee, lashing out with the sword as the monster passed her. More by luck than intent, the blade slammed into its ankle just above a huge, filthy foot and rebounded, nearly flying out of her hand. Bellowing in rage and pain, the orc came about, sword slashing wildly as it tried to hit her. Eddis fought her way back to her feet and backed out of reach as the orc tried to come after her. The wounded leg wouldn't support it, and it went down but fought its way back up again. Eddis glanced over her shoulder to make certain she wasn't heading into the arms of another orc, then backed up, yelling as she went.

"Someone with a spear—finish him!"

"Arrow!" one of the Keep men shouted back, and she dropped to one knee, flinching as a bowstring twanged from somewhere close behind her. The arrow, unfortunately, merely creased the orc's skull, but a half-breath later, one of M'Baddah's deadly steel sh'kuris sang across the clearing and buried itself in the orc's throat. The creature sagged, wavered, and finally fell over.

"Eddis!" Jerdren's bellow cut through the howls of furious or wounded orcs. "They're running!"

"Got it!" she shouted back. Apparently the orcs had had enough. Those who could still move were beginning to back away, leaving their wounded. When they reached the woods, they simply turned and fled. She turned to see two others running from Jerdren and Blorys. The only orcs over there were four wounded and three more dead.

She kept her sword at the ready and moved around the north perimeter of the camp as M'Baddah called out, "We're clear here, my son!"

"Coming!" M'Whan shouted back. He sounded short of breath, and looked it when he and the Keep man came into camp a moment later. "They're gone, father, across the road and still running. But one of them thought he'd climb into the tree with us, just now."

"What were you doing in a tree?" Jerdren wanted to know.

The youth shrugged.

"We hadn't much choice. One minute we two were alone out there, getting wood, and the next they were between us and camp. We got up high enough that the branches wouldn't have held their weight."

"Thanks to you, I'll have that story to tell, lad," the Keep man said. "Boy pulled me right up there with him, and me half again his size."

M'Whan shrugged that aside, but his color was high as he went to help his father pull dead orcs from the camp.

Jerdren looked around, then raised his voice. "What damage, people?" he asked.

"A few ugly cuts and bruises on our side, and not much worse," Eddis said. "M'Baddah, we can use you here, dressing cuts! Anyone who's not badly injured, help drag those brutes out of here."

"Search 'em first," Jerdren called out, as he looked up from an examination of one of the dead orcs hear the fire. "Remember what we found last night!"

"Orcs," Eddis muttered with distaste. She wasn't ready to search through one of those greasy leather jerkins. Fortunately, no one else seemed to share her feelings. She sheathed her sword and winced. Her left arm was beginning to ache in earnest where that shield had slammed into it.

Jerdren came up moments later, grinning cheerfully, a heavy purse swinging from his left hand.

"Well!" he said cheerfully. "There's one way to wake up the company, right, Eddis?"

"It's hard on the porridge," she replied dryly. "Why don't you get that pig out of the fire pit? The fire's going out, and the last watch hasn't eaten yet."

He tossed her the purse and bent to drag the smoking orc away. Eddis gazed at the bag with mixed feelings. It was heavy, but it was also soaked with blood. She dropped it on the ground and rolled it in the dirt and left it there for the moment. She clapped her hands together to get the men's attention. Her arm throbbed in protest.

"Anyone who's hurt, even a scratch, you know which of us has healing potions! Poisoned blades, remember? A dirty sword cut can kill you just as dead or cost you an arm! Those of you who haven't eaten, do that now! Rest of you, let's finish searching the dead brutes and get the bodies out of camp, and as for any orcs still alive—well, you know what to do. Let's get it done!"

She turned to look for Jerdren. "Jers, do we have someone on guard?

He nodded.

"Good. I'll help M'Baddah clean wounds. You finish searching those creatures, if you don't mind."

"Didn't realize you were squeamish, Eddis," her co-captain said. His glance flicked toward the filthy pouch under her toe.

"I'm not. I'm being practical. It's poorly tanned hide, and now it's soggy with orc blood. You put that in your pack, and the whole thing'll smell like rotting meat in a day or so. I'm letting the worst of the mess soak into the dirt before I pour out whatever's in there and count it, if you don't mind."

"Oh." He blinked. "Didn't think of that."

"No, you were thinking of gold and gems. Remind the other men, will you?"

"Good point." He turned away as Mead came back into camp. "What's still out there?" he asked.

"They are gone," the elf mage said. "Still running, as far as I can tell, but at this hour I have only charms to assure me of that." He pulled his book of spells from its leather shoulder bag.

"That's good enough," Eddis said. "You're exempt from cleanup, of course. You've got your own important task."

He merely nodded and settled close to the fire on his blankets once again, book open.

Blorys had come in and was watching her, she realized. "Let me worry about cleaning cuts, Eddis. Your arm is hanging limp, and I can see the pain in your face whenever you move it. Go, get M'Baddah to fix you up."

She nodded and he smiled suddenly. "You paid attention to what I told you back in the Keep, didn't you? I just happened to turn when you took down that last monster, and when you could see he was still a threat, you didn't try to finish the job yourself. Sensible swordswoman, that's you."

Eddis could feel her face redden. "Sensible swordswoman wouldn't be out here, fighting nasty creatures twice her size. But thank you."

"Of course. Stay sensible, swordswoman. Get M'Baddah to tend to that arm, will you?"

She nodded and watched him walk over to help Jerdren pull the dead orc from the fire pit. His words warmed her. Sensible, hah, she thought. Well, see you stay that way, Eddis. Because by this time tomorrow any of you—including Blorys—could be very dead. A wise swordswoman would think of any fighting companion as sword-fellow and friend, but nothing more.

7

It took time for the men to haul the massive bodies away. By the time Jerdren and the others returned to the camp, their provisioner had a fire going once more and the last of the porridge reheating. The men who'd been on guard when the orcs attacked ate as the others began packing up their blankets or retrieving what unbroken arrows and other weapons they could. Mead turned the pages of his book. Eddis sat cross-legged on her blanket, counting out the contents of the orc's purse Jerdren had tossed her—most of the weight came from copper pence and a small bar of silver that gleamed wetly in the early morning sun.

There were also two odd little bundles of sticks and string. M'Baddah, who sat close by bandaging one of the injured, looked them over carefully and suggested she give them to Mead.

"I think they are fetishes, but he may know what they are used for and if they are dangerous for us to keep."

"I didn't think of that," Eddis said. She dropped them atop the dust-coated bag and wiped her hands on her breeches.

It was quiet for some moments, except the crackle of the fire, and the faint groans of one of the spearmen who'd received a nasty crack on the back of his head. Fortunately, his helm had kept him alive.

Jerdren came back into the clearing and knelt at the fire to pour hot water over his bloody hands. None of it seemed to be his blood. He blotted them on his shirt and grinned at Eddis.

"There's one way to work up an appetite!"

"Not my favorite," Blorys replied. He'd come up behind her and settled down next to her. "Arm better, Eddis?"

She nodded.

"Good for your reflexes, a fight like that," Jerdren said. His grin faded. "We need to talk. The few orcs we left alive ran, and from what I saw, I'll wager they're still running. Maybe it was just our bad luck to pick a place to camp where we'd cross paths with 'em. Still—is it possible there's a hold of those brutes around here?"

The Keep men eyed each other. "There's no rumor of a hold," one said finally. "Now and again, hunting parties'll see prints that might be orcs or other such creatures. And they've been seen at a distance—but only a few of 'em at a time. Fewer than we fought here."

"But you don't send patrols eastward, do you?" Jerdren asked. "And you don't hunt this far into the wilds, so would you even know?"

"I would know if there was a hold close by," Mead said. He was stowing his book in its case as he came up to join the others. "I tested this area for evil before agreeing we should camp here, if you recall, and I made sure none of the orcs we fought last night had followed us."

"Oh, right." Jerdren rubbed his chin thoughtfully. "It just seems odd, as much wilderness as there is, that they just happened to wind up where we are."

"We didn't travel that far last night, and we weren't exactly being quiet, this morning," Eddis replied dryly. "And there's the fire. With this wind, they could probably smell the smoke for a long ways. But if you ask me, it doesn't matter if these orcs were part of last night's bunch, or if they're a completely different troop."

"It might matter," Jerdren said. "Because if there are bands of 'em wandering around out here, that just might mean we're close to a den. We aren't out here to battle orcs. They're big and nasty, and cursed few of 'em carry what I'd call a decent pocketful of coin. Besides, if there's orcs all over the place here, what chance is there we'll find that band of robbers in the same area?"

"I'm not arguing with you," Eddis said.

One of the spearmen looked up from his pack. "I'm remembering something," he said. "About two years ago, there was a company of men rode in from the east, early in the year. They told us they'd had one fight after another— orcs and all manner of other creatures—some distance from the Keep, where the road runs through heavy woods, down in a long, deep ravine. They broke free, finally, but half their number were dead, and most of their pack horses were gone, too."

"That long ravine is at least another day's ride from here," another said. "Up where the caves are, or so it's said."

"Caves?" Jerdren sat up straight and suddenly looked very interested. Blorys sighed quietly.

The Keep man shrugged. "Back when Macsen was still lord of the Keep, men went farther from the walls, and all this around here was peaceful. None of us here have ever seen the caves. There's always been stories, though, about a great run of caverns where monsters of every kind live."

"Oh." Jerdren waved that aside. "No robbers there, then. That's too far a distance for the men we're seeking, anyway."

He came partway to his feet and looked around. "We just about ready to move on?"

"Nearly," M'Baddah said. He was rubbing salve into an armsman's cut fingers, while Mead tended to the man with the aching head.

"Good." Jerdren broke out his map. "Anyone got an idea where we are? I mean, we're obviously somewhere in this area." He pointed at a place well within the woods, where they came down close to the road.

"More like here," one of the archers said. He indicated a place farther south. "We don't come this far to hunt, not often, but seems to me I've been here, time we came down the road last year. If I'm right, the river'll be right close to the road when we do come into the open, and there's the swamps just on the other side."

Blorys came around to look over his brother's shoulder. "You know," he said, "I've been thinking about the other side of the river—not where it's swampy, but back west. Here, where the water divides, those are islands, right? This time of year, will the river be low enough to cross?"

The archer nodded. "This time of year, water's almost warm, and it's low enough to ford, plenty of places. We haven't looked that far east of the Keep, partly for the distance, partly because they'd see us coming down from the Keep road and have all the time they'd ever want to set an ambush."

"Yes," Blorys replied, "but this time, they don't know we're out here."

"Unless they've heard all the fighting," Eddis said dryly.

"True. Even if they did, there's no reason they'd suspect who we are or why we're here. It just seems that this area is fairly close to the Keep, near enough to make it easy for men to see what's on the road and go after it, but still far enough away that men could bring their horses down to the river to water them and not be seen. Especially if they come down at dusk." He ran a thoughtful finger along the river. "Since they know the Keep isn't sending men to look for them, then I'd wager they aren't changing their camp very often. If at all."

Eddis nodded. "Makes enough sense to test your idea, Blorys. You think we should—what? Pick a couple good trackers and hunters, send them across the river to check the banks for prints, and see which way they go?"

"Exactly. Even if the tracks fade out on hard ground or stone, we'll know where to start. If I'm right, there should be plenty of signs of their passage."

"Besides, it's about the best choice left," Eddis said. "We haven't found anything to show they're north of the road. The other side of the river seems the next best chance for finding them, I'd say."

She looked around the fire. Everyone seemed ready to move on, and their provisioner was ready to douse the fire.

"Like you said, Jers, probably those orcs are still running, but I'd feel pretty stupid if we were still sitting here when they came back. I say we move out now and move as fast as we can. Once we reach the south edge of the woods, we can look over the land, make certain exactly where we are, and decide what to do."

Jerdren nodded and rolled up his map. "Good idea. Let's get going."

Eddis backed away from the fire pit as the cook emptied his pot over the fire.

"At least one of you hunters out front with me," Jerdren said. "And Willow? You've good good ears, I'd like you at the rear. Eddis?"

"Rear with Willow, or flank," she said.

He grinned cheerfully. "I was just thinking, way you carved up those two orcs just now, maybe we want you in back, in case they try sneaking up behind us."

"Funny man," she retorted and scooped up her pack.

The ground remained fairly level, the woods open. Eddis could see well into the trees on both sides, but steady wind high in the branches made too much noise for her to hear anything else. By the time Jerdren called a halt, she could clearly make out the road, and across it, a bright green line of brush that marked either the river or swampy ground.

Jerdren beckoned her over as two of the Keep men went a little farther on. They were back within moments.

"I was right," the archer said. "Fens and bogs are ahead, just across the river. That big mound is about dead ahead of us, and the river bends back south again." Jerdren had his map out, and the man pointed. "Just here."

"So the islands are back west along the road," Jerdren mused. "We'll stay in the trees, take a short rest there, then find a place to look out where they are. We can decide what to do at that point."

They went on, paralleling the road but still in tree shadow. Afternoon shade soon hid most of the land to the south, deep shadows cast by the hills rising steeply out beyond the river. Jerdren chose a small clearing a little farther back in the woods, and dropped his pack.

"Cold camp tonight," he said. "If the men we want are up on that hillside somewhere, a fire might be seen."

Eddis settled on her heels, back against a tree. "So—where from here? And who's going?"

"Best plan, I'd say, is you and I, M'Baddah, and a couple of the Keep hunters go down to the road, see what we can make out. Go from there."

She shoved to her feet for answer.

Willow came with them. "There is nothing coming along the road, in either direction," the elf said quietly. He couldn't have been heard at any distance beyond his companions. Wind blew dry brush and dust westward along the road. "I can see no movement south, toward the river, either, but there is plenty of tall brush out there, between us and water.

Jerdren peered and finally shook his head. "I can't even see that. No sign of movement up on the hillside, either, but it's kind of dark over there."

He took a step toward the open, but Willow held him back.

"There is still light on the road. If anyone was watching over there, you could be seen."

"Maybe," Jerdren replied with a shrug. "Still—I don't see anything high enough out there where someone could be spying on the Keep."

"We're too far east of the Keep for that," one of the hunters said, "but look a little farther west. The slope goes up sharply, and it drops off to the west. If I was setting a watch, it would be on the west edge there." He pointed.

"Then we need to go farther west?" Jerdren asked, but M'Baddah shook his head.

"Even if the watch is up there, I think no one would set a camp up there. Too much trouble to get in and out. Likely the camp itself is in thick woods, fairly close to the water. Soon there will be ice and snow on the heights, and if we are searching for signs of men and horses along the water," M'Baddah added, "then it makes sense to me that we start here and work our way back west, toward the Keep."

"I agree," Eddis said. "If there's nothing else we can see out here, I say head back to camp, and decide who goes . . ."

She fell silent as Willow held up a hand. He was gazing back the way they'd come.

"Enemy. Men there," he whispered sharply, and drew his sword.

Jerdren shook his head dubiously but drew his sword as a bowstring twanged loudly, and a man yelled in pain. Someone else swore.

M'Baddah and Willow were already running quietly and swiftly through the trees, Eddis and the others right behind them. The elf held up a hand as they neared the camp and gestured with his chin. A man lay dead a few paces ahead, between them and the camp. Three others were shooting arrows into the small clearing, and as they watched, one of the men fell. More yelling from the far side of the camp. Jerdren touched Eddis's shoulder to get her attention.

"We'll send M'Baddah and Willow around the north side. Keep those for ourselves." He grinned tightly as the elf vanished quietly into the trees. "I'd say—" he was counting under his breath— "about *now*."

There was more yelling north of them, all at once, and then M'Baddah's voice: "Eddis, go!"

She threw herself at the nearest of the archers with a hawklike scream. The man yelped in surprise as he came around, the bow falling from his hands, but as she closed with him, he drew a dagger from his sleeve and brought it up in a slashing backhand, inside her down-swing. Pain flared hot and sharp across her cheek. Her earlobe stung, and blood ran down her neck. She fell back a pace, and the man came after her.

"Fool!" she snarled and lunged. The sword went deep into his belly, and the hilt was torn from her hand as he fell. She set one foot on his chest, fought the weapon free, and brought it down in a hard arc across his throat. He shuddered, went limp. Cursing steadily, she shifted the blade to her left hand and felt her face cautiously. A long cut ran from her jaw nearly to her nose. It stung, and her ear throbbed. Most of the blood came from a small nick at the base of the lobe. Messy, a little uncomfortable, but nothing more

The clatter of fighting ceased, as suddenly as it had began. Jerdren had one of the men by his leather jerkin, a thick-bladed dagger held against the fellow's throat. He looked at her in sudden concern.

"Much hurt, there, Eddis? You're all bloody."

She shook her head.

"Good. Hey, the camp! Coming in!" Another glance at Eddis. "Need my help?"

"You deal with him. He clipped my ear, that's all."

She checked the fallen men. The one who'd been wounded just as they came up was huddled in on himself, moaning pitifully. She shifted the sword back to her right again and tapped the back of his head with it. "You're not dying. You're making too much noise to be hurt badly," she said harshly. "Get up. You wanted in our camp? Fine, let's go."

It took a little prodding, but he finally edged away from the tip of her blade and fumbled to his feet.

She gazed at him. Dirty, ragged. "You attacked us a couple nights ago, just inside the forest, didn't you?"

Silence. He stared at her slack-jawed.

She nudged him with the flat of her blade. "Go on, move it."

There were three other ragged, thin men already in the clearing. One lay on his side, eyes closed. His shirt was soaked with blood, and he seemed to be barely breathing. The one Jerdren had by the jerkin wasn't injured that she could tell. The other two bore cuts but weren't much hurt. Two of the Keep men took the man Eddis was guarding as Blorys came across the open ground, his eyes wide.

"You're hurt!"

"It's not bad, really," Eddis said. She was suddenly very tired and wanted nothing more than to just collapse. "My ear," she added with a smile. "You know how ears and scalp wounds bleed."

"Your face—gods, Eddis!"

"It's shallow, just a cut. M'Baddah can—"

Mead came up and took her arm. "I have a charm, Eddis. We'll heal it."

"You might need that later," she began, but Blorys and the mage both shook their heads.

"It would be bad for morale," the elf said, "to have our only swordswoman scarred. Besides, it is my charm, and therefore my decision."

"All right," she said, "but later. There's some unfinished business first."

One of their men lay facedown in the clearing, an arrow protruding from his back, and three others had been injured, though none badly.

Jerdren, M'Baddah and Willow had already begun questioning their prisoners, and the wounded man Eddis had brought in was stammering out answers, despite curses and threats from the man Jers had disarmed and dragged in. Two Keep men stood over him with drawn swords, which Eddis thought was all that kept him from throwing himself on the fellow.

"Yeah, we were with those guys that ambushed you the other night. But how'd we know you were gonna be down here by the road? Couple fellas followed your tracks the next morning, and you were going north."

"If you'd been smart," Jerdren said evenly, "you'd all have kept going the way you were running when we were done with you. Why didn't you?"

The fellow gave him a sullen look. "Because *he* said he knew where we could find these men." He pointed to the loud man under guard. "And because we're city men mostly, not hunters, and we haven't had a decent meal in days! We'd never make it back into the realm, so why try? What else was there—go up to the gates of the Keep and beg for bread?"

Jerdren was quiet for a long moment. The wounded man watched him warily. "Eddis," Jers said finally. "All of you. You know what we have to do here, right?"

Eddis nodded. "It was a mistake letting any of them go the first time. We do that now, and they'll attack us again. Or—"

"Or they'll get lucky, find the men they're looking for, and use the information about us to get into that camp," Blorys finished.

The wounded man paled. "You—you can't just . . . !"

"Can't just kill you?" Jerdren's lips twitched. "Would you rather we tied you up and left you here? There's a mountain lion out here, and there's orcs, and worse things. The castellan of the Keep's given us a charge. We have the right to execute lawless men like you." He turned and caught hold of the fellow he'd brought in, dragging him cursing and snarling to his feet. "You first. At least it'll shut you up."

M'Baddah came across. "Two men to hold him for me. I have done this before." He glanced at Eddis. "Let us do this and be done, quickly," he added. He turned and walked into the woods. Two Keep men came after with the ragged prisoner between them, and two others with drawn bows, in case he somehow broke free. The wounded man gazed after them, stunned, then buried his face in his hands and wept harshly.

Eddis took a deep breath, and Blorys wrapped an arm around her shoulder.

"Are you all right?" he asked.

She nodded, not trusting her voice at the moment.

The sun was nearly down by the time the last of the bandits was taken away—the wounded man, still weeping, had to be carried because his legs wouldn't hold him. The other bodies were dragged off into the brush. M'Baddah was gone for some time after that, dealing in his own way with cold-blooded killing, Eddis thought. Mead had tended to her face, and she was grateful for the sudden lack of pain, though all the fuss seemed foolish.

Jerdren looked around the clearing finally and sighed. "All that for seven miserable coppers. It seems we keep piling up dead enemies around the campsites, doesn't it? I say this time we leave 'em right here, and we move on."

"No argument," Eddis said, when it became clear they were all waiting for her. "And don't fuss over me, please. I don't ask it or need it. It wasn't cut that badly to begin with, and it's healed." The shoulder and sleeve of her shirt were stiff with blood. She'd have to change into her spare and wash the thing before she slept.

Jerdren gave his sword one more wipe before sheathing it. "Once we get settled, if there's still time, I'd like to send M'Baddah out with his pick, four or five men, to see if there's any sign of those men along the river."

The dark man merely nodded, and moments later, they were on their way.

Eddis found herself in the middle of the party, with M'Whan at her side, and Mead a few paces ahead, two of the Keep men a distance behind. M'Whan was quiet, his brows drawn together. She touched his arm to get his attention.

"Anything wrong?" she asked quietly.

M'Whan sighed faintly. "It's Father," he said. "This scouting party. I . . . he'll ask for me to go with him, I know he will. Though after what happened on our way up to the Keep, I wish he wouldn't."

"After—oh. Odd. I'd nearly forgotten about that ambush. M'Whan, it was *not* your fault that your father was wounded. Maybe one of us would have been killed, if you hadn't taken care of that man on the road."

Silence, which she finally broke. "You aren't as good as he is, but that is only because he's had more years of practice. Someday—"

"No, Eddis. He will always be my *Nehuah*, and I will always be his student. He has the greatness to be a master, a true *Nehuah*, and I do not. It is better that I accept that, don't you see?"

His voice was like M'Baddah's, Eddis thought—low and non-carrying.

"I don't believe that's true, M'Whan," she said, as quietly. "Remember, your father chose you as his *Nehuelo*, and he explained it to me. *Nehuelo* doesn't just mean apprentice. It means 'the one who guards the back of the master.' "

M'Whan shook his head, visibly frustrated. "If he chose merely because he and I are the last of our family, if he chose for love of a son, or pride in his family . . . ?" An abashed smile turned the corner of his mouth, very briefly. "I doubt my father ever would have spoken of such things to you, as I do now, when he was *Nehuelo*. That is another difference between us."

Eddis kept her eyes on the ground before her. Shadow was deep here and the ground uneven.

"All right," she said finally. "Perhaps he did choose you for family, or for love. But remember, when he and I needed another guard, he asked that I hire you. You're his son, yes, but if you weren't skilled enough to take care of yourself, why would he put you in danger that way—or himself, or the clients who hire us? Or me, come to think of it. He's fond of me—damned if I can think why, but it's so."

"If I fail him again . . ." The outland youth's voice was overly tight as it faded.

"You haven't failed him yet, M'Whan," she replied. "The mere fact you worry that you aren't good enough is reason to send you. The last person we'd want out there is someone like Jers—someone so full of himself that he'd wind up tripping over his own feet and putting everyone else at risk."

A familiar voice spoke up just ahead of her. "Someone mention my name?" Jerdren asked. "Just making sure my co-captain is all right," he added cheerfully.

Eddis rolled her eyes. "Save the sweet concern for your merchants' women," she replied crisply. Jerdren laughed and strode off toward the lead again.

M'Whan bit back a chuckle. He still looked tense when she glanced his way but not as bad as he'd been. "Thank you, Eddis," he said quietly. "If he does ask, I'll go, and I'll do my best."

"I know you will." She smiled. "You don't think I'd risk *your* life, do you? You're important to me, and I value your skills and your presence. Your sense of humor. Good enough?"

He nodded.

"Good. It looks like we've found someplace to stop," she added as they came into a clearing—this one longer than the previous one, with a shallow creek running along one side. She dropped her pack next to the water and knelt to bathe her face.

M'Whan went in search of his father.

* * * * *

The sun was near setting when M'Baddah led M'Whan, Willow, and two Keep men across the road and into high, frost-crisped grass. The air here was damp, and fog was beginning to pool in low places. They followed the west riverbank for some distance, then struck out due west as the shoreline became mucky and rank. The last of the tussocks behind them, M'Baddah again turned south and met up with the river almost at once, but now the ground was firm, sandy, and smooth and the bank lined with willow trees and bushes. Berry bushes, aspen, and the tall reeds blocked his view of the water, though he could now hear it, very close by.

The outlander signed for his men to stay where they were while he and the elf eased silently through the underbrush, stopping only when they could make out the ruddy light of sun on the water. It moved slowly here, a broad stream but shallow, the pebbly bed clearly visible. Partway across, massive black stones twice his height reared skyward, and the water boiled white around them. Not a good place for a man to walk, M'Baddah knew, unless he wanted the feet swept from under him.

There were two large islands midstream, the larger directly across from him. He couldn't tell much about the second because it was west, in deep shadow. Smooth water there, and he thought it might be deep.

The sandy bank was marked with prints, but none of them belonged to men or horses: there, the deep, pointed prints of deer, and beyond them a large bear.

The nearest island was nearly flat, and wooded, but not thickly. A long look told him it was uninhabited. From here, he could just make out the far bank of the river, and beyond it, rocks and trees climbing steeply toward the darkening blue sky. If they crossed now, there would be enough light for them to be seen, if there were any watchers, but they would need what light there still was to pick a safe way across and to see any prints on the south shore. M'Baddah thought this over as his eyes searched upstream and down once again. Nothing and no one in sight, and aside from the sound of water moving slowly over stones, he could hear nothing but the distant cry of a hawk. He still withdrew as quietly as possible, Willow right behind him. Once in the open, M'Baddah beckoned his company well away from the water and into brush before he whispered a description of the riverbanks, drawing a map in the soft dirt with his finger.

"I say we all cross to the island, but only two of us go on from there. Whoever has the best eyes among you, I want you on the island to keep watch, with Willow as your leader. That way, if the two meet trouble, someone will be left to carry news back to the camp. With me, I want the best ears among you."

They discussed this briefly and quietly and chose one of the spearmen. M'Baddah turned and led the way back to the riverbank.

Silence, except for the burbling of the river around the standing stones. The wind had died away completely, and the colors of sunset shone on the water's surface. M'Baddah took up a slender stick about half his height, removed his boots, and tucked them under his arm. He led the way into the shallows, feeling his way with the stick first, the Keep man a few paces behind him.

As he'd hoped, the water was merely cool this late in the season and never deeper than his ankles. The two men reached the small island without incident. There were a few willow trees here and a few thorn bushes covered with bright red berries. The outlander signed his companion to stay where he was, in view of those waiting on the north shore, and crossed the island barefoot, squatting behind low bushes to study what he could see of the far bank.

By the currents, the water was deep to the east but noisily shallow just to his left. He picked out what seemed the best crossing, eyed the opposite bank and the hillside. Still quiet, there. He backed away from the bank before standing and signing to his companion, who turned and waved to the others. The two men waited long enough to be certain the others were safely on the island before stepping into the water once more. Much later and it would be too dark to make out prints.

They crossed as quickly as they dared. M'Baddah emerged between two tall, bushy willows and slid into shadow behind smooth boulders, the Keep man right behind him. He stayed hidden, an arrow loosely held to his bowstring, while the outlander began moving slowly eastward, bent low, so he could study the damp, sandy bank.

Cat tracks here, plenty of deer once again, and what must be a sow bear, with at least one cub. He thought two, more likely. A bare space, where a rock ledge came far in to shore, and beyond that . . . M'Baddah crouched down and peered at the ground. Horses and horse droppings. Shod horses had come down to the water and gone away again, and there were enough overlaid tracks to show they'd come this way for many days. With them, boot prints—at least three men, possibly more.

They may be other men, and not those we seek, M'Baddah told himself, *but it's not likely.* He eased to his feet, but before he could sign to his companion or those across the river, he heard the soft plod of heavy, hooved feet behind and above him—up the steep hillside and still among the trees— and the low voices of at least two men. He slid back along the rock shelf, ran sideways along the harder, drier sand above the waterline, and went down flat in deep shadow under a low bush just as the men came into sight. They were leading three horses each and grumbling.

A splash along the bank, farther to the east—M'Baddah held his breath as both men turned to look. Finally one of them sighed gustily.

"Just a fish. Let's get these brutes their fill and get back to camp. I'm bored with horse duty."

"Fish?" the other replied gruffly. "Big for a fish, wouldn't you say? Besides, all the noise the horses make, we'd scare off a bear—and I didn't hear anything big running away."

Silence, as the two men listened intently. M'Baddah, scarcely daring to breath, slowly eased one hand to where he could reach his dagger hilt, and waited.

8

It was silent next to the river for some moments. The horse waterers were apparently listening intently. M'Baddah could hear his heart beating, the sounds of horses drinking and shifting their feet on the bank, the faint gurgle of water flowing by. Finally one of the men spoke again.

"It was a fish, like I said. You know what this country's like. There's no one about between here and the Keep, especially after sundown."

"Fine," the other said. His voice was reedy and sounded sullen. "These brutes done drinking? Because we still got another string to bring down tonight."

"You're forgetting orders. Captain doesn't like it when his black stallion gets restive up there in camp, on account he didn't get to drink his fill. You don't want the captain mad at you for neglecting his horse, not if you're planning to stay here. And you remember what he tells all you new men if he decides you don't get to stay."

"I remember. He said we earn his trust before we get to go on any raids, and if any of us tries to leave on our own, we get tossed off that cliff up yonder." He grumbled under his breath. "You'd think I was a spy from the Keep or something," he added resentfully.

"Happens I believe you aren't," the first man said.

"Well, then—"

"I said *I* believe you. The captain may be my brother, but he makes up his own mind about things."

It was quiet for a long moment. M'Baddah shifted his weight cautiously.

"You don't like how things are, that's too bad. At least with us, you don't have to walk perimeter guard that last cold hour before sunrise."

The sullen man replied, but too quietly for M'Baddah to make out what he said.

"Thought you understood that," the captain's brother said. "Fewer men we have wandering around the hillside, less chance the Keep men will see 'em. Besides, we've got a sentry box way up high on the mountain. You'll see for yourself, one of these days, but I can tell you that anyone goes into or comes outta the Keep gates, someone up there sees it."

M'Baddah could hear the stamping of restless horses, and the captain's brother spoke again, his voice unexpectedly warm.

"Get enough there, Night? Good horse."

The ground under the outlander's body vibrated with the thud of hooves on hard-packed sand, and he heard the scrape of a shod hoof on stone. Sounds of men and horses gradually faded.

M'Baddah counted time with his fingers against one leg. At twenty, he cautiously got to his feet. No one and nothing—then another scrape of hooves against stone, far enough away and above him that he barely heard it above the sound of running water. He crossed back to the rock slab and cautiously waved upstream. The Keep man must have been waiting for that because he immediately came downstream. He was dripping wet.

"That splash—it was you they heard?" M'Baddah asked, one hand continuing to press out the count, a finger at a time.

The man nodded.

"You heard any of that?"

"I was too far away."

A wary eye to the hillside, M'Baddah quickly filled him in. "Go back to the island," he said finally. "Tell the others. Send two back to camp with word for Jerdren and Eddis, but tell the rest to remain on the island in case I need them. Tell my son and Willow to come here but to wait for my sign. Those men will come back with another string of horses, but I will be able to hear when they are coming. Tell M'Whan, the usual signal."

The man merely nodded again and went.

Another count of forty. It was still quiet uphill. M'Baddah signaled, waited for the elf and youth to ford the river, and drew them down the bank a ways.

Willow listened for a long moment. "We're going up there?"

M'Baddah nodded. "The three of us. We will follow the two bandits when they take the second string of horses back to camp."

M'Whan was watching the river, though it was getting too dark to see much. "How far up there do you think it is, Father?"

"A distance. I am keeping count."

Both nodded. Willow eased back into shelter, and M'Whan settled down in the low brush with his father.

They didn't have long to wait, but this time down, the bandits barely spoke, and as the horses finished drinking, one of them uncovered a dark lantern—just enough to light the path. Then they started back uphill. M'Baddah rose cautiously, as the sounds assured him the party could no longer see him, and was rewarded with a brief glimpse of movement a distance overhead. It vanished into the trees almost at once. He stepped onto the bank, and M'Whan got to his feet as Willow came back to join them.

M'Baddah pointed uphill and whispered, "Stay away from the watering place. Leave no prints."

He moved out silently, over flat rock and onto wiry grass, his son right behind him, the elf bringing up the rear, a strung bow and arrow bunched in one hand. Just beyond the grass was more stone, and then a rough path—an ankle-deep, shoulder-wide indentation in the dirt. It led away from the water and up, into forest.

It was darker here. M'Baddah stepped aside, so Willow could lead the way, since the elf could see clearly here. They moved quickly, for the path was clear and smooth. It wound between trees and up a gentle slope, then took a sharp turn and began to switchback up steeper ground, littered with fallen trees, rockslides, and boulders.

Willow stopped abruptly and touched his ear—a gesture the outlander could barely make out, it was now so dark. Silence. Then M'Baddah could hear it as well: the clink of a harness, just ahead and a little ways on. A thin, flickering beam of light touched a tree ahead and higher up, then vanished.

"No danger," the elf whispered, "but we are close enough to them, I think."

Moments later, he was on the move again, but almost at once, he slid off to the side, behind a huge slab of rock and waited for the other two to join him.

"Fire, ahead there," he whispered. "I smell it, and I can just hear men's voices."

"What now?" M'Whan asked, as quietly. Both he and the elf turned to M'Baddah.

"We wait," the outlander said. "An hour or so and they will sleep. They do not post sentries, but it will still take all the care and quiet we three can manage. We'll map the place best we can."

Suddenly, sharply, he signaled for silence and lowered himself to the ground, dark cloak over him. On the other side of the stone, voices could be heard.

"Down already?" a deep voice asked. "Captain doesn't want the high sentry left untended."

A rough voice answered. "Let him keep watch himself, then. There's nothin' a man can see this time of night without a moon, and that Keep's locked up tight until sunrise anyway, you know that. Any bread left?"

"Might be. P'raps some of Blot's venison stew."

The second man snorted. "Won't be any bread, but plenty of stew. The wretched brat manages plain bread but can't cook anything else."

"Shhh! Captain's brother is everywhere these days, and he don't put up with anyone giving Blot grief, remember?"

"Huh. Why the captain had to send our only cook on that last raid . . . !"

"Because the man wanted to go, and that's his right—was. Same as yours."

"I know, I know." Silence. The man spoke finally, his voice quieter. "Any new raids in the planning?"

"Huh. What I hear, they'll wait as much as five days now."

"Better send soon," he grumbled. "It's fall, the grain carts come in about now. If we're to winter out here again, we'll want a proper share of that."

"By all the gods at once," the other hissed, "you trying to get us killed? Even his brother don't try to second-guess the captain!"

"Well, you asked me," the sentry said as the two men moved away.

M'Baddah waited to be certain both had gone on and only then raised his head. He grinned briefly at his son and the elf.

* * * * *

Middle night saw the three back across the river and struggling to get damp feet into their boots. The sky was clear, the stars casting just enough light to let them pick a path back to the road. Once across it, M'Baddah stepped aside to let Willow lead. Several moments later, he could make out the faint flicker of firelight through the trees and the unmistakable red of Jerdren's short-cut hair as the man crossed behind the fire. Moments later, they walked into camp.

"We decided against a cold camp," Jerdren said. "Anything out there can probably smell us out anyway, the fire can't be seen from the road, and most of us voted against cold stew." He and Blorys made room for the three. "Mind talking while you're eating? We know you found someone—couple of men and some horses."

"We found the camp," M'Baddah said. He smoothed the dirt before his crossed legs and began drawing a rough map of the camp with his dagger. "The camp itself is a long climb up, on a wide, forested ledge that overhangs the river. A good place for it. The trees are thick enough and the camp set back far enough from the edge that no one could see it until they came upon it. We were fortunate."

"No," Eddis said quietly. "You knew the right kind of place to look."

The outlander cast her a brief smile and went back to his map. Jerdren set aside his cup and rose to look over the man's shoulder. "The site is compact, built around three central fires. There is a trail, here, the way we came. We could not find another trail leading down from the camp."

"Then I'll wager there isn't one," Jerdren said.

"We were able to listen to men talking—at the river, outside the camp, and several in the camp itself. They see no reason to keep watch around the camp, merely a man or two awake at night in case creatures or men come upon them. This has apparently not happened, so the camp guard may be awake, but I doubt he is vigilant. There is also a path that leads up, and it climbs very steeply, from what we could see. That goes to the sentry watch we expected, and they do watch the road and much of the Keep from there. There are at least thirty-four men, and I think there may be as many as forty."

"Two or three apiece, with a few left over?" Jerdren grinned. "I'd call it bad odds for them, wouldn't you?"

"On ground they're familiar with and we aren't?" Blorys asked.

Eddis caught his eye and shook her head. Jerdren shrugged and gestured for M'Baddah to go on.

"There is a large tent here." The outlander indicated a place just back from the north and southwest fire pits. "It seems to be for their captain to hold meetings. He and his brother also sleep in there. The horse line is south, where the cliffs rise up steeply, and the rest of the men sleep under a long canvas, or in the open, according to their choice. The drop-off is to the north—there. It hangs over the river, I believe, but the edge is near enough the camp that we did not go there."

He glanced up and nodded to Willow, who took the dagger and his place at the rough-drawn map.

"To the west—here," the elf said, "I found crates covered in waterproof blankets. They are grain and food stores mostly. I checked what I could of them. No gems, gold, or coins there, but I would say that any wealth must be kept in the captain's tent. By what I overheard, he trusts very few of his men."

"The men who attacked you, Jerdren, were from that camp," M'Baddah went on. "It seems one of you cost them their cook. There was much grumbling over the lack of skills of this Blot, who has taken over his duties."

Blorys got to his feet and moved to where he could gaze over the elf's shoulder at the map. "Clear enough. One way in, but they aren't keeping watch over it—lazy or foolish, I'd say."

"Perhaps," M'Baddah said, "but it has worked well for them, until now. One thing you and your men did, Jerdren—they have no plans for another ambush right away. The last one was bad for the men's morale."

Eddis smiled at him. "Good work," she said. "We've found their camp, we know what it looks like, and we've got a good idea what we're facing here. I like that. Still . . ." She frowned at her fingers, then turned to her co-captain. "Jerdren, you may not like this, but hear me out, will you? I'm concerned about numbers. M'Baddah says probably forty of them. I know that you fought some of their men, and you weren't very impressed, but that doesn't mean all of them are poor fighters. They'll be on their home ground, fighting for their lives and a way of life that's been pretty good for them so far. We're good in a fight, all of us—we've proved that. But I want you to think about what the odds are really going to be like here."

His lips twitched, and he rolled his eyes.

She gave him a cold look. "I'm not done yet, and it's just a suggestion, but what if we waited for their next raiding party to move out, then ambushed those men *before* we went after the camp? Say they send out—how many attacked your wagons, twelve? Fine, that's twelve fewer men when we go after the camp itself. Now, I'd wager we could take the raiders by complete surprise. They'd be thinking ahead to the fight and what they could steal, and never expect to be ambushed themselves, would they?"

"It's an idea," Jerdren said. "Has its points. But two things. We can't be sure what parts of the road a sentry can see from up there. They see us attacking their men, and they'll know we're onto them."

"If we hit them after dark, it won't matter," Eddis broke in.

"Sure, but one of them might get away from us in the dark, make it back and warn the camp, and there goes the surprise. I still say forty of them against us is bad odds for them, but only if they don't expect us. Other thing is, what would we do with prisoners? Tie 'em up and leave 'em for the orcs? Walk 'em up the road to the Keep, where their sentry could see us? I didn't much like having to order those men executed this afternoon, Eddis."

Silence. She finally sighed faintly and shook her head.

"Good," he went on. "Now, I say we send M'Baddah or Willow back up there, maybe a couple of our other quiet-footed men with 'em so more of us know what this place looks like. Make sure this evening was part of a regular pattern. The rest of us be ready, because once the camp's mostly asleep, we get into position and hit 'em hard, from all three sides, kill those we have to, make prisoners of the rest." He glanced at one of the spearmen. "The castellan got a lot of dungeon cells?"

"A few," the man replied, "but they're large and mostly empty. Keep folk tend to avoid 'em."

"Good. Maybe we even let a man or two escape, because that way word gets around that men of their kind would do well to avoid the Keep."

Eddis shifted. There must be a hole in his logic. At the moment though, she couldn't find it. Sleep on it, she thought.

"We'll need a real map, M'Baddah. Maybe he can make us one on the back of yours, Jerdren?" She gazed thoughtfully at the smoothed dirt and traced the line of the path up from the river.

* * * * *

Full dark the next night saw the company crouched along the north shore of the river, opposite the large island, waiting for M'Baddah's all-clear signal. Jerdren lay flat on the island, as near the water as he could go without breaking cover. Eddis was on his right and his brother beyond her, the rest nearby. The ground was cold and damp, and he was about to ease up onto his knees when the jingle of harnesses and men's low voices froze him in place. It was too far and the water just too loud for him to make out words.

Bandits bringing the horses to drink, Jerdren thought. He glanced up at the stars, west to where a little pale gray light still lingered. Right on time. He waited until it was quiet over there once again, then shifted his weight cautiously. Blor at his right elbow eased up to sit cross-legged. Eddis hadn't moved so much as a finger since her lieutenant had left them.

Across from Eddis, M'Whan rose cautiously, just enough to look out through the branches of the low willow he crouched behind. Eddis tensed, but the youth whispered something to her, and she eased over to talk to Blorys briefly, who tugged at his brother's shirt sleeve and murmured, "M'Baddah's on his way back. Willow passed word down that the south shore is clear."

"Good. We ready?"

"Ready." Eddis's whisper reached him. She was on her feet, checking her weapons one last time. A tense silence as the rest of the company made sure they were set, then Willow waded out into the water, Mead and Eddis right behind him.

It was now full dark, but with enough starlight so they could make out each other, provided they stayed fairly close together. There would be no moon.

M'Baddah had gone partway up the trail, but he came back as the last of the company reached shore. Mead and Willow passed him and started up the trail in utter silence. Jerdren beckoned the others close.

"This is it, people," he murmured. "No talking from here on out. Any questions? Anything?" No reply. "Good. And good fortune to all of us." He nodded and followed Eddis up the trail.

It was dark under the trees, and very quiet once they got above the river. Eventually, Jerdren was able to make out the least hint of ruddy light above them and to his right, and the faint sounds of men's voices. Moments later, the party halted as M'Baddah stepped into the path.

The others gathered around the outlander, who whispered, "They are still awake up there, but it is growing quieter. A rest, here. Mead has gone ahead."

Coarse laughter echoed through the trees. Some of the men up there were drunk, Jerdren thought. Good. Another advantage to us.

He found a place just off the path, between tall tree trunks where the ground was soft, settled his back against a tree, and prepared to wait. As usual, when things were this close to a picked fight, all tension left him. Everything was set—planned as well as it could be—and there was nothing else he could do, except wait. He rubbed his shoulders against thick bark to ease an itch between his shoulder blades. The Keep men who carried closed lanterns moved behind an overhanging boulder to light their candles. The flare of light illuminated the crouching shapes but nothing else, as the men quickly shuttered the openings. Moments later, two of the Keep hunters moved silently up the trail, to wait their opportunity to work their way over to the far side of the camp. Jerdren nodded his approval, then closed his eyes and listened.

Sounds from above slowly faded, though it seemed forever that the drunk men went on laughing and talking. Someone with a hard-edged voice finally snarled a curse, and there was immediate quiet. Jerdren opened his eyes and peered uphill. The firelight was dimmer—someone had banked the fires for the night, probably. When one of the Keep men stood, though, Jerdren tugged at his pants leg and shook his head. The man settled once more.

"Wait," Jerdren whispered. "Let 'em get to sleep, remember?" He leaned back against his tree once more, gazing around. Now that his eyes had adjusted, and with the faint firelight up there, he could see fairly far into the woods and make out his companion's faces. The wind picked up briefly, faded away to nothing. The light up there was fading, and he hadn't heard a sound in some time.

It's time, he thought, and got to his feet. M'Whan and Willow left moments later to take up positions blocking the path to the high sentry box. Eddis moved out onto the trail, Blorys just behind her. Jerdren joined them and began quietly counting on his fingers, aware Eddis was doing the same thing.

At a slow four hundred, Jerdren checked his sword and daggers one last time, then started up the trail. He stopped just short of the final switchback to listen and count off another slow four hundred. No sound from the camp, still; the others must be in place. He held up a hand briefly, then brought it down, and took the last section of trail at a fast walk.

M'Baddah had been good at description. Jerdren almost felt as if he were looking at a camp he'd seen before. The ground was fairly level, only the western storage and the horse-pickets out of sight. Two fires burned low. The third—near the captain's tent, mid-camp—was out. He could make out the long canvas shelter and the huddled shapes of men sleeping near the fires. No one moved out there.

He turned. Eddis and Blor were right behind him, the Keep men beginning to slowly fan out on both sides of the trail. He grinned at his brother, held out a hand to Eddis, who briefly gripped his fingers and mouthed "Good luck!" in reply. She moved off to his left, M'Baddah just beyond her. Blorys took his usual place at his brother's right. Jerdren planted himself mid-trail and drew his sword, slipped two daggers into his belt, and waited.

And waited. *If something's gone wrong . . . . If they knew we were out here all along, if it's their trap for us . . . ? If those men weren't the fools he'd thought them, if they'd been waiting for these invaders and taken each of them as they moved around the outside of the camp . . .*

He bit his lip. *It's your fighting nerves,* he told himself angrily. *Save it for them, why don't you?* If nothing else, he knew, their mage had an elf's night vision and both spells and charms at the ready.

He caught his breath in an upsurge of fierce joy. The clearing between the fire pits exploded in a glare of red and green lights, flame and sparks flying everywhere. The noise was deafening. Men came awake yelling in panic or fury, and someone screamed like a girl. Men bolted from beneath the canvas, rolled out of blankets on the ground, fumbling for swords, daggers, and pikes. Two of the Keep men he could see were ready to leap forward, then, but Jerdren gestured them sharply back. *We wait here for those men,* he thought, and hoped the men remembered his orders.

So far, things were going just as he'd hoped. Bandits milled dazedly mid-camp, though two of them tried to make a dash toward the higher ground. One fell with an arrow in his throat—M'Whan's, Jerdren thought—and the other turned and ran back to crouch behind one of the fire pits. Suddenly, a short, broad man emerged from the tent, a sword in each hand, and began to curse at them in a loud voice. Another followed, and ran forward to grab one of the men and shake him hard.

"What's wrong with you men? What was all that noise and light?" he demanded.

"Keep soldiers! I saw 'em! Blue shirts!"

"Save that!" the squat man bellowed and brandished both blades aloft. "Brother, get your squad moving. Make sure they don't cut us off! You and you, see to the horses! Rest of ye, come with me!"

Some of the men simply broke and ran for the path leading down the east slope. Jerdren grinned broadly and strode forward to intercept the first of them, sword in one hand and a dagger in the other.

The closest men yelled a warning and broke off to either side of the path, but one massive brute with a black beard and a curved sword raised his blade and ran straight for Jerdren, bringing the weapon down in a hard overhand. Jerdren parried that stroke and brought his sword back around. The bandit parried in turn. A fast clash of blades, sword to sword, before his dagger slipped under the other's guard. The man gasped, staggered away, and fell right in front of another who was pelting for the trees. The runner saw him but too late to change course. He fell hard, and one of the Keep men ran a spear through him. Jerdren was already righting another, vaguely aware of yet another charging up on his left, pike in hand.

"Eddis!" he yelled, but her sword had already cut through the pole, and her backswing slashed a long cut across the attacker's forehead. Blinded by his own blood, he staggered back. Eddis strode forward and lunged, her point catching him high in the arm before she brought the blade around two-handed. He folded in half and fell at her feet. Before the man behind him could reach her, Eddis was back at Jerdren's side, sword between her knees and the bow in her hands. The string twanged sharply, and the man fell, her arrow through his throat.

"Look out!" Blorys shouted.

Jerdren came halfway around to his right, sword coming down as his dagger came up. The ragged swordsman parried his big blade, and the dagger bounced off a small buckler. Blorys slashed at the man and missed as the bandit brought his sword up and around in a blurring movement. Jerdren ducked, but too late. The blade sliced through his left eyebrow and into his hairline. Blood blinded him. He cursed furiously and brought the dagger up—by luck and guess burying it in the robber's belly. The man gasped and went down, taking the blade with him. Jerdren went to one knee long enough to snatch up the dying man's long sword.

Behind him, Blorys shouted, "All right?"

"Fine!" Jerdren said. Blood ran down his face still, but by tilting his head, he had one eye clear.

"Spearmen!" Eddis yelled a warning from his left and tugged at his sleeve. He backed up with her as three men running shoulder to shoulder threw themselves at the path. All carried long boar spears.

"Room!" he yelled back.

Eddis moved away and launched an arrow at the nearest spearman. The man swung his spear wildly, possibly hoping to deflect it. The point sank deep in his eye, spinning him around and dropping him, dead before he hit the ground. Jerdren turned aside as the other two charged at him, let their momentum carry them on, then leaped back to slash at unprotected necks and heads. One man wailed and staggered off into the trees where two of the Keep men put him down for good. The other whirled back around, panic in his eyes as he looked at Jerdren, who was grinning like a madman, his eyes wild and blood running down the side of his face. The man screamed in terror, threw his boar spear aside, and sped on down the trail.

And there's our man to spread the tale, Jerdren thought. That's enough, I think. He spun back, blades at the ready, but for some moments, no one else came their way. He blotted the cut on his forehead and wiped his eyes clear. Off to his right, three of the Keep men had several bandits huddled on the ground.

Over between the two fires, Mead and M'Baddah confronted the squat man who'd come from the tent. Captain, that'll be, Jerdren thought. Another spate of fighting over near the ledge, and half a dozen men just beyond the canvas shelter seemed to be readying some plan of attack. Three men running toward the path were stopped by Blor and whoever was off to his right.

Eddis tugged at his sleeve. "You're cut! How can you see anything?"

"Still got one eye clear," he yelled back.

"You're supposed to be keeping an eye on things, overseeing! Like me!" She pulled a rag from her belt. "Hold still! And hold this for me!" She shoved her sword at him, roughly bound the cloth around his brow. He winced and swore as she took back her blade.

"Hurts worse than the cut did, woman!"

"So? You can see properly, can't you?"

Blorys was coming back, and all at once Jerdren could see Willow and M'Whan, heading into the firelight with five men, two of them limping badly, the other three bound and tied together. There was still some fighting beyond the fire pits, but as he watched, the last of the bandits dropped his boar spear and went to his knees.

"Where'd the leader go?" Jerdren demanded. "Eddis, if you cost us that man, wrapping my head up—!"

"Give it over, Brother," Blorys broke in. "He's there, Mead has him bespelled, I think. Got him before he could rally 'em."

"Oh? Oh. Good." Jerdren rubbed his forehead, dislodging the bandage.

Blorys tugged it back down into place. "You're a gory enough sight. Leave it be." He looked around. "Anyone get past you?"

"One here," Jerdren said. "On purpose. Other than him—don't think so."

"Not here," M'Baddah said. "Two of ours wounded up here, one badly."

"Get them into the firelight," Eddis said. She looked across the clearing as Mead came into the open. "Mead! All clear your way?"

"All clear!"

"Good!" Jerdren called back. "Let's get this mess cleaned up!"

* * * * *

It took time, building the fires back up, searching out the bodies and the wounded. Their own wounds were mostly minor, though the man M'Baddah tended had suffered a deep cut the length of his forearm.

Ten of the bandits lay dead, another twelve wounded. Several had been taken prisoner without any fight at all, Mead's spell and the suddenness of the attack having startled them so badly. Their captain was still under Mead's hold spell and now heavily bound as well. His brother had been badly wounded and was barely conscious. Three men, so far as they could tell, had escaped, and two at least had been unarmed when they fled.

Eddis was moving around the fire, sword still in one hand, checking the knots on the bound men, seeing that their own wounded were taken care of, then that the injured bandits were treated. When Jerdren would have protested, she gave him a cold stare.

"Act like a butcher, and you're no better than they are. Didn't you say that once? Besides, we'll get back to the Keep with them that much faster if we aren't transporting half-dead men. Unless *you'd* like to take M'Baddah's place as executioner this time around?"

She turned away before her co-captain could think of anything to say.

Mead, Willow, M'Whan, and Blorys were walking around the camp—the mage seeking any bandits who might be in hiding, his brother searching the tent for stolen goods, while the other two worked through the men's blankets and the canvas shelter. As Eddis moved out into the open, Mead came striding past the horse lines and beckoned her.

"There is someone hiding out there by the horses," he said very softly. "Not a bandit, no fighter. Someone very afraid. I thought perhaps you and I . . . ?"

Eddis nodded and went with him.

Most of the horses had calmed down, she noticed as they came up to the picket lines, but the two nearest the west end were restless, shoving against their neighbors. She met Mead's eyes, nodded again, and let him lead the way.

Hay was strewn along the picket lines, but at this end, the stuff was piled high as a horse's belly. Eddis slowed well short of the stack and gazed steadily at it. Not a trick of her eyes or the firelight—the hay had moved, ever so slightly. She gestured for the mage to go on around, until they had the pile between them. At her nod, the two dove into the stack, grabbing for whatever lay beneath.

A high-pitched yell of fright and rage. Startled, Eddis nearly let go, but Mead had a good grip, and the swordswoman grabbed at a flailing arm, got it by the elbow, and hung on. She shook her head to clear bits of hay from her eyes as she and the mage dragged their writhing captive toward the fire. She stopped dead and stared in complete astonishment at the furious, grubby little creature they held between them.

"Gods bless me," she said. "It's a child!"

9

The grubby little creature twisted furiously in Eddis's grasp and tried to bite Mead's fingers. Greasy hair, hacked short, slapped across the swordswoman's arms. Eddis was aware of the bandit captain trying to struggle to his feet, being shoved back down by Jerdren. The screeching child claimed her full attention once more as its teeth sank into her left wrist. She swore angrily, wrapped a hand around a knotted tuft of hair, and yanked. The child's head slammed into her forearm, and it shrieked.

"Let me go! You let Blot go! Lemme *go!*"

Mead's fingers began to glow as he murmured a spell. The child went wide-eyed and quiet, and it tried to back away, but Eddis had it.

"Be quiet," the mage said evenly, "or this spell will turn you to stone."

Blessed silence. The elf mage looked around them, his angry gaze sweeping across the prisoners. "What is a human child doing here and in such pitiful state? Where is its mother?"

"Maybe this fellow could tell you," Jerdren replied sharply. "Seemed awfully interested when you two hauled it out of hiding. Captain here, aren't you? Captain of this camp?" he asked.

Silence, broken by the sound of a hard kick and a grunt of pain. "I only ask nicely the first time," he said. "What about this child, eh?"

The child twisted half-around to screech at Jerdren. "Don't you hurt 'im. You got no right!" It tore at Eddis's fingers. "Lemme *go!*"

The swordswoman gave Mead an exasperated look, locked her other hand in the dreadful hair, and shouted, "Mead! Use the spell! Anything to shut the creature up!"

The child caught its breath in a gasp and cowered away from her. Eddis felt ashamed of her outburst and angry because of it.

The captain cleared his throat. "Leave the brat alone. It's done no harm. It's ours, honest like. Not stolen, it ain't. Born to us."

"Who's its father, and where's its mother, then?" Jerdren demanded. "Brat that size ought not to be without parents."

"It—which *is* the child? Boy or girl?" Eddis asked angrily. Her knuckles stung where ragged fingernails had torn at them, and the hair she kept in a tight grip was disgusting to the touch and smelled dreadful. "I can't keep saying 'it!' "

The man closed his mouth tightly.

She eyed the filthy child, bit back a sigh, and essayed a smile. Tried to make her voice soothing. "Little one, I'm sorry if we scared you. We don't mean to frighten children." Silence. "What's your name? Are you a boy, or a girl?"

"Told you, I'm Blot," it replied sullenly. Large tears pooled in the dark eyes and ran down thin cheeks all at once, leaving pale tracks in the dirt.

Eddis was suddenly furious with this captain and all the men who'd camped here with him. To so neglect a child . . . how low were they?

Blot spoke up, voice thick with tears, "What ye'll do with

Blot? With 'im?" Her eyes went toward the captain.

"Is he your father, Blot?"

"Don't know what that is. 'Im's just Captain. Lets me live here, sleep in the tent there with 'im 'n' 'is brother. I gotta do what they say, get wood for the fires, 'n' keep ashes cleared proper like."

Eddis met Mead's eyes, nodded to let him know she'd take control of the situation. She caught the child's shoulder gently as the mage released it and brought the suddenly quiet creature over to where the prisoners had been gathered. Her eyes were hard as they met those of the bandit captain.

"Suppose *you* tell me, then, Captain! Since the child doesn't seem to have any idea?"

He eyed her stubbornly.

"Fine! I guess I'll let Jerdren kick it out of you—be still, child!" she ordered and tightened her grip on Blot's skinny shoulders. The child twisted in her grasp, realized it was no use, and went still again.

The prisoner glanced at Jerdren, looked at the child for a long moment, finally shrugged. "Told you true, Blot's ours. We had a few camp women, last place we were. Bad idea, I knew it then, and so it proved. Women like that set the men against one another, always playing little games. And y'get byblows like *that* all too often." His gaze moved expressionlessly over the child and then beyond her. "Mother died when it was a year old—maybe two. I forget."

"It?" Eddis asked. The man glanced at her, away. Shrugged again.

"She. M'brother took to it—her. Kept her about, can't think why. Was it left to me, I'd've had it exposed and there's an end to it. Men like us got no use for something that young and useless."

Eddis's eyes narrowed.

The man went on, clearly unaware of her rising fury. "Turned out a useful creature in its way. We taught it to tend fires, fetch water—things like that. Taught it from the first that it didn't dare give over its chores, whatever it thought of 'em. Turned out my brother was right. Blot frees up a man or two when they're needed on important tasks."

Eddis drew a deep breath, let it out slowly. The poor child was probably expecting a beating. Clearly it was all she knew. She wouldn't understand the swordswoman's anger was for the man who'd so ill-treated her.

"She," Eddis said evenly. "So—how old is she?"

He considered this briefly. "Ten—twelve summers? Man loses count."

"Ten or twelve." Eddis stared at him. "And you kept her here, openly? Living with all these men?"

He scowled up at her. "Now, listen, there's none of *that!* Wouldn't ever have been, either. I run a clean camp! Didn't I say we was rid of loose women? Time came," he shrugged, "and Blot was old enough, we'd give the child a chance to learn weapons and join us."

"And if *she* didn't want to become a bandit, what then?" Eddis's voice remained soft, but the captain edged away from her, until Jerdren's boot stopped him.

"What d'ye think? We're not savages! My brother would've taken her to some town and turned 'er loose!"

"And, trained as you've trained her, of *course* she'd be able to find an honest way to earn her way," Eddis replied sourly. "Jerdren, get him away from me." She walked off, bringing Blot in tow.

"What'll ye do with 'im?" Blot asked in a small voice. "Y' can't kill 'im. 'E swore 'e'd protect me!" Another thought occurred to her. "Where's 'is brother? Where's Hosig?" She pulled against Eddis's grip, but in vain.

"M'Baddah?" Eddis turned to look for her lieutenant. "M'Baddah, where are—? Oh, there, thank the gods," she added as the man came out of the gloom to join her. "She's after the captain's brother—the man with the horses, down at the river, wasn't he?"

M'Baddah's eyes shifted toward the canvas shelter, where the more gravely wounded had been moved, and he shook his head minutely.

"Not yet," he said quietly, "but soon."

Eddis shifted her grip on the child's shoulders and went to one knee to be on her level. "Blot? We'll take you to see him. But . . . well, he's hurt."

"Hurt? 'E won't die, will 'e?"

Blot asked fearfully. Eddis looked up at M'Baddah, who knelt next to her and met the child's eyes.

"I do not think he is so badly hurt. Eddis tells you this only so you will not cry or look afraid when you see the bandages. He is your friend?"

Blot didn't seem too sure about "friend."

" 'E lets me have one of 'is blankets when it's cold out, and sometimes 'e helps me with the heavy pots and the wood and stuff."

"That is a friend," M'Baddah said gently. "Because he cares for you. Come. We will take you to your friend." He held out a hand.

Blot searched his face, sniffed quietly, and suddenly held out one of hers. Eddis bit back reservations of her own and released the child, who went quietly with her lieutenant. The swordswoman glanced at Jerdren, held up a hand when he would have trailed along, and went after the two.

The wounded man lay a little apart from the others. Someone beyond him moaned nonstop, though all the men here had been tended to. At first, Eddis thought he looked no worse than his companions. His leg had been splinted with a long stick of firewood. There was a spreading bruise on his forehead and a ragged, oozing cut that crossed his right hand. His face was tight with pain. M'Baddah spoke first to the robber and then softly against the child's ear before he gave her a gentle shove forward. The man made a clear effort to focus on her, and even managed something of a smile.

"There's my windflower. How's my little one?" he said.

Blot went to her knees beside him, eyes searching anxiously before she buried her face in his shoulder and burst into frantic tears.

"Don't die! What's Blot without ye?"

The man brought up a hand to pat her shoulder awkwardly. It had been bound by a loop of rope to his ankle, effectively immobilizing him, though Eddis doubted he could have moved, anyway. Pain-tightened eyes met hers, then moved to the child. *He does care for her*, Eddis thought. *More than his brother, at least, and I'll wager he wants my assurance we'll take her with us.*

She nodded, saw the look of relief on his face as he turned his full attention to the girl.

"Why, you'll be fine, child. It looks to me like my little windflower will have a chance to live somewhere clean and safe, just like we always wanted."

"Don't *want* that! Not without you!" The hands tightened on his arm. He winced, but when Eddis would have moved to loosen the child's grip, he met her eyes and shook his head. The eyes shifted. Eddis followed the man's gaze and briefly closed her own. The bandit's pale breeches were soaked with blood. She glanced at M'Baddah, shook his head again. The man didn't have much longer, then, and he knew it, but he was still doing his best for the poor little wretch. The swordswoman stepped back a pace and nodded. The bandit smiled his thanks at her, then gave his full attention to Blot.

"No, please don't cry. Remember what I told you, last winter? Remember our bargain? That you'd do your best to not anger my brother, and then I'd find a way to get us free of here, and we wouldn't be bandits anymore, you and me. I'd buy us a little house and some land, and horses, and a goat, and chickens. And we'd have a garden, and you'd have a place to sleep out of the wind and the cold, and you'd have warm water for washing, and real shoes, and clean clothes, and enough to eat. Remember?"

Silence. The child choked on her sobs and nodded.

"Well, I guess I won't be there after all, but you will. That's what I want for you, what I've always wanted, you know that, don't you? So I want you to promise me that you'll go with . . . ?" He looked up at Eddis, glanced at M'Baddah.

Eddis nodded, gave him the names he was clearly seeking. He coughed rackingly, patted the child's shoulder again as she drew back to eye him in sudden fright. "Go with Eddis and M'Baddah. They will care for you. They'll see you have the clean clothes, and a warm place to live, and enough to eat. I swear that to you, my small wildflower."

Silence, except for the child's soft weeping.

"Now I want you to go, and remember that I'm smiling at you now. Just like this. Remember that, because then I will always be smiling when you think of me."

The child didn't want to go, but somehow, M'Baddah persuaded her, speaking quietly against her ear, words only she could hear. Eddis knelt at the bandit's side as the two slowly walked away, M'Baddah still talking to the grubby little girl.

"We'll take care of her. I promise you that. Somehow, we'll keep her safe."

"Bless you—thank you," the man said, his voice suddenly very weak. He coughed again, and this time frothy blood spilled over his chin. "Haven't long, I—know. Never approved, m'brother keeping such an innocent with us. Back north and then here. Whatever her lineage, she's better'n that. Deserves better. Not . . . just a drudge to evil men. Tell her that, for me. If she ever doubts."

"I will. I swear it," Eddis said. She looked about for Mead, but the bandit coughed again, drew a sharp, pained breath, let it out on a long, faint sigh, and was quietly gone. Eddis looked down at his shell, closed his eyes with gentle fingers.

"May that one good deed survive you and keep you safe in the afterlife, for the child's sake," she murmured, got to her feet, and walked away.

It was still long hours until daybreak. Jerdren was portioning out watches and fire duty when Eddis beckoned him to one side.

"We're burying the captain's brother," she told him.

He frowned. "We're . . . we're what? Eddis, I thought we'd agreed everyone goes back to the Keep! What if the castellan decides to give us a bonus by body count?"

"Then we're one short, that's all. If you'd seen that child breaking her heart over the man, just now . . ."

"She's a child. They get over things," he said. "We agreed on this. I don't see why you're so hot to change things."

"It's no great matter," Eddis said flatly. "You've got the captain, we'll have whatever loot they've got up here. I don't want that poor child to see her only friend thrown over the back of a horse and hauled into the Keep."

"Poor child, is it?" Jerdren grumbled. "And *friend*, was it? True friend would've set her loose in some town or village—"

"Where she'd be ever after known as the raiders' bastard," Eddis broke in angrily, her voice low, so the child couldn't possibly overhear her. "You don't just take a child like this and hand her over to villagers or turn her loose in some town.

There'll always be someone who knows where she came from, or at least what she looked like when they got her, and they'd gossip, and you can imagine the kinds of things they'd say, can't you?"

"No," he replied blankly.

Blorys came up beside him. He'd clearly heard most of the argument.

"Sure you can, Brother," he said. "Remember that dark, skinny lad back home? One who hung himself? People like our aunt threw it at him for years that his mother had been a tavern girl and no one knew who his father was."

"Well, yeah, but that's different, Blor!"

The younger man shook his head. "No, it's not. And I agree with Eddis, anyway. Whatever that man did or was, the child deserves proper memories of a man she cared enough to cry over. And rites to remember him by. She'll have 'em. You don't like it, Jers, you can take any share his body might've earned us out of my portion." His gaze moved across the camp, settled on M'Baddah and his young charge. "Though he might have washed her, once in her life."

"No," Eddis said. "Maybe he did her a kindness. If she's twelve years or more . . . you can wager none of the men here looked at *her* as a camp woman."

"Gods," Blorys whispered and closed his eyes.

Eddis walked away.

Jerdren's bewildered voice followed her. "What? Leaving a kid all filthy— that's a kindness?"

* * * * *

A full day and a half later, nearly sundown, the company and its captives wound their slow way up the Keep road. Eddis walked ahead, leaving M'Baddah, Mead, and Jerdren to bring up the rear, the armsmen holding drawn swords, while Mead had several painful spells ready to invoke if any of the raiders decided to try escape. It might have been difficult for any of them, since the wounded among them were horsed but tied to their mounts, while those who had escaped injury were bound together in a long line, and afoot, under the watchful eye of the Keep men. Most of them seemed to have long since given up any hope of rescue or escape. The dead men were brought in at the rear of the long column, face-down over the remaining horses.

For most of the afternoon, the child Blot had walked between Eddis and M'Baddah, but only because M'Baddah stayed with Eddis, and the child was comfortable only with him and a little with Blorys. Try as she might, Eddis hadn't been able to breach the gap between the child and herself—the girl eyed her warily and avoided the swordswoman's touch whenever she could.

Thank the gods I have M'Baddah with me, she thought. The man had an instinct for communicating with shy, mistreated beasts of any kind, and on that count, Blot certainly qualified.

At M'Baddah's suggestion, he and she had heated water the morning after the surprise raid and did their best to clean the child. Blot objected, frightened of the mere idea, until M'Baddah convinced her that bathing was part of the funeral ritual for her friend. It might have been the first bath in the child's entire life, at least, after her mother'd died, Eddis thought. Her nose wrinkled. So many layers of dirt, grease, ash and cooking oils, mud, and anything else one could imagine. Underneath all that, the child was small even for ten years and incredibly thin—every bone in her body pressed against pale skin. There wasn't the least hint of fat anywhere on her. No outward sign of maturity, either. Eddis closed her eyes, briefly. Thank all the gods there might ever be that M'Baddah was the one man she felt safe in trusting to help her bathe such a mess of a child and that the child had in turn trusted him to sponge her clean and wrap her in his own blanket after. The hair still wasn't completely clean, but it was neatly cut.

Mostly clean and clad in one of M'Whan's tunics, Blot walked barefoot up the road, her hand in M'Baddah's. Well, Eddis, the swordswoman told herself dryly, you always knew you'd be a lousy mother.

The Keep road bent abruptly east, one of the final turns before the gates. Eddis glanced at those shuffling along behind her, was suddenly aware of the glad outcry from the walls above them. She bit back a smile. The gates would be open before they could announce themselves and their prisoners. This time, they'd be welcomed as honored guests, and tonight, they'd doubtless be feasted in the castellan's halls and properly rewarded.

They'd done well enough back at that camp. A chest in the captain's tent was full of bags of coin, gems, and Mead had taken charge of a bag of charms and potions. There'd been other wealth—mostly silver and copper pence—scattered elsewhere in the camp. It came out to a good-sized purse each. Jerdren hadn't been convinced that they'd found everything, but the bandits one and all denied there was any further hidden trove. With so much forest around them, it was possible they'd simply hidden things outside the camp or buried their wealth. In that case, the castellan's dungeonmaster might manage to wring the location out of them.

On Jerdren's orders, the men had gathered together the bandits' weaponry and brought it along. Most of it was inferior stuff, but the metal could be melted down for new blades. They'd also retrieved the hanging sides of meat that were still fresh. Both metal and meat would add to their shares, of course.

Could've been worse, Eddis thought with a sudden grin. We didn't get as rich by this as Jers expected, but it paid a lot better than caravan guarding. At the moment, she was glad to be coming back to civilization and the chance for clean hair and clothes, and decent food that wasn't coated with ash from an open fire.

She looked ahead as they came around the next bend, past the southeast corner of the Keep, and smiled. Sure enough, the gates had been thrown open, and there were guards in the road, cheering them on. On the walls, men and women were waving and cheering.

Jerdren edged his horse forward, dropped to the ground, gripped her wrist and flung up his arm, dragging hers high.

"Victors!" he shouted.

Eddis felt her face turning red, and she tried to tug her arm free. He grinned at her and tightened his grip.

She smiled up at the people on the walls and muttered, "You'll pay for this, Jers."

"Bah! Enjoy it while you can," he replied cheerfully. "Nothing like it, is there?"

* * * * *

That night, the castellan held a special banquet for the company. The last time they had been here, the main hall had been a vast, shadowy, and echoing place just inside the main doors. Now the chamber blazed with light, every candle in the elaborate, massive, sconces aflame. Long tables that had lined the walls were arranged to fill the great space, and Eddis gave up trying to count the number of people who had been invited. She recognized the taverner and his wife far across the chamber, and not far from them, the smith. Familiar faces were everywhere. She was abashed to find that she and Jers had been given the high-backed, padded chairs flanking the castellan himself. They were both clad alike in fine silk, their feet shod in soft suede boots made for them that afternoon, eating from silver dishes and drinking from gold-rimmed goblets, while their fellows were ranged at the heads of the tables abutted to the main one.

The bandit chief and his uninjured fellows had been consigned to two of the deepest dungeon cells, close watched by guards. The injured men had been placed in another nearby, one of the company medics and his aides treating them before they were locked in for the night. The dead had been counted, named in the few cases possible, and set outside the northeastern walls for burning at first light.

Eddis, M'Bhaddah, and a nervous Jerdren had explained about the captain's dead brother and about the child called Blot, but Ferec had waved this aside as their personal choice and not mentioned it—or the child—again.

Our problem, that child, Eddis thought. Gods, I'm afraid she really will be our problem, won't she? She tried to forget about the girl as yet another toast was made to the heroes of the day, but that particular worry wouldn't stay gone.

It had taken all M'Baddah's patience to get the frightened child into the Keep and into one of the inn's private rooms that she would share with Eddis. It had taken a good deal of explanation to convince her that this arrangement was the only one possible, and Eddis still wasn't sure the girl believed they would return to her after the banquet. She had been curled in on herself against the far edge of the cot when they left. We left her clean, she has blankets, water and food, the swordswoman thought. We certainly couldn't have brought her *here* tonight.

Another toast. She smiled, held up her goblet, and dutifully sipped the wine. What, she wondered, are we going to do with the child? She's used to a rough life, but even so, to take her on the road, guarding caravans?

The banquet was nearing an end, finally. The last sweet had been served, followed by a bowl of water to dabble honey-sticky fingers, that followed by a cool vinegar marinade of thin strips of venison—she managed to set that aside politely, aware of the scent of onions that pervaded both the meat and the liquid. Lastly, a silver bowl of mint leaves to chew, and through them, sip a final chilled tea.

The castellan waited until she and Jerdren had drained their cups, then stood, raising his arms for silence, shaking his head minutely as the co-captains sought to rise with him.

"Keep your places, my friends," he said, his voice filling the vast hall.

Loud cheers echoed from every corner. The castellan waited, smiling, and finally waved them down. Silence, which he broke, and for the first time, Eddis thought, he sounded like a city leader. The words had obviously been prepared ahead of time.

"Long have we thought, my council and I—all the folk of the Keep!—how best to reward you! "Eddis, Jerdren, your kinsmen, and fellows! Those of our own who chose this dangerous and dire journey with you!" Brief silence. "The reward you earned is yours in any event, but it seems little enough for all that you did for us. Were our Lord Macsen yet alive, and the Keep as it was in his day, a bountiful place, a mark on the map where the wealthiest and most skilled of artisans came to bargain and trade, then would we heap you with gems and gold, and wealth of every kind!"

A rousing cheer at this.

I swear, Eddis thought tiredly, that I know what he's up to. Is it another horde of bandits, or what?

She glanced at Jerdren. From the look on his face, he'd reached the same conclusion. He raised an eyebrow. She shrugged. Your turn, this time, she thought cheerfully, and sat back in her chair. Ferec let this go on for some time, finally raised his hands for silence, and looked down at Jerdren.

"My lord—I mean, Ferec," Jerdren said with an abashed looking smile as he ducked his head. "We don't ask any additional reward, really. What we did—well, that makes it safe for everyone on the road, doesn't it? Including us? And—well, that we were able to help out . . ." He cleared his throat. "Well, maybe there'll come a day you can heap those gems on us." He smiled at the castellan, who smiled back.

"Well, of course!" Feric broke in. He was smiling broadly, his arms up, encouraging the guests to cheer loudly. "However, I closeted myself with my advisors for most of this day, and we thought hard, how best to reward you, since we cannot offer the gold and gems you so richly deserve."

Eddis's skin felt cold, all at once.

"We offer you another challenge, Jerdren, Eddis. Once again, we will supply all equipment you need—up to a reasonable cost, of course. A hundred gold each, say? That should easily cover weaponry, supplies, food, anything you require, and allow you to find and attack the Caves of Chaos, and clear them of all evil creatures!" His voice rang from the rafters. People cheered. Ferec smiled at Eddis. "If you choose, that is."

People were talking excitedly, all around them, but their own company was utterly still. Ferec smiled at Jerdren, at the startled company grouped around the head table.

"Any gold, gems or other things of value you find are yours, entirely, as before. Any aid we or the master of arms, or the curate—any leader or any citizen of the Keep can offer—we will freely give. Any additional warriors or others to aid you, we will help you find them." He looked around the table, leaned back in his chair, and drank from his silver cup. "I see that you are amazed—perhaps surprised to be so honored, all of you. So I will ask no response from you now, yea or nay. You Keep men who served as part of this brave company, you may sleep in your barracks and eat with your messes, if you choose, but you are exempt from other duties for now. When you all decide what your course will be, send word. Whatever you choose, I wish you all the blessings of the gods, and that of myself and all who dwell within the Keep."

Sure we can say nay, Eddis thought. I can imagine how welcome we'd be here after that.

Ferec was speaking once more. "Whatever you decide, the thanks and the blessings of those who now will feel free to come and go in more safety!"

A roar of applause met this. Ferec smiled and waved, then raised Jerdren and Eddis to their feet.

The noise redoubled, and under its cover, the castellan said, "Our greater gratitude, if you can find it in you to aid us further."

He was gone, then, his aides and assistants surrounding him. It was some time before the cheering ceased and Blorys was able to pull the two of them aside.

"Well!" Eddis wrinkled her nose. "That was a proper show, wasn't it?"

Jerdren looked around and shushed her anxiously.

"There's no one close to overhear me—if anyone could in all this din. I'm not a fool, Jers!"

"Ask me," Blorys replied gloomily, "we've been set up. Proper, as you say, Eddis."

"Proper?" Jerdren looked from his brother to his co-captain, back again. "Set up? Are you both mad? D'you know what that man's just offered us?"

"No," Blorys said tiredly. "No idea, Brother. What?"

"What?" Jerdren eyed him sidelong, visibly puzzled. "Chance at fortune, glory, and the gods know what else!"

Blorys cleared his throat cautiously. "Um, Brother? I'm wondering, just what is there in these particular caves?"

Jerdren grinned broadly. "Orcs! Remember, our Keep men said there was supposedly some at these distant caves?"

"Oh, that's right," Blorys said. "Caves—except 'our' Keep men, as you call 'em, have never seen these caves. Frankly, everything I've heard is a tale told so many times no one knows what of it's true. If anything."

"What about the men from the East?" Jerdren asked. "Remember? Two years ago—that's not so long. There'll be people here those men talked to."

"It's still stories, Jers."

Jerdren shrugged. He was still grinning. "So?"

"Besides," Blorys said evenly, "think about this, before you get too excited about the possibilities. Good against bandits—we're that. Good against orcs who weren't expecting us—we're that, too. What else might be out there, though. Ask yourself, Brother, before you agree to this mad venture. What's in those caves? Sounds to me like the castellan is afraid enough that he's willing to offer just about everything he can promise."

Eddis shook her head. "Blor, he probably doesn't know any more about them than anyone else—just rumor and gossip. He's probably peopled those caves with every evil being that was ever said to walk the realm and the lands beyond!"

"Well?" Blorys asked quietly. "That's all I'm saying, Eddis. Maybe that's exactly what's out there."

He looked from her to his brother, but for once, Jerdren seemed to have nothing to say.

10

It couldn't last for long, of course. By the time they were halfway across the inner bailey, Jerdren's spirits were again soaring high.

"Look, it's an honor, Eddis," he said, waving the rest of their company close. "Being picked to—"

"We still don't know *what* we're supposed to do," Eddis put in as he paused. "Jerdren, we can't talk out here like this."

"The tavern won't be any better," Blorys said. "Now the banquet's over, the place will be packed, I'll wager. People wanting to talk to the taverner and his wife about it, the usual crowd, and I'll also wager there'll be plenty of men looking for us already. Word will get around fast, Jers. People will assume that of course we'll take the castellan up on his offer, and they know that the men who went out with us last time came back with fat purses."

"Those who survived," Eddis said.

"True, but the men who left family here at least got their share. Most soldiers would find that acceptable, if they weren't going to make it through themselves."

"What about the inn?" M'Whan asked, but Jerdren shook his head.

"There's always men asleep in there," Blorys told him.

"Like the barracks. Personally, I'd like somewhere private, if we're going to talk."

"The private rooms at the inn are too small," Eddis reminded him.

"I know," he replied. "Wait, though. Private—that reminds me. Jers, that was our hide merchant at the far end of my table, wasn't it? Because if so, he'll be coming this way any time now, and they're staying at the Guild Hall, aren't they?"

Jerdren nodded.

"So, if you asked, he might get them to let us in, give us some place to talk this over."

"Can't get ale at the Guild Hall," Jerdren reminded him.

"So? It's a trade-off, if they'll let us in. And there might be someone there who can answer some questions for us." Blorys was scanning the crowd of people crossing the inner bailey. "Anyone wants a cup of ale after that, I'm for it."

Jerdren looked at his companions. "Sounds good to me. Why don't you all head out, and I'll see if I can't find the man. If not, Blor, you should be able to catch him at the gates. If you can't, we'll head over to the Guild Hall." He was gone before his brother could form a reply.

"He's right. No reason for us to wait right in the middle of everyone's way, is there?" Blorys asked as Jerdren vanished into the crowd, and started back the other direction. "So. Eddis, I think we're of the same opinion. But the rest of you—any thoughts yet?" He smiled faintly.

"I . . ." Eddis sighed. "I just don't know about this, Blor. I'll wait to make up my mind until I hear something that doesn't start with 'I've heard', or 'they say.' "

One of the Keep men spread his hands. "It's more of the same, I expect. All any of us knows is what we told you, out there. Old tales from the days when Lord Macsen first began to build here, about caves and the monsters that live in 'em.

Stories all differ about the size of the caves, where exactly they are, what lives there and why. The only thing they all say is that if you travel far enough along the east road, you'll find them. Or the creatures that live there will find you."

"Don't forget the other tale," another man said. "Those traders who came from foreign lands east of here. The castellan and his advisors talk to any strangers who come in from distant lands, and it's certain they talked to those men."

"That's better than a story passed through half a dozen mouths," Eddis said with a shrug. Though it would be better to my thinking if I'd had the chance to talk to those men myself." She looked up as Jerdren came hurrying through the gates. He was smiling widely.

"Found him!" he announced, "and he said he'd be happy to ask. Just asked that we give him time for that, then follow. If no one minds?"

Eddis cast up her eyes, shrugged.

"Well, then?" He started off, but Blorys caught hold of his arm, dragging him to a halt. "What?"

"Brother, give the poor merchant time to reach the Guild Hall, will you? Maybe even ask the favor?"

"Oh, right. Sure." Jerdren looked around, waved at a clutch of people who were smiling at him and talking in low voices, finally strode over to the fountain, and hoisted his backside onto the rim, one leg jiggling. The rest of the company followed. Eddis settled cross-legged on the paving. "Now, I say first thing is, we separate fact from tales. Best we can, of course. Any argument?"

"What—you're not going to demand we choose to go right now?" Eddis asked dryly.

"Well, sure I am. Why not? Even if we didn't find these caves or anything out there to fight, we'd still get decent equipment and provisioning out of it," Jerdren replied promptly.

"C'mon, Eddis, why not? If we do find caves and monsters and all that—well, we get better at what we do, we probably find a lot of gold and gems they've stolen from travelers, and we come back heroes." He waited. She cast up her eyes. "Hey, Eddis, same terms as this last time—equals in everything, huh? Wasn't so bad, was it?"

"The pay was all right," she said. "Though I'm not sure I like Ferec's idea of a reward. Say we did find caves and all. Say we did win through. I don't want to think what the man would consider a proper reward for *that*. It doesn't matter, because until I know more than I do right now, I'm not jumping either way."

"She's right, Brother." Blorys settled down next to her. "If we're even going to think about fighting orcs and worse things, we need to have some idea what to prepare for. We lost men on this last journey. This one—well, if we underestimated the enemy, none of us might come back." He glanced at Eddis. "I wouldn't like that much."

"You need to talk to the castellan tomorrow," Eddis told Jerdren. "Find out what they actually know, if they talked to those foreigners, what they learned. Anything that's fact. The rest of us can split up tomorrow, talk to people, especially anyone like us who's come in with a caravan. Maybe someone should visit the chapel. Didn't Ferec say the cleric would help us? They should have records, if there's anything known."

"Don't forget the Guild Hall," M'Baddah said. "They also keep records, and they learn much from the merchants who come here."

Jerdren nodded. His leg was still jiggling up and down. "We can work that out tonight." He looked around, up at the sky. "Been long enough, hasn't it?"

"May as well go," Eddis said and pushed to her feet.

She'd half expected the man's excitement—rudeness, to

her thinking—to get them turned away. If the merchant had even asked, of course. The man might feel Jers had put him in a difficult position. But as they walked back around the inn and along the stables and barracks, she could see the hall and light shining through an open door. Two tall men-at-arms flanked the door, and just within, clearly awaiting them, was an elderly but vigorous-looking man with long, white hair and very blue eyes.

He smiled and inclined his head as they came up. "I am the master of this house. Welcome. I recognize each of you from your entry to the Keep yesterday morning. You are Jerdren, you Eddis, and these the men and elves who went with you after the bandits."

Eddis wasn't quite sure what the protocol was. She bowed her head much as the master had, as he stepped aside to let them enter a hallway that stretched to both sides.

"The hide merchant tells me you need a quiet place to talk for a time. I fear we cannot offer you strong drink, or indeed food at this hour, but—"

"We need nothing, save a quiet place to talk," Blorys assured him.

"That you shall have." He stepped back to let the two men-at-arms lead the way down the hall and through a door. The passage here was narrow, and nearly as long as the first, with a flight of stairs at its end. The steps curved out of sight to the right.

It was dark here, except for the master's lamp behind them and another carried by one of the armsmen. At the top of the stairs, another empty hall with a closed door at its end. One of their guides opened the door for them, then the two men-at-arms went back down the hall and could be heard clattering down the stone steps. The master remained while they were shown into yet another hallway and from there into a long, windowless chamber. A narrow bed, a desk and several chairs were the only furnishings. A fire burned low in the fireplace along one wall. The second-floor guard knelt to build up the fire. The master gazed around the room, nodded as it apparently met his standards, then went back to the door.

"If there is anything you need, these men will be nearby," he said. "I will see that fresh water and some fruit are sent up for you."

"Ah, sir," Eddis said, ducking her head politely again. "One additional favor, if we may. It's said that your people may have some knowledge of these caves—caverns?"

"Not so much knowledge as rumor," the master said. "But what we have, my clerks will find for you. I fear you will need to read it here, as we have no spare copies of such old records."

"That will be acceptable," Blorys said. "Our thanks, sir. And when we're ready to leave?"

"The guards will escort you down and into the open once more."

He was gone moments later, the door quietly closing behind him and the two guardsmen. Jerdren eyed the door thoughtfully, finally shrugged.

"We're speaking no secrets here, small matter if anyone listens, and we won't be constantly interrupted, unlike any other place I can think of within these walls. Good enough, I'd say." He glanced at his brother, then at Eddis. "I suppose you two want to wait for whatever the man's clerks can turn up?"

"Not necessarily," Blorys said. "We can talk about it. I'm not going to be swayed by the castellan's fine speech and all that cheering, though, Jers. I know—that wasn't all that took your eye, it was the adventure itself. All the same. I want as much idea of what we're getting in for as we had this last time. Makes it easier to decide on who and what we need to take."

"It's vital that we know as much as we can," Eddis said evenly. "Not knowing could get us all killed, and there is nothing heroic about foolishly throwing your life away."

They talked generally, the Keep men reminding each other of various rumors they'd heard over the years. Most of it was like the things they'd mentioned in the inner bailey after the feast, Eddis thought. Eventually, the men ran out of what they'd heard. Then one of the hunters tugged at his ear.

"Don't know what reminded me of it. There was a feller who came through here—must be three years ago, now. Claimed to be a monster-fighter, just come down from wiping out a clan of kobolds up north somewheres."

"Huh," Jerdren said shortly. "Unless kobolds seriously outnumber you, *anyone* can do that." Blorys tugged at his sleeve, and he subsided.

"Well, what he said, at least. Don't remember as any of us were so impressed with him and his tales, 'cept I remember him tellin' us at some point that if you're fighting goblins and one of 'em yells out, 'Bree-yark!' that means they give up." He blinked in surprise as Blorys and Jerdren broke out laughing. "What?"

"He must have been army, wager anything!" Jerdren said finally. He was still chuckling. "*We* got told that when our company first went north to fight orcs. Bunch of green recruits, most of us were, and that nearly got us killed!"

Blorys shook his head. "It's an old army joke. Just about every green village recruit in that company I ever talked to had heard that one. I'm not certain what it really means, but it's something like, 'Hey, you idiot!' Bad insult, anyway. We didn't get nearly killed, Jers. None of us was fool enough to stop fighting and wait for 'em to toss down their weapons, were we?"

"Stupid kind of joke," the hunter said earnestly. "What if a man took it serious like?"

Eddis bit back a smile. She'd already noticed most of the Keep guards lacked a sense of humor. Blorys tipped her a wink, then went to open the door as someone tapped at the panel. A nearly bald old man in clerk's robes came in with a small basket containing several dusty scrolls and another containing a stoppered ewer of water and plain wooden cups. The man murmured something rather anxiously. Blorys nodded and took the basket. The clerk scurried off, closing the door behind him.

"Wanted to know if we needed anyone to read Common," Blor said as Jerdren raised an eyebrow. "Said some of these are old, the writing's bad, and some are fading."

"I'll try," Eddis said. She unrolled the first, shifting around until light fell on it, and pored over the contents. "Here," she said at last. "This is from when Lord Macsen first began to build the Keep. He sent a large armed company on a long scouting party up the east road to see how far they could safely journey and what was there. And with orders—" her gaze flicked toward Jerdren—"to not take serious chances or engage the enemy, if there was one, because they were there to bring back information.

"Macsen's men took their lord at his word—particularly the last words, because most of them returned alive. They'd spoken of orcs in a long, deep ravine where the road went northeast, of kobolds and something very large and dark that followed alongside them, back in the trees where all they could make out was the general size and shape and speed of it. It hadn't come close, perhaps fearing their numbers, good arms and armor. They hadn't gone after it, nor had they ever strayed from the road. They'd built large fires at night and kept watches by twos and threes, had heard plenty of wolves and other odd, disturbing cries in the night but saw only a huge flying shadow cross the fire once, nothing else."

The second scroll yielded nothing but most of the rumors they'd already heard and a few new ones.

"Eater of men?" Jerdren scoffed. "That could be nearly anything! Orcs, lizardmen, ogres, too, though it's said they prefer dwarf, and . . ." He faltered to an embarrassed silence, eyed Willow and Mead from under his brows.

"And elves," Willow said dryly. "We know. Never mind, Jerdren."

The third scroll was newer than the other two, less dusty. Eddis examined it for some moments, then glanced up. "I think I've found something. It's—let me see—a new copy of a very old scroll, one Lord Macsen brought with him when he came here. There's some notes here, see?" She indicated the beginning of the neatly written text. "It says, 'I, Veriyan, make this fair copy of a scroll scarce ten years old but damaged by the damp, and it was in turn a copy of one brought to these lands by the Lord Macsen himself. Some say the lord had that scroll from a kinsman who rode these lands and saw in person the wonders written down here. Others say that he bought the scroll or was given it, and this I believe to be true, since it was not ordered to be placed with histories."

Jerdren cleared his throat impatiently. Eddis shrugged and began scanning down the document as quickly as she could.

"Ah," she said finally, "here is the most detailed thing so far. 'To me it was told by one who journeyed there, a hero who knew nothing of the caverns until he drew near them and was accosted by dire and diverse enemies. Vast they are, with many ways in, and often the passage in is the only way out. Many the sorts of monster which dwelleth there, but like men and monsters, oft the varieties of these do not or cannot live together. For many long, weary days did this man and his followers battle the small dog-men armed with spears who withdrew from bright lights and fled from greater numbers.

There they found the hyena who stalks on two legs and bears weaponry. Here were orcs, and traps, and the strange creatures that often inhabit the dark places of the world, and serve no one but themselves and their own hungers.'" Her nose wrinkled. Caves were all right, but nasty creatures lurking in the darkness . . . " 'And in yet another place, a vast silence and stench and a fear so great even the hero himself would not tread the darkness there.

" 'Often he spoke of these matters I here record and often told me how he came to believe all the foul creatures had been gathered by one master. Or, perhaps, dwelling there separately, they had come to serve a single master. But of this, he could provide no proof, though he said there were many caves he had not yet entered, or even discovered, when he and his men wearied of the battle.

" 'Here ends the tale of the caverns wherein dwelleth chaos.' "

She read silently and rapidly down the rest of the scroll, but it was short, and she soon rolled it up and laid it back in the basket with the others.

Brief silence. Blorys broke it. "It's something, I suppose— let me finish, please, Jers. It seems to match with the other stories, so if it's simply a tale, it's consistent. That makes it more likely to have some basis in fact. We ourselves have seen orcs, and some of the Keep men have seen lizardmen. We have Mead's word that there's a strange or possibly mad man out in the north woods, in control of a mountain lion—but he may not be connected to the caves."

"Maybe he was," Mead said. "Maybe *he* was the one this hero suspected of controlling the caves and their evil occupants."

"Anything's possible," Jerdren said. "To me, this scroll and everything else we've heard tells me we wouldn't simply be riding out the east road to enjoy the falling leaves and the chill nights. And I'll tell you what—me and my brother, we've fought not just orcs but worse monsters, way up on the north borders. We were part of an infantry company, sure, but we learned a few things there about fighting the brutes. They can all be killed, if you know what you're doing."

"And," Blorys said, "if you have plenty of luck."

"Same as for anything else, Brother," Jerdren said, "but this I can tell you for fact. Creatures like that kill travelers, villagers, whatever's handy or whatever they want. And they keep *everything* those folk had. Remember that one cave, Blor? It was the nastiest mess I'd ever seen—clothes and mail-shirts piled in heaps, rusted blades and arrows with the points all brittle and the feathers long since molted and half-eaten by bugs. Chests, locked ones, full of gold and silver coin, so much of it that it took three of us to carry it back to the commander's wagon. And two others, filled with cut gems and jewelry, that made the dimmest man of us want to plunge his hands in it. Those bandits we just took maybe weren't smart enough to hold onto much treasure, but you can trust orcs and the like to do just that."

Blorys eyed him tiredly. "You're still as much for it as ever, aren't you?"

"Didn't listened to what Eddis read just now, did you?" Jerdren countered cheerfully. He settled his shoulders against the mantle and gazed around the room. "Now—ah, Eddis, you've your own decision to make on this. And I'm not pushing you for any word tonight. So far's I'm concerned, it's the same deal as we made last time. Equal shares in decisions and responsibility, and equal shares to everyone of whatever treasure we find."

"*If* I say yes," Eddis replied, "and that's only after M'Baddah and M'Whan and I have time to talk it over privately.

That will only be after we've gathered as much information as we can tomorrow. This—" she tapped the nearest scroll— "is fine, so far as it goes, but it's still too much 'they say' for my taste."

"No need for anyone to decide tonight, then," Jerdren replied. Sleep on it, all of you. We can meet early tomorrow in the tavern."

"Preferably," Eddis said, "after the taverner's had time to finish his bread and porridge *and* properly open the doors."

"Huh?" Jerden looked at her blankly. "We'll decide who goes where, talks to whom, and once that's done, we can meet again—late afternoon, maybe. We should know pretty well by then where we stand, I'd say."

Eddis glanced at Blorys, who gave her a faint smile in reply.

"And then, since Ferec's being generous with weapons and supplies again, we can get going on lists of what we'll need, how many of us there'll be, and so on. Only a fool'd go after monsters in caves with one decent sword if someone'd buy him a second to keep it company."

"We'd want warmer clothing, decent food, plenty of lanterns, charms for making light and making fire," Blorys said. He sounded resigned.

"Extra water bottles and plenty of travel rations," one of the Keep men put in.

"And plenty more volunteers," Jerdren finished.

"We could use someone who's good at planning battles inside caverns, Jers," Blorys said. "Last time you and I did that, we were following someone else's orders, and that's been a while ago. We have you two, for seeing far in the dark." He indicated Mead and Willow with a nod. "If you decide to come along, of course. I'm thinking back to when we fought up north, and I'm saying dwarves."

Jerdren frowned. "Dwarves? Why?"

"Because that kind of fighting is what they're best at."

"Dwarves," Jerdren said again, darkly. "Doesn't matter. Not likely you'll find any around here."

One of the Keep men cleared his throat. "Um, actually, there's a pair of 'em came in just after we went out, down the walls. They were pretty beat up, from what I hear. Might not want to go anywhere, but just maybe . . ."

"Great," Jerdren muttered. "Dwarves no one knows, dwarves no one here can vouch for, and wounded to boot."

Eddis glanced at Blorys, question in her eyes.

He shook his head minutely and mouthed, "Tell you later."

"Jers," he said. "The dwarves who tried to betray us—that was an isolated incident, a clan that had been so ill-treated by men that it's no surprise to me they turned to evil and joined the orcs. They'd been tortured, remember?"

"They *said* they had," Jerdren replied.

"Why would they have lied about it? Doesn't matter, though, Brother. These won't be the same dwarves. I'm at least willing to talk to them without judging them by others of their kind." Stubborn silence. "You know how angry you used to get when one of the officers looked at you and you could tell what he was thinking—'Villager, country boy, common lout. Maybe he's smarter than the deer he hunts, but probably not by much.' Now listen to you!"

Jerdren's mouth quirked. "All right, Blor, I know. I just . . . doesn't matter. Each of you think about this tonight. If you want it, any of you, so far as I'm concerned, you're in. Think about what you'd want for extra weapons and supplies, what we'll all need."

"Maybe," Eddis replied sourly. "Personally, all I'm planning on is a decent night's sleep. I don't know when you slept last night, Jerdren, but I'm a much nicer woman to deal with when I've had a full night of unbroken sleep."

"Fine. That's it then. We're done here?" He went to the door and knocked. One of the guards ushered them into the hall and another came from the head of the stairs to escort them down and turn them over to the main-floor guards.

There was no sign of the master and even less light along the walls. Somewhere in the distance, Eddis could hear someone snoring lustily. Sleep, she thought. I'm half sick for it. Until she'd had several hours of oblivion on that nice, soft pallet back at the inn, she wouldn't give any further thought to this mad notion of the castellan's—or Jerdren's.

Jerdren, predictably, had the last word as they parted outside the tavern. Some of the Keep men had gone off to their barracks, and the elves were heading for the inn. M'Baddah and his son had already gone, and Blorys had followed the other Keep men into the tavern to secure a table and order wine.

"One more thing," he said.

Eddis fought a yawn. "A quick one more thing," she said. "I meant that about sleep."

"Well, all right. One person I've already decided we need, if we can get him. I don't know if you've battled in caves, gone looking for things hiding in them . . ."

She shook her head.

"Elves and dwarves are useful for seeing in the gloom, and Blor's right, most dwarves are born to that kind of fighting. But when you're up against foul things living in dark, twisty places, and they've been there a long time . . ."

"There's a point here?"" she asked as he hesitated.

"Thing is, we used the fellers back in the army as well, and dursed useful they were."

Silence. She folded her arms and waited.

"Well, thieves. Remember that long-fingered lad who snipped your purse and nearly made off with it? That one—he's good, Eddis. We could use him. And I wager if we asked nice, old Ferec would make us a present of him. Dungeons are rather full just now anyway, aren't they?"

Before she could think of anything to say to this outrageous proposition, he smiled and strode into the tavern. A roar of excitement filled the room.

"I'm not going anywhere with him," Eddis snarled under her breath, "because I'm going to murder him!"

She turned and stalked off to the private room she shared with Blot. Halfway there, she slowed her pace and began counting, up to ten and back down again, until her fit of temper eased. The poor child was no doubt still in terror of her. Not point in scaring her worse than she already was. Gods, she thought suddenly. If for some fool's reason I do decide to take on this mad venture, what ever will we do with that child?

II

Eddis woke with a start in the gray light of early day. The small sleeping room she ordinarily enjoyed so much all at once felt confining. I dreamed of caves, she thought, and shuddered. She tried to remember anything about the dream but couldn't except a sense of dread and darkness. Well, it wasn't dark here and now, but the room was overly warm and stuffy. The wind, if any, wasn't blowing through the window slit, as it usually did at this hour. After so many nights of sleeping in the open, it was small wonder she'd had bad dreams about close places.

Eddis edged onto one elbow. The door was still barred from the inside and there, on the floor, she could make out a small huddle of blanket just under the window. Blot slept, so far as she could tell.

Gods, she thought in sudden panic. What are we—what am *I* to do with a child? A half-grown girl who's been ill-treated by hard men all her life? A child who barely trusted her and was afraid of everyone else except M'Baddah? She sighed quietly. Worse yet, if M'Baddah, M'Whan, and I decide not to go back to guiding, if we take up this new fight. . . . It's astonishing she survived so long in a robber's den. She wouldn't stand a chance in those caves, but how could we simply leave her here? There are good, honest people here, and they'd do their best by her, but they'd never understand her. All she'd know is that M'Baddah befriended her when we took her away from the only life she ever knew—and then we abandoned her.

At the same time, Eddis knew she wasn't much of a person to deal with ordinary children, let alone this one. Somehow, she'd managed not to lose patience with the little one's fears the night before and simply let her sleep on the floor.

"A bed," she had said, "was not a place for a Blot."

Eddis gazed down at the still bundle, eyes narrowed as she remembered. "I could kill those men," she whispered.

The child knew only what those men had told her: Townfolk and such were "nocks," good only for the money, gems, and grain others could steal from them. She'd protested staying with Eddis and had difficulty understanding when M'Baddah explained that in towns and in houses, women and girls shared private rooms while men all slept together. Eventually, he and Eddis realized the child had no concept of sex. There were only "nocks," men like the bandits, and Blot. When the outlander had tried to explain that Blot, Eddis, and the merchant's ransomed lady were all "she," the girl had stared at him in visible disbelief.

One thing for certain, Eddis decided as she swung her legs to the floor. First thing this morning, before she and Jerdren started butting heads over their "reward," she and M'Baddah would go buy proper clothing for Blot. *We can't keep calling her Blot. It's cruel.*

A tap on the door brought her back to the moment. It was growing lighter outside the window, and she could hear people moving about. She dragged on breeches and padded barefoot across the little room. Blot came awake with a start as she opened the door. M'Baddah came in, bearing a thick clay pot filled with steaming hot tea and a cloth bag full of warm, spiced rolls. Eddis rummaged in her pack for her cup.

"The taverner gave me leave to brew my own herbs over his fire," the outlander said. "He also sent along the rolls. Good morning, young friend," he added with a smile. Blot sat in the midst of her blanket, rubbing her eyes. "Here is food for you, and drink."

He was quiet and patient, persuading the girl that she had no early duties, that he and Eddis wanted her to eat and drink with them, that she could have as much of both tea and bread as she liked. Two small rolls and a cup of tea later, the girl handed M'Baddah back his cup and sat back against the wall, tugging the blanket over her bare feet.

"She needs something decent to wear, M'Baddah," Eddis said then.

"I agree." He settled down next to the child while Eddis ate, telling her what she would see outside and where they would go. "You need clothes of your own," he said.

She fingered the loose jerkin she wore—M'Whan's spare, which itself had been bought secondhand.

"But this is nice stuff." She looked up at him. "Too good for a camp brat, maybe, but big enough, it would last a while. Blot don't need more."

Eddis sat back and waited. Her lieutenant was getting further with the girl than she might. It took time, but finally the girl agreed to leave the little room if M'Baddah agreed to stay right with her.

The short journey from the inn into the fountain square was slow. The girl was wary of everything and everyone, though at this early hour, the area was relatively deserted. The market was better. There were things to look at: piles of fruit and bright-colored cloth. Blot hid behind M'Baddah as the stall-holder gave her a kindly smile.

"You buy often enough from me, Eddis," the old woman

said, "and you've done us all good service. We'll see you get a good bargain and proper garments for him."

Eddis smiled and let the mistake pass. Blot was won over by the woman's quiet manner, entranced by the clean, colorful jerkins the old woman held against her skinny shoulders to test for fit. Eventually the little girl came away clutching two changes of shirt and trousers, as well as a pair of boots and soft foot-wraps to go under them. She even relaxed enough to walk between the two fighters.

But as they came abreast of the tavern, the clothing was forgotten, a fallen heap at her feet. Blot clung to M'Baddah, her face buried against his chest as men just inside the open doors started a cheer for the new heroes. The outlander moved aside, drawing the girl with him. Eddis scooped up the fallen bundle and followed. Once the noise had faded away, she knelt and laid a gentle hand on Blot's shoulder.

"You *don't* have to go in there. Are you hungry, though?"

A muffled, tearful voice finally said, "Got 'em rolls still. Where us slept."

"We'll take you back there, then. Would you like that?" Eddis asked.

Blot nodded, finally easing her grip on M'Baddah's arms, and took back her bundle and followed the swordswoman.

Once back in the small chamber, Eddis said, "You can bar the door so no one can open it, and you'll feel safe. But you have to promise to open it for us, when we come back."

"Promise" took a little explaining. The child finally nodded and rubbed her hand across her eyes and sniffed loudly. Eddis gave her lieutenant a frustrated look.

"M'Baddah, we can't keep calling her Blot. That's not a name!"

"What they said I was," Blot offered sullenly. "My . . . my friend didn't never like it. Called me Windflower, but that was only for him and me. He said, rest of 'em'd make fun. Was our secret."

Eddis sat cross-legged on the floor and beckoned the child close. M'Baddah had turned away to gaze out the open door. She lowered her voice.

"You and I have a secret, too. Know what my name is?"

"Eddis," Blot said promptly.

The swordswoman shook her head.

"Yes, but when I was a girl, about your size, before I learned to use a sword, my name was Flerys. It means 'flower' where I come from."

Blot looked at her, visibly puzzled.

"See, I didn't think that was a good name for a swordswoman. So I called myself Eddis. Maybe we could call *you* Flerys. That would be nicer than Blot." Silence. "Just . . . if you think you'd *like* to be called Flerys."

"Flerys." The girl tried it and smiled tentatively.

"It fits you." Eddis reached cautiously, and to her surprise, the girl let her lightly pat her shoulder. "Now, you can stay here and feel safe while we go back to that tavern. Eat all the rolls if you're hungry. We'll bring more later."

A few moments later, she and M'Baddah walked away from the little chamber, having heard the bar drop into place.

"Gods," Eddis said feelingly, "I hope she'll open it again."

"She will. That was kind of you, my Eddis. Flerys suits her better than it would you."

Eddis rolled her eyes. "You sneak! I should have known you'd hear all that!"

He laughed quietly and clapped her on the back. "I wondered often what kind of village woman would name a baby girl Eddis. Flerys is a good name, and a proper one for the bright poppy I see in that child. Not *ever* for my Eddis," he added.

The sun was well above the Keep walls when Eddis and her second headed back to the tavern. "Jers is probably going mad, waiting for us. Where's everyone else?"

"Jerdren left the inn when I did, but he went back to the Guild Hall to speak with the master. Blorys went to the chapel to see what aid the curate might provide. Our Keep men are talking to their fellows to see who might come to talk to you and Jerdren this evening. My son is at the provisioner's, making certain that we will be able to get all the oil and lamps we need—if we do take up this journey."

"Efficient," Eddis said. She stopped short as they came up to the tavern doors. Sitting outside, basking in the early sun, were two dwarves. Both wore sleeveless leather tunics, heavy pants, and thick boots, but they were otherwise unclad and unarmed. Eddis could see bruises and half-healed cuts on their bare forearms, and the older-looking of the two was missing most of his right ear. They looked up as the swordswoman drew near and respectfully inclined her head.

"I'm Eddis," she said. The younger of the two cleared his throat with a deep cough.

"Know who you are," he said evenly. "And that's M'Baddah. Everyone in the Keep, even us, knows that." The older one touched his arm, and he fell silent. "My uncle," he said with a nod at the older dwarf.

"We were once from the far north," said the other dwarf. "Most of us got driven out of the mountains though, and some of us went east, but we found little to mine and came back along that road, yonder, a few days ago. Turned out to be a bad choice." He let his eyes close.

"We're the last. All our folk—and now just us two," the younger said bitterly.

"Easy, lad," the elder said. He looked up at Eddis. "Word has it you and yours may ride out that way soon. Don't ask us to go. We won't. Bad that way. Bad luck for us dwarves anyway."

"You don't look ready to face it again, and no blame to you," Eddis said evenly. "But I wouldn't have asked you to go. If we go, it's strictly a mission for volunteers."

"Fools," the dwarf said.

"Perhaps, but if you could tell us what you saw, show us on the map we have . . ."

She let the suggestion hang. The younger looked as if he wanted to refuse, but the uncle sighed and nodded.

"Tonight, here?" Eddis asked. Another nod. "We'll buy—food and ale for you both."

The dwarf smiled faintly. "Of course you will." He got carefully to his feet. "Tonight, then." He let his nephew lead him off in the direction of the barracks. Both dwarves were limping.

Eddis and M'Baddah watched them out of sight. "Should I have offered to pay for the information, M'Baddah?"

"With some dwarves, that would be insult—as if they thought only of coin. If what they tell us is of value, you can offer a small purse, and leave them free to take it or refuse." He bowed her ahead of him, into the tavern.

There were few people in here at present. The taverner smiled as they passed him, heading for their usual corner. Eddis settled against the far wall, facing the door, and accepted the cup of fresh-squeezed apple and pear juice the barmaid brought her.

"We'll need lists," Eddis told M'Baddah as she set her cup aside. "Everyone should be responsible for his own weapons and personal supplies, but we'll need a central list for some things, and I say we write everything down as we think of it, because there's going to be too much to remember. Like healing potions—as many as we can get our hands on. And someone besides Mead—if Mead and Willow decide to come—who can use them, or better yet, who can heal more than small wounds. We'll lose people out there otherwise."

"You've decided to go, then?" her lieutenant asked.

She sighed faintly. "Part of me would rather not. Most of me thinks it's foolish and dangerous both, and we still don't even know how much of what we've heard is based on fact. Last night, before I fell asleep, I thought I'd find another client, and we'd head back to the realm. But the past days were . . . some of it was scary, but mostly there wasn't time for fear. And the bandit camp . . ." She tugged at her plait. "Planning that, having the plan come out just like we'd hoped . . . that was exciting. Fighting all those men on rocky, uneven terrain and in the gloom, discovering that I could not only defend myself but really *fight*. Gods, I sound like Jerdren," she mumbled.

"No. Like a swordswoman who understands the need to fight, does what she must, and does it well."

"Maybe." She shook her head. "But . . . Blot. Flerys, I mean. If we hadn't raided that camp, if we hadn't found her—"

"We did. So there is no use to think on it."

"No. But I realized just now, when we were talking to those dwarves, there could be prisoners held in the caves. For ransom or—"

"Or by those who like to hurt others. Or for a beasts' banquet," her lieutenant finished grimly as she hesitated. "I remind you of this because that is something you must think about Eddis. Can you face such creatures?"

"I . . . don't know, but nobody deserves to die like that. I'm afraid right now, but that's because I don't know what we're going to face out there. I'm just not afraid to go looking for it."

"Hey, that's great!" Jerdren had come across the room from the direction of the taverner's counter, a full mug balanced in his hands.

Eddis sighed. Woman, you have got to keep your eyes and ears open, she told herself. This time it was only Jers coming up on your blind side.

"You're up for it, then?" he asked as he settled across the table from her.

Eddis shrugged. "So far," she said cautiously. "Keeping in mind what I said last night, about proof of some kind. We need to talk, though."

"Knew that." Jerdren took a pull at his ale and smiled. "Why I'm here right now. Same rules as last time, right? You and me giving orders, me not pulling any fast ones on you?"

"Something like that." She told him about the dwarves. "We need to start writing things down." She glanced at her lieutenant. M'Baddah had pulled out a flattened tube of paper, a quill missing most of its feather, and a box of dry ink powder. He mixed a little of this with tea from his cup, began stirring it with the quill. "Maps," she said once the man was ready, "if there are any."

"There aren't," Jerdren said. "I asked everywhere. Best we can do is the one we already have, I guess. I can't even get a good fix on where the caves are, except somewhere east and near the road. Let's forget that for the minute, because while we've got this corner to ourselves, we need to get it straight about that thief, Kadymus."

Eddis drew a deep breath, let it out slowly, and brought up a smile. "Fine. We'll do that. Then we need to talk about the child."

* * * * *

Jerdren didn't like it and said as much at some length. "You can't take some grubby, howling brat into—"

"She howled when we first found her," Eddis broke in flatly. "Since then, I wager you haven't heard a sound out of her. She cleans up, same as anyone. We can't leave her here, though."

"She will not remain here without us," M'Baddah said. "She will find a way to follow us, if we do leave her."

"She's a child!" Jerdren protested. "Children don't remember things. Leave her here, some nice family, she won't recall who we are by the time we return. Won't care, anyway."

"That's not so," Eddis said. "Weren't you ever a child? Don't answer that," she added. "Just . . . you want this Kadymus? Fine, I'll agree so long as the girl comes, too."

"*If* she insists," Jerdren said flatly.

"She will, Jers. And if they keep her from following us, she might just throw herself off the walls."

Jerdren gave her a dubious look, but he finally shrugged and took another drink.

"Maybe Kadymus can teach her things. She might even be useful."

"Don't even *think* about it, Jerdren," Eddis growled. "That's another thing. The girl will be our responsibility. That light-fingered creature is all yours."

Blorys showed up moments later, visibly excited as he strode across the room, which was slowly beginning to fill for midday meal. Blor dropped onto the stool next to his brother, waved away the potboy, and planted his elbows on the table. "There's a man staying in the chapel, did you know?"

"I heard there was a madman being kept somewhere in there," Jerdren replied.

"He's not mad, though you might think so, the way he talks. He's a mercenary from the east. Speaks Common but not well. If I understand right, he was guiding a company here, and most of 'em were taken from around their campfire late one night. He remembers what sound to me like orcs and gnolls—like spotted dogs but man's height, two-legged like men, and armed. The curate thought him mad on that count alone. Guess he's never heard of gnolls."

"Not supposed to be any this far south," Jerdren replied.

"I asked the curate if we could send Mead in to try *his* spells on the fellow and got permission. The elves are there now. With luck, we may get more information out of him, and the curate said he'd find us a priest, if we decide to go."

"There's that other priest," Jerdren said. He wiped foam from his lip. "You know, the one at the inn? Has a couple novices, both under some vow of silence, I guess. But the priest himself—he's a cheerful sort. Comes here at times to talk with folks, drink and all. I hear he's been talking lately about going out to smite the wicked, or some such thing."

Blorys glanced at him. "I don't think we'd want him with us."

"Why, Brother? Supposed to be a powerful priest. Seems we might need one of those."

"I agree we might, but I got the feeling the curate doesn't trust the man. He's master of the local house, so I say we'd be wise to listen to him."

Jerdren considered this. "Maybe. This madman maybe could draw us a map?"

"He has one," Blorys said. "He wouldn't let me have it, but maybe Mead can persuade him. From what I saw, it's much better than what we have now."

A short while later, Eddis and M'Baddah left to check on the girl and take her food and drink. She still wore M'Whan's old jerkin, but her new things were spread out across the bed. She had readily opened the door when M'Baddah asked her, but she wouldn't move beyond the entry.

When Eddis broached the subject of leaving the Keep, Blot—now Flerys—nodded vigorously.

"Good. I go, too—with you." Her eyes were anxious.

Eddis nodded in turn. "You go with us," she agreed. The child settled cross-legged on the floor, sniffed cautiously at her bread and cheese, and bit into it, sighed contentedly as she chewed.

A few minutes later, the two fighters walked back to the tavern. "Gods, M'Baddah. If I get her killed . . ."

"She is safer with us than where she was," M'Baddah said, "and she is not as helpless as you fear, my Eddis."

Most of the company, including the elves, now occupied the far corner. Blorys smiled as Eddis got settled.

"The child is doing well?" he asked. She nodded. "Bad news is the madman won't come here—won't set foot outside the chapel," Blorys said. "But . . . well, Mead can tell you."

"He is not mad, but he has reason for his fears," the elf said. "After he was made prisoner, he and the others were moved from one cavern to another. It was always dark, there was always the smell of old death, and each time they were fewer until he was alone. Often he was tortured, but he does not know why, since they asked him no questions. One day, he found himself chained to a wall, and there were two other prisoners. Their guards were hobgoblins. He gave himself up for dead then, but all at once he heard the sound of battle, and men charged into the chamber, led by a huge fellow in black furs and bright armor. The hobgoblins died or fled, the men released the prisoners and started for the outside world. Just as they could see light in the distance, they were attacked. The man was knocked unconscious and woke in a silent, dark corner. He made his way to the road. After many days of walking and hiding, a hunting party from the Keep found him. He sent this." Mead handed over a much-folded piece of parchment. Someone had drawn a rough map. The lines and writing were very shaky. "The curate says he began that not long after he first came here."

"Any chance it's useful?" Eddis asked.

"I think so," Mead said. "The man is not mad, and though he remembers little of his journey here from the caves, he recalled much of the caves themselves. He also mentioned rumors of a human priest inside the caves who often demanded victims for sacrifice—and something about the undead." He looked around the table. "I have no magic to turn the undead."

"No," Jerdren said, "but a priest would. That man of yours, Eddis—Panev. He said he'd come and gladly. The curate says he'll do well by us. I talked to Ferec just now. He's got a man looking for whatever hard information there may be in old Macsen's records."

By late that night, he and Eddis had a solid count of twenty to go with them. The dwarves met with them only long enough to eat, answer a few questions, and add to Jerdren's map of the lands outside the Keep. They left as soon as the meat and beer were gone.

* * * * *

The next few days were busy. Jerdren ran them all through some maneuvers, and they laid in provisions. Eddis made arrangements with the castellan to have emergency supplies of food and other needs ready for them, if they had to come back for such things, and he arranged for horsemen to escort the mounted party as far as a base camp well up the east road, to keep the horses and return every few days, so they could be reprovisioned, and any wounded could be returned to the Keep, if need be.

Finally, there was nothing left to do except choose a day and hour to set out. Jerdren called a last meeting at the tavern late in the afternoon. Eddis settled as far as possible from Kadymus. The little thief was too smug for her taste, and she still didn't trust him to keep his fingers to himself.

She and M'Baddah sat against the wall, a wary Flerys between them. She wore sturdy boots and dark pants and shirt. M'Baddah had found a hardened leather vest that would serve her as armor, as well as a shortbow and arrows, and three long throwing knives on a belt, and he'd persuaded her to join him them for target practice. Eddis knew Jerdren was still unhappy about the girl's presence, but he'd seen the results of the outlander's lessons: The girl was reasonably accurate with the bow and not afraid to use the knives.

Jerdren brought her attention back to the moment as he clapped his hands to get the party's attention. "One last meal here tonight, then everyone off for a good night's sleep—ah, right, Eddis?"

She nodded.

"We'll leave tomorrow at first light," he went on. "Wager whatever you like, tomorrow will be a very long day."

It had been Eddis's suggestion that they leave so early. "We can come back to cheering crowds, Jerdren. Better we simply go and get this done, don't you think?"

* * * * *

The company of men who would take care of their horses and bring them supplies led the way out the gate and down the still-shadowed road. Flerys rode behind M'Baddah, one hand clinging to his belt. The rest were strung out along the road.

They stopped an hour later to rest the horses and refill their water bottles. The familiar swampy country went by on their right, and now Eddis could clearly see the mound where lizardmen were said to live. It was far enough away that she couldn't make out anything else.

Midday came and went. The company halted briefly for food. The air was clear and cool, and there was open ground all around them. Soon after, the ground began to rise and the hills to close in. Before long, the sky was a strip of deep blue, high above, and shadow lay heavily. The road wound down into a ravine, the sides rising steep and crumbly above their heads. Now and again, rock scree slid down toward them, but Eddis saw no sign of anything that might have loosened the slide.

On Jerdren's suggestion, the company made no more stops but walked the horses to rest them instead. Now the lead and rear guards rode with drawn swords and strung bows, and the elves kept watch on both flanks.

The afternoon dragged slowly on. Either the land was as empty as it appeared, or perhaps the company presented too large a threat for anything to challenge them, but they heard and saw nothing.

An hour before sunset—as best Eddis could tell by the deeper blue of the sky—they halted in a large clearing on the east flank of the road. There had been plenty of travelers here, over time, though the two blackened rings of stone looked long disused. The tattered end of a rope that might have once been a horse picket remained.

Men moved out to find wood, with guards to watch over them, while others went for water, taking the horses with them. By full dark, there were two fires and food, and Jerdren had posted guards all around.

Eddis felt edgy, and Jerdren looked it. He spent most of the dinner hour discussing plans that had already been set back in the Keep, mostly the disposition of the horse guards.

Blorys finally murmured something against his ear, and the older man sighed and set his bowl aside.

"All right, we'll stick with things as we planned 'em. You men ride back tomorrow, and three days past that, come back with spare horses and the provisions. Someone'll be here to meet you, but if not, you stay the night and go back at first light. Come back three days later."

The guard knew all this by heart; Eddis could see it in his face. He merely nodded, and Jerdren turned to the next matter—choosing watches for the night.

After that, the men fell silent. With luck, Eddis thought, they'd find the caves somewhere nearby. With better luck, they'd win through, though at the moment, she didn't feel as confident as she had the night before. Finally, she settled down close to M'Baddah and Flerys, snugged the blanket under her chin, and turned her face from the fire. She was asleep in moments.

12

It was much colder and very quiet when she was wakened for her share of the watch around middle night. No wind, no insects or frogs down by the water. That means you'll hear anything coming after the camp, she told herself. Of course, it might mean they were near enough the caves that the creatures there had killed off even the smallest game. Not a good thought, here and now. Jerdren's right, she thought. Why should you care if something eats your carcass, once you're dead? A short while later, she went to waken Blorys and sought her blankets once more.

By daybreak, the Keep men and horses were gone, and most of the party was ready to move out, waiting only for for Willow and M'Baddah, who had gone across the road to check the lay of the land and see if they could locate landmarks on what Jerdren called the "madman's map." As Eddis checked the last of her arrows and strung her bow, elf and outlander came back, and she could tell by M'Baddah's normally impassive face that they had found something. A faint smile curved his lips, and his eyes were alight.

She was nervy, all at once. Ready to start moving, to do *something*. Jerdren caught her eye, and she went to join him and the two scouts.

"We're somewhere close," her co-captain said cheerfully. "Just as I said last night."

She shrugged. "We knew that much. Everything I read mentioned that ravine."

"Sure, but that madman—"

"Zebos," Willow corrected him quietly. "Zebos told us his company did not like the look of the road ahead, where it plunged into a ravine. The big deserted camp they had just passed seemed too open. So they set up for the night in the trees just past the camp. M'Baddah and I found traces of such a camp, just down the road. Across the road, we could just see pale stone, rising above the trees. It is . . . not a good place, I think. Mead will be able to tell more, when we go."

"I felt nothing," M'Baddah said, "but it will be hard work, making our way through those woods. There are no paths visible from where we were, and the undergrowth is thick."

Jerdren grinned. "I'd say luck's with us, so far."

"So far," Eddis replied dryly. She went back over to finish stowing her gear. Flerys sat nearby, listening to M'Whan, one hand clutching her small bow. She looked interested in their surroundings, and if she was afraid, it didn't show. The swordswoman got to her feet as Mead restored his precious book to its bag and stood. The priest finished his prayers, tugged at his armor, and came over to the firepit. Moments later, the company started across the road and began working their way up a steep bank and into the woods.

It had been gloomy coming up the ravine and shadowy where they'd camped. On this side of the road, it was worse. Half-dead trees clung to each other and thorny vines twisted across the ground, clawing at her boots. Behind her, someone stumbled and nearly fell. Even where the trees were thin and wide-spaced, they managed to keep overhead light from penetrating. It might have been an hour after sunset, for all she could see. The ground was hard, but the air smelled damp and moldy.

She became increasingly aware of the furtive little noises around and above them. There was nothing to see, no hint of a breeze. They could be anything, she told herself. But nothing as big as an orc. *Something I could step on, more likely.*

The thought was reassuring, though she was grateful when the ground began sloping up and the worst of the brush was behind them. It was very quiet, all at once, and the moldy odor had faded and changed to the least hint of long-dead things.

Finally, she could see far enough to either side to make out pale, rough stone rearing high above them. From the looks of things, they were heading into a broad-mouthed ravine.

Don't think mouth, she ordered herself. Ominous as the place looked, her heart rose. This bore a strong resemblance to everything she read in the castellan's scrolls, and it was laid out just like Zebos's map.

She glanced back as they slowed, so Jerdren could choose a direction. Flerys was right behind her, staying close to her and M'Baddah as the girl had promised. Her dark hair was covered by a leather cap, and like M'Baddah, she carried her bow strung, an arrow fitted to the string.

Jerdren called a brief halt and sent Mead and M'Baddah a short ways ahead. The two were back almost at once.

"We chose right," the mage said quietly, as the others gathered close. "There are caves on both sides of this foul glade, and evil creatures are there as well, but none are nearby."

"Good," Jerdren murmured. "Remember what the madman told you, Mead. The nastiest things were living farther from the road, and higher up. We'll start low and near."

The mage nodded.

Jerdren shifted his grip on his sword and led the way once again.

It was mid-morning when they halted again. Rock walls climbed steeply north and south, and a high crag straight ahead. Shadow lay thick everywhere, though Eddis caught occasional glimpses of sunlight on the highest spires of stone. Caves—perhaps some of the darker blots along nearest ledge were caves—but the thin, light-starved trees all around made it difficult to see very far.

Jerdren beckoned everyone close. "All ready?" he asked quietly. "Our cave is just over there. See it? Dark opening, right at ground level. You three, get those oil lamps lit and shuttered. Luck, people." He turned away to check his weapons one last time.

Eddis gave Flerys what she hoped was a confident smile, sheathed her sword, and knelt to rest her feet a moment and set an arrow to her string.

The ground was littered with small stones, bits of bark, and other hard things. She brushed them aside, froze briefly as something small and white rolled away. Finger bones, she thought. She pushed them under a drift of leaves and got back to her feet. They moved on a moment later. Jerdren was back in the lead with M'Baddan and three of the Keep men. Eddis dropped back behind Flerys, and Blorys gave her a faint smile as he moved up next to her.

Sudden movement ahead and up caught her eye.

"Something there!" she whispered.

As Jerdren passed under a black-trunked tree, doglike creatures half her size and armed with blades threw themselves from the branches. Jerdren, startled, went down under two of them, his sword swinging, but he rolled and was on his feet almost at once. Keep men closed in from both sides, spears ready. Eddis set her shoulder against Blorys's and drew back her bowstring. Mead pushed his way forward and, raising his hands, brought his palms together silently. Something flew from between them, something that scared the little brutes. With shrill cries, they turned and pelted uphill, past the cave entrances she could see, and vanished into the woods—leaving behind one dead comrade, a wounded one, and half a dozen roughly edged small swords.

"Kobolds," Blorys breathed against her ear. "Nasty little things."

Eddis nodded and eased the pressure on her string. Jerdren dispatched the wounded kobold with a swift stab, straightened his mail shirt, and looked at Mead, who signed, "Gone."

Jerdren jerked his head toward the nearest dark opening and set out once again, Mead at his side, but when the man would have gone on in, Mead touched his arm and shook his head.

Willow entered the cave, then quickly came back out and gestured for them to join him.

"There are guards, back in a ways, but there is a deep pit just inside, where you humans will not be able to see it. Stay as close to the walls on either side as you can. It is perhaps four paces inside, and it will take four paces for you to pass it. I will lead," he added.

"Good," Jerdren said. "You with the lanterns next, archers after."

Eddis clutched her bow and the arrow in her left hand and felt her way along the wall with the other. Once inside the cave, darkness was complete. Four steps, five. Her foot tilted out and down as the ground fell sharply away. She pressed against the wall and moved past as quickly as possible and kept going to make room for those behind, until someone's still form brought her to a halt.

Guards, Willow had said, but wherever they were, they weren't making any noise. Maybe they'd run when so many large, well-armed people came into the cave. Surely they had seen their visitors? Something off to her left was producing a stomach-turning stench, and she wondered if she was going to be able to deal with all this.

"Light!" Jerdren's voice was painfully loud in the enclosed area, and a way ahead, something yelped. Three oil lamps were unshuttered. Eddis could make out armed kobolds frozen against the far wall, their eyes screwed shut tight. Before they could recover to fight or run, Jerdren charged forward, with a Keep spearman at his side. Two of the small guards went down in that sudden attack, and two others fled into darkness to the right, yelling shrilly. Eddis stayed back out of the way as Jerdren and the Keep man cut down the other two guards.

"They're warning the others," Jerdren said as he wiped his blade on one of his fallen enemy. "Leave the lanterns open. Wager they all know we're here now."

By that light, Eddis could make out rough-hewn walls that were wide enough for two grown men to walk abreast and higher than she could reach. The corridor the kobolds had taken ran fairly straight at a right angle to the entry and was very dimly lit, but she thought the far end might be blocked by a curtain. The other way, a heavy, dark cloth blocked the passage just across from the pit they'd come around. The pit, she could see, was at least as deep as she was tall, and it was spiked.

"We're in luck," Jerdren murmured. "It's cowardly little kobolds, all right, and I don't think they dug this cave. Ceilings would be lower."

"Good," Eddis said quietly. "I don't fight well on my hands and knees. We'd better get after them, don't you think?

Keep in mind this place might hold a lot of them—enough they'll be willing to turn and fight. Or they might have bigger allies back there."

"Allies, huh," Jerdren said.

"What's that way?" Kadymus whispered. He was gazing at the curtained-off passage across the pit.

"Worry about it on the way out," Jerdren replied. "Guards went *that* way."

"Nothing there but very dead things," Mead said, and his face twisted in disgust. "Dead things—and rats."

Jerdren looked at him, astonished. "You wasted a spell for *that?*"

"I used my nose," Mead replied shortly.

"Dead things," Eddis said, as shortly. "He's right, trust me. Let's get moving, before they get a chance to plan something."

They hurried down the long corridor after the kobolds. It was very quiet that way at the moment. When they reached the curtain, another gloomy passage branched to their left—a fairly short one. Eddis and the others waited while Willow and Kadymus slipped past the filthy cloth. They were back at once.

"Nothing in sight," Willow said quietly. "We've come about halfway down this passage. There's a chamber down there. I could see light, and there are kobolds down there. I don't think the guards went that way. It's too calm."

"We don't go on and leave anything behind to set an ambush for us when we're going back out," Eddis said.

"Let's go," Jerdren said shortly and slipped past the curtain. The others followed.

The passage itself was gloomy, but Eddis could make out what seemed to be a large chamber. The air was still and smelled of damp dirt, sweat, poorly cooked food, and something long dead. The last fortunately could not have been close by. Willow took back the lead, and the men carrying lanterns had them shuttered once more.

Eddis glanced at the priest, who now walked next to her. The man carried a mace, and his face was grim. Odd, she thought. He'd been so quiet and placid all the way to the Keep, she'd once thought him half-witted.

Flerys was right at M'Baddah's side, bow slung over her shoulder and a long knife in her hand.

Gods, I must have been half-witted myself, bringing a child here, the swordswoman thought. At least the child didn't seem to think it odd. Eddis made sure her own bow was secure and drew her sword.

Panev suddenly eased to the fore and pointed.

"Evil is there, hiding," the priest whispered, then yelled a warning as a dozen or more kobolds erupted from the chamber beyond. Most were armed with dagger-sized swords and long, slender metal pikes. A few wore bits of armor, but many—likely females—wore only ragged tunics and clung to even smaller creatures. Perhaps they were merely seeking a way of escape, but most of those with young held knives or daggers. Eddis blocked a long, wild swing and countered with a pivot and stab. The kobold howled in pain and tore itself from her blade, but staggered into the wall and fell. She brought the blade down across the back of its neck and swung at the next. Four long steps—and two more dead— brought her into the chamber itself, her back against the wall, bloody sword in one hand, long-bladed dagger in the other.

This chamber was wide and deep, the ceiling vaulted, and only a few tallow candles burned here, the smoke thick and cloying. Eddis was grateful when one of the Keep men opened his lantern, illuminating the place in all its dreadful fouled state. A few kobolds—smaller and half-naked—knelt mid-chamber, clinging to each other, and these were guarded by females.

Many of the fighters were still trying to cut their way through the company—seeking simply to flee or perhaps hoping to escape with the females and young. Several of the Keep men, like M'Baddah, were using bows to bring the creatures down from a distance. Eddis decided to stay where she was, in the doorway, sword ready to bring down any who made it past the archers. As she freed up a throwing knife, Blorys came over to set himself at her left shoulder. Three of the Keep men ran into the chamber, boar spears ready to throw.

"Arrow!" M'Baddah's voice rose above the noise, and the spearmen ducked, staying low as the outlander, his son, and Flerys shot together. One arrow buried itself to the fletchings in the nearest kobold, and the other two wounded their targets, though not badly. The other kobolds abandoned their fallen comrades and retreated toward the far wall.

One of the spearmen yelled in pain and fell, two black arrows in his shoulder, another wobbling back and forth in his hardened leather armor.

Eddis glanced at Blorys. "They aren't trying to run, but they can pick us off from across the chamber," she said.

"Two can play that game," Blorys said and drew her across the opening and along the wall, so they had a clear view of the enemy. "Watch out," he added. "If those are females, they aren't exactly helpless!"

"Got it!" she replied.

The smaller, unarmored females had put aside their young and were now retrieving bows and spears from the messy pile of things littering the floor around them. She drew down on the nearest, dispatched the creature, and began firing arrows as quickly as she could. Blorys's bowstring sang non-stop.

Seven of the armed kobolds and at least as many of the others fell dead or dying. Four went down squealing and bleeding heavily. The remaining young and females ran wildly for the passage, and many of the armed creatures threw aside their weapons to follow, but others seemed grimly willing to cut their way through the tall invaders blocking the way out.

But the invaders were no longer there. As the kobolds came running, Jedren drew his men aside and let them pass. The men who'd been left to keep watch at the joining of passageways were ready for that. By the time Eddis and Blorys came to where they could see the corridor, Keep men holding swords blocked the way. The startled kobolds milled in panic and were cut down.

M'Whan came back to illuminate the cavern with one of the lanterns. The chamber had been fetid with body odors, rancid food, and less pleasant things. Now it reeked of blood. Blorys gripped her forearm and gave her a reassuring, if faint, smile. She nodded and drew her sword as she followed him back into the passage. Flerys joined her at once, with M'Whan at her side.

"Nothing in there worth having, I'd say," Jerdren remarked. "Those entry guards weren't in here, so we still have to face whatever they've gone to warn. Let's go."

Mead, who had taken a few steps up the short side passage, came back to say, "We go back the way we came in. There is no way out up there. There are enemies, but I cannot tell how many or exactly where they are."

"One way to find out," Eddis replied.

The lanterns were again mostly shuttered, only a dim light from one showing that the way was clear. Just ahead, another hewn corridor crossed this one at right angles. Eddis could make out flickering lantern light on the far wall.

"We might as well yell out, 'Here we come!' " she murmured crossly.

"Well, but they know we're here anyway," Blorys replied. "Why *not* let 'em see us coming and maybe scare most of 'em into running?"

"Where'll they run, if there's no way out up there?" she countered.

He laid warning fingers on her arm as they reached the passage end. Jerdren had somehow got himself ahead of Willow here. He leaned into the open, yelped in surprise, and jerked back. A crossbow quarrel vibrated in the shoulder of his chain mail. He yanked the deadly little bolt free with an effort, then threw it aside.

"Three, I think," he said softly.

Three guards, but there might be more, and the creatures were either trapped or safe behind some barricade because they weren't giving up or trying to run.

She heard a sharp *ping!* as a quarrel missed Jerdren's head by a finger's worth, slammed into stone, and bounced off. Her co-captain ducked back out of sight. Two more bolts followed in rapid order, clattering off stone some distance down the side passage to his right, but they came nowhere near him. Jerdren grinned.

"Lousy shots!" he mouthed and crooked a finger for them to join him.

Mead moved to the fore and gestured for the others to stay put as his lips began moving in a spell. Willow was right behind him, and he murmured something in Jerdren's ear that Eddis couldn't hear. Jers nodded, and he and the elves suddenly leaped into the corridor, yelling loudly. The irregular volley of quarrels ceased. Jerdren turned to loose several quick arrows, then threw himself after the elves, down the right-hand passage and into darkness.

Mead followed. "Fire spell!" he yelled, and got an answering, distant reply from his brother. A fireball crackled to life between his outspread fingers and launched itself along the west passage. The mage threw himself after it.

"Wait." Mead had stopped just short of a left bend in the passage a long way on. He had to raise his voice to be heard, when the rest of the company would have surged past him and around the corner. "Only three kobolds there, and my spell has neutralized them, but Jerdren and my brother would doubtless have killed all three by now anyway."

Eddis flinched aside as the whine of a sword cut the air, ahead in the gloom. Then two kobolds made bulky by chain mail came running up the passage straight toward her, throwing aside their crossbows as they ran. The sight of Eddis, Blorys, and Mead blocking the way stopped them short, and they spun around and ran back the way they'd come. There was another, very brief, clash of metal on metal, and Jers's triumphant yell. Blorys, sword in one hand and spear in the other, sprinted down the passage, but Jerdren came back into sight, a small cut on his ear bleeding freely. Willow followed, his nose wrinkling in distaste.

Eddis moved warily around the corner and into an alcove, one of the lantern-holders illuminating the way for her. Ahead she could make out a heavy-looking wooden door that was closed tightly, and just short of the door, a sentry area. Two low stools and a table littered with cups and scraps of an old meal had been shoved against the right wall, and on the floor nearby stood a basket stuffed full of quarrels and a wound crossbow shoved in with them. The creatures that had been on guard here were dead.

Jerdren spoke quietly. "Don't know what's in there, but we don't want to leave it there to cut us off from the outside."

"Don't even think about that," Eddis replied.

Willow moved past her to lay his ear against the rough-hewn surface. He nodded and then backed away from the door.

"I can hear voices but cannot say how many. They do not seem to have heard the fighting."

"Ridiculous," Eddis began, but the elf shrugged.

"It is a very thick door. Perhaps for privacy?"

"Chief's room, maybe?" Jerdren asked. He was grinning widely. "There's where any treasure will be."

Eddis was aware of Kadymus for the first time since they'd gotten past the pit. The little thief was grinning even more widely than Jerdren. She tapped his shoulder, hard.

"Share alike, remember? If there's an armed chief in there, do you really want to be the first in to fight him, little man?"

He gave her an indignant look and fell back as Mead again took over.

The mage laid both hands against the portal, then stepped back and spoke under his breath. To her amazement, Eddis heard the mage's voice from the *other* side of the door, scarcely muffled by it.

"Fly, all of you!" he ordered, "for you are discovered!"

He retreated just in time. The door slammed into rock, and armed kobolds fled into the passage, engaging the Keep men and the priest. Eddis let Blorys pull her aside to let the creatures go. She sensed a large room beyond that door. M'Baddah came up on her other side, opening his lamp wide with one hand as he drew his curved scimitar with the other.

"That's no kobold!" Eddis protested as she got her first look at the fellow. He was nearly twice the size of the others, and he seemed unaffected by the sudden flare of light.

"Their chiefs are chosen by size and skill!" Blorys hissed, then set his shoulder against hers as the brute strode through the open doorway and straight for Jerdren.

"Two others in there that I can see, Blor," Eddis said as the chief brought his two-handed axe down overhand at her co-captain.

Jerdren yelled, "He's mine!" as he jumped nimbly out of the way and stabbed at the leader, but his blade slammed into the face of the heavy axe and went flying. Off balance, Jers flailed for balance and went down.

M'Baddah slipped between the fallen man and the axe-wielding brute, deflected a wild overhand blow that might have separated the man's head from his body. The outlander countered the attack with an overhead, slashing blow of his own. His enamel-hilted dagger buried itself to the hilt in the kobold chief's chest.

At M'Baddah's warning yell, one of the Keep men ran at the enemy with his spear, but heavy mail turned the point and sent the man reeling back into the wall. The kobold dragged a long-bladed knife from its belt but slipped in its own blood and went down hard. Jerdren, back on his feet, snatched up the battle-axe and brought the weapon down across its owner's neck.

Eddis stayed where she was for a long moment, then skirted the mess, heading for the last armed kobold, hesitating in the doorway. It wasn't running—possibly there was no place left to run to—but it wasn't giving up, either. Female, Eddis thought as she drew near. Possibly protecting its young, and now she could see two such little creatures. They weren't cowering, either. They were trying to sneak around—possibly trip her or help the female in some attack.

Blorys was a reassuring presence against her left arm. He swung at the monster holding the doorway as Eddis turned sideways to stab at sudden movement on her left.

A sudden, dreadful, high-pitched squealing filled the chamber and hurt her ears. One of the little creatures who'd tried to flank her staggered back, into the open room. Long, pale, bony fingers clutched the hilt of a dagger buried in its belly. The other shrieked and tried to flee, and to Eddis's horror, Flerys ran past her into the chamber where, one of M'Whan's spears in hand, she ran the little thing through, pinning the now squirming body to the floor.

"Flerys! Get back!" the swordswoman yelled.

"They'd hurt you!" the girl protested, but at M'Baddah's command, she edged back out of sight.

The kobold Eddis fought was distracted by the injured and frightened youngling and went down a moment later, impaled on the woman's sword. Blorys left the one he'd fought gravely wounded and leaped beyond it—or her—to the next of them. The fight had gone out of the last of the creatures. It dropped its weapons and huddled on the floor. The remaining two young ran to it and clung.

Blorys shook his head and swore softly. "Gods. I can't kill that!" he protested.

"*I* can." Jerdren pushed past him and swung his sword hard, several times. Finally he turned away to finish off the wounded creature Flerys had attacked, retrieved the spear, and wiped it on one of the room's rough hangings. He met his brother's eyes.

"Any of those might have killed you, female or not. And the little ones grow up, remember?"

He stepped back into the passage. "All of you out here! Keep watch. We don't know what's left in this cave that needs fighting. I think this is the chief's room, and I believe whatever treasure we find will be here. Mead, you should help us look, in case there are potions or charms. Otherwise—Eddis, I say that you, me, the child and Kadymus have the best chance of quickly finding whatever's here."

"Keep in mind," Eddis said, "that we came up the right-hand

end of this passage. We don't know what's down the other way. So far, I haven't seen anything resembling those two guards from the entry. Maybe there's another horde of creatures behind us that they went to warn?"

"Let the guards worry about that," Jerdren told her. "Work fast. Check anything that might hold coin or other trove, and remember, anything locked probably holds something of great value. If this is the chief's chamber, he wouldn't have locked everything of value away—not with that door and guards to keep him feeling safe."

Kadymus was already rummaging through a pile of dirty bed clothes. He sat back on his heels suddenly and gave a sharp little whistle.

"Don't do that!" Eddis turned from the small chest she'd found.

"Got something," the youth said and scooted backward across the floor, dragging something into the open: a small wooden chest, with dulled metal banding. He chuckled softly. "Hidden pretty well. Heavy, too." He peered at it. "And locked."

"That's yours to open, then," Eddis ordered. "*Open*, not keep to yourself. Got it?"

Kadymus gave her a sour look but sat down cross-legged to fish out his special lock-wire.

Blorys came across the room, a blood-soaked chain dangling from his fingers. "Found a key around the chief's neck."

Jerdren's eyebrows went up as he fingered the links.

"That's gold! I don't know what the gem is, but it's big. I'll take the key. Blor, you hold the rest."

"Lookit this!" A jubilant Kadymus sat back on his heels. "It's all coins—hundreds of 'em!" He pawed through the top layer, sighed. "No gold I can see, but plenty of silver."

"Some of that's platinum, unless my eyes deceive me," Jerdren told him. "Good work, lad!" He looked around as his brother suddenly laughed.

Blor had torn one of the moldy-looking hangings from the wall and was slicing it to shreds. A pile of gold coins glittered in the lamplight, spilling over his fingers.

"Funny," he said. "I remembered one of our aunts sewing her egg-coins into the hems of her curtains and blankets."

"I'd forgotten that. Bundle 'em up, Brother," Jerdren said, "and be quick about it. M'Whan, you and Kadymus divide up that chestful, so we can spread out the weight among us. Once we're back in camp, we can make a fair count and sort out what to do with it all."

"We're going back to camp already?" Kadymus asked.

"Why go looking for another fight with what we've got?" Jerdren replied. "We've killed plenty of 'em, and whatever's left down that last passage—well, we can come back and finish 'em off another day, if we want. All the same . . ." He thought a moment. "Let's have a look at that key and see if we can figure out what it's for."

Eddis was wiping her blade on one of the hangings when Flerys came up beside her. The girl looked nervous for the first time since they'd left the Keep.

"Eddis? You mad at me?"

It took the woman a moment to remember yelling at the child to get out of the way.

"No, I'm not mad at you, Flerys. I just didn't want you to get hurt. You mustn't ever get in front of anyone swinging a sword the way I was."

"Oh." The child puzzled at this. "But I was afraid for you, Eddis."

Eddis managed a smile, though the girl's words worried her. Flerys had already lost her friend back in that bandit camp. I can't be sure the child won't lose me either, Eddis thought. I can't afford to let her care that much.

"Just . . . stay close to M'Baddah for now, will you? Or me, if I tell you to. You've got good aim with that bow, but I don't know that you're ready for close fighting, and you aren't big enough to bully things bigger than these kobolds, all right? There is a lot of training you'll want, so you know how to hurt only your enemies in close fighting. Blorys and I are trained, so it's safe for us to fight together."

"Yes, Eddis."

The company moved back along the passage toward the outside world, but at Jerdren's insistence, made a quick check at its far end. There was a locked door, just to the left of the short tunnel, and the key the chief had worn fit the lock.

"Treasure," the man breathed as he turned the key and the door swung open.

Eddis caught her breath in a gasp and thrust Flerys behind her. The elves backed hastily away as a foul odor assaulted them. Jerdren, undeterred, took one of the lamps and stepped into the chamber to look around. The swordswoman closed her eyes. *It's a larder. The chief's larder. That was a human head I saw on the shelf there—and next to it, a human skull.*

13

Early morning found them waiting once more just within the clearing while Willow and M'Baddah searched for enemies out in the open. They lay low for a while when Willow signed he could hear things flying overhead, fairly low to the ground.

"They may be stirges," he whispered. "Small but unpleasant."

Unpleasant, he calls the nasty bloodsuckers, Eddis thought, and wrinkled her nose. Each was as long as her arm, and enough of them attacking a woman her size could leave her dead and completely drained of blood in no time. After a while, the elf stole back into the clearing, listened, and motioned them on.

Furtive noises and rustlings followed them as they worked their way toward the south ledge, where another cave loomed dark and forbidding. Blorys touched Jerdren's arm to get his attention.

"I think this might be the cave Zebos described," he whispered. "All that prickly brush around the entrance and that fallen tree—the forked one—see?"

Jerdren nodded, then beckoned the others close to pass that on.

"Keep in mind what he told me," Blor added quietly. "There are lots of long passages and guards everywhere—even where you might not expect them. Goblins and orcs and possibly hobgoblins."

"And remember what we discussed about prisoners," Eddis added. "Rescuing prisoners here is a high priority, right?"

Kadymus looked as if he wanted to disagree with her. She quelled him with a hard look.

Jerdren nodded again. "Sure. Any prisoners would be grateful to us, and that could mean a reward. Or they may know where their captors have hidden treasure."

The little thief brightened at that.

Unlike the previous day's cavern, this seemed to be a naturally formed cave—at least for the first part of it. Here, it wasn't entirely dark. Eddis could see faint light far down one corridor, enough that they could walk at a good pace. It was quiet for some distance, but as M'Baddah started into the main passage, he pulled back, gesturing urgently for his companions to get out of sight. Moments later, Eddis heard guttural-voiced beings come clomping and grumbling up the passage from her left. Two burly, shadowy forms passed the entry without slowing. The sound of their footsteps slowly faded. Willow eased into the open briefly to gaze after them, then came back to whisper.

"Goblins. Taking messages and food to guards on duty up there. The guards are orcs, I think. One of the goblins asked, 'How's old Bear-face?' and a guard cursed him."

The elf moved silently into the passage once more, then beckoned. "It is all right. They kept going that direction, away from us."

"Then we'll go the other way," Jerdren indicated the long passage with faint light at its end.

It took time, moving quietly down the rough-hewn way and making sure they weren't seen or heard. They could hear others, though. Harsh, guttural voices echoed along the stone ceiling. Several of them. They could make out moving shadows, cast by the dim light.

"Guard room," Eddis murmured, and Willow nodded. The swordswoman checked to make sure Flerys was staying close to M'Baddah and nocked an arrow.

Light shone on the left-hand wall of the passage, and another step would bring Jerdren into view. He met Eddis's eyes, indicated the right wall with a jerk of his head as he moved that way. He edged along in shadow for several steps, back to the wall, bow drawn partway. Eddis was right behind him, and M'Baddah came after her.

Five steps, six. Jerdren threw himself across the passage and into the light, firing three arrows rapidly and seemingly at random into the chamber beyond. Fire flared up in there, casting dark, long shadows in all directions. Startled yells filled the corridor as Jerdren pelted back out of sight, and Eddis took his place. She could make out little because of the light and commotion—creatures running in all directions— but she fired two arrows into the confusion and ran. M'Baddah was already in front of her, shooting with his usual deadly precision. Willow and M'Whan faced a volley of spears and arrows, but none of the weapons came anywhere near them.

Eddis stiffened as a squat, nasty-looking creature came into sight, sliding along the shadowed wall, spear in one hand, and braced itself to charge.

"M'Whan, your right!" she shouted and drew back her own string.

The orc's head snapped her way, and she could make out an evil gleam of teeth as it grinned, and shifted direction— toward her. Her arrow buried itself deep in the brute's eye, more by luck than aim, and the orc sagged to the floor.

There was a sudden silence in the chamber, except for a pained whimper. What are they up to? she wondered. Running feet alerted her, but the sound faded, going away.

M'Whan darted into the chamber, bow clutched in one hand, a throwing spear in the other. Eddis threw herself after him.

She drew her sword as she came into the chamber, but there was no need. The low-burning fire against the far wall showed dead and dying orcs. There was no sign of M'Whan, though. She turned on one heel as the others came up. Flerys had a tight grip on one of her spears, and her eyes went wide as she gazed around the room. Blood ran across the floor and pooled in low places, and now several of the Keep men moved from orc to orc, finishing off the wounded. Aside from the bodies, there wasn't much in the room: a barrel of water, a table and benches, a barrel full of spears. Eddis could see a passage in the far wall that led into darkness.

"M'Whan must have gone that way," she began but stopped, as a breath later M'Whan came into the light.

"Passage there," he gasped, out of breath. "Goes down, around a corner. More stairs and a closed door at the top. The one I followed went through it."

"And may bring others back here," M'Baddah said. He, Willow, and two of the Keep men went back the way they'd come to keep watch, and Mead took up a position just inside the lower corridor.

"Or it might've just run," Jerdren said. He retrieved his arrows, tossing aside one that had snapped against the wall and another that had fallen into the fire pit.

"These don't look like rich goblins to me. Ratty clothes, lousy leather bits for armor—nowhere to hide a bag of gems in that, and nowhere in this room, either. I say we go back the way we came and on up where those guards were before we worry about that runner. No sense getting caught between two bunches of goblins, even if they aren't much to fight. Besides, if the guards are eating, they'll be as easy as this bunch to catch off guard."

"Not much to fight," Blorys said dryly. "They just sneak up on you and ambush you. No danger of dying from *that*, is there?"

"Don't make assumptions like that," Eddis added flatly. "We've been blessed lucky, two fights in a row. Only a fool would think they're all going to be as easy as this was."

Jerdren rolled his eyes ceilingward and led the way back out, beckoning M'Whan to join him. The rest followed.

Near the end of the passage, where they could see light from outside, Eddis called a brief halt for water and a rest. When they moved on, she and Willow were in the lead, several paces ahead, the elf listening intently for the sounds of goblins or other creatures moving around the passages. For now, there didn't seem to be any, and within moments they reached a four-way branching passage. A faint light flickered straight ahead—perhaps a candle or oil lamp in a deep niche, Eddis thought. Otherwise it was quiet and dark that way and utterly dark to their left. She glanced at Willow, sent her gaze that direction.

The elf listened and sniffed cautiously, then whispered, "It's a dead end, I think."

To their right, however, came a sudden burst of coarse laughter. They'd found the guards. These were laughing at some joke, or maybe simply drunk—she couldn't tell. Ruddy light flared as though someone had tossed a log on a fire, and by that she could make out that the whole south wall of the chamber—a large chamber—was open to the passage. Great, she thought. We won't be sneaking up on anyone *here*. She and the elf drew back to describe the layout to the others.

Jerdren thought for a moment, then listened as the priest spoke into his ear. The swordsman nodded vigorously.

"Eddis, M'Whan, and two of you Keep men who can run fast, we'll go first," he whispered. "Arrows ready. We're gonna sprint along that passage, fire, and keep going until we reach the far end of the chamber."

"Where they can pick us off one at a time?" Eddis objected.

"No. Panev says he has something that will distract 'em."

He was gone before she could say anything else, moving along the tunnel until a step or two more would bring him into the open. Blorys sighed faintly and gripped her arm as she swore under her breath. She smiled at him, fitted an arrow to the string, and went to join Jerdren. Two of the Keep men and the priest were right on her heels. A glance over her shoulder as she settled in to wait. Panev tilted his head back and began to pray quietly.

Jerdren went into a low crouch, then burst into the open, Eddis right on his heels. She could hear the pounding of boots right behind her. Movement—there, to her right, and not as far away as she would have liked. She swerved as her co-captain came to an abrupt halt and turned to fire an arrow, then took off again. She shot two arrows wildly and ran, slamming hard into Jerdren's outstretched arm. She had a sharp mental image of stunned goblins staring at them, mouths agape, until Jerdren's arrow brought one of them down yelping. The Keep men ran up, and the orcs were coming for them.

We're dead, Eddis thought, and was suddenly angry.

"Jers, you brainless oaf—!" She caught her breath in a startled gasp. Brilliant light, painful as lightning, flooded the room.

"That's Panev," Jerdren hissed. "Back the way we came—now!"

If he'd run fast coming over, he was almost flying now. Eddis stretched her legs and tried to keep up.

All four made it back across without incident. Most of the goblins were clutching their eyes and wailing, but as Eddis ran for the relative safety of the corridor, two of the goblins scooped up a bundle from the floor and fled through a massive wooden door she hadn't noticed before. Two others drew short swords and swung them wildly, as if they expected the crazed humans to sneak up on them and kill them while they were blinded. One accidentally slashed its companion in the forearm.

He screeched in pain and flung himself away from the blade, crying out, "*Bree-yark!*"

Kadymus pushed past Eddis, laughing. "Hey, get that! Hit 'em with a little light and a few bad shots, and they give up!"

Jerdren snatched at the youth's sleeve but too late. The young thief was already halfway across the room, swaggering toward the huddled creatures, sword in one hand, long dagger in the other.

"Gotta be one of you understands some Common, I bet, just like I know that surrender word of yours. So you just drop those swords and give up n-now . . . ?" His voice rose to a girlish squeak. Two of the goblins were coming for him, still blinking but ready to kill. As he retreated a pace, the door slammed against the far wall. A massive brute filled the doorway, huge club clutched in one hand. It raised a meaty fist and leered at the youth only paces away, revealing brownish, ugly teeth. Kadymus's sword fell from his hands, and he staggered back into the nearest wall. Jerdren darted into the open, grabbed him, and dragged the youth back into the passage.

"Gods," Blorys said reverently. "It's an ogre! Willow," he added urgently, "you and Mead, back, out of sight!"

"It knows we are here," Willow replied calmly, though

he'd gone pale. "It can smell us, but I will not run from it."

"Now what?" Eddis asked. Her sword felt puny, all at once. The creature was head and shoulders taller than she, if not more, and muscled like a blacksmith. Still, there was only one...

"We fought one in the north," Borys said. "They're mean and strong but not smart or fast. Remember, Jers?"

"Sure. You remember what we did to stop it?" his brother replied, as tersely.

"Hope so."

"You'd better remember! M'Baddah, you and M'Whan come with us, and the rest of you, deal with those goblins, so we can concentrate on that ogre!"

Jerdren moved out into the chamber again, sword drawn, and his back against the nearest wall.

The ogre was in the chamber now, the goblins backing warily away from it, though two had begun a slow stalk along one wall.

"Watch it," Eddis said and indicated the two with her chin. "They're trying to flank us."

Willow brushed by her and shot two arrows at them. One struck its target, and the goblin sprawled across the passage, twitching and snarling. The other yelped in surprise and darted back to join his companions near the doorway. The ogre growled at them, and they backed hastily from the door, edging along the north wall, out of his reach.

Jerdren yelled something guttural, a single word. The ogre's eyes narrowed, and it drew itself up straight, grip tightening on the club as the man ran for the far wall, just as he'd done earlier. This time, he didn't stop. The ogre, astonished, turned to watch him. Blorys and the outlanders flung themselves into the room, M'Whan clutching a throwing spear, M'Baddah his bow, Blorys his sword.

Gods, it'll kill them! Eddis knelt, bow in hand and tried to sight on the brute's eye or its throat—either was big enough to make a decent target. The Keep men moved around her, staying close to the wall, and began firing arrows and spears at the goblins.

The ogre spun around as M'Whan's spear missed it by inches, and it swiped at Blorys with one massive hand. Blorys leaped out of the way, ducking as M'Baddah's arrow sang over his head, and sliced across the monster's shoulder. It didn't even notice, Eddis thought, and shifted her attention to the orcs, who had been bullied into a pack by one of their number and were charging the Keep men. She fired several arrows at them, but most were foiled by armor or went wild. They slammed into the humans, and she didn't dare shoot any more. Willow eased past her, sword in one hand, dagger in the other, and went to help.

M'Baddah's second arrow bounced off a bony hip. The next sank deep into the ogre's belly. Behind Eddis, Mead was muttering—setting up a spell. Off to her right, one of the men yelled and went down. Another slid down the wall.

The ogre plucked at M'Baddah's arrow, snarled, and left it where it was. Its filthy leather pants were slick with blood. Eddis stared in horrified astonishment as Blorys darted back and forth in front of the massive creature, waving his arms and shouting taunts. She brought up her bow and shot high. The arrow tore through the air where the massive head had been, but the ogre was on the move, its attention locked on Blorys as it swung the club.

Too hard. It overbalanced and fought to regain its feet, but as the man ran in, sword swinging, it smacked him with an open hand, sending him rolling across the floor, half-stunned. His helm rolled the other way and cracked against Eddis's knee. She dropped her bow and drew her sword, throwing herself into the open between Blor and the brute. The ogre laughed, an evil sound that filled the chamber and left the orcs drawing back in a terrified huddle. Brushing past M'Baddah and M'Whan, the creature raised its club high.

Eddis slashed wildly with her sword, hoping to force the ogre back. Behind her, Blorys was fighting to sit up and gasping for her to get away.

"Don't distract me!" she yelled.

The ogre bared its ugly teeth in a savage grin and reached for her.

Eddis tightened her hands on the sword hilt and swiped at the ogre's hand. The blade rebounded. She staggered back, off balance, and Blorys shouted a warning. Jerdren came running then, sword a blur as it cut the backs of both the ogre's legs. The brute snarled and fell hard, one or both of the long tendons cut, but it was fighting to turn and bring the club down on the head of the man who'd injured it. M'Baddah, M'Whan, and Willow threw themselves at the brute, stabbing at its throat and eyes. The ogre jerked once and was quiet. A little blood trickled down its filthy cheek but soon stopped.

Blorys staggered to his feet and fell back into the wall. Eddis wrapped her free arm around his shoulder to draw him away from the fighting, and when he tried to resist, her hand tightened.

"Come with me! You'll get someone else killed trying to protect you!" He went with her then, back into the passage where Mead, the priest, and Flerys waited. He was still panting for air and not walking very well, but he wouldn't go any farther than the entrance.

"Gotta . . . see," he gasped.

Eddis swore under her breath as she eased him down to the floor and handed him her water bottle. A glance over her shoulder assured her that the goblins were retreating.

"How bad?" she asked quietly.

"Just . . . knocked the wind . . . out of me," he replied.

Eddis tensed and spun around, sword ready to slash, as Jerdren yelled. She couldn't make out what he said, but the few goblins still standing shrieked in what sounded like pure terror and ran through the open door.

Blorys laughed. "Jers . . . learned a word or two of Goblin . . . back in the army. When . . . we . . . fought 'em. Forget . . . what that means. Don't think they'll . . . come back, though."

A moment later, he let Eddis help him back to his feet as Jerdren came running across the guard alcove to join them.

"Blor! You all right?" Without waiting for answer, he said, "Ogre's chamber beyond that door. Know what that means, don't you, Brother? Come on, all of you!"

Eddis kept a steadying hand on Blorys's arm as they went back into the open. Two of the Keep men were down and still. Another leaned against the wall, lips tightly compressed while one of his fellows wrapped his forearm. The man's fingers were bloody. Several goblin bodies were scattered around as well. M'Baddah and Willow moved around the room, dispatching the wounded creatures.

Jerdren paused as they started past the dead ogre. "Got an idea," he said. "Those goblins that ran? I'm pretty sure I could see daylight on the far side of the ogre's den. So, I'm thinking they just kept going, all the way out of the cave. It looks to me like there could be more chambers on ahead, but if anything's there, they aren't coming at us."

"There are creatures that way, I think," Mead said, "but not near."

Jerdren nodded. "So what if we drag this monster back into his lair? Some other goblins come through here later, and they'll see all this blood, all the dead guards, they'll figure the ogre went nuts and killed 'em. Won't go looking for him, then, will they? And they won't suspect we're here, and we still have surprise on our side."

"You're forgetting the guard who ran back the other way," Blorys said. "Still . . . it might work to our advantage, and we're a couple of men short."

"What about our men?" Eddis asked.

"Bring them into the ogre's den as well," Jerdren said. "Best we can do for them, don't you think?"

Eddis glanced at the remaining Keep men. They looked grim to a man, but no one protested.

M'Baddah shoved a last arrow into his quiver. "My son, two of you others, keep watch up and down the passage. Only fools would let themselves be surprised now."

It took time. The dead men were brought in first and laid against the wall, behind the door. The ogre was awkward and heavy, and it took four of them dragging at the massive arms to get it moving. They hauled the body just far enough inside the chamber that the door could be pushed shut.

Jerdren strode into the darkened cave, hands on his hips, looking around. Eddis's nose wrinkled. A faint breeze rustled dry leaves piled here and there on the cave floor, but the air remained utterly foul, like poorly tanned hides and meat gone rotten.

"What's that?" Flerys demanded sharply and brought up her spear. "Nasty brute keeps a bear?"

At first glance, the thing near the far walled did look like a sleeping bear. Eddis drew her sword and stalked warily toward it, but after a few steps she realized it was a hide. Probably the source of the odor, she thought and backed away from the thing.

"Just a skin," she said.

Flerys gave her a doubtful look.

Jerdren was rubbing his hands together and grinning

cheerfully. "Only other ogre I knew kept his treasure close—and he had plenty of it. Too bad for me and Blor that was when we were infantry, because the officers got most of it. Still . . . some of you, look under things and in things. Coin, gems, gold, jewelry, any of that should be just what it looks like. Anything you see that doesn't look like that or like food—"

"Like garbage, you mean," Blorys said.

"Food or garbage." Jerdren shrugged. "Ogres collect stuff. Magic devices and amulets among 'em. Anything that looks odd, you let our priest or our mage check it before you touch it, got that? I think I'll start—there." He pointed.

There was a large leather sack that smelled nearly as revolting as the bear hide did. Eddis decided to keep an eye on the outer door for the moment, dividing her attention between Jerdren and what she could see outside. The sky was bright as midday, but the twisted forest was gloomy as ever. Nothing moved out there. The ex-soldier cut the ties on the huge bag and pulled several smaller bags from it, examining each in turn.

"Cheese—too old for any but an ogre to appreciate. Whew! Mmm—this is brandy by the smell. Nice little keg but awkward to carry around, and here's no place for a drink."

"Save it for a toast, back at the Keep," Blorys suggested. He sounded normal once again.

"There's a notion. Ah! Here we are—coins. Clever brute to sort 'em by kind, so far's I can tell. Gold here, copper here—here's some silver." He hefted one. "Eddis, any notion of how late it is?"

"Midday, maybe," she told him.

"M'Baddah, anything the other way?"

"Not a sound, but they will change guards at some point," the outlander said quietly.

"I know. If we plan on going back the way we came, we'd better go soon. Eddis, you think you could find this cave from outside?"

She shrugged, eased through the opening, and after a cautious look all around for enemies, she backed away to study the door and the rock face surrounding it. The door was ordinary, the trees and brush and rocks no different from any others she'd seen. She drew her dagger, made a small cut, just above the handle, and eased back into the chamber. After a few breaths of fresh air, the ogre's den smelled worse than ever.

"I can find it," she said.

"Good. Remember we came this way to clear the cave of goblins, so they wouldn't catch us between 'em—the ones here and the ones beyond that door back yonder. Now, we can either quit fighting for the day and carry all this trove back to camp, or we could take it with us and go jump those brutes on the other side of that door. But we'll be overloaded, and most of us will be thinking more about gold and silver than about fighting." He grinned. "Me included. It's natural. I say we leave the stuff here—under that hide, maybe—and come back for it from the outside when we get the chance."

"I agree," Eddis said. "You saw how scared those goblins were of their ally. They won't come in here looking for him after they see the mess out there."

She looked up as one of the Keep men exclaimed in surprise. One of his fellows had just dragged a clinking, heavy bag from the ogre's water barrel. Across the room, mage and priest were rummaging through a heap of bones, and as she watched, Panev pocketed several small items, while Mead wrapped a bit of cloth around a handful of arrows and slid the bundle into his quiver.

"Eddis is right," Jerdren said. "But just in case . . ."

He separated out three of the bags and piled them by the door where anyone pulling it open would be sure to see them. "Leave that wet bag here, too," he added. "That's the one they brought in here. Must hold his pay for taking us on. They'll expect to find it, if they look, and they'll also find a bag of silver, the cheese, and the brandy. Wager my share of what's hidden that they won't look any further."

"What if they do?" That was Kadymus, of course. "We fought pretty hard for this stuff!"

"*You* sure did," Eddis replied bitingly. "Took their surrender, didn't you?"

He flashed her a dirty look but fell silent.

"I agree with Jers," she went on. "We've spent enough time in here. Shove the rest of those bags under that hide, and let's get out of here."

They retraced their steps, back into the other guard chamber. It was still empty, except for the dead goblins. The fire had burned to a sullen red glow. Willow and M'Baddah listened intently at the entrance to the next passage and pronounced it empty.

It was very dark here. One of the Keep men lit his lantern and opened the shutter, just enough that they could make out the way ahead of them. There were stairs here, rough-cut and uneven. The passage turned right, and another, shorter flight of cracked stairs went into a flat passage blocked by a heavy door. Skulls were nailed to the walls and door, and someone or something had scrawled a message in Common: COME IN! WE'D LOVE TO HAVE YOU FOR DINNER!

Kadymus stared at the message, looked at the skulls, and licked his lips. "Have you for dinner? Who'd eat with whatever lives in there?" he mumbled.

Eddis felt Blorys bite back sudden laughter. She swallowed

her own mirth and murmured against the thief's ear, "Wrong meaning. Not *to* dinner. *As* dinner."

He gave her a sick look and moved away.

Jerdren eyed the door for a long moment. He stiffened as faint, coarse laughter came to them from the other side, followed by what sounded like a snapped order, then silence. He stepped cautiously back and beckoned the others close.

"Someone's on alert in there. Mead, can you tell how that door's locked?"

The mage nodded and moved toward the portal, hands spread wide. He was back in a moment. "It's both locked and barred. I have a device that will move the bar, quietly, but the lock is a fairly simple one, I think. Your business," he added to Kadymus. "If I explain this thing, will you be able to move the trigger and open the door?"

"Open?" Kadymus looked at him, round-eyed. "Me? Open that? You see all those skulls? See what it says on that door?"

Eddis tapped his shoulder with a hard finger, silencing him. "Open the door, little man," she said softly. "Because we're going to open it one way or another. You do a good job like a nice little thief, we just might surprise whatever's in there. Probably more goblins." She couldn't resist adding, "Get the door open, and yell *bree-yark!* They'll drop their weapons and surrender."

He glared at her but went with the elf, drawing his lock picks from a small pouch at his belt.

"Ease up on the lad," Jerdren murmured. "I think his first ogre startled him." His eyes stayed on the door, and a moment later, Mead held up a warning hand.

"Stay alert, people," she said quietly as she freed her sword and a throwing knife. Blorys came up and settled in at her left shoulder, two long spears in his right, sword in his left. He still looked a little pale, she thought, but he no longer sounded winded.

Kadymus had the door ajar. He and Mead stepped back as Jerdren took their place. She could hear low, rough voices—not goblin voices—and a sudden yell as Jerdren pelted into the chamber. Eddis and Blorys were right behind him, then Mead, who moved along the inner wall, two of the Keep men between him and the room's occupants.

She had no time to see where anyone else went.

"Hobgoblins!" Jerdren shouted the warning. Hulking, heavily armored and armed brutes leaped to their feet as what must have been females caught up little ones and backed away behind a pile of broken furniture.

"I hate hobgoblins," he snarled and ran straight at the nearest, attacking before the creature could bring his sword up.

Blorys swore in frustration as he and Eddis came after, blocking the poleaxe of a second hobgoblin who was trying to get behind Jerdren. Eddis's sword rebounded, but so did the long pole, and Blorys jammed his spear at the monster's eye. Eddis brought her blade back around, slashing at his knees. The brute fell back, startled and bleeding but not badly hurt.

The company swarmed into the room, driving the startled hobgoblins back, but only for a moment. The fellows had been clad for a fight. They were big, fast, and skilled. That lousy goblin guard must have warned them, Eddis thought. She lunged and slashed at a huge back as one of the hobgoblins roared past her, but hardened leather foiled the blow, and the thing turned on her, teeth bared. She swung again, and this time the blade clove through leather and deep into the arm beneath it. The monster bellowed in anger and pain, slapping the sword from her hand. As good as gone, Eddis thought as she shook out her hand and tried to free up another throwing knife. Her fingers wouldn't cooperate.

"Change sides!" Blorys shouted.

She nodded and took the spear he held out. He shifted his sword to the other hand and turned to check on the brute she'd wounded. The hobgoblin was staggering a little and bleeding heavily but still full of fight. When one of the Keep men ran at it with a boar spear, the monster batted it aside, snatched at the man, and threw him against the wall. He wobbled there, trying to gain his balance, but when the hobgoblin started after the man, Kadymus came up behind the creature and plunged a knife deep into the back of its neck. He skipped nimbly aside as it howled and slapped at the air, trying to grab him.

"Cover me!" Blorys yelled and brought his sword down two-handed on the brute's neck. The first time, the blade hit something hard and rebounded with a clang, nearly flying out of his hands, but the second time it cut deep. Blood poured from the long wound, soaking into the shuddering monster's clothing and hair, pooling around the suddenly still body. Another of the hobgoblin's fellows came running, eyes fixed on Blorys, who freed his sword and let Eddis guide him back with a hand clutched in his near sleeve. The hobgoblin's boots slid across a suddenly slick floor, and it went down, hard. M'Whan and another Keep man were there to make certain it didn't rise.

Eddis yelled as something slammed into her left arm. She stared in surprise as blood welled from her sleeve and ran from a long, ugly cut just above her elbow. Blorys swore, snatched at the long knife caught in her torn sleeve, reversed it and threw, hard. The dagger sliced the ear of the hobgoblin who'd thrown it at her. If the brute hadn't ducked, it probably would have hit its eye. Eddis set her teeth against her lip and tried to press her sleeve against the cut. Ugly, not dangerous, she thought, but it hurt damnably, and from the elbow down, her arm wouldn't respond. M'Baddah had her by the other elbow, drawing her back out of the fray. He thrust her into Flerys's trembling hands and strode out to take Eddis's place at Blorys's side.

"Hurts?" Flerys asked. Her voice trembled.

"It hurts," Eddis agreed, "but it won't so much if you can tie my sleeve around it."

The child nodded and leaned her spear against the wall, but it took her three tries to get the ends fastened.

"Better," Eddis managed, with what she hoped was a reassuring smile, though with the added pressure, it hurt considerably worse. "You stopped the bleeding, and my father used to say that if it doesn't bleed, it doesn't hurt."

Flerys clearly didn't understand a word of the weak joke, but the smile did seem to reassure her, a little. She retrieved the spear and scrambled to her feet to guard the swordwoman. *Though I don't know what she can do against one of those,* Eddis thought. *Or what more I can do.* Her left arm hung limp, and the fingers of her right still smarted, but they'd hung onto Blorys's spear, somehow. She tightened her grip and watched the fray.

The fight was nearly over. The last two hobgoblins were tottering, and as she watched, they fell, one to a Keep man's spear, the other to a joint attack by Blorys and M'Baddah.

Jerdren had already sent Willow over to listen at the far door. "Bless me if the entire cave shouldn't be down around our ears by now, all the noise we made in here. Maybe we're still in luck, and that door's as thick as the one we just came through."

He eyed the cowering huddle of females and young. "And

bless me if I don't want to run 'em through. I've had enough of killing beast babies and their cowering mothers. Suggestions, Mead? Panev?"

The priest came forward, mace in hand and his eyes glittering. "If you cannot kill them, I shall. The females of their kind often fight and kill as well as the males. The young will grow up to become fighters. But—" he shrugged. "If you choose to bind them instead, I will strengthen your ropes with a charm I have that will keep them enthralled for several hours."

"All we need is enough time to see what's beyond that door and get back out this way, if we need to." Jerdren's brooding eyes fixed on one of the fallen hobgoblins.

Blorys picked his way across the room, his eyes dark with anger.

"Beyond? Are you mad, Brother? We have injuries here, and Eddis is bleeding! And all you can think of is—?"

Jerdren's head came up at that, his color high. Eddis dragged herself to her feet and stepped between the two men.

"Let's not waste time arguing. Blor, I'll be fine, M'Baddah will tend this. Blor, remember the description Zebos gave of the way to that torture chamber, where he was chained to the wall? I think this is it, and I still say we are bound by honor to free prisoners. This is a cut, nothing more. It's not—" She became aware of Flerys right behind her and shook her head, her eyes warning Blorys. "It's nothing. Let's finish up here and *go*."

"She's right, Brother," Jerdren said. "There's the least chance new guards will find that dead ogre or the dead guards just back there—or this room. We're leaving a trail, and I wager they'd be ready and waiting for us if we came back tomorrow. With things like hobgoblins, I'd rather have surprise on my side when I attack."

"Never mind that," Eddis said. She bit her lip as M'Baddah began working on her arm. "These creatures might simply kill prisoners, once they realize we're here. I'd hate that."

"If there are any prisoners alive," Blorys said as he retrieved her sword and wiped it clean.

"We won't know until we look," Eddis told him.

The rest of the party members were tending wounds or working their way around the chamber, looking for coins and other wealth. Panev watched two of the Keep men tie the unresisting females and young. When they were all knotted together, the priest waved a short black wand over them and spoke under his breath. Moments later they all slept, and when Jerdren nudged the nearest female with his foot, she didn't move.

"Good work, man," he said and headed toward the far door. Willow had it open and was already out of sight. "Good work, all of you. Eddis?"

She nodded. Her arm still throbbed, and she might be weak for a while, but her fingers and elbow were working once more. Blorys patted her shoulder awkwardly and went after his brother. Eddis stayed back with Flerys and Mead as the brothers strode through the door.

14

A long, shadowy corridor, cut into the rock, meandered ahead of them, fire or torchlight turning the stone ruddy some distance away. No sound, except for their own breathing. Eddis listened intently. No good. She wondered where the goblin had got to. If it had gone on this way, it could be anywhere by now. They could be heading for an ambush.

They were moving slowly, making as little noise as they could, but the passage was dark, the floor uneven, and complete silence impossible. Eddis's boots shuffled aside a spill of gravel. Someone else's foot scraped across stone. Each sound seemed loud in the narrow place.

When they halted so Mead, Willow, and Kadymus could check ahead for side passages, Eddis leaned against the wall. Her arm throbbed despite the thick stuff M'Baddah had rubbed across the cut, and she felt lightheaded. She dredged up a smile as Flerys tugged on her sleeve. The child looked worried, and not much reassured when the woman breathed against her ear, "I'm fine." She took a sip from the water bottle the girl held out to her. Beyond Flerys, M'Whan looked no less concerned.

The passage seemed to go on forever, but Eddis felt a little better for the water, and her sword hand no longer tingled. A short jog right, then immediately left, another right a short distance beyond that—places where a small group of enemies might lie in wait, but each was deserted. All at once there was enough light from well-spaced torches that they could make out the hallway for quite some distance ahead.

They paused again while Mead, Willow, and Jerdren scouted. The three were back in short order, and Jerdren beckoned the party close.

"A tunnel cuts off to the left, just short of that second torch. No guards near, Mead says, but there's hobgoblins down there, he thinks. Willow could hear someone wailing. I think you're right, Eddis. This might be where Zebos was held."

Blorys leaned forward. "What Zebos told me—if that's where we are—is that there's only one way into that chamber and only a couple guards. But if you keep straight on this way, you'll come to a guard room beyond that last torch somewhere. Hebold and his men were taking him that way, said it was how they'd come in, when they were attacked. The guards came from their left, I think, but he could see daylight at that point."

Jerdren nodded. "Good, but one thing at a time. We'll be able to tell if it is a prison cell, once we get closer. If it is, we hit it hard, fast, and quiet as we can. Grab any prisoners. Kadymus, that'll be your task. Once we distract the guards, you find keys for the cells or manacles, and be ready to use 'em once we've killed the guards." He met Eddis's eyes. "You all right?"

She nodded.

"Good. In and out as quick as we can, kill the guards fast and quiet. Prisoners will be our only concern here. If there aren't any, we kill the hobgoblins and make sure we find any wealth they've got on 'em. Let's go."

Eddis stayed with Flerys as M'Baddah went ahead with Willow. The child clutched a spear nearly as long as she was tall in her right hand—one she'd picked up during that last fight. She gave the swordswoman a round-eyed look and a faint smile that was gone as quickly as it came, but she seemed merely awed by the strangeness of her surroundings and not afraid of them. *She'll probably have nightmares for the rest of her life if she survives this,* Eddis thought.

And if we're headed into a dungeon, a prisoner's cell? She'd seen what was left of tortured, dead men just once, and it had sickened her to her very soul. *Better if Flerys didn't see. How to shield her, though?*

They reached the branching of ways without incident. Once they stopped, Eddis thought she could hear faint noises down the left passage. Mead went on ahead but came back almost at once, shaking his head. No one that way—at least close by. Jerdren indicated the left way with a jerk of his head, and started off at a ground-eating long stride. As he fetched up against the first bend, he set his back to the rough stone and listened intently. Eddis could now see her companions clearly. There was plenty of light ahead. Someone down there moaned non-stop, and someone or something else was jabbering in what sounded like Orc or Goblin to her. A deep voice snarled threateningly, and the shrill one was momentarily still.

Willow took the lead then, arrow nocked to the string of his longbow, and stopped just short of the light, Mead right behind him. Blorys slid into place at Eddis's left and gave her a questioning look. She held up her right hand, flexed the fingers, so he could see they were working again, then drew her sword.

He murmured against her ear, "Good. All the same, stay out of this fight if you can. Keep the girl back." She nodded, drew the child to her side, and let Panev go by. The priest's eyes were black, his face stern, and his lips moved silently.

M'Baddah knelt to draw on his thick gloves and hooked the leather envelope of sh'khuris to his belt where he could reach them. That done, he tested his bowstring and joined Willow. M'Whan followed, one arrow nocked to the string, a handful stuffed up his sleeve where he could grab them quickly and fire. *How he can do that without losing them all or slicing his arm?* Eddis wondered. The youth's points were long as her finger and wickedly sharp on all four sides.

Tense silence as Willow held up a hand and touched it briefly to his lips, then held it out as a warning to be ready. The high-pitched voice was whimpering once more. *It sounds like a dog that's been beaten,* Eddis thought. Flerys bit her lip. Her hands tightened on the spear. The elf brought his hand down sharply and sprinted around the corner, Jerdren and M'Baddah right on his heels, the rest following. Eddis kept the girl back with her.

The passage bent once more, then opened out into a small, brightly lit chamber. Eddis could make out humans shackled to the far wall, and near them, a gnoll hung from chains. The wall was pale rock, splattered with blood. Eddis drew Flerys aside with her as men and elves slammed into the hobgoblin guards. Already the fighting was so fierce that it took the woman a moment to figure out there were only two of the monsters, but both were armed with thick-bladed swords. They were swinging the blades with vicious intent and not much skill—which could be just as deadly in close combat. One of the Keep men fell back, sword dangling from his hand, blood pouring down his arm. Mead dragged him aside, and Jerdren bellowed an order for the swordsmen to get back.

"No arrows!" her co-captain yelled. "You could hit the prisoners!" He pulled back himself, freed up his short boar spear, and waited for an opening.

One of the guards slashed a wild path through the attackers and charged past the Keep men. Eddis drew Flerys farther into the chamber in case the thing was trying to escape, but it turned sharply, sword still swinging, and threw itself at Blorys. Blor parried an overhand blow with his blade and was sent sprawling. Eddis started but subsided against the wall as Flerys snatched at her arm.

Somewhere deep in the turmoil of bodies, M'Baddah shouted, "Down!" A moment later, he broke free and began working his way around the creature, a glittering, deadly metal star gripped in one gloved hand. M'Whan's spear broke against the brute's armor. Another hit and clattered harmlessly to the floor.

The hobgoblin was starting for Blorys once more when the sh'khuri thudded home, lodging in its throat, just above the armor. Blood ran down the monster's throat, but it seemed merely enraged by the wound. A second deadly missile sank in deeper, just above the first. Men and elves scattered as blood sprayed everywhere. The hobgoblin pawed at the sh'khuri but succeeded only in slicing its hand open. It toppled slowly backward. Blood shot high briefly, slowed, and stopped.

The second hobgoblin was trying to gain the entry and escape. Eddis brought up her sword, took two long steps to put herself squarely in the creature's way, and thrust Flerys behind her. The priest was back in the hallway. He was armed, and a good fighting man, but if he was distracted by prayer, he'd be caught unawares and probably cut down. Not, Eddis thought grimly, while I'm here to prevent that. She was aware that Flerys had moved a pace to one side, could see the steady spear. But two of the Keep men knocked the brute flat from behind, swinging mace and morningstar in a smooth, precise maneuver. Before it could struggle to its feet, Blorys and Jerdren finished it off.

"Good work, people," Jerdren said. He sounded out of breath.

"Noisy," Blorys objected as he sheathed his dagger.

"Only in here, Brother. Panev said he'd make a silence spell back there, across the passage."

Eddis glanced across her shoulder as the priest came into the open.

"Anything?" the ex-soldier asked.

"I saw the fight but heard none of it," the priest replied. "Nothing is moving this way, just yet."

"Good. Let's be quick about this." Jerdren turned on one heel as Kadymus came hurrying up, a clanking batch of heavy keys in his hands. "Fast work, lad," he added, and the thief smiled.

"Was hanging just there, in plain sight," he said, and to Eddis, he sounded smug and self-confident once more.

Leave be, she thought tiredly. *If he's cocky, he's probably more use to us.*

"Good," Jerdren said. "Stay close. If these don't work, we'll need you and your lock-picks."

"I'll use 'em anyway," Kadymus said. "Free 'em all so much the faster."

"Good thinking." Jerdren slapped the youth on the shoulder, staggering him, then turned to survey those chained to the far wall. "Only release the humans, though. We'll need to be sure what the others will do, if we let 'em go."

There were four humans, and two—a chubby older man and a ragged-looking woman with wild, staring eyes—couldn't have been here long, Eddis decided. The man would've lost the belly straining at his filthy robe, the woman's hair was still partly a mass of worked curls atop her head, though some of it was plastered to the side of her face and stiff with dried blood. The other two had the look of armsmen, though they wore only torn jerkins and trousers. Both were barefoot and bloody, but they looked alert enough as their eyes moved across the invaders.

Just beyond the merchant, an orc cringed away from the party, babbling or muttering in its own language. The gnoll stared fearfully at the far wall or at some nearer delusion, panting and licking its lips.

"We're here to get you out," Jerdren said. He began trying keys one after the other on the older man's fetters.

"I know him!" one of the Keep men said. "He used to sell pottery in the Keep!"

"Get us . . . get us out, by all the gods, please get us out of here!" the man begged, his teeth chattering. "They'll kill us, me and my wife!" He swallowed. "They keep saying they'll kill us tonight, and . . . and there's a b-banquet, and—"

"Don't, man," Blorys urged. "We'll keep you from that, I swear it. Kadymus, free the lady, will you?"

"We . . . haven't anything to give you." The potter's voice quavered. "They . . . took everything, but I have gold, a bag of it, I left it in the Keep. It's all yours, every gold piece, if you'll only—!"

"We don't ask a reward," Eddis said as she came up. "Just hold still, if you can. The manacles will come off faster."

"We were guarding the merchant's wagon," one of the other prisoners said. "Bunch of those things came down on our camp, late at night. We didn't have a chance. Free us, and we'll serve you. Though I wouldn't blame you for doubting we can fight, seeing where we are."

"She just said," Jerdren replied, a nod of his head to Eddis, "this isn't for reward. Likely you'd do the same for us, but we can talk it over later, after you're all safely out of here."

The merchant's wife seemed to come out of a half-swoon, and began shaking her head frantically. "Out of . . . no, you can't, we can't! If we even think about escape, they'll . . . they said that they'd—" She broke into terrified, wracking sobs, and tears ran down her face.

Blorys caught the woman's shoulders in a gentle grasp. "They can't do anything, because we'll be gone from here before they know you've escaped. The two who guarded you are dead. We'll see you safely away from here, back to the Keep."

The woman beat at him with soft little fists, and when her husband staggered the few paces to take her arm, she shook him off, her voice spiraling into hysteria.

"Here, let me have her," Mead said. He drew the woman aside, speaking quietly. The shrill cries broke off suddenly, and when Mead turned to lead her back, she came willingly and quietly. Her eyes were unfocused, and the merchant eyed her, then the elf, with fear.

"I bespelled her. A simple and harmless charm. She feels none of the terror that crippled her mind, and now she believes herself safely home. I will waken her from that spell once we are far from these caves." He beckoned to Jerdren. "That orc told my brother that he will aid us against the hobgoblins if we give him a weapon."

"Oh?"

"I do not trust him, any more than you do, but to leave him here for other hobgoblins to find, and their two comrades dead on the floor . . . ? Or that poor, mad thing," he added, his eyes flicking toward the gnoll.

"*I* don't trust either of them," Blorys said, before his

brother could speak, "but if you want to free them, mage, I'll watch them. Neither looks strong enough to be a threat."

"Don't trust that," Mead warned.

"We won't." Jerdren looked around the room. "We'll have to take turns to lead the woman—or carry her. Anyone have spare daggers or spears for these two men?" In short order the two were armed with boar spears and a long dagger each. "Priest, still quiet out there?"

Panev smiled narrowly. "Of course it is, since the spell holds. Beyond it?" He walked out of sight, was back in moments. "Still quiet."

"Good. Kadymus, free that gnoll. I'll deal with the orc. Most of you get back over there, ready to move. Eddis, you and Blor stay here, help me keep an eye on these two until we're certain they're not up to some trick."

Silence, as Jerdren fought the key into rusted locks. The gnoll hung limp in his restraints, but as soon as Kadymus jiggled the last lock and opened the final leg iron, the brute leaped forward, barking and giggling madly. It flung itself at the youth, who whipped out a pair of daggers, but went sprawling as it knocked him aside. M'Whan let it charge past him, then brought his spear around two-handed across the back of its head like a club, reversed his grip and plunged the point through its chest. The gnoll twitched feebly.

The orc stared at the fallen creature, fell back trembling as Jerdren freed it.

"Tell it, Willow," the man said. "I haven't the words for it. Tell it that it can *earn* a blade from us if it behaves. Ask if it knows the way out."

A short exchange of guttural, clicking speech.

"It claims to," Willow said. "What it says agrees with what Zebos told us."

"Good. We go now, then," Jerdren said. "Prisoners in the middle, and no stopping this side of that barred door!"

The passage to the main door was shorter than the one they'd just traversed, well-lit and smooth-floored and very quiet. The orc stayed well ahead, with two of the Keep men and Blorys watching it closely. The men traded off carrying the merchant's wife once it became clear she was too weak to walk very fast, and Willow kept a supporting arm around the merchant's shoulders. The two rescued guardsmen clutched their borrowed weapons, their heads moving constantly, jerkily, as if they expected an ambush momentarily. Fortunately, though they appeared to have been worse used by their captors, they had been stronger than the merchant or his wife to begin with, and even barefoot they managed to keep up with the company.

The lights were left behind, all at once. They stopped for a long moment while Mead and Kadymus went on to scout. Some long, anxious moments later, a door eased inward, creaking slightly and letting in a little daylight. The party hurried through the portal into a short cavern, waited for the mage and thief to close the way behind them.

If they can replace the bar on the inside of that door, somehow, Eddis thought, *we'll leave a pretty riddle for those monsters to sort out.*

Willow had gone ahead to check the lay of the land, returning as Mead came away from the door.

"It is sealed," Mead said quietly.

"It is very still out here," Willow said. "We have come out partway up the south flank of the ravine and well west of where we went in. It is late afternoon. If we want to reach camp before sundown, we had better go now."

Several long, tense moments later found them back on level ground. There was a path leading down, but it was steep, riddled with loose stones and thick with dust. The Keep men simply lifted the merchant off his feet between them and strode downhill, leaving the path entirely.

On the floor of the ravine once more, they made the best possible time they could through the trees, until the merchant finally sagged between his supporters, air whooping into his lungs. Jerdren called a halt, waited while Panev tested their surroundings for evil, then ordered a brief rest in the dark shade of a small, tight copse of trees. The orc sank down warily, its back to one of the trees, eyes flicking from one to the other of the company, most of whom were watching it as closely.

Eddis stayed on her feet, looking around. "Jers, we're close to that door I marked earlier. I'm pretty sure we just passed it, back that way."

"Think so?"

"Pretty sure. I think we should bring out those bags now, if we plan on getting them at all. Chances are that dead ogre hasn't been discovered yet, so we can likely slip in, grab those bags, and get back here without a problem."

"What if they've found him, though?" Blorys asked.

Eddis shrugged. "We left the door ajar. Sensible goblins would close and bar it again, wouldn't they?"

"Unless they left it open as a trap," he countered.

"Sure, but why would they? The way we left things, it looks as if he killed some of the goblins and was killed by them in turn, remember? Why would they expect someone to come back and spring such a trap? Besides, we fought hard for what's in those sacks—including you, Blor. And you, Jers. If we wait another day or so, anyone walking through that guard room will know there's a dead ogre in that den. And there goes our chance to retrieve any of those bags."

Jerdren considered this. "Your call, Eddis. We need a proper rest here anyway, so it's not like we'd be waiting for you."

She looked over the rest of the company. "M'Whan and Willow?" The elf stood and drew his sword for answer. "And . . ."

"I'll come," Blorys said.

"And I." Mead drew a slender wand from his belt and got to his feet.

"Good. Let's go. And let's get this much straight ahead of time—we're not taking chances here, all right? If it looks wrong, we don't go in. If we decide to go in, we grab what we left in hiding and get out, fast." She glanced at M'Baddah, at Flerys sitting cross-legged close to him. The child's eyes were closed, her head bobbing close to his shoulder. He glanced at the child himself, smiled faintly, and waved her on her way.

It was a little farther than she'd thought but not much. The door was still ajar, the chamber beyond utterly silent. Willow made them wait while he listened, but when they finally entered the den, there was nothing in sight but the dead ogre and his possessions, and the fallen goblins they'd dragged in to keep him company. Eddis kept guard at the inner door while the others worked to separate out the bags of coin, the brandy, and other things of value. Blorys came over to join her, then.

"We've got it all, I think. Let's get out of here." Eddis nodded and strode across the fetid chamber, only drawing a deep breath when she was finally outside.

* * * * *

They made it back to join the rest of their company and distributed the bags among those who'd be less vital in a fight, should anything fall on them between here and the camp.

The orc was still huddled on the ground, back braced

against a gnarled tree. It looked up warily as Jerdren came over to stand before it, but the man merely dropped a dagger and a pair of silver coins at the creature's feet.

"Tell it we kept our word, and tell it to go," he said to Willow. "We will let it live if it does that."

Willow spoke for some moments in the rough-sounding tongue. The orc replied briefly. Without another glance around at the humans and elves, it scrabbled for the blade and the coins, leaped to its feet, and raced off through the trees, heading farther up the ravine.

Jerdren turned away. "Let's go. It'll be dark soon, and this will be no place for us."

As they came back into relatively open ground, a bowstring twanged from nearby. Willow gasped and fell bonelessly. A dark-fletched arrow quivered in his back. Jerdren urgently waved the ex-prisoners and those helping them back into the copse. Mead gazed in horror at his twin, then knelt to lay a hand against his throat.

"He is breathing," the mage said unsteadily, "but I cannot—"

"Wait," Panev said and gripped Mead's forearm. "Find the ones who did this, lest we are all killed here. I will save your brother."

The mage swallowed hard. Trembling fingers sought something in a small pouch at his belt and drew it out. He closed his eyes and concentrated, tears slipping silently down his face.

"Tree," he mouthed to Jerdren. "There! Up above us!" He drew back as M'Whan and M'Baddah moved into position. They had seen what Mead had found. Half a breath after, two arrows tore through the leaves and branches from opposite sides. With a gurgling cry, an orc fell to the ground and lay in a still huddle, M'Baddah's arrow deep in its chest, M'Whan's nearly as deep in its back.

"That it? Just one?" Jerdren whispered.

Mead nodded. His dark eyes, his whole attention, was fixed on his fallen brother who lay as still as the dead orc.

Panev had drawn a small wooden box from his belt-pouch, and, having prayed over the contents, he sprinkled a few grains of a yellowish powder all around the arrow. Head bowed over the slender elf, he remained still for some time, praying in a breathy whisper. Mead started, hand outstretched in protest as the priest slowly withdrew the arrow. The priest's other hand clamped down on the mage's arm.

Eddis watched, astonished. Willow was still breathing in shallow gasps, but the outpouring of blood didn't follow the point. Willow fetched a deep breath, let it out on a sigh, and seemed to sleep. The priest sat back on his heels, his face gray with exhaustion.

"You . . . restored his life?" Jerdren whispered.

"No," Panev replied softly. "Though I think he would have died quickly, without what I used." He sighed. "Mind no one else takes such a blow between now and morning, because I cannot use that powder again this day."

"We're going, now," Jerdren informed him.

They reached the campsite not long before the sun set. A cool wind sprang up as the last rays of sun left the treetops, and Eddis pulled her cloak close. Two of the Keep men went for water and another built a fire in the second pit, over the trove they'd already buried. Jerdren set another to dig out the other. There were two spare blankets and an extra cloak to share out for those they'd rescued. The merchant and his still-bespelled wife were huddled together under the cloak, close to the fire, the two guards each wrapped in a blanket. M'Baddah, Mead, and the priest tended to wounds and the torn bare feet of the rescued guards.

There was hard bread to begin with and a thin soup once

the fire was properly going. Willow woke long enough to drink a little broth and eat the bread his brother held for him, then fell asleep once more. The merchant and his wife lay sleeping close to the fire.

"They are exhausted only, I think," Mead said, "and afraid. The armsmen will be all right."

"If we can send them back to the Keep, they'll recover," Jerdren agreed. He raised his voice a little to include all the company. "That was good work today, all of you. By tomorrow evening, our horses should be back here. Any of you wants to go with 'em, there's no shame in that, and you've earned your share of what we've found so far. But I say we've got a rest coming. We'll stay here tomorrow." He glanced at Eddis, who nodded.

"Sensible," she said. "We can use the time to upgrade your map and plan our next move."

"I thought so," he said. "How's the arm?"

"Just stiff." She glanced at him. "We've found a fair amount of treasure so far. Maybe we should send it back with the merchant and his wife, lodge it with the castellan?"

"You think that's wise?" Blorys asked. "I mean, the man's honest, but what if we finish up here and for some reason some of us would rather not return to the Keep? Makes sense to me not to keep everything out here, of course. It could be found by accident—someone coming by and digging the ash out of the fire pit, going a little too deep. Or if something followed us back here and saw where we'd buried their coins and such? Eddis is right though. There's a fair amount of gold and all and that after just two days. Maybe we're lucky, but maybe there's that much more, back there. In which case, we'd be wise to send some back to be locked in Ferec's vaults. Make certain we'll all get a fair share, whichever way we go."

Jerdren considered this, finally nodded. "Makes sense. We'll do that." He looked at Eddis. "So. What's next?"

"Why ask me?" she said gloomily. "You may as well toss M'Baddah's fortune-sticks and ask *them*. Still, we know there's more caves, we've seen some of the openings, and what Zebos told Blor bears that out. It's odd, though. Kobolds, hobgoblins, orcs, and goblins all living that close together. From what I've always heard, they'd be warring with each other, and it would be nasty and brutish. But so far, all we've seen is barred doors and guards."

"Maybe someone's brought them together," Blorys suggested.

Jerdren laughed shortly. "Why anyone would—"

"Why not, Brother? Some warlord ousted from another land. Maybe even a powerful sorcerer who's been chased off by others of his kind. Someone who wants to rule the lands hereabout, possibly take over the Keep—maybe eventually rule all the realm." He looked at Jerdren, who grinned and gestured for him to go on. "It just seems to me that anyone with such ambitions and half a brain wouldn't flaunt himself right under the castellan's nose the way those bandits did. You'd want time to build a fighting force, time to acquire funds to buy weapons—all that."

Jerdren considered this but finally smiled and shook his head.

Blorys sighed gustily. "Don't discount the idea. Probably it's wild and foolish both, but I'm just saying it's possible."

"I won't, Brother," Jerdren assured him. "Not here. Only a fool would do that, and I'm foolhardy—according to you, anyway. But even you wouldn't say I'm foolish."

15

"Things are working out well," Jerdren told himself as he paced around the camp perimeter and watched his company getting ready for another day of fighting. "Our company," he added and cast a sidelong look at Eddis, who was some distance away, checking her arrows. "A full day to rest up, thanks to those prisoners we rescued, a good hot soup last night, thanks to the riders, and fresh supplies." His map was up to date, showing the caves they had cleared thus far, how many monsters they'd killed. He had a separate list he kept deep in his belt pouch of how much trove they'd amassed and where they'd hidden it.

Now the guards were gone again, heading back to the Keep at first light with the four rescued prisoners, and Jerdren—and Eddis—had three more men-at-arms.

He cast Eddis another sidelong glance. She'd recovered nicely from that wounded arm, though she'd been cross most of the previous day.

But she's never been cut like that before, he reminded himself. First one's always a shock. At the moment, she was talking to the girl Blot. No, Flerys. Funny, insisting on the name change. The kid was used to being called Blot, wasn't she? Odd, too, the way the swordswoman left the girl in

M'Baddah's charge most of the time. I thought women doted on children.

Mead had stowed his spellbook and was dividing the arrows he'd found in the ogre's cave, half to his brother, half to M'Baddah.

"Magic arrows—huh," Jerdren said dubiously. *He* hadn't felt anything unusual about them, but since elf and outlander were the best archers, it made sense to give them the extra shafts.

The company was about ready to move out. Time for a last look at the map.

Eddis came over as he unfolded the thing. "I thought we worked everything out last night," she said. "We're still going back after the rest of those hobgoblins, right?"

He shrugged. "I was just thinking. Usually, there's one torture chamber per clan—or so I've heard. Sure, we didn't take out the leaders or finish 'em all off like we did the kobolds, but I'm thinking they'll keep."

"The leaders know by now that we're out here someplace," Eddis reminded him. "*You* said only a pack of fools would give them the chance to come at us."

"Yeah. We killed just about every hobgoblin we found. Why would they come looking for us? Anyway—" he shrugged that aside—"you got me thinking about prisoners. Maybe you're right, Eddis. Nobody deserves to die like that. Remember that madman's story about the fellows who rescued him and then got grabbed themselves? Way he described 'em, I'd say it was bugbears."

"I wouldn't know, but those men are probably dead by now, Jers. It's been too long since Zebos got out." She sighed faintly. "If we aren't going back to that last cave, what's your idea?"

"Farther in and up," Jerdren said promptly. "Something

else the madman told Blor—how the creatures close to the road weren't as deadly as those farther in and higher up? We can waste a lot of time killing kobolds and their kind, Eddis. Creatures that are a nuisance but not deadly, and there's a lot of ground to cover here—more than I would ever have thought back at the Keep. I'm thinking we get farther back in and up on the ledges, where we can get a better feel for what's here. Me, I'm all for scouring out these caves entirely, but even I can see that isn't likely. Snow'll bury us to our chins before we get that far. Autumn's well on, and this summery heat can't last much longer. Besides, say we completely clean out one cave like we did with those kobolds, maybe something else comes along right behind us and fills it up, and there we are again? I say we start picking our fights, get smart about it. We kill off bugbears and others like 'em, maybe the goblins and orcs'll see the damage we can do, and they'll up and run for it."

"Could be. Good point, though—picking our fights." Eddis took the map from him and eyed it for some moments, finally shrugged and handed it back. "Farther back in it is. Keeping in mind that we've got a few new fighters to break in."

"They'll do all right, and we still have our priest and our mage," Jerdren reminded her.

"Yeah, well, whatever else we accomplish here, we can at least leave something of a map for any who follow us."

"Don't talk like that, Eddis!" Blorys protested. He'd come up behind them. "You sound like you think we'll all die here!"

She shook her head, smiled up at him. Her eyes were warm. So were Blorys's. Jerdren blinked and looked away. *Eddis and my brother? When did that start? Blor'd never smiled at a woman that way in his young life, and Eddis . . .*

Even more unnerving, he felt disappointed. *As if I would have a chance with her* ... He shook the thought off, let his eyes wander. *Man like me hasn't any business wanting a woman, even a fighter like Eddis.*

"I'm not planning on it," Eddis told him, "but I agree with Jers. Let's pick our fights from now on. It's no good battling rats when there's bear in the woods. Another thing," she added with a sidelong glance Jerdren's direction. "We did all right against that ogre, but if we find ourselves in a spot like that again, and it looks like we're losing—well, that won't help the Keep or us. At that point, there is *nothing* wrong with turning tail and running."

Jerdren stared at her, astonished.

"Dead heroes don't kill anyone," she reminded him. "Smart heroes back off and go find another cave to play in."

Jerdren let his head fall back, and he laughed heartily. "Gods, but you have a tongue on you, woman! Don't look at me like that, Brother. She's right, and I'm smart enough to see it." He folded the map and put it away as he got to his feet. "If everyone's ready," he added, "we'd better move out."

* * * * *

They hadn't gone far when Willow, who was ahead, stopped and held up a hand for silence. "I hear something overhead," he said softly. "A droning noise."

"Stirge," Jerdren said flatly. "Stay close, all of you, and keep your eyes open. If one lands on you—"

He spun around as Flerys yelped. An insect as long as her upper body was clinging to Eddis's back, its long proboscis feeling along the side of her face as she swore under her breath and furiously swatted at it.

"Hold still, I'll get it," Blorys said, but Eddis spun around and slammed into the nearest tree, squashing the thing between her and the trunk. Green muck and blood splattered. The swordswoman staggered away, nose wrinkling at the foul odor and the mess. M'Baddah was at her side then, rubbing briskly at her neck, armor, and leather cap with the cloth that held his spare bowstrings.

"Get moving, now!" Jerdren ordered. "There's never just one of those things."

Eddis nodded, dragged out her own bowstring cloth, and mopped at her face as they started out again.

They heard the deep, whining buzz several times but saw no more of the bloodsuckers. Once within the ravine, they moved north, staying fairly close to the rock wall, moving warily but quickly now, crossing the few open places at a near run.

When the ledge at their right hand began to curve south, Jerdren called a halt so they could get their breath back and study the lay of the land. The trees were very thick here, the air musty and humid. From the little he could see, he thought they might be near the inner curve of the ravine. Good as anywhere for a start. A few moments later, they went on.

The rock face rose steep and crumbly here, but there were plenty of handholds, and Blorys found a way up they could all negotiate. In the thick dust, Jerdren could make out footprints. Lots of them, and very big. A few paces on, Willow found a rough trail that worked its way up the ledge.

The trees came together again, leaving them in a twilight-like gloom. The cave that came into sight among the trees was even darker. There were signs on both sides of the entry, written in several languages, including Common.

"Safety to humanoids," Eddis read in a low voice. "Welcome!" Her lips twisted. "Someone has a sense of humor."

"Hope it's not more hobgoblins," Jerdren murmured. "Man could get bored, fighting them twice in a row."

He sent M'Baddah and Mead on ahead, holding back the rest of the party until they could check the opening.

Silence, broken only by the echoing *kruk!* of a raven, somewhere off to the south. The scouts returned quickly.

"I sense large beings, evil ones," the mage said, "and the passage smells like wet dogs."

Jerdren nodded grimly. "Our luck's holding," he said quietly. "We've got bugbears in there. Watch for traps. They'll have 'em all over the place. Remember—they're big and fast but not very bright."

There was no door on the cavern entry and no guards, though they could hear harsh laughter coming from their left. The passage ended almost at once, joining another that went off right and left. Distant torchlight faintly illuminated the right passage, and Jerdren could make out a room the other direction by the flickering light of a fire. Low voices came from that direction.

The air in this tunnel was cool and unpleasantly moist. It still smelled like wet dog, but he could also make out the savory odor of roasting meat.

"Left," Jerdren said quietly and stepped back to let M'Baddah and Willow take the lead as he drew his sword.

The passage was quiet and empty. Just short of the room, they passed a flight of stairs going up into gloom on their right. M'Baddah stopped just short of the light, and Jerdren came up behind him. It's a guard room, he thought. Cots, blankets . . . and guards.

Two cots piled with filthy looking furs and cushions had been shoved against the far wall, a massive bronze gong suspended from the ceiling between them. Three bugbears, clad in leather armor, sat around a brazier mid-room, keeping a close eye on long spits of meat. Some guards, Jerdren thought.

He beckoned Mead close and murmured against his ear, "Make sure none of 'em get to that gong."

The mage nodded.

Eddis set an arrow to her bowstring and glanced at Jerdren, nodded once, and moved quietly into the room, back against the wall, M'Baddah right on her heels. Jerdren tapped two of the Keep archers to watch the stairs and the passage behind them. Blorys sheathed his sword and drew a pair of throwing knives.

The three bugbears turned slowly as someone's foot scraped across the stone floor. Only just aware they've been invaded? Jerdren wondered. They didn't seem too concerned about it. One bared its teeth in what might have been a smile, scooped up the nearest skewer, and bit into the meat, then slowly got to its feet, holding it out to Eddis. The other two followed his lead.

"Don't trust that, you men," Eddis warned and leaped aside as one lunged, trying to pin her to the wall. She let go her bowstring, but the arrow merely sliced along the bugbear's neck. Bleeding but barely damaged, he lunged at her again.

Off to Jerdren's right, someone yelled in pain, and one of the bugbears snarled triumphantly. Jerdren slashed at the bugbear after Eddis, fell back as the brute swiped at him with the skewer. Eddis's second arrow clove deep into the bugbear's arm, but didn't slow the creature at all. One of the Keep men jammed his spear between flaps of leathers and yelped as the wood was torn from his grasp.

"Get back, Jers!" Eddis yelled, and he realized he was between her and the bugbear. The end of the spear barely missed his head as he ducked and got out of the way, coming up behind the creature and throwing himself on its back. The bugbear swung partway round to deal with this new threat, flailing wildly with the skewer. Chunks of meat went flying, and hot grease burned the back of Jerdren's hand.

Eddis came around the brute, caught hold of the spear, and shoved with all her strength. Jerdren was slammed into the wall, the breath knocked out of him, but the bugbear slowly sagged at the knees and went over. Eddis ran her sword into its eye, to make sure of it, then came around and hauled her co-captain to his feet.

"What were you doing?" she demanded.

He grinned and forced air into battered lungs. "You said get his back, right?"

A quick glance assured him that the other two bugbears were engaged and that neither was anywhere near that gong. "Come on," he added. "This is taking too long and making too much noise."

The second bugbear went down moments later, but three of the Keep men were bloody, and one wasn't moving. The third bugbear began to back away, then turned and ran for the gong. Jerdren threw himself after, but Mead grabbed his arm.

"Wait," he said. The bugbear caught hold of the heavy club used as a striker, but couldn't seem to lift it. "Enfeeblement," the mage said.

"Hah! Well done!" Jerdren pelted across the floor, sword up and out. The bugbear turned and slapped him backhand, throwing him into the wall where he sat, dazed and blinking. He watched the creature go down under the attack of four spearmen and M'Baddah, who finished it off with his sword.

"Brother?" Blorys came running.

"Thought . . . Mead said he used . . . Enfeeblement . . . on it," Jerdren gasped.

"I did." The mage laid gentle hands on the man's head, then helped him to his feet. "That blow would have killed you otherwise. Can you stand?"

"I'll take care of him," Blor said. "You deal with our wounded so we can get moving."

"Good . . . idea," Jerdren said. "Don't . . . need any more of 'em in here."

"One man dead, Jers," Blorys told him. "One of the new fellows got tangled up with someone else, and they both went down. Second man'll live, though."

"Which way next?" Eddis asked as Blor helped Jerdren over to join the others. "Up or down?"

"There is great evil up those steps," Panev said. He was turning one of his short wands in his hands. "Down the passage, I sense pain, but it is too far to tell much else."

"Masters live up, dungeons are down—usually," Jerdren said. "If we go after the prisoners right now, we'll be done fighting for the day, and we'd be fools to leave any bugbears alive here. Those hobgoblins might not come after us, but bugbears *would*."

"There can't be many of them," Blorys said. "They don't crowd together like kobolds, but a bugbear chief'll be as hard to kill as that ogre."

"I know," Jerdren replied. "All right, we're going up first. You wounded, stay back, out of the way, keep watch for us. Mage and Panev, if we find a chief's quarters up there, we'll need you to hit them first, hard as you can. Get 'em off balance for us. We're not going for a fair fight here."

The steps were very steep, but fortunately there weren't many of them. A short corridor with a closed door branched off to the left. Jerdren led the way past that and down a right-branching passage, but it ended almost immediately with a padlocked door.

"Nothing to sneak up behind us there," Jerdren murmured and started for the other door. Panev took up a position near the wooden panel and began to pray. Another of those silence spells, Jerdren hoped. Mead drew a slender wand and pressed past him. At the mage's gesture, two of the Keep men caught hold of the latch, ready to pull the door open.

"The rest of you, stay back," he murmured.

The men yanked hard, and the door slammed into the outer wall. Jerdren was aware of massive clutter and a huge bed. Two bugbears piled out of it, one female, the other a scarred brute with graying fur. The male was reaching for his battle-axe when Mead's wand spat a gout of flame. Fire roared through the room and as suddenly vanished, but the bedding was smoldering and the female's fur ablaze. She howled and rolled on the floor. The male caught up his axe, but now the metal handle glowed dull red, and he dropped it with a shout of surprise. Eddis, M'Baddah, and Blorys crowded the entry then fired arrows at the chief, moving into the room so others could deal with his mate. Hit several times but not badly wounded, the chief began backing slowly away. All at once, he turned and vanished. Part of the wall had turned with him, and now clicked back into place. The bugbear was on the far side.

"Don't let him escape!" Eddis shouted. "He'll alert the others!"

Panev crossed the chamber to lay his hands on the wall.

The female lay still, blood pooling around her singed body. Blorys was fighting to retrieve his sword from the back of her neck. One of the spearmen had found water to pour on the bedding, and black smoke was suddenly everywhere. Furs smoldered, giving off an awful smell.

"Quick look around in here, folks," Jerdren ordered.

"There's bound to be wealth here, but no sense getting killed by smoke trying to find it. You, by the door—the smoke may bring guards, so you keep a good watch. Impressive, Mead," he added.

The elf mage smiled. "You said to slow them. It seems to have worked."

"I found the mechanism for the secret door," Panev said. "The passage beyond is dark, and I think it is blocked not too far on by another such door."

"We better check that," Jerdren said, and he sent Blorys and two of the armsmen to guard the priest. They were back in short order.

"Beyond the second door is a very evil place," the priest said. "I sense twisting passages, lost souls, and a reek I only encountered once before. I think there is a minotaur."

"Minotaur!" Jerdren's eyes lit.

Eddis hauled him around by the shoulders and gave him a good shake. "I've heard about them, Jers. Damned few of us would survive an encounter with a minotaur, and that's if we got far enough into the maze to find it! We're not done with these bugbears and any prisoners they're holding. Or did you forget?"

Jerdren sighed, shook his head.

"The smoke's starting to clear out, but we're still at a dead end passage, because I am *not* counting that secret door. I say a very quick search here and we're gone before we're trapped."

"What—by half a dozen bugbears?" Jerdren demanded. "We're better than that."

Eddis scowled, and he turned to shuffle his feet through the things on the floor as he moved toward one of the tables.

"Her's got gold earrings," Flerys said, pointing at the dead female with her spear. It was the first thing Jerdren had heard her say all day.

"So she has. You take them, girl, and put them somewhere safe," Jerdren said. He abandoned the table and went over to where Mead was slowly moving, his eyes searching along a high shelf.

"Thought so," the mage said. "There—a chest, see it?"

It proved heavy, and Mead insisted they use care getting it down. Kadymus broke the lock, to reveal a heavy, pale statue.

"Worth something," Jerdren said, "but too heavy to bother with, leave it. Look—there's a pile of coins under it. We'll divide that for carrying. What's that leather tube, Mead?"

The mage drew it out and turned it carefully in his hands, then peered down the open end. "Potions for healing. Good! They'll be needed."

Jerdren waited while the party divided up the silver, then led the way back out. "Quiet here?" he asked the men on guard, and one of them nodded.

Back down the stairs, and along the main passage. It was quiet here at the moment, and Jerdren could smell smoke from the chief's chambers. Fortunately, it didn't seem to have alerted anyone else up this way. Where the long passage ended, he could make out low voices off to his right.

The other direction, a natural cave sloped up, heading roughly north and out of sight around a bend. Willow went a ways along the slope and stood listening, then came back.

"There are more bugbears that way, but not close, and I believe there is a closed door between them and us. Sleeping quarters, I would say."

Blorys came back from the right-hand passage. "Steps heading down, just up there. I can hear guards down there and someone moaning."

"That'll be the dungeons, then," Jerdren said quietly. "Leave the barracks for the time being."

Panev went ahead, hands clasped together and lips moving silently, the rest following. At the base of the stairs, the priest stood aside to let the others pass. Jerdren paused while they were still in shadow. There was no door.

It's a dungeon, all right, Jerdren thought. You couldn't mistake the sounds or smells of such a place. He could see guards now: five bugbears sitting at a table right in front of the entry, though they weren't watching it. Jerdren quietly drew his sword and started forward, the others right on his heels.

Just inside the chamber, he slapped his sword against the wall, and shouted, "Who wants to fight?"

The bugbears leaped to their feet, catching up spears and throwing them in one lightning-fast move. Jerdren dropped to one knee, swearing through his teeth as bruised bone protested.

Behind him, someone cried out, and Eddis yelled, "Are you *mad*, Jers? No, Flerys—behind me and stay close, do it now!"

She brushed past him then, knocking him off balance and back into the wall, leaping out of the way, sword swinging in a shining arc as M'Baddah's bowstring twanged and one of the black-fletched arrows Mead had found buried itself in a hairy shoulder. The bugbear roared a curse and clutched at it but couldn't pull it free.

Spears were flying both ways. Jerdren shoved to his feet, got a two-handed grip on his sword-hilt, and settled in next to Eddis, hacking and slicing, though so far all he'd done was leave cuts in poorly tanned, hardened leather armor. He ducked as one of the brutes jabbed at him with a thick spear, slammed his blade down across the exposed forearm. Blood ran down the bugbear's fingers and pooled on the floor, and it lost its grip on the spear. M'Baddah's arrows finished it in short order.

A crossbow quarrel pinned one bugbear to the wall by its hand. The beast snarled and strove to tear it free, but too late. Eddis stabbed high, plunging the sword deep into the female bugbear's throat, angling up. The creature sagged, quarrel tearing through its hand as it went down. A little blood trickled from the gaping wound, then stopped.

"Good one!" Jerdren shouted. Eddis rolled her eyes and backed away from the entry, drawing Flerys with her.

"Move!" she ordered him. "You want to get pinned by one of your own spearmen?"

Another cry of pain from up the hallway, then Mead strode into the open, lips moving and hands out before him. A spear whistled by his head, barely missing his ear, but he stood his ground and brought his hands together.

It was the same spell he'd used on the bandits, Jerdren thought, but in this enclosed place, the result was incredibly bright and loud. The bugbears were caught dead center. By the time the light faded, all the guards lay unmoving, and the air was filled with the stench of burning hair. Sword at the ready, Jerdren moved forward to check the bodies, but Mead shook his head.

Brief silence, broken by a sudden clamor of voices from the far ends of the chamber. Men, Jerdren thought—but other things, too.

"All right, people! We've got the guards down, and we've got locked cells at both ends of the room here! Anyone hurt back there, get help from our priest here, or Mead, or M'Baddah. Kadymus, I need you!"

He was aware of Eddis's sneer as the young thief swaggered into the dungeon and edged around the dead guards to search for keys.

Willow joined Jerdren, who was looking up and down the

long, narrow chamber. "Panev's silence spell is holding. Any guards up that slope won't have heard anything."

"Good. We'll move fast anyway," Jerdren said. "We don't know when they change guards here, and we'll be slowed by our injured and what hurt men we find here."

The priest nodded and went back to keep watch partway up the stairs, taking two of the archers with him.

"Kadymus, keys?" Jerdren added tersely.

"Ahead of you," the thief announced and handed over a heavy ring of them before producing his bundle of lock-picks.

"You go to the right, boy, but wait until Blor or Eddis checks that pen before you open it. I'll take the other. Two of you Keep spearmen come with me, in case there's trouble."

He strode down the passage and peered into the gloomy pen. The air was fetid, close, as though the straw littering the floor hadn't been changed in a long time. There were several beings inside, chained together, but the only light was down by the entry, so he couldn't make out much else.

"Light," Jerdren demanded, and one of the Keep men broke out a candle lantern and flint and tinder.

An odd lot, Jerdren thought as he peered into the cell: three hobgoblins, two gnolls and—yes, a bugbear. And a wild-looking, wild-eyed man, who blinked and threw up an arm to shield his face from the light. The bugbear grumbled as his chains tightened, and the man kicked at him.

"Die of it, ye filth," he growled.

Jerdren grinned.

"Wouldn't be a feller named Hebold, would you?" he asked.

"Might be. Who asks?"

"Fellow who's talked to a merchant named Zebos. Fellow who was rescued from hobgoblins a while back, just around here. Said he'd appreciate if we found you and got you out."

The man stared at him for a long moment, then began to laugh. "Beats all, how the luck follows a man! Aye, I'm Hebold, all right. Break me out of this foul pit, and I'm for another chance to smite a few monsters."

"I'll see you get it," Jerdren said. He finally had the right key, and the lock turned easily. "But what about these others?"

"Don't speak Kobold or Gnoll myself, but *he* does." Hebold indicated the bugbear with a jerk of his head. "And, being here as long as I have, I've picked up enough Bugbear to get by on. *He's* in for leading a revolt against their chief. Was a lot more of 'em, but they're all gone now. Likely dead and probably eaten as well. Him and them other creatures have been planning how to get free, kill what bugbears are still around here. I was trying to get 'em to take me along, but not getting too far." He grinned fiercely. "Seems they don't think a man's strength counts for much, compared to theirs, and they weren't too sure they could trust me."

"Would you trust *them*, if we were to let 'em out of here?" Jerdren asked.

The man shrugged. Didn't know or didn't care, perhaps.

"Mead!" Jerdren called out, and when the mage came up, he explained. "Any way to tell if we can trust 'em not to pick a fight with us if we loose 'em?"

"They'll die if they stay here," the mage said. "They'll starve, if nothing else. Wait." He stepped into the cell, squatted down, his hands moving in a curious gesture as he asked a question in some language Jerdren didn't know. The hobgoblins sat up straight, and one of them replied, the words spilling from it. The gnolls spoke then, more haltingly. The bugbear merely growled deep in his throat.

"I asked if they would fight bugbears if we released and armed them. They said yes, and they told the truth."

"Great," Jerdren said. "I think. Someone find these fellows weapons! Those dead guards won't be needing theirs."

"I will go talk to the others," Mead said and strode down to the far end of the chamber. Jerdren ran through a number of keys before he found the one to free the chain from the wall and then the one to undo the shackles. Hebold came into the passage blinking and stretching.

He was a big man, Jerdren realized: as tall as he, but half again as broad through the shoulders, and his neck was massive. Hair paler gold than Eddis's was tangled wildly with a red-gold beard and moustache that Jerdren thought must ordinarily be very neatly trimmed. His eyes were an unexpected brown—so pale as to be nearly tan.

"By Kord, it feels good to move again. I owe you a life, man. Now, where's these bugbears?" he added eagerly.

"Soon," Jerdren promised as they started back toward the entry. "There's a few more prisoners there. We'll free them before we move on" A look assured him that Kadymus had the cell open.

Mead emerged moments later, two wan-looking men following him, and an assortment of thinnish kobolds, goblins, and orcs stumbling in their wake. A dwarf came last. He gazed down at the dead bugbears and spat, then reached into the mess to come up with a battle-axe. His eyes gleamed as he patted the haft.

"All clear down there?" Jerdren asked.

Kadymus nodded.

"All right, let's do this fast. Mead, you translate for me. You prisoners don't owe us a thing, but if you want to help us, there is a guard room or a barracks up the passage from here, beyond the stairs. We believe all the other guards here are dead. The chief's wife is dead, but he went out a secret door, and our priest says there's a minotaur on the other side.

Now, he may have run, but I think myself he's gone to find help. Any who want to come with us when we leave here, so long as you swear not to harm us, you can do that. We'll know if you lie. Any who want to stay and fight—that's your choice."

"Minotaur!" Hebold's eyes gleamed.

Jerdren winked at Eddis, who sighed. "Any of you men, or you, dwarf, who want to stay with us, we'll arm and feed you best we can, and see you're rewarded for helping us. We're doing our best to cleanse these caves, though. You might find yourselves dead, just as any of us might."

"Better than what the bugbears offered," one of the men said.

"For a chance to avenge my murdered clansmen?" the dwarf demanded in a harsh voice. "But I am armed already, human. This axe was taken from me when I was brought here, ten days ago."

"Good. Stay with us, and stay close," Jerdren ordered. "We're getting out of here and back to our camp, fast as we can. We'll talk then."

The kobolds, the bugbear, and gnolls needed no urging to attack the remaining bugbears. Jerdren led the way up the stairs then stood aside to let them race up the passage. He grinned at the ensuing howls of surprise and pain. There was a very brief clash of weapons up the sloping passage. Eddis tapped his shoulder and gestured the other way, then started out at a long-legged stride for the outside world, Flerys right on her heels, and M'Baddah behind the child. Kadymus, a heavy sword in one hand and a bugbear mace in the other, came on behind them.

They made the outside without incident, but the sky was a dirty black. Thunder rumbled in the distance, and a muddy flare of lighting briefly lit the clouds, somewhere to the south.

More thunder—distant, for the moment, but by the wind and the look of the sky, the storm was moving straight for them.

"Not good!" Eddis had to raise her voice to be heard above the wail of wind over stone and through trees. "We'd better find shelter, unless we're going to run all the way back to camp! But under all those trees is the worst place to be in a storm like this!"

"It's not that close!" Jerdren replied. "If we go now...."

He looked back to make sure everyone was out of the cave. The rest of his company—their company—was out. Two of the hobgoblins, one bleeding from a head wound, came into the open and tore down the hill, running as fast as they could for level ground.

Hebold was staring all around him, teeth bared in a fierce smile. "Know this place," the man said suddenly. "There's orcs over yonder—east of here. The filth. I owe 'em something."

He swung around jerkily, waved an arm. The rebel bugbear came into the open, two bugbear heads dangling from one hand, a heavy broadsword in the other. The gnolls were with him. Hebold shouted something Jerdren couldn't understand, slapped his chest with the axe, and took off running. The bugbear threw aside his trophies and followed, the gnolls and a hobgoblin loping after.

Blorys stared after them. "He's mad!"

"No," Jerdren said. "Angry. Do you suppose we should go after—"

"You're the madman, Jers!" Eddis yelled. "We've got wounded, we've got rescued prisoners, and there's a bugbear chief probably making a deal with a minotaur right now, and it's not gonna be good for us if we're here when that deal's made! We are not in any shape just now to take on a twisty cavern full of orcs!" Tense silence, which she broke. "That—

that 'hero' doesn't have any responsibility except to himself, Jers! You and I have others depending on us not to get them killed for no good purpose, remember?"

He sighed and finally nodded. "You're right, of course. Let's go."

16

They made it to level ground without incident, but as Jerdren turned to lead the way east, lightning flared, turning the forest blue-white, and a nearby tree exploded. Thunder shattered the air. Jerdren staggered to his feet, but his legs gave way. He looked dazed, and blood trickled from his nose.

"Back!" Blorys shouted above the din of sudden wind, drenching rain, and more thunder. "We could all die out here! Back to that cavern!"

Thunder roared, drowning his words.

"No!" M'Baddah blocked the way. "We would never make it, not in this weather!" He pointed. "This way—against the cliff! Perhaps we can find an overhang! Everybody move—now!"

Eddis helped Blorys get Jerdren moving, letting Flerys carry her bow. Another brilliant flare of lightning and a loud crack! M'Baddah jumped back just in time to avoid a huge branch that crashed down from high above, then leaped over it and kept going.

There was no overhang, only more trees, and the lightning had intensified as they fled, thunder deafening and non-stop. Wind drove the rain sideways, lashing their faces and hands, soaking everything.

M'Baddah waved his arms and pointed as they came into

the open. Just ahead, a vast, dark opening loomed. Eddis caught up to him, and her nose wrinkled.

"Gods, M'Baddah! I never smelled anything so horrid!" She had to yell to be heard.

"You want to look for another shelter, woman?" Jerdren yelled back.

Lightning stabbed into the trees a short distance away. Flame and smoke licked greedily up the branches but was doused by the rain.

"Or you want to die out here? Come on, we won't go in very far!"

"You got that part right!" Eddis screamed and ripped her sword from the sheath as she stepped into darkness. Flerys hesitated, then dove after the woman as thunder cracked across the sky. The rest followed hastily.

They huddled together as near the entrance as they dared.

"Keep watch," Jerdren ordered. "Every last one of us, both out there and behind us. And we'll stay close together, if no one minds."

"What are you watching *for?*" Eddis snarled at him. "Anything in here is dead. Very, very dead."

"Who knows? Whatever killed what you're smelling?"

The storm raged on. Bushes bent to the ground under the intense downpour and more branches came crashing down. Lightning was everywhere and though the storm seemed to be gradually moving away, each time Jerdren started to get up, another strike hit close by.

"I swear," he mumbled, "the filthy storm is trying to *keep* us here!"

"None of that," M'Baddah said sharply, before Eddis could reply.

Flerys hunkered down between M'Baddah and Eddis, her face buried in the outlander's cloak. She started violently whenever thunder cracked nearby. Kadymus alone seemed unfazed. He was wandering around, straying farther from the others by the moment.

"Wretched little dungeon-bird, you stay put!" Eddis ordered him, but the thief shook his head. "Don't disturb anything in here!" she added sharply.

"You said it yourself, Eddis," he replied with the smile that so annoyed her. "Everything in here's long dead. But, you know, with such a mess all around, there's just *got* to be something valuable hidden!"

He'd search for golden eggs in a pile of chicken droppings, Eddis thought. "Listen to me, you light-fingered little man. You come away from this cave reeking of dead things and you will sleep in the road. Because you will *not* have a place around the fire tonight!"

Kadymus held out his hands and laughed. "I won't touch anything dead, all right? But it can't hurt to look, can it?"

"If it's you that's looking, it just might—" Eddis said, then shrugged and fell silent.

Jerdren shook his head. "Blor, keep an eye on him. Kadymus, you stay where we can see you. You should know by now that any cave in this place can hold just about anything. And I'm not talking about treasure."

"If there is treasure—" the thief grinned— "I'm the one to find it. C'mon, Blor. You hold the lamp for me, and I'll share evens with you."

"You'll share evens with all of us, you little rat," Eddis growled, but she doubted he'd heard her. He was already wandering around, peering into the gloom while Blor got out flint and tinder and lit the stub of candle in his lantern. "Keep him quiet and close, will you, my friend?" she asked quietly as Blorys looked down at her on his way back into the reeking cavern. "This place is—I don't know! I just feel like something's back there in the dark, watching us."

"I know what you mean, Eddis." He smiled. "Though, if you ask me, something killed whatever lived here and left. The place feels deserted." He looked around in alarm as Mead got to his feet. "What?"

The elf shook his head. "Do not alarm any of our wounded, please. I just wish to test the place. There is no life in this chamber, but . . ." His voice trailed off, and Eddis could hear him mumbling under his breath. "I cannot detect anything close by," he said finally, and he sounded frustrated. "But I feel something wrong."

"Oh. Great," Eddis muttered. She came halfway around and onto her feet, sword and dagger out, as Kadymus's low mumbling suddenly stopped.

"Hey!" he announced. "There's an odd thing over here!" And as Blorys came up with the lamp. "Oh, sorry. Guess it's just a puddle, but it looked strange, like it was moving, and I—" He yelped. "Gods above, it's coming at me! Look out!"

Eddis threw herself to her feet, sword in hand as Blorys caught the thief by his collar and yanked him back. Candlelight shone on something pearly, gray, and snakelike. It reared from the cave floor to snap at Eddis, who threw herself to one side. The thing followed, and Blor hauled out his sword to slash at the thing.

Mead's voice echoed. "Get away from it!"

Blorys stared. "My sword! What's it done to my sword?"

The blade was smoking, dissolving. Molten metal splattered to the cavern floor, and he threw the hilt with an oath as it began to steam. Eddis tugged at his arm.

"Get away from it!" the mage yelled again. "It is gray ooze, and it eats anything metal!"

Kadymus shrieked and pelted back across the chamber, stopping only when he reached the mouth of the cave. The ooze puddled on the bone-littered floor, but it was already beginning to form itself for another strike. Eddis hauled Blorys around with all the strength in her, and they ran.

"Eats . . . metal!" Blorys sounded as stunned as he looked. He rounded on Kadymus. "That was my best sword! I've had it since before I went in the army! You filthy, wretched, light-fingered, little—!"

"Be grateful you still have your armor," Mead said sharply as the man paused for words. "And the metal buckle of the belt that holds up your pants. Jerdren," he added, "it seems to me that the storm is moving on. So, unless *you* know how to stop gray ooze, we had better get out of here. That thing knows we are here, and I have nothing that will even slow it!"

"Out," Jerdren ordered sharply. "Everyone, out—now!"

It was still raining heavily, and the wind blew hard, tearing small branches free to pelt down on the company as it wrapped sodden cloaks around their legs. But the storm was as short-lived as it was fierce. By the time they reached the road, the rain had turned to a thin drizzle, and the sky overhead was a deep blue.

It took time to get a fire going, since all their wood was soaked. The company devoured the bland mess their provisioner cooked up for them, then spent the remaining daylight hours tending to minor wounds, drying cloaks and blankets. One of the Keep men brewed hot mulled wine.

"Wonder where our big, bad hero wound up," Eddis remarked sourly as she sipped the spicy, steaming liquid. "One muscle-bound brute and a handful of weakened monsters taking on an orc den? He must be mad."

Jerdren shrugged. "Really? He impressed me. Think how long those bugbears held him, and somehow he kept himself fit and fed, ready to fight his way out if he got the chance."

"I hope he will work off his rage against his captors, if he comes here," M'Baddah said. "But against so many orcs—"

"Wasn't so many as all that." Hebold's voice boomed out.

Eddis snarled a wordless curse as the man strode into the firelight.

"Lost most of my allies, worse luck, but I did all right myself. Just look here!"

He hauled a length of rope from his belt. Eddis peered at his hand, realized what she was looking at, and thrust Flerys behind her. Severed orc hands were strung on the rope.

The "hero" grinned at her proudly, then looked at Jerdren, his chest expanding.

"Jerdren, isn't it?" Hebold asked. "Thought you might be camped hereabouts—this was the safest spot we found, anyway." He brandished his trophy. "Proof of my kills."

Eddis glared at him, her eyes narrow slits. "Get that mess out of this camp. Now!"

He stared at her blankly.

Eddis freed up a dagger and bared her teeth. "Far, far out of camp! Or you can take yourself back to that bugbear cell and lock yourself in, for all of me, but you won't stay here!"

He took a step forward and scowled. Eddis held her ground, jaw set, and freed up another dagger.

"Woman," he snarled, "where I come from, your kind tend fires, provide pleasure, and nurse babes."

"Go back there, then," Eddis overrode him. "In this company, Jerdren and I are equals. Captains. If you're thinking of fighting with us, or even staying here the night, you'd better remember that."

Hebold gazed down at her for a long, utterly still moment, then turned and strode from camp.

"Nice going, Eddis," her co-captain said mildly. "He's big

and tough, a good fighter, and he knows more about these caves than we do. And you've alienated him."

Blorys caught hold of her shoulders. "Are you mad, woman? He's big enough to break you in half!"

"He won't, Blor. Don't you know? The gods protect the mad," Eddis replied.

Blorys laughed quietly. Jerdren shook his head and went off after Hebold.

She sighed faintly. "I'm just glad we got all that silver out of sight before he showed up. I don't trust him."

She looked up as Jerdren laughed aloud. He and the big man were standing together at the edge of the clearing, talking quietly. Trading exploits, no doubt. So long as they don't trade stories where *I* have to listen to them, she thought. Or Flerys. She turned to look for the child and found her waiting quietly.

"I'm sorry if I hurt you," she said. "I didn't want you to see what he had."

"Didn't hurt," Flerys replied. "I saw, but bandits took hands sometimes." She shrugged. "Is just hands, not anything messy." She shivered into her cloak as a cool breeze sprang up and went back to the fire.

Eddis glanced at Blorys. "Gods. That poor child. You think regular guard'll be enough to keep an eye on that Hebold tonight—if he stays?"

"Oh, he'll stay, all right," Blorys said glumly. "But Jers'll probably be up half the night, trading war stories with him."

* * * * *

Near dawn Eddis was wakened by men shouting and a clash of weapons. She snatched up her sword, but Jerdren and two of the Keep spearmen were already on their way back to the fire. Jerdren grinned and wiped his bloody sword.

"Orcs," he said as Eddis looked at him. "We killed three, and Hebold went after the last two."

"Great," she muttered and tugged the cloak around her shoulders. "They've found us."

"If they were a scouting party, there won't be any of 'em left to report what they found," Jerdren replied. "It's early, Eddis. Go back to sleep."

* * * * *

When she woke again, it was full day. We're waiting for the men from the Keep, she remembered. No fighting today—unless more orcs or other things come looking for us. Just as well, she thought as she sat up. Everything ached at the moment.

Jerdren had posted guards. She could see a spearman out there, pacing the road. A few others sat together talking quietly and honing their blades, and Flerys was getting another archery lesson from M'Baddah.

Across the firepit from where she lay, Jerdren and Blorys had Zebos's map out. Hebold was looking over their shoulders.

"First place we went was there. Rumor had it the worst and toughest creatures were as far from the road as they could be, and that seemed a likely start. Turned out to be gnolls. Handful of coins, no gems that we found, and a pack of cowardly dog-monsters aren't worth fighting." He shrugged. "Next place we went was that hobgoblin lair, worse luck. Couple of my men were full of 'emselves for killing off gnolls, got too loud, and drew down an ambush on us. Lousy hobgoblins must've been lurking while we went in for the prisoners. They were waiting just short of the door when we came back."

"Heard about that," Jerdren said. "Still a bunch of 'em left, if you want to finish 'em off." It wasn't quite a question.

Hebold grinned. "May not have to bother. That hobgoblin—the one I shared a cage with, I told 'im the bugbear lair's empty, and that their chief kept his treasure in chests, lots of 'em in the secret passage behind his bedroom. Fool creature believed me, too. That minotaur'll do for 'em."

"Could work." Jerdren grinned.

"So—" Hebold stretched long and hard. "You find much trove so far?"

"Oh, you know. Few coins here and a few there. We sent most of it back to the Keep, of course."

"Sounds foolish." Hebold squatted on his heels next to the fire.

"Some fools we'd be if we buried it here and came back to find it gone." Jerdren turned back to the map. "So . . . you've emptied that cave, and that one's where the orcs were. And the small one here. Bugbears—here. Gnolls are gone, or as good as, and so're the orcs, and your goblins are done for. We wiped out the kobolds, first day. What's it leave us, then?"

The big man shook his head. "Didn't get much chance to look around. Still . . . while back, late one night, I was trying to sleep, and I could hear one of the bugbears challenging someone. Then he backed away, and all of 'em looked flat-out scared. Here comes this—figure. Black hood, cloak the color of dried blood. Never saw its face, but its voice gave *me* an unpleasant feeling. Said something in Common about sacrifices. Went to the other cage, looked in and said, 'That one and that.' Bugbears dragged out two of my men and hauled 'em up the stairs, and that hooded thing went off behind 'em.

"A priest," Panev murmured. He had come up quietly behind Eddis. "A black hood and red cloak, you're sure of that, man?"

Hebold nodded.

"The curate may be right after all. He has heard rumor these past years—disquieting tales of men and women who travel along this road from the east, but they do not seek the Keep. He questioned the man Zebos, who said he had seen strangers who passed through his town, and all of them wore dark red cloaks. They did no business with the local merchants, he said, and never spoke to any but their own kind. The curate asked that I serve as priest in this company, rather than either of his acolytes, because he fears the red-cloaked ones to be part of a cult of the undead."

"Undead?" Jerdren asked. "Why didn't we hear of this before now?"

"Because it seemed unlikely to us that such a temple would be here—so far from any town. But if this man has seen the priest he describes, then I believe the temple must be nearby. Of the priests in the Keep, only the curate and I can turn powerful undead."

"Turn?" Blorys asked. He looked bewildered.

"You cannot stab a skeleton to the heart—it has none. I have spells to force them away from me. From us. Or to unmake them."

"Great," Jerdren muttered. "So, where's this temple? Every cave opening on this map of Zebos's, we've marked. We know what's there—or was."

Hebold studied the map closely, holding it nearly to his nose. "No. There's one missing. Should be just . . . here." He pointed. "When we went after the gnolls, we could see it. Another cave, a little lower down the slope and nearer the center of the ravine."

"Undead," Jerdren said. He thought, finally looked at Eddis. "We need to talk."

"Yes," Panev said. "And each member of this company must decide whether to continue to fight. Such a temple will be a place of great evil."

In the end, the entire company—including Flerys, who was startled to be given a vote—chose to go.

Kadymus grinned widely. "A temple! Think what treasure we'll find!"

"No!" Panev shook his head fiercely. "In such a place, you touch things at your peril. I will instruct you before we go into battle."

* * * * *

The party from the Keep arrived early the next afternoon. Eddis was beginning to feel nervy. Every weapon she owned was freshly edged, and there was nothing left to do but wait.

M'Baddah, Willow, and Mead had gone up the ravine that morning, to see if they could locate the cave Hebold claimed to have seen. They'd found it, but hadn't dared go too close. Mead's reveal spell showed danger and great evil, but he couldn't tell anything more specific than that. They had also seen twenty or more dead hobgoblins near the foot of the cliff near the bugbears' cave but had no explanation for what had killed them.

The Keep guards brought food and a hide full of new arrows and quarrels, spears and daggers—and a parcel and message for the priest.

Panev read the message and drew Eddis and Jerdren aside. "The curate tells me that visiting priest and his two acolytes have been arrested. A search of their rooms revealed evidence that they are not the holy men they pretend to be but servants of a secret, evil brotherhood. They also found a map that shows these caves. The curate sends his blessings to the company and all the potions and wands he could gather. I see Hieroneous's hand in this." He smiled. "Things will go well, if we are all well prepared." He walked off, deep in thought.

"Always do, don't they?" Jerdren asked of no one and went over to talk to Hebold.

Eddis gazed after him, then went in search of Blorys. Jers had been acting odd—like his old, wild self—ever since Hebold first showed up. Blorys might not be able to do anything with him either, but he'd stand a better chance.

* * * * *

Eddis took third watch with M'Baddah and one of the spearmen. It was very dark and cold, and utterly silent except for someone snoring near the fire, and the occasional shifting of the picketed horses. The hour over, she woke Jerdren and lay down close to the fire.

A man's yell of pain and the screams of terrified horses had her on her feet scant moments later. There was chaos all around the fire, as men ran to protect the horses, and others headed toward the clash of weaponry, far enough into the trees that it was hard to tell who was fighting whom—or what.

"Lights!" Eddis shouted. "You and you, let's get some lights out there, or we'll wind up killing each other!"

The battle had moved to the road by the time she and Blorys came running, each carrying a lantern and drawn sword. Three men were down, one wailing in agony. Beyond them, five heavily armed hobgoblins fought furiously. Jerdren and Hebold were battling side by side, finishing off one fallen brute, but the others seemed unharmed as yet.

The unexpected light distracted one of them. M'Baddah and his son charged it, M'Whan lunging as his father swung the curved blade, two-handed. Blood ran down the creature's face, blinding it, but as M'Baddah brought the blade around again, it caught him by the forearm and yanked, dragging the outlander onto his blade. The outlander shouted in sudden pain, the outcry drowned by M'Whan's, "Father!"

The youth stabbed, again and again. Eddis handed the lantern to one of the bleeding men stumbling back from the fray and ran to help. Blorys came hard on her heels, and as Eddis jabbed at the brute, Blor shoved the lantern at its face. Momentarily blinded, it snarled and slapped the thing aside. Blor staggered but managed to stay on his feet. Eddis was behind it, then, out of its reach and safely away from M'Whan's flailing sword.

No room to swing the sword, without cutting one of their own, she thought, and lunged, plunging the point into the unprotected back of the hobgoblin's knee. It bellowed in rage and pain, dropped M'Baddah, and swung around to face her, but M'Whan and Blorys attacked now, cutting it badly. It was swaying as it turned from her to face this new threat, and it went down. Eddis brought her sword down hard across the back of its neck, again and again until it no longer moved.

She fell back, winded. Two more hobgoblins had fallen since she had sprung to the attack, but more men littered the road, and she could still hear the high-pitched, shrill cry of a terrified horse, back in the camp.

M'Whan knelt to help his father, and Eddis came around to steady the man as the youth got him on his feet.

"How bad?" she asked. Her lieutenant's face was ashen.

"My arm—above the wrist. I think it is broken." He gripped M'Whan's shoulder tightly. "Thanks to you three, it is only that."

"Gods," Eddis whispered and shook her head to clear it. "M'Whan, get him out of the middle of this. Blor—?"

But Blorys had already moved off to help his brother and two spearmen take down another of the attackers. Eddis ran to aid three of the Keep men who'd ridden out that day. They were backing nervously away from a massive brute who bled from a dozen or more shallow cuts, their spears trailing in the dirt.

"Don't run!" she shouted. "You'll give him a better chance to cut you down. Stay there, keep those spears at the ready!"

The creature turned to face her as she ran in, yelling wildly, her sword swinging. Two more cuts—a deep one across the back of its sword hand, another down the side of its face, and the hobgoblin backed away and bounded forward and took a vicious swipe at her head. Eddis's heels caught on one of the fallen men, and she went down. The brute loomed over her, teeth bared in a horrid grin, sword raised to pin her to the ground. She rolled, coming up onto her knees, staggering to her feet. Furtive movement caught her eye. Kadymus, a thick-bladed dagger in each hand, was sneaking up on the creature, and Flerys came flying out of the dark, spear ready to thrust. The brief distraction cost Eddis, but a quick jump back kept the hobgoblin's sword from more than scratching her arm.

With a yell of fury, Flerys jabbed her spear at the creature's back but lost her balance as the point bounced off armor. The little thief brought one dagger down, the other up, burying one blade in the hobgoblin's sword-arm, the other in its neck.

It bellowed and turned to strike. Eddis's sword bit deep across the backs of its legs, felling it, and Kadymus leaped to slam two more daggers deep in its neck. It shuddered and went limp. Flerys edged around it and came running, clinging fiercely as the swordswoman stroked her hair. Eddis's eyes moved, taking in their surroundings. No fighting close by, and the monsters still standing were surrounded.

"Are you all right?" she asked the girl finally.

A sharp nod.

"Sure?"

The thin body trembled against hers. Afraid, Eddis thought, but a moment later, Flerys burst into tears.

"Thought it killed Eddis," she whispered tearfully. "Don't want filthy monsters killing Eddis."

The fighting was over as suddenly as it had begun. The last hobgoblin tried to flee, but Hebold ran after it and cut it down with the double-bladed axe he'd picked up in the dungeons.

Eddis surveyed the damage. Four dead hobgoblins—five now, as spearmen dispatched the last of the wounded. Men seemed to be everywhere, fallen, bloody, moaning. Some weren't moving.

"What damage?" Eddis asked generally.

Mead looked up from the armsman he was tending. "At least ten wounded. Two horses dead, that I know for certain. Four men dead."

"And all those filthy hobgoblins," Hebold announced. He was bloody, filthy, and grinning hugely.

"Good," Eddis told him. "Why don't you get a couple of the men to help you drag them away from camp, so the horses can start settling down."

To her surprise, he did what she asked without comment. M'Baddah—over there, with M'Whan; Blorys moving along the far side of the road. No sign of Jerdren, and she couldn't recall the last time she'd seen him. Hard to tell who was where, with only two flickering lanterns out here.

"Jers, where are you?" she called out. "Someone get a couple more lanterns out here, and any of you who aren't hurt, set a guard here, on the camp and on the horses, so we don't get caught like that again!"

"Here he is!" Blorys called. "I think he's—no, he's breathing, and that's not his blood."

Eddis made her way past fallen and shocked-looking men, and knelt to feel Jerdren's throat for pulse. The man groaned faintly.

"Got the wind knocked out of him," Eddis said.

Another groan, and Jerdren fought his way to sitting, gingerly cradling his head in his hands.

"Gods, what a headache," he mumbled. "Brute got the spear away from one of the men and cracked me across the skull with it."

Blorys gripped his shoulder and fetched a quiet sigh of relief.

"What's the damage?" the older man asked after a moment. Eddis told him. "That's not so good, is it?"

"It could have been a lot worse," she assured him. "All those inexperienced Keep men, all those horses, and a surprise attack. Except after last night, we should have been expecting it."

Jerdren shrugged, then winced and clutched his brow. "Know what, Eddis? I owe you an apology. Think you're right—they know where we are, all right. Tells me that we take on this final cave, one last battle, and ride away."

Blorys stared at him. "You're giving up? That must have been some crack to the head, Brother."

Jerdren managed a faint grin. "Didn't say that. Just doesn't seem sense to sit here and wait for 'em to finish us off a few at a time. There's no reason why we couldn't come back later—next spring, say—and finish the job."

"Sounds like a plan to me," Eddis said and got back to her feet.

Someone needs to keep an eye on things here, she thought. With M'Baddah and Jerdren both down, that meant her. "One last battle," she whispered. Jerdren's words sounded like an ill omen, all at once.

✦ ✦ ✦ ✦ ✦

Cleanup took hours, and it was nearly dawn when Eddis settled down close to the fire and closed her eyes. Sleep evaded her. Four dead horses, two badly injured, another two simply gone. Most of the dead men were those who'd ridden out from the Keep to bring them supplies. Panev had healed the worst injuries, Mead using potions to close cuts and a spell to sooth and quiet the horses.

Too much blood, she thought wearily. The sight and smell of it sickened her, all at once, and Jerdren's words still rang in her mind. One last battle. They'd lost so many men already. If this temple was as dire as Panev thought, how many of them would survive?

17

Morning came with a chill wind, and a ruddy glare filled what could be seen of the eastern sky. Eddis woke to the jingle of harnesses and the thud of restless horses stamping their feet. The party returning to the Keep was ready to ride out. Anxious, she thought, and who could blame them? All around her, the armsmen were quietly stowing their belongings and readying their weapons. Blorys, seeing her sit up, brought her a steaming mug and a bowl of porridge, and someone else doused the fire. Eddis managed a smile as she took the food and drink. Blorys looked distracted and worried, but he said nothing while she ate.

"What's happening? Is Jerdren all right?" she asked finally.

He shrugged. "We buried the dead men a little while ago. Mead gave Jers something for the headache last night, and he was fine after that. He's just . . . well, you know Jers." He shook himself and smiled, warmth kindling his eyes. "Take care today, Eddis."

"I will." She hesitated, then took both his hands in hers. "If you swear to do the same."

"As best I can. Jers may—"

"No," she said quietly. "Swear you'll take care of yourself." Silence. "Blor, he won't thank you for getting killed trying to protect him."

He sighed quietly. "I know. It's just—" He gripped her fingers, then brought one hand up to brush against his lips. "I swear, Eddis."

Moments later, Panev called them all together. "I have told you a little of the dangers that may await us. Even I cannot be sure what we face, if we enter a temple of evil. Listen to your leaders—and to me—and you may well survive this day. You men who return to the Keep—my blessings and the strength of the gods guide you safely home. You did not expect to battle monsters, and yet you did, and you live to tell the tale."

He was silent as the Keep men mounted and rode out, then turned to look over the armed company surrounding him. "Kneel, all of you," he said. "This blessing may give you courage when you most need it."

He spoke quietly, and even Eddis—who was nearest—heard little of what he said, but she felt calm wash through her, and a sense of *rightness*.

Hebold came back through the trees as Panev was finishing his prayer. His lips twisted, and he turned away. Dolt, Eddis thought. I don't believe in the priest's gods or his religion either, but I'm not fool enough to spurn them. Jerdren got to his feet and strode out of the camp, across the road, and into the brush. The others followed.

They passed the kobolds' lair, halted abruptly as harsh, wild laughter echoed all around them. Willow and M'Baddah ran that way, slipping from tree to tree, out of sight moments only, before they came walking back. Eddis had nocked an arrow to her string, but her lieutenant's familiar hand sign told her there was no threat.

Willow beckoned them close and said, "We saw hobgoblins going from the orc caves to their own hold, carrying orc and kobold dead."

Eddis's nose wrinkled. "Filling the larder, no doubt. Not our business, if that's all."

They were on their way moments later and made the westernmost end of the ravine without further incident.

They paused for breath and to ready their weapons. Eddis gave Flerys a reassuring smile. The child waggled her spear and made M'Baddah's sign for luck, though Eddis thought the child looked anxious. When they went on, Panev led, Eddis, Willow, and M'Baddah close behind him with their bows ready. Hebold was on their heels, battle-axe in one hand and the hobgoblin club he'd picked up the night before in the other.

The few trees on the heights here looked frost-burned, blackened leaves hanging lifeless, the trunks thin and twisted. The air was musty and still.

"Wait," Panev ordered quietly and clambered up a few paces to survey the heights before them. He nodded sharply and gestured for them to come on.

Eddis stared as she came up. There was a true path here, edged in broken stone and worn down into the rock itself. How can that be? she wondered. There's no trace of a path leading to this place! Magic, she thought unhappily. Her feet tingled as she reluctantly stepped down into the trail.

Panev beckoned Mead to his side, and the two led through a copse of bloated trees and twisting vines. The musty smell increased. Free of the close-growing trees, Eddis could see a cave looming just above them. The odor was much stronger here, borne on chill air that seemed to flow down from the entrance and wrap around them.

The priest nodded, as if satisfied on some count. "Quickly," he hissed. Mace in one hand, a slender gray wand in the other, he strode through the wide opening and vanished into darkness.

It was deadly quiet in here. What Eddis could see was hard to distinguish—murky, as though the air itself were dark. A few lamps were set in niches, enough she could make out a vast, vaulting roof, veins of black and red stone writhing across the dull surface of the rock from which a wide, long corridor had been hewn. The floor was smooth and clear and faded into gloom, north and south.

Panev's lips and hands moved. "As I feared. It is a temple, a cult to worship chaos and death, served by the undead. There are many of the undead both ways," he said quietly. "A few living, perhaps priests and some guards, but these are few in number. The greater foe in number and evil is that way, which tells me that the priests—and the chief priest—are there." He pointed north. "None of you," he added as he gazed around the company, "must touch anything, unless I say it is safe!"

Jerdren nodded. "Pay heed to what he says. We'll go south first. Make sure there's none left to attack our rear once we go after these priests."

Panev drew forth a small, sun-shaped pin and pressed it reverently to his lips before fastening it to his surcoat.

The long south passage took a bend to the right, and just past the bend, the wide corridor split, both passages leading to poorly lit rooms. What they could see of either was empty: no guards, no furniture or furnishings.

Panev indicated the right passage with his wand and quietly said, "There are guards. Undead guards. Be warned."

To the left, the passage was blocked by a huge fall of stones. Blocked deliberately, Eddis thought, and fought a shiver. Gods, what was so dire that priests who could raise the dead would fear it?

Panev hesitated just short of the left opening to shift his grip on the wand, turned the corner, and strode rapidly into a room lit by guttering torches. Eddis was aware of vast space and a dais at the far end: a throne that glinted red in the dim light. Flerys caught hold of her arm and pointed. Along the walls on either side of the dais, statues of foot soldiers stood or sprawled. She could make out ancient, rusty mail and helms, and here one guard held a heavy, curved sword.

"Gods," she whispered. "Those aren't statues! They're skeletons!"

"Who'd leave bones to guard a throne room?" one of the Keep men murmured.

"They are the enemy," Panev said sternly. "Fear them, and be wary!"

"But they aren't moving!" Jerdren whispered in reply.

Kadymus pushed past him, Hebold right on his heels.

"That throne! Look at them jewels!" the youth whispered.

Eddis looked. What she'd taken for fading torchlight shining on metal turned out to be gems—enormous rubies, unless her eyes deceived her.

"Do not touch them!" the priest warned, but Hebold rolled his eyes and passed the little thief at a bound, dagger ready to pry the ruddy stones free.

"Fool of a priest, what's the danger in a gem?" He chuckled softly as his blade popped one free. "Hah! One of these and a man's set for life," he said softly, shoving Kadymus aside as he tried to help.

The breath caught in Eddis's throat. The skeletons along the south wall were stirring, and a wordless gasp of warning behind her assured her the others were as well.

"Back!" the priest ordered. Kadymus looked up, yelped, and fled the dais. Hebold ignored priest and thief both. He was busily freeing a second stone. The rest of the company backed toward the doorway, Panev setting himself grimly as rearguard against the undead. Bony figures raised their swords and slowly stalked toward him, but two rounded on the barbarian, who suddenly came alert to his peril. He dropped gem and dagger, rolled across the dais as a sword crashed down where his neck had been, leaped to his feet, and swung the battle-axe two-handed, shattering both helm and the skull under it. A second swing and the skeleton broke apart, bones flying and bouncing across the stone floor.

Kadymus yelped as one detached arm clutched at his leg, and he went down. Jerdren swore and grabbed him by the sleeve, dragging him across the floor to relative safety. Hebold snarled curses as the second skeleton's blade slashed his hand. He tossed the battle-axe from his right to his left and swung it flat on, slamming the bony guard into the wall. The man looked around wildly, found the company, and ran.

Jerdren pushed past Panev to go to his new ally's aid, but the priest yanked him back. He was muttering under his breath, and the small, dark wand he held turned briefly a pale green. The remaining skeleton guards backed away from the party and began stalking along the walls. Trying to get around us to flee—or to keep us here, Eddis thought.

"Back!" Mead hissed and pressed past her. She expected one of his fireballs, but the mage threw a clay jug of oil into the chamber, splashing many of the skeletons. A burning candle stub followed.

Flames roared high. Dry, rotting cloth burst into flames, and several of the nearest undead simply fell over and were consumed. The five still on their feet ran for the doorway, but Hebold and two of the Keep men who carried battering weapons blocked the way and battered them into bone shards and dust.

"Damage," the priest demanded sternly, and to Eddis's eyes, he'd grown and changed since entering this cave—turning from mere priest to a deadly force. "Let no cut go untended in such a foul den as this!"

Jerdren turned to stare from the room. "Not yet!" he hissed. "Something's out there, coming this way!"

The priest's eyes closed briefly. "Coming, but not close enough to be a danger." His dark eyes fixed on Kadymus, smoldered as they picked out Hebold. "I warned you. But take the gems, if you wish. Nothing will challenge you for them now." He strode over to stamp out the few remaining flames.

"Don't doubt that I will," Hebold replied stiffly. "*Priest.*"

The word sounded like a curse, and Jerdren spoke quietly but urgently against the man's ear. Hebold nodded, then turned away to scoop up his dagger, so he could free the other stone. He shoved the last in his belt and brought up his chin to meet Eddis's glare with a challenging stare of his own.

She turned away as if disinterested, then froze. Something was moving out in the hall—close by. Uneven footsteps. Lame guards? she wondered.

What came into sight didn't look lame so much as corpselike. A zombie, she realized, and swallowed hard. The reek of long-dead bodies filled the chamber. Eight of the foul undead approached slowly, bulging eyes or empty eye sockets fixed on the invaders. They carried no weapons that she could see. She set an arrow to her string and moved offside to get a clear shot. M'Baddah thrust Flerys behind him as he put himself against her left shoulder and drew back on his own bow. Her arrow slammed into the nearest zombie with a nasty squelching sound. M'Baddah's went clear through its neck and into the shoulder of the one behind. Neither seemed affected.

More arrows: Between them, Willow and M'Baddah had neutralized three, but they were both running out of the magic arrows. Jerdren caught up a spear and swung it at a shuffling corpse. The zombie's head went flying, and the body collapsed.

"They die like the skeletons!" Jerden shouted. "Take 'em apart and they're worthless!" He darted forward, Keep men following, maces and axes swinging.

One cried out and fell. A zombie had him by the ankle. Another man hacked the arm from its body and kicked at it. Blorys hauled the man to his feet and passed him back to Mead. Hebold slammed his heavy axe into one fallen zombie, cutting it nearly in half. Another man cried out in horror and pain.

Sudden silence.

The hall reeked of long-dead flesh, and the floor was slick with black, oily fluid that seeped from severed limbs and heads. Most of Eddis's arrows were worthless—coated in foul ooze, broken, or the fletches soaked. M'Baddah and Willow retrieved what they could but finally gave up in disgust. Eddis held her breath as they edged past the horrid mess and into the open.

"So far, so good," Jerdren said as the priest came up to join him.

Panev pointed across the hall. "The other undead at this end of the temple are in that chamber," he said quietly. "They are bound to that chamber, or the noise of battle would have brought them out to aid their fellows just now." He eyed Jerdren, glanced at Eddis. "We can leave them alone for now. But if we did, their high priest could summon them against us."

"We fight them, then," Jerdren said with satisfaction.

"We fight," Panev said. "Though I will turn them, if I can. Wait, all of you, until I order an attack."

His black gaze rested on Hebold, who rolled his eyes and shrugged.

"It is seldom given to a man of my calling to turn the undead—but perhaps the gods of order will aid me in this.

When we are done there, I will help Mead with the wounded."

Eddis thrust herself forward. "You who've been hurt—stay out of this fray, and watch our backs."

Panev beckoned as he strode into the room. Zombies—eight more of them—came to staggering life as he entered the chamber. Eddis moved to M'Baddah's side and drew back her bowstring.

Her lieutenant hadn't been quick enough to get Flerys behind him this time—or more likely, the smell of rot and decay from the hall behind them had already affected the girl. She stumbled away from him, clutching her stomach, and vomited. M'Whan snatched at her arm and dragged her back to the nearest wall, where he thrust her into Mead's grasp.

Eddis and M'Baddah shot and shot again, moved sideways as one, the way he'd taught her. But the two zombies stalking them seemed unfazed by the arrows. One of the spearmen came from somewhere to bury his weapon into the nearest, angling up from the base of its neck and into the skull. The head popped off, and the body went down like a sack of pudding. The undead at its side pawed at the man but slid in Flerys's mess and fell on its back. Hebold was there with his axe before it could rise, and across the chamber, Jerdren came darting up behind two more undead, beheading them both in one mighty swing.

"Back!" That was Mead, who thrust Flerys back at M'Baddah and strode forward, unstoppering a gourd of oil as he walked. He whipped the thing back and forth, then backed away himself as he tossed a lit candle stub into the spill of liquid. Fire roared up. The three zombies still on their feet went up like torches.

Mead was already back in the short, broad corridor. "There is no one and nothing out there just now. Catch your breath, all of you, drink water—no, not here, out in the passage, where the air is cleaner. Let me know which of you was wounded in that fray. We cannot afford to lose anyone here."

Eddis hugged Flerys close as they left the chamber. The child was pale, and her lips trembled.

"Here," the swordswoman whispered. "Eat a little of the travel bread, it won't hurt your stomach."

"I'm sorry." The girl's eyes filled with tears. "I didn't mean to."

"You couldn't help it. It's all right, Flerys. I almost got sick in there myself. A little bread and a drink of water. You'll be fine."

Flerys took the wafer and tucked a bite of it in her cheek, sipped water, and leaned back against the wall, spear clutched to her body.

Mead's voice roused Eddis. "Anyone so much as touched by those foul creatures, come to me or Panev now and let us heal you."

Hebold sighed heavily. The mage eyed him with disdain.

"Of course, a man like you bears his wounds bravely, but the least touch from these undead may turn you into one of them. Do you want that, hero?"

Time passed. It was deathly quiet here. Eddis thought she heard something like a distant flute once, but when she held her breath to listen closely, there was nothing.

"So." Jerdren came up quietly behind her. "What next?"

The priest answered for her, as he pointed north. "There are men. Fewer than we but strong in evil. We must be careful."

Jerdren smiled grimly and got to his feet. "I can deal with men."

Back past the entry and a like distance on, the passage ended in a door ahead and a door on their right. Panev brought out a stubby black wand and gazed at it, then turned to look from one door to the other. He nodded toward the one straight ahead, but as Jerdren and Hebold surged that way, the priest blocked their way.

"There are priests within," he murmured. "Four priests. Trust nothing they say or do!"

Hebold shrugged and slammed into the door. The panel gave way. Four hooded, red-robed men snatched up weapons and ran to put themselves between the invaders and two other priests who had been reading a text.

Mead fired a glowing dart across the chamber into the nearest standing priest. The fellow's hood smoldered, and he flung his mace aside to beat at the thick cloth. Mead jumped back, M'Baddah and Willow brushed him aside and blocked the entry, firing two swift arrows each. M'Baddah's bounced off the robed being with a clang. Willow's lodged deep in the hood, and the unseen priest sagged and fell across the table. Hebold and Jerdren charged into the room then, as outlander and elf swung away from the doorway. Two Keep men followed, bearing down on the priest with the still-smoking hood.

Eddis and Flerys stayed in the hall, the swordswoman with her blade out and her free arm around Flerys, her eyes searching both corridors. Panev said noise would bring the undead down on us, she thought. *If this isn't noise, I don't know what is.*

It was abruptly quiet back in that chamber, all at once. Someone was moaning in pain. A sword clanged into something hard and metal, and the moaning stopped. Eddis looked that way. Blood splashed the far wall, and all four hooded men lay still.

"It's all right, child," she told Flerys. "We've won again." She hoped. There were men down in there—one she could see with a long dagger sticking out of his neck, his eyes open and vacant.

Panev walked around the chamber, spoke a blessing over their dead. "Everyone out," he said tersely, and began pouring oil on the bodies. When Hebold protested the waste of oil and time, the priest gave him a chill look. "Would you be foolish enough to leave a body in *this* unholy place?" Without waiting for a reply, the priest strode on down the west-facing passage.

At its end, he paused once more. There was a chamber to their left. Eddis could just make out a large, red stone block that might be an altar and farther in, a great tapestry that covered most of the wall behind it. She shuddered and turned away.

Panev led them past the room, then paused. "There is a door ahead—perhaps two doors. Men are there, and evil surrounds and fills them. The gods grant us courage."

Jerdren nodded grimly and led the company on.

Another closed door. Hebold broke this in and threw himself at those inside. M'Baddah fired his remaining magic arrows, and the battle was quickly over. Hebold came back into the open, bleeding from a head cut, which he grudgingly let Panev heal.

Another chamber, more priest-clad enemies who grimly swung maces. Two Keep men went down under the attack. Eddis leaped back as a priest evaded Hebold's axe and pelted straight for her, hand snatching at her. Blorys's sword came down across the robed back, and Flerys lunged, spear stabbing deeply into the hood. The enemy sagged, dragging the spear from the girl's hands. Blorys pulled it free, and she snatched it up.

Another hooded man burst free, and his mace knocked Blorys to his knees. Eddis jammed her blade two-handed into thick cloth. The weapon felt sluggish, her arms weak, and the point seemed to hesitate just short of flesh.

"Foul thing!" she yelled and used her legs to drive the sword in. The man wailed, staggered back into the wall, and slid down it.

More dead men, more injured, and another room ablaze. Where does it end? Eddis thought wearily. Panev looked as exhausted as she felt.

"Undead hold the way against us, up there," he said. "We will avoid them, if we can." His eyes kindled. "The center of evil is here—so close!"

"Let's get 'em, then!" Hebold snarled, but Jerdren pressed him back.

"Wait," he said. "Any other place, I'd be with you, friend. Here, we let this priest guide us." He caught Eddis's eye and managed a faint, wry grin. "Didn't you tell me once that dead men don't kill anything?"

"Hah," Hebold retorted but stayed where he was.

"Rest, all of you," Panev said. "Our greatest challenge lies ahead. And I warn each of you—touch *nothing!* We approach the heart of evil, and the thing that catches your eye may draw you from us and turn you into its slave. Do not let any creature touch you or hold your gaze. And let no priest escape!"

"Great. So, if he's that powerful, how does a mere man like me kill him?" Hebold asked. He scowled at his broken battle-axe and tossed it aside.

"The priest who controls this place is still mortal, though harder to kill than most men." Panev paced while the others drank water or checked their weapons, then led them swiftly on.

All at once, the passage widened into a chamber, a dark void at their left. Panev drew them close to hiss, "There are undead waiting beyond the wall, to our right. Keep still if we are to avoid them!"

They moved slowly and cautiously now, easing into the large, open room. Light flared. Black candles burst into flame, illuminating the chamber suddenly and painfully. Panev ripped a scroll tube from his pack, though he did not yet open it.

The wall ahead glowed as if covered with fresh blood, then seemed to shift and change. Eddis hastily turned away.

It's a temple! she realized as her eyes adjusted. There a black stone dais, here benches and pews for worshippers. The vast dais took up much of the room and was topped by chairs of the same stone grouped about an enormous throne. Gems glittered—the dais and the chairs were covered in them. Kadymus gasped then spun away, hands clasped together behind his back. Even Hebold seemed subdued.

As they passed a great iron bell, Hebold's face lit up, and he tapped Mead's arm, pointing at something Eddis couldn't see. The mage shrugged, brought up the wand he was carrying, and finally nodded. Hebold grinned hugely, sheathed his sword, and scooped up a pair of heavy mallets, knocking them together with a dull clank. Mead gestured urgently for silence and hurried to catch up with the priest, who had reached the far end of the room.

A long purple drape covered the wall. It shifted, colors swirling wildly, curious writing and symbols filling the space.

Panev drew Eddis and Jerdren close and whispered, "There are small passages beyond the cloth and three undead at guard. Beyond that is a small room where the priest dwells. He is the one I seek, the one we must defeat if this place is to be taken back from chaos."

Jerdren nodded and signed for Willow and M'Baddah to stay with him.

Eddis glanced at Blorys, who waited only long enough to see that Hebold wasn't on his brother's heels.

"Gods, Blor," she whispered. "What are we doing here?"

"The best we can," he whispered back. "Remember your pledge to me!"

She nodded. "Remember yours."

His eyes warmed. Panev laid a hand on her shoulder in passing, and her heart lifted briefly. When he pressed the drape aside, she followed close on his heels, sword in one hand, dagger in the other.

Her nose wrinkled as they came into the passage behind the drape. There wasn't much room for maneuvering here. Too much fancy and luxurious furnishing—couches, carpets, odd bits of statuary here and there—and not enough bare floor. The space reeked of long-dead flesh. Zombies. She could see one now, shuffling toward her, sword in its rotting hand

A loud clang brought her around. Hebold had leaped to the attack, beating down a zombie with his long-handled bell mallets. M'Baddah pinned another to the wall with his sword, ducking back as the thing continued to swipe at him, but M'Whan charged in to behead the thing with a two-handed swipe of his sword.

The third turned from her and staggered toward Mead, giggling madly, but the mage snatched up a spear from one of the Keep men. The creature veered away, right into Jerdren's reach, and he smashed it down, bones and black fluid spilling over the tiled floor as he reversed his grip on his sword and beat at the thing with the heavy hilt.

Another door loomed. To Eddis's surprise, it opened easily when Mead pressed his spear against the latch. A small chamber was beyond, nearly as obstructed with furnishings as the last space had been.

"Great," she murmured sourly. "No room to fight... now what?"

Panev strode past her, Mead on his heels. The priest's scroll crackled as he read the spell aloud—odd words that echoed in her mind and made her skin crawl.

The words meant something to his enemy, clearly. Wild, deep laughter filled the room. Eddis shuddered.

"Why do you invade my private sanctum, priest of Law?" a voice demanded from the shadows "What fool are you, to invoke a spell of lawful holding, here? Do you think me a weakling that I will fall to such simple words as that?"

"Foul creature of chaos!" Panev replied, "I knew you would turn that spell! Because you turned it, you have torn down the wall you built against lawful spells such as mine, and now you are open to both my magic and the weapons my allies bear! You cannot overcome us, dark one! Die, you and your undead servants! Sink into darkness forever!"

Eddis stopped just inside the doorway, fingers clutching her bow and her sword. The priest who strode into the open was tall and thin, clad in red and black. But as Panev spoke, the least wind soughed through the chamber, and the other's robe shifted, revealing a gleam of mail under it.

His eyes were black, luminous, eager pinpoints. After one glance, the swordswoman knew she dared not look on his face again. Blorys was a sudden, comforting presence against her left arm, his sword in his left hand, throwing-dagger held by the point in his right.

The evil priest darted aside to snatch up a staff, lips moving. Mead raised his hands to begin a spell, then went flat as the priest launched the staff at him. Eddis ran to help him up, then jerked away as the weapon clattered to the floor, writhed, and became a serpent. It twined around the elf mage.

"Get away from it, woman!" Panev ordered her sternly and began to pray aloud. A snake grew between his hands, twisting and hissing. With a shout of triumph, Panev cast it at the dark priest, but the dread creature clapped his hands together, and the snake was unmade in a coil of black smoke just short of his feet.

Teeth gleaming in the gloom, the dark one drew a bludgeon from his robes. Panev pressed Eddis aside and brought up his mace.

The two priests swung furiously at each other, but their blows missed. The dark priest spat words and darted forward to backhand Panev out of his way. Blood ran down Panev's cheek from a long, narrow cut, as though he'd been knifed. He gritted his teeth and swung the mace again, this time catching his opponent's weapon firmly against the head of his own. Eddis waited for an opening and threw one of her daggers. The blade sliced through the red cloak but clanged off metal and fell useless to the floor.

Blorys's sword ripped at the priest's neck, and blood followed.

"Look!" he shouted above the din. "He isn't proof to a blade!"

Eddis laughed wildly and stabbed. The man now bled from several wounds, but nothing seemed to slow him, and Panev could make no headway. The evil priest shouted, and the sound ground against Eddis's skin like sharp-edged stones. Blorys gasped and went down. Eddis cursed furiously and set herself between him and the evil one.

Behind them, sounds of fighting ceased. Eddis hoped, but didn't dare look to see which side had won. Slowly, Panev was gaining the upper hand. A finger's worth at a time, he pressed the evil priest back, but every step took them both closer to Mead, who stood helpless, eyes black with fury as he remained bound in a serpent's coils.

Blorys swore weakly. Eddis helped him up.

"This has to end. Now," she said flatly.

Blorys nodded. He was short of breath, but his eyes were dark furies.

"We end this. If we can," he added.

The two ran forward, swords high, and brought them down across the priest's neck. Blorys's sword rebounded with a loud clang. Eddis's slashed through flesh, and the priest howled, staggered back, breaking away from Panev, who staggered and nearly fell on his face. The foul priest spun around, eyes glittering with hate, the mace a blur as he swung at Eddis, but she darted back out of reach, and Panev's mace slammed down on the priest's exposed head.

Eddis ducked as somewhere behind her Willow urgently shouted, "Arrow!"

One of the black-fletched magic arrows sang across the chamber and buried itself deep in the priest's eye. He fell to his knees.

Horribly, Eddis realized, he wasn't yet dead. But as he strove to rise, Blorys lunged, stabbing through his throat as Panev brought the mace down two-handed.

The snake released Mead, vanishing in a roil of oily black smoke. The elf came slowly across the room as Panev gazed down at the fallen priest, mace ready to strike if he moved again, but the man's blood no longer flowed, and his eye stared glassily, unseeing at the ceiling. Panev staggered back into the wall, eyes half-closed, his breathing shallow.

Mead felt in his pouch for a healing potion and came up with a small, dark bottle. "A good thing you aren't much hurt, priest. I'm running low."

"It scarcely matters how I fare, if he is dead," the priest replied.

"But others depend on us to escape this place," Mead reminded him.

The priest took the little bottle and drank down the contents.

"That's him?" Jerdren peered around the doorway. "That's . . . that's it?"

Panev nodded.

"Anything here we dare take?"

The priest shrugged. "I am too worn to dare trust my own thoughts about that. Mead?"

The mage shook his head. "I used my last reveal spell. Still . . ." He drew a slender scroll from his pouch, unfurled the thing and read it under his breath. "It is safe now. Search for things of value if you wish, but do not touch that priest or any scroll or bottle."

"Good. Because we need to . . ." Jerdren frowned, turned. "Where's Kadymus? He's the one who wanted to search this room!"

M'Baddah leaned against the doorway, Flerys holding him upright. The outlander reeked of things long dead, and his armor was black-splashed.

"The thief? He ran past me, a little while ago. I heard him say something about gold, a statue of a golden beast. One of the guards got between us about then, and I lost sight of him."

"How long has he been gone?" Jerdren asked.

"Saw him go," Flerys told her. "Just when Eddis went in here. Little sneak went out past the long cloth."

"He's lost, if that is so," Panev said. When Jerdren moved to go after the youth, the priest caught his sleeve. "Search for him, if you will, but there are still undead here. Perhaps this death has released such slaves and unmade them, but I cannot tell, for I am worn." He turned abruptly and left the chamber.

Jerdren shook his head, then turned away, joining Hebold as the man searched through a deep coffer. Two of the Keep men crowded in to help, but after a few moments, they gave up.

"Too many hiding places here," Jerdren said. "Panev's right. This place doesn't feel any safer, even with that one dead. Let's go."

Panev, the cut on his face healing at what Eddis thought to be unnerving speed, stepped aside as Mead splattered oil around the chamber and tossed in a guttering torch. Flames exploded, licked at the dead priest, and roared up from the bedding as the elf mage shoved the door closed.

It was quiet here once again: no guards, and no sign of Kadymus, though Eddis wondered if there were fewer stones on the great throne. Any thief who'd try to cut-purse a swordswoman in a village tavern isn't bright enough to leave cursed gems alone.

* * * * *

Sun gleamed pale in the west. They rested a few moments, then set out for level ground.

"Stay alert," Jerdren warned as he waited for the last ones to join them—Blorys, Panev, and Hebold. The priest looked less grim than he had in a long while, but the supposed hero was muttering to himself, eyes flickering from his two-handed sword to Jerdren, Eddis, the priest, and back again. Blor met Eddis's eyes and smiled. She smiled back.

Hebold abruptly sheathed his sword and drew a long-bladed dagger, turning it in his hands as he strode down the shelf. He hauled Blorys off balance, fingers gripping his hair, the knife pressed against the young man's throat.

"Hebold, what're you doing?" Jerdren said, bewildered. "That's my brother! Don't—!"

"Brother!" Hebold spat. "I saw you both drooling over the rubies I pried from that throne. You want 'em, don't you?"

"I don't—!" Blorys managed, then fell silent as the blade moved slightly.

"I know you all took things in that cave, gold and gems! You hid 'em from me when I wasn't looking!" Hebold shouted. "I'll have all of it now, every last single penny! Or this man dies, and he won't go easy!"

Eddis took a step toward them. Hebold grinned at her mirthlessly, and the tip of his knife broke skin. Blood seeped down Blory's throat.

"Don't hurt him," she said, her throat tight and dry. "He's no threat to you, Hebold."

"He may not be. But you—!" His eyes gleamed and he licked his lips. "One more order from you—one more *word!*— and you're dead, woman! But I'll kill him, no matter what!"

Eddis gazed into Blorys's eyes, then met Hebold's mad glare squarely. "Why kill him? *I'm* the one you hate—aren't I? You'd like to cut my throat, but you won't. Because you're afraid. Aren't you?"

"Eddis, no!" Blorys croaked.

Hebold's arm slacked a little, and he looked confused, angry, nervous all at once. The men around her seemed frozen, except for Jerdren. She could sense him moving cautiously up alongside her. Hebold gave him a mad glare, and he stopped. Behind the barbarian, Eddis realized something was moving. Flerys, spear in hand, edged up a slow, cautious step at a time.

If Hebold knew she was there . . . He'd never get the chance, Eddis thought in sudden fury.

"You want orders, you barbarian bastard? I'll give you

orders!" she snarled. "Drop that blade and turn him loose, or I'll gut you where you stand!"

Hebold stared, astonished, eyes shifting from her to Jerdren and back again. He bellowed in surprise as the girl's spear bit into the back of his knee, and he spun around to slap her down, but Flerys had let go the shaft and fled into M'Baddah's arms. Blorys surged against the man's grip and half-spun out of it. Hebold came back around, dagger swinging. The point sank into Blorys's shoulder. He sagged as the barbarian laughed and threw a second blade at Eddis, but she'd dropped flat.

Behind her, Jerdren choked and went down. Hebold staggered back, his wounded leg collapsing under him. M'Baddah, Willow, and M'Whan finished him off.

"Oh, gods." Eddis scrambled to her feet and ran to Blorys. There was blood trickling from the corner of his mouth, but his eyes were clear. "Blor—gods, don't move, Blor! Panev can—"

She turned. The priest was bent over Jerdren, who lay flat and still two paces away. She touched Blorys's face gently.

"Wait, just *wait*. Promise me!"

He nodded, and his eyes sagged shut, but he was still breathing. Eddis's legs gave way. She crawled over to Jerdren on her hands and knees, swallowed dread.

Bloody froth covered the man's chin. Hebold's dagger protruded from his belly, just below his short leather armor.

"All . . . right," he whispered and tried to smile as she leaned over him. His eyes shifted, flicked over his fallen brother, then met Panev's squarely. "Priest," he said. "I remember what . . . you did for Willow. That . . . box of powder?" He swallowed, raised his voice a little. "I know you can heal us both. I'm . . . not as bad off as Blor, though. Take care of . . . of him first, will you?"

Eddis's throat closed. "Jers!" Her voice wouldn't rise above a whisper. "Gods, no, don't do this!" His fingers gripped her hand, his eyes warning, and she fell silent.

"Do it, Priest," Jerdren said, "before . . . one of us . . . dies . . ."

Panev gripped Jerdren's fingers and signed a blessing over him.

"That's right," Jerdren whispered. "Go. Save him. I . . . can wait."

Eddis's eyes filled with tears. Jerdren clung to her fingers. "You can't do this," she choked out.

"Shhh." His eyes flicked warningly toward his brother. She could see the priest sprinkling his powder around the knife, remembered the man's words as he brought Willow back from near death. Panev could use this cure on one man only. Her tears spilled over and fell on Jerdren's face. He laid his free hand gently against her cheek.

"Don't cry, Eddis. You're . . . my kind of warrior, remember?" He coughed and brought up a smile. "Tough, skilled. And so . . . so beautiful. Did I ever tell you that? So . . . gods' blessed beautiful." He swallowed, grimaced as pain knifed through him. "Take . . . care of him for me."

She brushed her lips against his fingers as they slipped from her hand, as the breath eased out of him on a long, quiet sigh. Eddis closed his eyes, dashed tears aside with the back of her hand, and let M'Baddah help her up and hold her. Flerys clasped her close, tears plowing a muddy path down her face.

The priest staggered up. "The man will live. He will sleep for some hours, though. Those of you with the strength for it, carry him." He made another sign of blessing over the still Jerdren. "And his brother. We will not leave such a hero behind."

"What about 'im?" Flerys demanded, black eyes fixed on Hebold.

Eddis stroked the girl's hair. Her eyes were hard.

"We leave him where he fell, child. He's got everything he deserved."

* * * * *

Ten days later, Eddis sat cross-legged and barefoot in the open doorway of the small, private sleeping room of the Keep's inn, staring blankly at the paving stones, fingers absently working through a long strand of clean hair. Even that seemed too much of an effort all at once, and her hands fell to her lap.

They'd been welcomed as heroes, and Jerdren had been given a hero's funeral pyre. Not one of them could enter the tavern or walk into the open without folk cheering them or asking about their great adventures. The castellan had brought out the treasure they'd sent ahead, and with the rest they'd brought in, each of them was wealthier than they could have imagined, even after shares were set aside for the families of men who'd died out there.

"Adventures," the swordswoman muttered. She felt old and used, too tired and disinterested to even rise from the floor, though her back was beginning to ache and one foot had gone to sleep. "Heroes," she said bitterly. "We had luck and skill, and even then . . ."

Even then, they hadn't finished the job—not the way she and Jerdren had planned. There were hobgoblins and goblins still alive, including their chiefs. Possibly these would scatter, now that the priest was dead and his temple and chapel burned. The minotaur might keep to his maze and be no threat to those who traveled the road. It didn't matter, she thought. *I won't go back there again.*

Just now, she wasn't certain she'd go back out to guarding caravans. People here were friendly, but she didn't feel like one of them. Nothing in the realm called her back there, and now M'Baddah was talking about returning to his homeland. M'Whan would go, of course. She wasn't surprised when Flerys decided she wanted to go with them.

"She's a good child, and I'll miss her, but M'Baddah's better for her than I would ever be."

Eddis knew he'd stay if she decided to go back to the road. He'd welcome her if she chose to travel with him. It was too much effort to think about, at the moment.

One good thing had come out of all this: Flerys. It was hard to remember the wild, filthy creature who called itself Blot. Now the girl walked confidently about the Keep. She kept the golden earrings Jerdren had told her to take from the bugbear chieftain's wife, wearing them on a chain around her neck since they were much too large for her ears.

"I'll wear them and remember him that way," she said.

Odd, Eddis thought. Other than that brief kindness, Jerdren had paid little heed to the child.

Blorys—she hadn't seen him in days. Not since Jerdren's funeral. *I should find him, tell him* . . . She couldn't complete the thought. Tell him she was sorry his beloved brother had chosen to die, so he could live? Her throat tightened.

To her surprise, most of the Keep men had quietly returned to their companies, and those she saw seemed little changed by what had happened.

Willow and Mead had left hours earlier, stopping to talk to her on their way out. Willow had been sympathetic. Mead tried to talk her into sense. It didn't matter.

"If I hadn't dropped when he threw that second knife, Jerdren would still be—" She swallowed hard, shook her head.

"Don't think that." Blorys's voice.

She started, blotted her eyes and looked up, then away.

"Eddis . . ."

She shook her head again, and this time he dropped down next to her.

"Mead told me. I . . . gods, I should have come to see you before now. I didn't know you thought . . ." His voice tightened. "It's not your fault. How can you think that?"

"He's dead, isn't he?"

"He's dead because he chose to let me live. If you're placing blame, lay it on Hebold. Black hells, lay it on Jers for taking the man into that temple with us." The man's voice was suddenly tight. "You can't just sit here, brooding on it. Jers would hate it."

She frowned, puzzled.

"I saw how he looked at you, Eddis. I know how he felt, because I feel the—never mind." He got to his feet, reached down and waited until she finally took his hand to let him pull her up. "I know my brother. Wherever he is now, he knows he died doing something heroic and tragic at the same time." He managed a faint smile. His eyes shone with unshed tears. "I'd like him alive again, so I could strangle him just for that. But it won't help anything, and it won't change anything."

"I—" She tried to smile at the awful joke, bit back a sob. "He was the most annoying, frustrating, crazy—! And I hate that he's done this to you."

"What?" Blorys asked quietly. "Left me? Left me in his debt? Stepped aside with a noble bow to leave the field to me? I'm angry with him right now, but that's grief. He'd have been angry if our places had been changed that afternoon. There *was* no easy way out of this one, Eddis. No way out at all."

She shook her head. "What do you mean, the field?"

"I know how he felt about you, Eddis. We both did. I still do. I know it's hardly the time to talk about it. But, if you'll listen to me for a little, an idea I had . . . Well, maybe we'll have the time, later. To decide, anyway."

He folded his arms, leaned against the wall.

"I'm done with the road and guarding caravans. Too many memories in that, and the gods know I don't need the coin. I can't go back to our home village. I'd be stifled in a fortnight. And you?"

He let the question hang. She shrugged.

"M'Baddah's restless," she said after a moment. "Wondering what's happened to his homeland, thinking that if things are still bad for his people, he might be able to help shift the balance. M'Whan will go with his father, of course. And Flerys—"

"I thought the child was staying with you."

She smiled faintly. "She sleeps here. Finally understands propriety, at least in a place like the Keep. But no, she's bonded with M'Baddah, and he's very fond of her. I'm . . . I'm glad for the child. She'll be happy with him, and safe, I think."

Silence, but a comfortable one. Eddis looked up to see Blorys watching her, his eyes warm. "You said you had a plan?"

He blinked. "Oh—oh, that. Yes. Panev is readying to journey on east, and he's looking for an escort. I know," he added with a small laugh as she shook her head. "No more guarding, I said, and I mean it. But this would be one way only, and for my own purposes. You know that the realm used to trade with the lands to the east."

"Of course. Trading silks and other rare fabrics. It always sounded to me like the kind of fable that grows up when the truth has been lost."

"Sounds it, but I spoke with Ferec yesterday. The old records from Macsen's days show that silk and emeralds were traded here, and fine pottery. Maybe those people have fallen on hard times as well. If we went there, we'd know, wouldn't we?"

Silence.

"Think of it. Not the wealth, we both have plenty of that. But new lands, new faces. Maybe a chance to begin trade for the Keep once again, now that the road's fairly clear."

He stood, gripped her shoulder gently. "I need to go see to the horses. Decide whether to sell Jerdren's gelding or keep him as a pack animal."

Silence.

"I won't press you for an answer now, Eddis. Think about it, though. Please?"

She nodded.

"Don't rush it. We have time." He hesitated a brief moment, then turned and left.

Eddis gazed down at her hands. The room felt empty without him. Time. Jerdren thought he had all the time there was—until it was too late. She jumped to her feet, leaned out the doorway. Blor was already out of sight, then she saw him striding toward the smithy's.

"Blorys! Blor!" Her voice echoed, and he turned around as she ran toward him. "I . . . you don't need to wait. It's all right." The rest of the words wouldn't come.

He took her hand in both his. "You'll come with me? Friends? I won't ask more."

"No," she said. "I know what I want." Her face felt flushed. "Besides, you're good at guarding my side."

He smiled and leaned forward to kiss her. "Four horses, then," he said. "Unless you think we can manage with one packhorse between us."

She smiled back. "Four. Just make sure that you don't get me one named Feather!"

She turned and ran back to her room, her heart suddenly much lighter. East might be an error, or guarding that grim priest once again might be. It might be a serious mistake getting anywhere near those caves again, however briefly. But they'd come through all right. The two of them. Wherever they finally chose to go.

Legend of the Five Rings

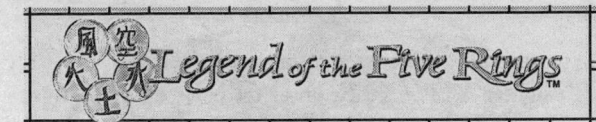

The Phoenix
Stephen D. Sullivan

The five Elemental Masters—the greatest magic-wielders of Rokugan—seek to turn back the demons of the Shadowlands. To do so, they must harness the power of the Black Scrolls, and perhaps become demons themselves.

The Dragon
Ree Soesbee

The most mysterious of all the clans of Rokugan, the Dragon had long stayed elusive in their mountain stronghold. When at last they emerge into the Clan War, they unleash a power that could well save the empire . . . or doom it.

The Crab
Stan Brown

For a thousand years, the Crab have guarded the Emerald Empire against demon hordes—but when the greatest threat comes from within, the Crab must ally with their fiendish foes and march to take the capital city.

The Lion
Stephen D. Sullivan

Since the Scorpion Coup, the Clans of Rokugan have made war upon each other. Now, in the face of Fu Leng and his endless armies of demons, the Seven Thunders must band together to battle their immortal foe . . . or die!

November 2001

LEGEND OF THE FIVE RINGS is a registered trademark owned by Wizards of the Coast, Inc.
©2001 Wizards of the Coast, Inc.

DRAGONLANCE

The War of Souls
THE NEW EPIC SAGA FROM MARGARET WEIS & TRACY HICKMAN

The New York Times bestseller—now available in paperback!

Dragons of a Fallen Sun
The War of Souls • Volume I

Out of the tumult of a destructive magical storm appears a mysterious young woman, proclaiming the coming of the One True God. Her words and deeds erupt into a war that will transform the fate of Krynn.

Dragons of a Lost Star
THE WAR OF SOULS • VOLUME II

The war rages on . . .
A triumphant army of evil Knights sweeps across Krynn and marches against Silvanesti. Against the dark tide stands a strange group of heroes: a tortured Knight, an agonized mage, an aging woman, and a small, lighthearted kender in whose hands rests the fate of all the world.

DRAGONLANCE is a registered trademark owned by Wizards of the Coast, Inc.
©2001 Wizards of the Coast, Inc.

MAGIC: The Gathering®

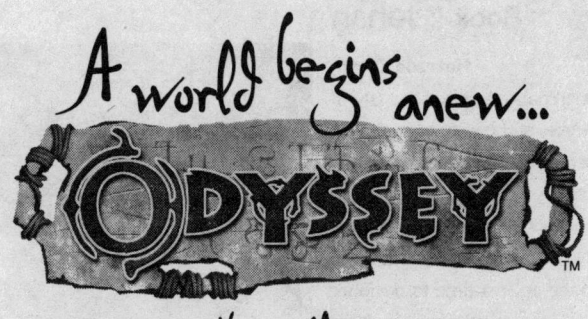

A world begins anew...

ODYSSEY™

Vance Moore

**A hundred years has passed since the invasion.
Dominaria is still in ruins.**

**Only the strongest manage to survive in this
brutal post-apocalyptic world. Experience the glory and
agony of champion pit fighters as they enter the arena
to do combat for treasure.**

In September 2001,
begin a journey into the depths of this reborn
and frighteningly hostile world.

MAGIC: THE GATHERING is a registered trademark owned by Wizards of the Coast, Inc.
©2001 Wizards of the Coast, Inc.

MAGIC: The Gathering

Legends Cycle — Clayton Emery

Book I: Johan

Hazezon Tamar, merchant-mayor of the city of Bryce, had plenty of problems before he encountered Jaeger, a mysterious stranger that is half-man and half-tiger. Now Hazezon is caught up in a race against time to decipher the mysterious prophecy of None, One, and Two, while considering the significance of Jaeger's appearance. Only by understanding these elements can he save his people from the tyranny and enslavement of the evil wizard Johan, ruler of the dying city of Tirras.

Book II: Jedit

Jedit Ojanen, the son of the legendary cat man Jaeger, sets out on a journey to find his father. Like his father, he collapses in the desert and is left for dead until he is rescued. But rescued by whom? And why? Only the prophecy of None, One, and Two holds the answers.

December 2001

MAGIC: THE GATHERING is a registered trademark owned by Wizards of the Coast, Inc.
©2001 Wizards of the Coast, Inc.